NO BETTER MAN

NO BETTER MAN

A Heart of the Rockies Novel

SARA RICHARDSON

FOREVER

NEW YORK   BOSTON

Copyright © 2015 by Sara Richardson
Excerpt from *Something Like Love* copyright © 2015 by Sara Richardson

Forever
Hachette Book Group
1290 Avenue of the Americas
New York, NY 10104

HachetteBookGroup.com

Printed in the United States of America

First Edition: May 2015
10 9 8 7 6 5 4 3 2 1

OPM

Forever is an imprint of Grand Central Publishing.
The Forever name and logo are trademarks of Hachette Book Group, Inc.

The Hachette Speakers Bureau provides a wide range of authors for speaking events. To find out more, go to www.hachettespeakersbureau.com or call (866) 376-6591.

The publisher is not responsible for websites (or their content) that are not owned by the publisher.

*To Will: Thank you for making me
believe in love.*

Acknowledgments

It seems impossible to express the depth of my gratitude for everyone who has walked this journey with me, but I'll do my best.

First, there are countless people who have helped make this writing dream a reality. To my editor, Megha Parekh, I am still amazed you chose my story. Thank you for your brilliant vision and your incredibly hard work on my behalf. I have learned so much from you! Thank you to the whole team at Forever for being the absolute best at what they do. To my agent, Sue Brower, and the entire team at the Natasha Kern Literary Agency, thank you for your guidance and unwavering support.

While writing this book I had so many questions about the foreclosure process. A big thanks to Matt Metcalf of *Simply Denver, Real Estate Made Simple* for answering every question and explaining things I didn't understand.

I am incredibly blessed to have a close, supportive family. Thank you to my husband, Will, for being whatever I need at any given moment: a friend, a drill sergeant, a motivational speaker, a laundry expert. I can honestly say this story never would've seen the light of day without your faithful persistence. To my sweet boys, AJ and Kaleb, thank you for teaching me how to love deeper than I ever thought possible. To my parents, Phil and Emy Remley, thank you for making me believe that nothing was out of my reach. To my sister, Erin Romero, and my sis-in-law, Traci Remley, thanks for being just as excited about this as I am. And, of course, thank you Kyle Remley, my little bro, for always making me laugh. A very special thank you to Keith and Wanda Richardson and the Guhlke family for accepting this quirky writer into your hearts and making me feel like I belong. Without your support, this wouldn't have been possible.

During these past few months of deadlines and an intense writing schedule, I was reminded that I also have the best friends a girl could ask for. To Melissa Anderson and Erica Meikle, what can I possibly say? You two get me. Your friendship means the world to me. Jenna LaFleur, I am so grateful for your energy, creativity, and friendship. I'll forever treasure our visionary coffee dates. Thank you Elaine Clampitt for putting wind back in my sails at a time when I didn't know which way to go. I'm so grateful for our conference experiences and lengthy brainstorming sessions. To my very first writing buddies, Patti Lacy, Tiffany Kinerson, and Kasey Giard, thank you for helping shape my writing journey.

To every family member and friend who has touched

my life (there are way too many to list here), I hope my stories will carry on the legacy of grace, encouragement and love you have shown to me.

Above all, I am so thankful for the faith, hope, and love that give my life meaning.

NO BETTER MAN

CHAPTER ONE

Some girls claim the spa or a favorite mall as their happy place, but Avery loved Wrigley Field. She loved the blaring red sign, WRIGLEY FIELD, HOME OF THE CHICAGO CUBS. She loved the smell of popcorn and hot dogs and stale beer, the sticky crunch of the concrete beneath her feet. It was her haven, almost as familiar as her own home, which smelled like the hazelnut lattes she made every morning, for the record. Didn't matter if the Cubbies were trailing by 12 or up by 10—every time she sat in section 14, row 4, seat 12 (right behind the home dugout), she was utterly, completely, divinely happy.

Which was why she never should've let her father sit next to her.

The day should have been heavenly—a shining Sunday afternoon complete with a jewel-blue sky and hints of fall crisping the air. The Cubs were up on the Yankees by three, which was a miracle in itself.

Dear Old Dad, AKA the infamous Edward King, sat next to her, dressed in a tailored gray suit, if one could imagine. His million-dollar hair was slicked back from a widow's peak. Silver Armani shades deflected the sun. He leaned forward, hands securely fastened to his knees so his bare skin wouldn't graze the defiled concrete rail in front of him. Really, though. Who's afraid of a little stale beer? They were at a baseball game, for crying out loud.

"Did you have time to read the Aspen briefing?" Dad shouted over the roar of the crowd.

Ignoring the question, she glanced at Vanessa, Dad's assistant and one of her best friends. The woman was supposed to be her buffer at the game so Dad wouldn't pull her into some big work discussion, but at the moment, Van happened to be otherwise occupied in a nonverbal flirting contest with some hot guy sitting halfway down their row.

"Hey." She jabbed an elbow into her friend's ribs. "A little help here?"

"Excuse me." Van flipped her curly black hair over her shoulder and gave her a girl-code glare for *I'm busy.*

Avery rolled her eyes. *Please.* Vanessa could get any man she wanted. She had the diva look about her, dark even skin that didn't need make-up, round innocent bedroom eyes accentuated by thick lashes, also natural, of course. She could have that man down the row eating out of her hand with a *hello*, but there was one problem. "I didn't drag you here and sit you between my father and me so you could troll for men." She needed her right now. "I will personally go get the guy's phone number if you shut up my father," she whispered.

"Avery? I asked you a question," Dad broke in. "Have you read the briefing on Aspen?"

She raised her hand toward Vanessa. *See?* The man was relentless. How could he even *think* of work at time like this? Two more outs. They only needed two more outs and they'd be back up at bat...

"Of course I sent Avery the briefing," Vanessa said as she waved to Mr. McDreamy eyes. "She's looking into it."

He leaned over to see past Vanessa. "Don told me an old ranch is about to foreclose. He sent me some pictures. It's exactly what we've been looking for."

Don Pendleton, the mayor of Aspen and an old friend of her father's, had been trying to get King Enterprises to build a resort out there for the last ten years.

Dad went on and on about the unique location, about the natural spring on the property, yada, yada, yada. "Your mom would've loved it."

That snapped her out of her baseball stupor. "I know, Dad," she said, softening. "I was copied on the e-mail, remember? Don't worry. I'm watching it." Without looking over, she reached across Vanessa and gave him a consoling pat on the arm. She loved the man and everything, but nothing ruined a good baseball game like talking.

To tell him as much, she scooted to the edge of her seat and refocused on the game. One of the Yanks' best sluggers who'd been on a hot streak since...well...forever, was up to bat. *Great.*

"We have to do more than watch it, Avery." Her father used his stern lecture tone, which had stopped working when she was eight.

But he'd never known when to quit.

"It *will* go fast. There will be multiple bids. You know what I always say—"

Crack!

He hit the ball high and long, sent it sailing straight for the right-field stands. *No!* She jumped to her feet. The outfielder—Colvin?—sprinted hard, arms pumping, head angled back and up, watching...

He leapt, arm outstretched, reaching...

She squeezed a hand over her mouth.

Smack! The ball hit his glove. It hit his glove!

"Yes! Way to go, boys!" She fell back to her seat, heart pounding with the thrill of a close call. "Did you see that circus catch?"

Clearly Vanessa had no time to actually *watch* the game. She was too busy mouthing *call me* to her new boyfriend. "I'll be right back." She stood, smiling in that coy way that brought out her dimples, and sashayed over people's feet to make a love connection.

Shaking her head, Avery pressed her fingers against her lips and gave a good, solid whistle. "Come on, guys! Don't let 'em back in it!"

Her father winced and stuck a finger in his ear. "How much longer will this thing last, anyway?"

"It's only the top of the seventh, so it'll be awhile." An eternity to him. Baseball had been Mom's passion, not his. Family outings at Wrigley Field painted Avery's most vivid and cherished family memories. For three seasons, before Dad became "America's favorite tycoon," they'd all tromped to the field in matching jerseys, her and Mom's blond hair tied back into swinging ponytails like the perfect picture of the American dream. They'd buy tickets for the cheap seats and sit way up high, peering through second-hand binoculars. She and Mom would put on their pink mitts just in case someone's rogue hit made it all the way up to the nosebleed section.

Oh, how things had changed. Ever since Mom's death, her dad had despised America's favorite pastime. But then, he despised anything that reminded him of her.

That thought was all it took to turn her to mush. There was a reason he hid inside his work. There was a reason he was desperate to complete the Aspen project. In his mind, the resort would be Mom's legacy. She'd always loved it there.

Tuning out the game, she faced her father. "The ranch in Aspen is on two hundred forested acres. Located on Maroon Bells Road. Built in 1956 by the Walker Family," she intoned as though doing a voice-over for a documentary. "The projected foreclosure date is not until January. So far, there are no other known interested parties." See? She really did do her job. "I'll travel out there in a few weeks to make Mr. Walker an offer before he loses it. By then, he'll be desperate to sell. Trust me. It'll be the biggest bargain we've found in years."

"That's my girl." A look of pride dawned in his dulled gray eyes and made them come alive again. But he never looked into her eyes for too long. They must've reminded him too much of her mother's. She saw it every time she looked in the mirror, too.

"Now can I watch the game in peace? Please?" she mock-whined. "You know how I feel about mixing base-ball and business." She rustled a bag of sunflower seeds out of her purse, ripped it open, then dumped a pile into her lap.

He gave her a disgusted look, but a slight smile relaxed

his face. "I don't see how you can watch an entire game in these ungodly seats."

"And I still don't see why you had to sit with me. Are they renovating your box?" That was where he always hid, far away from the memories, distracting himself with members of the board or potential investors or unsuspecting business associates being buttered up for a negotiation.

He shifted with an impatient grunt and straightened his suit coat. "Logan asked me to join you. Down here." He said it like they were in some third-world country.

"Logan?" She flipped up the bill of her hat and stared at the pitcher's mound. Though he'd never jinx his concentration with a glance back, she waved and gave him a thumb's up. "Logan doesn't care where you sit." Sure, Dad and Logan had chummed around since she'd started dating him last year, but it wasn't like things had gotten that serious. He was on the road half the time. And she worked sixty hours a week. He was a great guy, but... they'd never had what her parents had in those early days of their marriage, that fiery spark of energy that seemed to charge the space around them.

Speaking of Logan...She glanced at the scoreboard again. *Holy moly!* Two balls, one strike. Two outs? She cupped her hands around her mouth. "Come on, Logan! Strike 'im out!"

"Did you wear makeup today?" Her father's tanned face slid into view. "Or brush your hair?"

"Why?" She smiled sweetly. "Am I embarrassing you?" Lord knew, it wouldn't be the first time. There were certain expectations for people in their position, as he always reminded her, but she'd given up on meeting expectations in the looks department a long time ago.

"Of course you're not embarrassing me." He waved her off like that was the most ridiculous thing he'd ever heard. "You never know when the media will take a shot, that's all. I want you to look your best."

"This is my best," she assured him. Maybe her current attire didn't scream business executive, but it sure beat the hell out of those tight skirts and starched button-ups and godforsaken, ass-pinching pantyhose. "I haven't washed my jersey all season. It's good luck. See this mustard stain?" She pointed out the yellow blotch just below the V-neck with a proud smile. Proud and maybe somewhat mocking. She couldn't help it. He sometimes had that effect on her.

"Whatever makes you happy, Aves." Over the years, it had become his favorite platitude. Hers, too, actually. The thought was nice. Even if he rarely meant it.

"Can I start wearing my jersey to work?" She bounced her eyebrows.

"Once you take over as CEO, you can do whatever the hell you want," he grumbled.

Yeah, right. Edward King would never retire. He was only fifty-five, and healthy as a Clydesdale. Besides that, she had no desire to take over as CEO of King Enterprises. Not that she'd tell him that. It'd break what was left of his heart.

"Let me know when it's over." Dad dug out his iPhone and started to peck away.

Good. She could finally refocus on the game…

Out on the mound, Logan wound up.

She hunkered down, held her breath.

The ball zinged past home plate.

"Strike!" The ump signaled.

"Whoo hoo!" She leapt to her feet and screamed with the rest of the Cubbie faithfuls. "Way to go, Logan! One more!" Leaning forward, she gripped the concrete bar in all its sticky glory. *Come on . . . you got this . . .*

Logan wound up and let it fly.

Strike!

She high-fived the men behind her, her throat raw from another high-pitched squeal.

"Seventh inning stretch." Sliding back into her seat, she flung an arm around Dad and rattled his shoulders. "Isn't this the best?"

"The best," he parroted as he shrugged from her grip.

Waiting for the tune that exuded Americana, she hummed to warm up her vocals, find the right key. It was the best part of the whole game! Everyone singing about America's beauty, then pining after peanuts and Cracker Jacks . . .

Except the music didn't start. Instead, an announcer marched across the infield and handed a mic to Logan. He trotted toward the dugout.

Dad straightened his suit coat. "You might want to wipe that mustard stain off your shirt now." He reached over and brushed a pile of sunflower seeds from her lap.

"Hey!" She dusted his hand away from her beloved snack and looked up.

Logan didn't stop at the front of the dugout. He kept going, all the way to the end of the bench. Closer, closer . . . until she could see his smile, his eyes. What was he doing? He would ruin his concentration!

Vanessa rushed back to her seat. "What's happening?" she whispered.

"I have no idea," she hissed. "Vanessa, what is he doing?"

"Got me." Her eyes were as wide as Avery's. "I thought *you* knew."

No. She didn't know. But she had a bad feeling...

Logan hoisted himself up on the dugout roof and knelt in front of her with a nervous grin. His blond curls poked out from beneath his baseball cap in that endearing little-boy way.

She tried to focus on his eyes, brown and calming, the same color as a sweet, foamy latte.

Behind him, his teammates whooped and hollered.

"Time's a wastin', big boy!"

"Man up, Schwartz!"

"Logan?" The mic caught her whisper and carried it into an echo. A pound resounded in her chest. Her heart. Yes, that was her heart getting ready to gallop away...

"Pardon the interruption everyone, but I have something to ask my girlfriend." His voice sounded so different in the microphone, low and manufactured. Like something out of a reality show.

"*Mierda*," Vanessa choked.

Shit was right. Her palms broke out in a sweat. She couldn't breathe. Couldn't move. More whoops and hollers dented the silence, but the longer Logan stared at her, the quieter everything got. Muffled. Like she was sinking into the ocean.

"Avery..." He took her left hand in his. "You mean everything to me."

"Awwww," reverberated around the stands.

Gasp. Choke. Gulp. She couldn't utter a word, but she managed to peek over his shoulder. There, on the Jumbotron, was her mustard stain, glowing in the neon way of projection images.

"I love you. I want to share my life with you."

Another *awww* stretched into a deafening chorus.

Oh, dear God. Oh, no. He wasn't proposing. Not like this. Not in front of 20,000 people. Whatever happened to baking the ring in a cake? She'd gladly chip a tooth over this any day! Whatever happened to discussing things like marriage? A lifetime? Forever? Those weren't exactly spur-of-the-moment decisions.

"Make me the happiest man in the world." The goofy grin expanded. "Marry me."

"I'll marry you!" some woman behind her screamed.

Logan handed the mic off to Dad and dug in his pocket. Out came a baby blue Tiffany's box. When he flipped it open, a gargantuan emerald-cut diamond caught the sun.

A collective gasp hushed the crowd.

"*Mamacita!*" Vanessa yelped.

"Look at that rock!" someone else shouted.

Jaw hinged open, she stared at the prism-like diamond. It was wrong. All wrong. She'd always pictured her wedding ring as something of an antique, tried and tested by two people who'd weathered year after year of storms together. It would be a family heirloom, handed down to her future fiancé as a blessing when the stars aligned and he found his soul mate...

Logan slipped the imposter-ring on her finger and gazed into her eyes. "Avery?" The mic was still close enough to project his voice to the crowd.

Everyone quieted in anticipation of her answer.

Vanessa had officially invaded her personal space to inspect the ring.

Her body trembled. Could Logan feel it? Could he feel

that she didn't love him? She *liked* him. A lot. A whole lot. They had fun. But love? Marriage? Forever?

Extreme terror scorched her cheeks and made her feel like she'd sat in the sun too long. *Oh, no. I'm gonna throw up.* Chest heaving, she wrapped her free arm around her stomach.

Logan squeezed her hand a little too desperately. "Avery King, will you marry me?" he repeated in case the whole world hadn't heard him.

"Uh…um…" The stares of twenty thousand people burned into her. "I…well…"

His arms flew around her neck. He kissed her hard, his lips like steel. Then he let go and waved to the crowd. "She will! She said she will!"

What? Wait! No! She'd said well. *Well.* For the love of everything holy, it was a completely different vowel sound! The words remained trapped in her frozen throat. Her hand was still splayed in front her, weighted down by at least three carats.

A cheer rose from the stands and swelled into a roar.

The loudspeaker played a wedding march.

Edward stood next to her, stiff as one of his marble statues, clapping like he was at the opera and the fat lady had sung.

Only Vanessa seemed to get it, seemed to realize she was drowning.

"Oh, boy," her friend muttered, mimicking her own look of fear.

Hands jostled her shoulders. "Wanna chug?" The guys behind her held up their plastic beer cups in a mock toast.

"Ohhhh! How romantic!" shouted females, from ages

eight to eighty. Best wishes for a happy life mixed with music and chants.

Her heart palpitated. Not in a happy, *ohmygoodness I'm getting married* pattern, but in a dreaded *thud, thud, thud*, that made her chest feel too crowded and small. Oh, this was bad. So very bad.

"I didn't say yes," she whispered.

Vanessa nodded discreetly. She got it. Her eyes shifted as though searching for an escape, some way to end this before it got too ugly.

The blood drained from Avery's face and pooled in her chest. She couldn't marry him. She couldn't.

But...maybe she should go with it and give everyone a good show, a happy ending. It was the King thing to do, as her father would say. She glanced at Logan, at his broad, friendly smile. At the generous way he waved to all of his fans.

Her heart felt steeped in pain. She couldn't live a lie. Not even for five minutes.

He deserved more than that. She couldn't lead him on.

Slowly, she rose, legs shaky and weak.

Vanessa stood, too, arms outstretched, eye blaring a warning... *Don't do it, Avery. Not here. Not now.*

But she had to.

Logan finished waving to the cameras and leaned into her for another hug.

"Wait." She jutted out her arms to stop him. *Stop.* It had to stop. Her hands rested on his broad, muscular shoulders.

His eyes met hers.

Slowly, she shook her head back and forth.

A frantic look of understanding cranked open his

mouth. "Oh, no. I...I thought you knew...I'm sorry..."

He was sorry because he realized it, too. What would happen if she said no in front of 20,000 of his most devoted fans? He had to realize it. He was Chicago's Golden Boy. Everyone loved him, which gave them every reason to hate her right now.

The crowd hushed as if they'd caught on that their little fairy tale wouldn't have a happy ending. She hated to burst their bubble, but the popping had to start somewhere.

"I'm sorry." She tuned out the horrified gasps around her and kept her eyes trained on him. Because this was right, even if breaking his heart broke hers. "I can't do this. I can't marry you, Logan."

For a moment, a deafening silence smothered everything, then a horrible booing rose up from the crowd.

Logan said something, his eyes worried and sad, but she couldn't hear...

Cold splashed against her back. The smell of beer overwhelmed her. Things flew at her—cups and hats and...oh no! Popcorn rained down over her head, the kernels sticking to the mess on her clothes.

"Avery!" Vanessa huddled against her and raised her coat over their heads.

"Get her out of here!" Dad yelled at some security guards who'd sprinted over to help. Hands gripped her shoulders and ushered her down the aisle. She couldn't see. Beer and soda dripped down her face. Ice cubes slid down her matted hair.

"That's right! Leave, bitch!" A woman yelled.

The hands of her security entourage pushed her forward, shielding her with their coats and bodies, following her father's directives.

Vanessa found her again, threw an arm around her and somehow kept her moving. Her feet stumbled down a series of steps.

"Don't come back!" a kid shouted.

"How could you do this to him?" some lady wailed.

"Go!" Dad commanded behind her. "Bring the car!"

Locked inside the security guards' shelter, she and Vanessa staggered on and on for what felt like miles. Her body shivered from the way her wet clothes clung to her skin. Boos still echoed from the stadium, but they grew softer.

Finally, the momentum stopped.

Wheels screeched somewhere nearby. The hands herded them into the limo and slammed the door.

Avery sank into the leather seat next to Vanessa and tried to remember how to breathe. Breathe. Just breathe.

"Here, honey." Vanessa handed her a soft towel from the minibar.

She mopped her face. When her vision cleared, she saw her father's expression, the worry lines engraved in his forehead, the sad pull of his lips. It was the same look he'd worn at Mom's funeral, and then again every time he saw Avery in pain.

"Everything'll be fine," he insisted, even though everything was *so* not fine. His eyes brightened. She could practically see the light bulb flicker on over his head. "Schedule the jet for Aspen," Dad said to Van. "As soon as possible. We need to get her out of the city for a while. Might as well get some work done."

There was no point in arguing. Logan's botched proposal was destined to be tomorrow's YouTube sensation. She wouldn't be able to walk down the street without getting yelled at. "Let the death threats commence," she muttered.

"I'll get the PR department on it. We'll release a statement," Dad said briskly, as if that was all that mattered. Like her ruined public image was what had finally freed her tears.

He should know better. She didn't care what people thought. She didn't care if the whole world hated her.

She gazed out the window at the place she loved so much, the only place where her mother's laugh came back to life in her memory.

An overwhelming sense of loss weighted her heart.

She'd lost so much more than the city's respect.

After what had just happened in there, she'd never be able to show her face at Wrigley Field again.

CHAPTER TWO

"Hey batter, batter! Swing batter!"

Bryce Walker positioned himself behind home plate and glared at the woman who taunted him from the pitcher's mound.

"Love that tight t-shirt, baby!" Meg Carlson called, then bounced her curls like a blonde Betty Boop. He shook his head at her. What was she thinking, wearing that low-cut white t-shirt and short skirt to a damn baseball game? She wasn't careful, someone might mistake her for a cocktail waitress instead of an ER doctor.

"You been lifting weights or what? Those guns are gonna tear your sleeves!" she crooned.

If it hadn't been for the bat, he'd have flipped her a one-finger salute, but as it was, his hands were occupied. "No weights, sweetheart," he called back, making sure to smile real big at Nelson, her nurse fiancé who manned the outfield. "Just the usual mountain man stuff. Wood choppin', tree haulin'. You know the drill. Tough stuff for delicate hands like yours." Or for Nelson's, but he didn't say it. That might be one step too far over the line.

"Can you bend over real quick?" she shot back. "I want to get a picture of that tight ass of yours."

"You wish."

"We want a pitcher, not a belly itcher!" someone yelled from the bleachers, but he couldn't see who. The floodlights above him cast a glare right into his eyes. It was the perfect night for a game at Lower Moore Field—cool and crisp, the smell of campfire lingering in the air. With the fall tourist season in full swing, it seemed the stands were fuller. Or maybe they'd all turned out to see Aspen's prodigal son make his return to the town baseball league.

Whoosh! The ball sailed past him and smacked into the catcher's mitt.

"Hey." Bryce lowered the bat. "I wasn't ready."

Meg shrugged. "Always gotta be ready, Walker."

Trash talk flew from his team's dugout.

"Don't let her ruin your concentration!" Mom shouted. Even the sweetest woman in town knew Meg's M.O. She'd earned a reputation as the biggest flirt ever to grace the mound, and her strategy usually worked. She made half the guys in town practically swallow their tongues when they stepped up to bat, which meant she had the best pitching record in the history of the league. Lucky for him, he'd known her since he was old enough to open his eyes, so she didn't do much for him. Kind of like that annoying older sister who's always humiliating you in front of your friends. Or the whole damn town, as the case may be.

Not tonight…

"You know, that whole shaggy mountain man look is really working for me," Meg tried again. "Love a man who's not afraid of a little curl in his hair."

"Put a sock in it!" Mom yelled from behind the chain-link fence. "For goodness' sakes, Meg, don't encourage him!" She'd made it pretty clear she didn't appreciate the way he'd let his dark hair grow down past his ears. Wasn't too keen on the stubble he'd started to keep around, either. What could he say? Hadn't been much time lately for standing in front of a mirror. She, on the other hand, went to the beauty shop twice a week to keep her Betty White hair perfectly sculpted. He glanced over at her. On the street, you might mistake Elsie Walker for a sweet, little old lady with that white bob and the deep laugh lines accentuating her bright smile, but underneath that exterior she was a force to be reckoned with.

"Take it easy, Ma," he called over. "I can handle her."

"Yoo hoo! Bases are loaded," Meg reminded him with a wicked smile. "No pressure."

Bryce widened his stance and raised the bat. No pressure his ass. This was his first game in the town league since his stint in rehab. Not to mention, they happened to be playing their biggest rivals for ten years running. Aspen Valley Medical Center versus the Walker Mountain Ranch. He glanced over at his motley crew made up of river rats and ski bums, many of whom had worked at the ranch when it'd been operational. Before he'd gone and screwed everything up.

Next at bat would be Paige Harper. Growing up down the road, she'd always been like his little sister, though she'd changed a lot since her days of tagging along with him during the summers he came home from college. She'd always been a pretty girl, with long, wavy hair the color of Ponderosa pine bark—a cross between red and auburn. Back when they'd chummed around, she'd been in high school. Mom hired her to keep up the grounds and gardens at the ranch. Since then, he'd heard she'd become a damn good boater. Good skier, too. She worked for some rafting company in the summer and the mountain in the winter.

Then there was Sawyer Hawkins, a cousin from Mom's side, but everyone said they looked more like brothers. If that was true, Sawyer would've been the big brother, the way he always got Bryce out of trouble. Didn't hurt that he was an Aspen deputy. He was the one who'd finally convinced him to go to rehab. Said he'd beat the crap out of him if he had to drag him to detox one more time. As usual, Sawyer's wife, Kaylee, was attached to his arm. Newlyweds and all that.

Standing next to Kaylee was Bryce's buddy Shooter, who didn't much care if a woman was married or not. He still wasn't shy about looking. Shooter was tall and bulky, played wide receiver in high school. Still could, if he would've kept himself in shape. For a while, he tried to get himself cut enough to go pro, but no one drafted him so he'd fallen back on his other hobby in high school—skiing. He'd worked his way up the ski patrol and was now assistant director on the mountain. He was also obnoxious as hell, but he'd do anything for a friend, and Bryce figured it didn't hurt to have people like that around.

After Shooter came Yates, then Simpson, then Timmons, who'd all worked maintenance for his family at one time or another. When they could fit it in between bar tending and skiing, that was.

Looking at the two teams, it wasn't hard to pick out the underdogs. But as it stood, their team was only down by three. One long hit could hand them the victory.

"Oh, Bryce." Meg turned his name into a song.

"Hit a line drive! Nail her in the face!" Paige yelled.

"Tune it out, Walker! Get in the zone!" Sawyer chimed in.

No pressure.

"You ready, Slugger?" Meg taunted. "'Cause I've got a curveball with your name on it."

Grinning, he grabbed his crotch and spit like a professional ball player. "Send it in, sweetheart."

From the outfield, Nelson flipped him off. Didn't he know better? Stuff like that only egged him on. "Give it to me hard and fast. You know how I like it." There wasn't a lick of truth to that statement. Meg had no clue how he liked it, but two could play her game.

An outraged growl screwed her face into a look of fiery disgust.

Mission accomplished.

She planted her feet and drew back her arm. "Don't say I didn't warn you, Walker." With a loud grunt, she let it fly high and wide.

"Ball one!" The ump signaled.

He lowered the bat. "That all you got, Meg?"

Her face darkened—mouth taut, eyes narrowed like she was calling on some inner power.

Time to trip her up. Bryce backed out of the batter's box and threw a few practice swings, making sure to engage his biceps. One hit, that was all they needed to pull out a win. If he could catch a break, he'd hit the winning run, and that'd mean more than anyone could've guessed. After two years of letting the ranch slowly die, he'd come back to change everything. Right now it was more than just winning this game. He did this, maybe he could win back the ranch, too.

Before the bank took it away.

"Come on! You got this, Bryce!" Paige rattled the fence. She knew how much he had to prove to everyone sitting in those stands.

"Send the boys home, son!" Mom clapped and whistled.

Now or never. He jammed his big toe into the dust inside the batter's box and nodded at Meg.

She launched it in, straight and low.

His upper body strained and he came at it with everything he had.

Smack! The ball sailed over the outfielder's glove, hit the ground and rolled all the way to the damn sidewalk.

The Walker Mountain Ranch Misfits whooped and hollered.

"Run, Walker. For shit's sake, run!" Shooter sprinted along the fence just like he had back when they were ten. Bryce dropped the bat and took off for first, keeping an eye on the outfielders. Nelson had the ball, but he was still a ways out and he threw like a girl. Sure enough, he lopped it up, but it didn't have the distance.

Bryce rounded second, then third before Meg somehow came up with the ball. She chased him all the way home, but he had a longer stride.

Two steps. He'd beat her by two steps.

The dugout went wild and bum-rushed him. They swarmed him with congrats, high fives, and hearty slaps on the shoulder, with one on the ass, courtesy of Shooter.

When the racket settled, Meg trudged over. "Good game, Walker," she grumbled as she punched him in the shoulder.

"Yeah. You, too, Meg." He punched her back.

Surprisingly, she smiled. "It's good to have you back. How are things with the ranch?" Her eyes shifted away from his and told him she already knew the answer.

Gotta love a small town. He wouldn't be surprised if she'd found out before he'd even received the Notice of Election and Demand from the bank, informing him that he had 120 days to catch up on payments or they'd send it to auction. The thought wrenched his gut. While he'd been getting sober, things at the ranch had piled up, and now he had no idea how to dig out.

He tried to shrug it off. "Things have been better."

"Anything I can do?"

"Don't think so." He glanced past her at Mom, who was handing out homemade post-game cookies like it was some Little League Championship game. He hadn't found a way to tell her about the bank yet. Hoped he didn't have to. "I'll find a way to make it work." He had to find a way.

Meg reached into her pocket and pulled out a business card. "Bill Rhodes is a friend of mine. Go talk to him. Tell him I sent you."

He took the card and studied it.

Bill Rhodes, Senior Loan Officer
First Bank of Aspen

Despite the show she'd put on out there, he smiled at her. Felt damn good to have people on your side, even after being away for a while. "Thanks, Meg. Really."

"Yeah, sure. Least I can do."

Across the field, her fiancé waved her over. "Let's go, babe! Got the early shift."

Her hand patted confidence into his shoulder. "It'll work out, Bryce. Something will work out. Let me know if there's anything I can do."

As she jogged away, he dug his cell out of his pocket and punched in Rhodes's number.

After that hit he was feeling lucky. Time to go for another win.

* * *

Italian leather. Man, how he hated Italian leather. Bryce tried to get comfortable on the stiff couch and tapped the sole of his mud-caked boot against the marble tiles. They didn't belong in a place like this, those boots. Hell, he didn't belong in a place like this, but he'd run out of options.

"Mr. Rhodes will see you now." The secretary—admin assistant?—didn't even look up from her computer screen.

He stood and glanced at the nametag proudly displayed on the lapel of her swanky suit jacket. "Thanks, Chrissy."

She still didn't acknowledge him with a look, but her eyes narrowed like he had no business calling her by her first name. Yeah, he probably didn't. Even so, he passed her with an exaggerated smile. Her nose got any higher in the air, she'd scrape it on that golden ceiling and ruin her perfect nose job.

He clomped down a short hall and stopped in front of a door clearly marked, *Bill Rhodes, Senior Loan Officer* over frosted glass. He'd never been one for titles. Person could add as many adjectives to their name as they wanted and it still wouldn't impress him. Senior, President, Chairman, Superman, whatever. Didn't change much about a person, and he was about to find out exactly what kind of guy Bill Rhodes was.

The door opened.

"Mr. Walker?" Rhodes was dressed in one of those neatly trimmed suits that looked like something out of the old Bond movies. He had dark hair, cropped short and sculpted into stiff spikes.

A man who uses hairspray. Never a good sign.

Still, Bryce stuck out his hand. This guy held the cards for his future. Wouldn't hurt to make a good impression. "Yeah. Name's Bryce. Nice to meet you."

"Come on in. Have a seat." He stepped aside and gestured to his palatial office.

Apparently being a Senior Loan Officer meant you got a corner office that looked more like an apartment— a granite wet bar with a stocked wine rack, two black leather couches squaring off over a rustic coffee table, a black poplar desk that could've easily sat eight. All with a million-dollar view of downtown Aspen.

Bryce glanced at the door. This had been a mistake. He was way out of his league.

"Have a seat." Bill Rhodes gestured to the couches. "I'll grab your application so we can chat."

A man who says "chat." Another bad sign.

Suddenly too aware of the dirt trail his boots left behind, he tromped to the couch and slouched into the cushions. *Let's get this over with.*

"Would you like something to drink?" Bill Rhodes shuffled his loafers across a Persian rug to the wet bar and swung open the mini-fridge.

"No." He hadn't come for a drink. He'd come for a verdict. "Thanks."

"All right, then. Let's see…" Bill snatched a Perrier for himself and popped the top. "We've reviewed your application." He strode back to the couch and sat across from Bryce with what could only be described as a plastic smile, similar to the ones on all those mannequins that stared out the gold-trimmed windows in the shopping district.

"I'm sorry, Mr. Walker. Bryce. We've decided to deny the loan. It's too risky." He sipped his sparkling mineral water, then set it carefully on a marble coaster.

Bryce said nothing. He'd expected to hear that, but he wanted to watch Bill Rhodes squirm.

"The ranch hasn't been operational for a few years. There's no guarantee your improvements will pay off." His hands laced together into a patronizing configuration. "If you make the improvements and get things running again, we'd be open to seeing a new application."

"How would you suggest I do that without a loan?" A familiar knot lodged in his throat, a tangle of the guilt and grief that followed him around. "All due respect, Mr. Rhodes, but this bank used to be a big supporter of what my family did around here." The mountaineering trips, the backcountry education. And now...without their help—his help—he'd lose it all.

"I'm sorry. We're all sorry about what you've been through."

The words sounded like a monotone recording... *thank you for calling, your call is important to us.*

"But with the economy in the tank, there's nothing we can do. We need a guarantee before we give out that kind of money." He stood quickly and smoothed his hands down the sides of his suit in a dismissive gesture. "I suggest you do some marketing. Start taking guests again. We'd be a lot more comfortable if you could show us revenue."

Revenue? Bryce shot to his feet. "The place is falling apart. No one's gonna come stay there until it's fixed up. Where am I supposed to find revenue?"

Bill stretched out his arm, glanced at a pricey silver watch. "Look, Bryce. I'm glad you got yourself cleaned up. Really."

So Bill knew why the ranch hadn't been operational for two years. Of course. Everyone knew, read about it in the papers. How the son of such a respected family dove headfirst off the deep end after the accident. Bryce fisted his hands. The drunken bar fights, the nights in jail, the five-day benders. Everyone knew and no one believed in him. Not anymore.

Bill blazed a path to his office door and opened it. "Sorry. I wish I could do more but my hands are tied."

Yeah. So were his. He crossed the room and sized up Bill with a long glare. If he hadn't wasted two years with alcohol, they would've handed over the money. The ranch wasn't the big risk. He was. "Thanks for your time." He caught Bill's flimsy handshake in a firm grip. "I'll be back. Give me a few weeks." He'd prove himself, fix the place up all on his own, and when they saw what he could do with a hammer and nails, they'd give him the money.

Then he could start to reclaim everything he'd lost.

CHAPTER THREE

This voice mailbox is full—"

I know, lady. I'm the one who filled it. Avery stabbed her cellphone's off button and tossed it in her purse. She didn't blame Logan for ignoring her calls. Not only had she rejected the man in front of the whole world, but the Cubbies had lost. They'd blown a three-run lead and lost, thanks to her. Logan had played terrible. The Yanks hit four home runs off of him in the last two innings. And she hadn't even had the chance to talk to him. Right after the game, he'd hopped on a plane for a three-game series in San Francisco. She'd tried to explain herself, but you could only apologize so much on voice mail.

She held her breath until the ache in her heart subsided, then pulled back onto the highway.

Outside the rental car's windshield, the sky radiated a three-dimensional blue—liquid and electrifying. Pure. So pure. Gold leaves, dangling from clusters of white-trunked aspen, danced in the breath of innocence that whistled through the cracked window.

For the first time in three days, she could breathe. It didn't matter that the air in Aspen was thin as gold filament. She had space, quiet, anonymity; everything she'd craved since she'd watched the end of that ill-fated Cubs game on TV.

"In half a mile, turn right," the friendly GPS reminded her.

Sure enough, just up the road, a sign announcing *Walker Mountain Ranch and Outfitter* swayed in the wind. It'd obviously been there awhile, judging from the chipped log frame and the way the wood had weathered and faded. She made a quick right on the dirt road and maneuvered the rental car over a rutted, gravel driveway. If Logan wouldn't take her calls, she'd have to write him a letter. That's what she'd do. As soon as she was settled in her room, she'd send him a nice long e-mail.

Already feeling better, she eased the car over the grooves in the driveway. Thick clusters of aspen and pine trees lined either side, swathing her in their soft shadows, but then the forest opened into a clearing. Avery eased her foot on the brake. The first thing she noticed was a modest log building nestled in a meadow blushed by blue columbines and fiery Indian paintbrush. The scene could've been an oil painting, smudged in the impressionistic style, with golden leaves backlit against the glowing blue sky, deep green pine needles contrasting against pewter cliffs. Snow-swathed peaks stood in the distance, safeguarding the lodge into a fortress of peace and solitude.

She pushed out a long sigh, and with it came the regret, the humiliation, the utter ugliness of the last few days. Every second glance at the Rockies, at the blue sky and expanse of freedom, eased the tension in her neck.

She'd always loved the mountains, ever since their first camping trip to the Aspen area when she was six, before Dad had built his empire. That was when Dad had made his promise to Mom. They'd been in town, walking past The Knightley Hotel, when he'd stopped suddenly. The place had looked like a palace to Avery, with those faded bricks and manicured gardens and towering walls. There was no way they could've afforded to stay there, then. They were lucky to be able to scrape up the gas money to drive out here. But on the sidewalk that day, Dad had taken Mom's hand and pointed up at the hotel. "Someday we'll build our own resort here," he'd promised. "And I'll call it the Mirabella," which was Mom's middle name. Both Mom and she had giggled, never thinking it would actually happen. Back then, she'd never thought a lot of things would happen. She'd never thought she'd lose her mom when she was a kid…

Suppressing that familiar throb of sadness, Avery looked around the property. This place was a refuge. No wonder Dad had insisted on making it the site for the Mirabella. It was perfect.

Easing off the gas pedal, she pulled into what she assumed was a parking spot in front of a carved sign that said OFFICE. The building itself didn't look like much. The logs were peeling and cracked, the windows filmed with grime. Still, the whole place had this wise, grandfatherly presence about it, like its history had established its permanent legacy.

Warmed by the thought, she slung her backpack over her shoulder and climbed out of the car.

If nothing else, this assignment was the perfect opportunity to dress down. She'd let her hair go curly instead of straightening it into a sophisticated sheen. She'd dug through her closet and found her old frayed jeans and flowered long johns top from the hippie phase she'd gone through when Dad tried to send her to finishing school. When speaking with a true mountain man, it didn't hurt to look the part. Besides, she felt more comfortable in these clothes than she did in the clothes she wore to work every day. Don't tell her father.

She tromped up the steps in her brand-new hiking boots and rapped her fist against a splintered door. It creaked and inched open as if she'd stepped onto the scene of some horror flick.

"Hello?" The room was eerily dim. "Anyone in there?" She stepped inside and let her eyes adjust. Ancient oak floorboards creaked. The room smelled like sunbaked pine sap and dust—plenty of dust—which coated the counter where a lone computer sat. Two bookshelves bulged with colorful hardbacks. Square windows let in just enough light to unveil the framed pictures that occupied nearly every inch of wall space: an old black and white of a happy couple posing in front of a lake, a faded picture of a little boy climbing a boulder. Too many skiing photos to count. It was a fixer-upper, no doubt about that, but it had obviously been a beautiful place at one time.

"*Mwwufff.*" A low bark sounded from the far corner of the room.

Avery looked over. A massive, furry, black, brown, and white dog lay on a square pillow next to the counter.

"*Mwwufff,*" it droned again, then rolled onto its back and exposed its belly. Definitely a he. None too shy about it, either.

The adorable beast wagged his tail, sweeping it furiously over the ground.

How could she resist that? She walked over and knelt next to him, gave his belly the good rub he obviously craved. His humongous paw rested right on her chest, and she could've sworn the dog smiled.

She laughed. "Hey, there, buddy. A little soon for that, don't you think? We just met, after all, and I don't even know your name."

"Moose."

A man's baritone voice froze her.

"His name is Moose." Footsteps pounded behind her.

Crap. This wasn't exactly how she'd envisioned introducing herself to the Walkers—hunched over on the floor with a dog feeling her up. She scrambled to her feet and whirled just as a man came around the counter.

He had tousled dark hair and a shadow of stubble across his chin. The sleeves of the green flannel shirt he wore had been rolled up to the elbows, exposing forearms that bulged with solid, sinewy muscle. His tanned skin had a weathered quality that showed a love of sun and wind and snow. *Mamma mia.* Heat rushed through her, made her skin feel all flushed and tingly. Emphasis on the tingly. He was average height, but something in the way he carried himself seemed so...imposing.

His fiery green-eyed gaze trespassed into hers. "And you are...?"

Totally checking you out. She couldn't stop. The lower she went, the better it got. He wore some kind of khaki work pants that looked like they'd been custom-made to fit his solid body...

Her cheeks flamed. She had to stop. With a hefty clearing of her throat, she looked back at Moose so she could think. "Avery." Her skin still smoldered, but she'd recovered enough to offer the man her warmest smile. "I'm Avery King."

He raised his head in recognition, but said nothing.

Something cold and wet scraped against her hand and startled her. Moose licked her hand again, then nudged his nose into her crotch.

"Whoa!" she yelped.

"Watch out for that," the man said with a straight face. "He's right at that awkward level."

A nervous laugh made her sound like a drunk cheerleader instead of a business executive. *Okay.* Time to rein it in, get those pheromones under control. She'd come to negotiate with Bryce Walker, not to lust after some caretaker.

Giving Moose a good scratch behind the ears, she applied gentle pressure to keep his nose far away from her lower hemisphere. It was already on heightened alert, what with this man's overwhelming presence in the room.

"I'm here to see Bryce Walker." She worked hard to maintain an indifferent, professional tone, but her eyes betrayed her and lowered for another shameless glance at his broad chest.

"Why?" Those eyes inspected her with a cold precision. "What'd you want with Bryce?"

What *did* she want with Bryce?

The land...the resort...

She gave herself a mental shake of the head. *Snap out*

of it. So he had a nice body. An extremely pleasant face. That didn't mean this man was a pleasant person. "I'm a representative for King Enterprises. I believe Bryce will know why I'm here."

The man didn't move, didn't speak. He simply stood there, staring at her in all of his manly glory. If he stood that way much longer, she was pretty sure something inside of her would explode.

The dog rubbed his head against her leg, nearly knocking her off balance, and nudged her hand again. *Thank God.* The perfect distraction. She knelt to the dog's level and scrubbed his soft fur. "Aren't you a pretty doggie? Yes you are. You are a pretty doggie Moosey woosey."

"Don't talk to him like that," the man said in his flat tone. "He's a Bernese Mountain dog, not a Shih Tzu."

Well he may have been a big, bad Bernese Mountain dog, but Moose didn't seem to mind her tone at all. His massive tongue swamped her face, which unleashed her juvenile laugh again.

"All right, Moose. That's enough. Go lay down," the man commanded in a gentle but authoritative voice that tempted her to go lay down, too.

Moose gave a woeful look, his eyes wide and wondering, but then he trotted to his pillow, turned two circles, and lay down with a grunt. He rested his head on his paws and continued to stare at the man as if he had the biggest, juiciest steak hidden in his pocket.

Yes, she could relate. Did she stare at the man like that, too? *Ahem.* She shifted her weight and rose with as much grace and dignity as she could muster. Business. She was here on business. "Listen." She stitched her lips into a professional smile and faced the man directly. "I'd really

like to speak with Mr. Walker. We have things to discuss.
So if you wouldn't mind—"

"What'd you say your name was?"

"Avery. King." She enunciated each syllable just in
case he had a hearing problem.

His mouth cemented into a straight line and concealed
any hint of emotion. He stared at her like she was a mark
on the wall, annoying but at the same time insignificant.
"Bryce isn't here."

After all that? After he'd tortured her with those omni-
scient stares? Bryce wasn't even around? Anger pricked
her face, but she gazed right into that man's eyes and
matched his indifference in her own expression. "When
will he be back?"

A smirk dimpled those stubbled cheeks. "Dunno."

Her hands fisted. "Listen, Mr. . . . ?"

"Trust me. You're wasting your time." He leaned
against the counter, all casual and unaffected, damn him.
"You're not getting his land." Those unreal eyes looked
down on her as he secured his ultimate fighter arms over
his chest.

She diverted her gaze to the wall behind him. He really
needed to stop with the bulging muscles. It was kind
of distracting. "Fine. That's fine." Glancing around the
room, she spotted a rickety hardback chair in the corner.
"I'll wait for him to come back." She held her head high,
marched to the chair, and sat herself down.

"He won't be back today." Heavy footsteps punished
the old floorboards. Brown work boots emerged in her pe-
ripheral vision.

She crossed her legs all ladylike and studied her nails.

"You can't wait here. I'm about to tear out the floors."

Gazing up through her eyelashes, she blinked sweetly. "Then I'll wait outside. On the porch." Though she'd hate to miss this man doing some manual labor...

He muttered something she couldn't hear and marched closer. "The day I sell my land to your *daddy*"—his tone mocked her—"is the day hell freezes over. Last I heard it was still all fire and brimstone."

"Wait." She shot off the chair. "The day *you* sell?" He'd totally played her. Nobody *ever* played her. "You're Bryce."

A slow smile spread across his face.

They resumed their staring contest, but this time it was different. So. Different. This man, the one who'd done things to her body without even touching her, was the man she had to negotiate with? *He* owned the ranch?

"Disappointed?"

Disappointed? Hadn't he noticed her ogling him? Oh, lordy, hopefully not. "Of course I'm not disappointed." No woman with any sense of desire could be disappointed in a specimen like him. "You're just...not what I expected." The lodge had been built in the fifties, so she'd pictured someone with gray hair and a limp. She'd pictured the mountain man aged like good cognac. Not a mountain cowboy fantasy, all dark and brooding and completely irresistible. He'd totally caught her off guard.

"Anyway, Miss King. Like I said, I'm not interested." He stepped closer. "So you might as well go back home."

He stood so close she could smell cedar and sweat, so close she could see the ridges and lines in his lips. *Wow.* He had nice lips. Smooth and pliable...

Her throat knotted. She had to stop thinking about his lips. His lips were not helping her with this negotiation...

"Tell your daddy to find another place to build his swanky resort. Try Telluride." Bryce dodged past her and headed for an open door behind the counter.

"Hold on." She shook herself out of a swooning shiver and chased him. "I'm not leaving until you hear me out. It's a generous offer."

"Won't be generous enough."

"You haven't even seen it." She snatched her backpack off the floor and rifled through until she found the print-out. "If you'll—"

"You're wasting your time." Bryce peered over his shoulder as he walked away.

"I have nothing but time." She tossed the backpack on the ground, assuming the stance she'd perfected in all of her business negotiations; feet rooted into the floor, hip jutted. Bryce Walker would sell his land. Give her two days with the man. "I'm not going anywhere. I think I'll hang out and see the sights." She shuffle-kicked her back-pack to the counter. "My flight doesn't leave until Friday. I'd like to stay here."

He laughed, but it was breathless and garbled. "Bad idea. You might ruin your perfect hair."

Her hand reached up to pat the curls that kept dipping over her eyes. "No one's ever accused me of having per-fect hair." Especially when she didn't bother to straighten it. "But I'll take that as the highest compliment, coming from you," she sassed, just in case he could tell he was getting to her. Because he was.

She'd stood in front of two hundred board members and investors on numerous occasions to articulate good news, bad news, boring news, and never once had her heart drummed like it did when Bryce Walker looked at her. She'd done press conferences for King Enterprises for years, with the media rapid-firing question after question, and not once had she fumbled her words or resorted to the drunk cheerleader laugh. Yet somehow this man managed to make her feel like a silly, socially awkward girl who got all warm and flushed when a member of the opposite sex noticed her. It brought her right back to those memorable junior high days.

And he was doing it again, the jerk! Staring at her long and hard, as though cataloging a list of her physical features.

Avery fought a desperate urge to adjust her posture and make her B cups more impressive. She had to get out of there and regroup.

"So what's your nightly rate?" She dug through the backpack pockets until she located her wallet.

"You're not staying here," he said in that same voice he'd used to command Moose, low and resolute.

Except she wasn't a dog. She didn't have to obey his commands. "This is a guest ranch, isn't it?"

"Was." Bryce's jaw set into a hard line and erased the smirk. "It was a guest ranch. No one's stayed here for two years." His gaze roamed over her body again.

Wait a minute. Was he ogling her, too?

Finally, his gaze made its way back to her eyes, his stare so intense it left her breathless.

"It won't be up to your standards," he muttered.

She fought for a full, deep breath of air and raised her brows in a challenge. "You'd be surprised."

"There're plenty of five-star resorts in town. Perfect for people like you."

People like her. Why did everyone always do that? Assume that she was one of those entitled heiresses who spent her days partying and shopping with her father's credit card instead of working her ass off? She glared at him. "You don't know me." Her father had made sure she knew how to work hard to get what she wanted. Even after all his success, he'd made her work and save every penny until she could buy her first car herself, a 1989 Toyota Corolla with rust creeping up the fenders.

Unfortunately for Bryce Walker, she'd learned how to scrap and fight to get what she wanted. He hadn't seen perseverance, didn't know the true face of stubbornness. She twirled to face him. "A thousand dollars. Will that cover four nights?" She lifted each c-note from her wallet and held them out.

His eyes focused on the money. "I'm... I haven't set prices yet."

"Good. I'll help you. Two hundred and fifty a night would be competitive in this area." Maybe not in its current condition, but something told her he already knew that. She shoved the money into his hand and tried to ignore the glorious pull of her insides when his skin grazed hers. Then she traipsed to the rack of keys dangling on the wall behind the counter and selected one. "I'll stay in Room 5. Will that work?"

Bryce's arms dropped to his sides. "I think it's clean."

How encouraging. "Where is it?"

His forehead wrinkled like he wondered how they'd gotten to this point. "Out the door, down the steps, take a left," he said slowly, like he had to think about it. "But—"

"Got it." She gathered her bag and bolted for the door before he could get to the "but."

"I'll come and find you after I freshen up. We can continue our discussion then."

"I already told you. I'm not—"

"See you soon." Without looking back, she jogged down the steps and made her exit, the suitcase bumping an encore behind her.

CHAPTER FOUR

Bryce jabbed the hammer into the crack and ripped out another floorboard. *Jab. Rip. Screech.* The work was loud, messy, painstaking, but nothing compared to listening to Avery King talk. The sight of her kneeling next to Moose had given him a good jolt, and it wasn't because he'd been surprised to see someone. No, it was something about the way her curly blond hair fell down around her shoulders, something about her silky, flushed skin. Then there was her body, slender but athletic. When she'd looked at him, her topaz eyes glimmered with humor and life.

She had some spark that'd lit his fuse...

Then she'd opened her mouth. Avery King. Just his luck. He finally sees a woman who intrigues him and she happens to be the ranch's biggest threat.

He tossed down the hammer and shoved the old rotted floorboards into a pile. Couldn't tell if the heat crawled off his skin because of the manual labor or the fact that, right now, that woman was unpacking her things in Room 5. Staying there for four nights. If he didn't need the money so bad...

A car engine hummed outside. Monster wheels grinded gravel and skidded to a stop.

Bryce pushed off his knees and wiped sweat from his eyes. Had to be Mom. Hopefully she'd gotten his message. Without her help the next few days, he'd be in big trouble.

Sure enough, petite footsteps scurried across the porch, barely louder than a squirrel's.

The door swung open.

"Bryce! I came as soon as I heard." Mom rushed in, her Birkenstocks clacking the barren floor. "Is it true? We have a guest? How wonderful!"

Wonderful? "Not really." What could possibly be wonderful about the King family eyeing his land? The land his grandparents had invested their entire lives in? The land he'd grown up on?

"Well..." Her outstretched hands demanded an answer. "Don't keep me in suspense! Who is it?"

"Avery King." The name tasted bad in his mouth. "That guy's daughter. The one who owns half of Chicago." And New York. And L.A., according to Google.

"Avery... gracious!" She gasped. "You mean *the* Avery King? The heiress?"

"That'd be her." Unfortunately for him.

"How exciting! Well?" Mom shook his shoulder like a five-year-old begging for a thick slice of chocolate cake. "What's she like?"

Where to start? "She's... annoying, relentless, irrational, stuck up." At least that's what he'd keep telling himself. Because the thought of her spending every night in the lodge had his imagination wandering places it hadn't for a long time.

He kneeled back to the floor and swiped the hammer off a chair, pried out another floorboard.

A wave of Mom's hand dismissed him. "Oh really, Bryce. She can't be that bad." She knelt to his eye level. "What does she look like? Is she pretty?"

Warmth swelled through him. No. She wasn't pretty. She was perplexing. Stunning and strong and obviously determined to get what she wanted. He'd never met any woman quite like Avery King.

Mom stared at him, waiting.

He shrugged. Hopefully she couldn't see him sweat. "She's average." After what she'd pulled earlier, he wasn't about to pay her a compliment.

Studying him carefully, his mother stood and clasped her hands. "We should invite her to dinner. Don't you think?"

He pried up another floorboard and tossed it on the pile. "Nope. No way." That would be a bad idea, and not only because it would make her think he actually wanted to hear her offer. Staring at Avery King across the table for an hour wouldn't help his imagination. "We have a baseball game at seven. She can grab dinner in town."

"Now, Bryce. That won't do. That won't do at all." Her bracelets clanged around her wrist. She always talked with her hands when she felt passionate about something.

Here we go. He tried not to shake his head.

"We have to impress her. Show her why you don't want to sell this place. I mean, once she realizes what happened to Yvonne—"

Yvonne. Every time he heard her name, he still saw her, that silky dark hair falling over her shoulders, those maple-colored eyes that never failed to pry him open, the lift of her lips when she smiled. Even after three years, he still saw her, still heard her voice. He still felt her presence with him, like she was simply upstairs in the apartment they'd shared instead of in a grave.

Then Avery King had walked in and for those five minutes, he'd forgotten. She'd made him forget. A surge of anger fisted his hands. "My past is none of her damn business." The hammer stilled, but his pulse kicked up. He did a silent count to ten before he looked at Mom. "I'll only do the dinner if you promise not to say a word about the accident." Avery King had no right to his memories. She didn't deserve to know.

"Fine, fine. Of course that's your decision." Pity glossed her eyes.

He'd seen that look too many times. Didn't need to see it in Avery King's eyes, too.

"But we can still tell her all the wonderful things this ranch has done over the years, can't we? We need to show her why you'll never sell. So she understands."

"She won't understand." He'd only spent a total of ten minutes with her and he already knew that.

"You're impossible. So quick to judge." She waggled her head as if wondering where she'd gone wrong with him and teetered over the missing floorboards to make her way to the counter. With a mischievous look directed at him, she picked up the phone and dialed.

"Yes, hello, Miss King. This is Elsie Walker, Bryce's mother."

A pause, then she smiled. "Why, it's lovely talking to

you, too dear. I was hoping you could join Bryce and me for dinner tonight."

Bryce closed his eyes and shook his head. Perfect. Just what he needed.

She switched the phone to her other ear and gave him a double thumbs-up. "Wonderful. We'll see you in the dining room at five o'clock."

Another pause, then Mom waved a hand through the air like Avery was standing right in front of her. "Oh, no, no. Don't you worry about bringing anything. We'll take care of it."

God help him. Mom was giggling. She was actually giggling like her best friend was on the phone. He swiped a hand down his face. This would not end well.

"Okay, dear. We'll see you then. Looking forward to it! Bye, now." Mom cradled the phone. "Well, isn't she just the sweetest thing?"

Bryce stood and posted his hands on his hips. "You do realize she wants our land, right? That's why she's being sweet." That's why he couldn't let himself look at her—really look at her—or think about her, or let her inspire his imagination more than she already had. Someone had to be sensible.

"She seems very genuine," Mom insisted, patting his hand. "Let's give her the benefit of the doubt, shall we?"

Much as he'd like to, he couldn't afford to. She'd unlocked something in him when he'd seen her, and it wasn't just a fleeting rush of admiration. It went deeper. It made him want her. And he hadn't wanted anyone. Not since Yvonne.

Damming back that flood of desire, he picked up his

hammer and ripped out another floorboard. It would be a long four days.

Mom peered down at him. "Look at you, doing all this work. Your grandpa would be proud, you know."

No. He didn't know.

"We'll bring this place back from the dead, you and me." Her eyes misted. "You wait and see. It'll all work out, won't it?"

"Sure it will." He hoped his lost faith didn't haunt his features. He'd neglected to mention his visit to the bank. She knew they were behind, but she didn't know how bad it had gotten. He couldn't break her heart that way. Couldn't tell her until he had a way out of it...

"I'd best get on to the market, then. I'll make a delicious dinner for the three of us. My Sunday best," she declared with a confident nod.

He smiled down at the floor. Good old Mom. Always believed home cooking could solve all the world's problems.

"Oh, it's been so long since we've had a guest. We'll make it pleasant, won't we? Please, Bryce?"

"Pleasant? Hmmm." He wasn't about to give in to Avery King again, like he had when she'd asked to stay, but he could be polite. He'd have to be smart about it, keep his distance so he didn't get sucker-punched by her spark again. But it could be done. As long as she didn't push him. "I'll try."

"Now, now," Mom wagged her finger. "We can find the good in anyone, can't we?"

"I don't know about 'we,' but you definitely can." She'd sure waited patiently to find it in him.

"I will. You can count on that." She tiptoed to the door,

carefully stepping over loose nails and scraps of wood. "Oh, and Bryce?"

He looked up.

"You will shower, won't you?" Her nose wrinkled and softened the blow. "In the interest of making a good impression and all? It wouldn't hurt to shave, either."

He gave her a disgruntled look, but didn't argue. "Good thing I've got you around. Who else would tell me when I stink?"

She waved cheerily and scooted out the door. "See you at five, dear. Don't be late."

* * *

The coast was clear.

Keeping an eye out for Bryce, Avery darted up the lodge's grand staircase, which was flanked on either side by the loveliest hand-carved banisters. Shadows flickered on the log walls in a rhythm of swaying evergreen trees, and within the window's light, dust particles glittered in the glow of a setting sun. She ran her hand along the hewn log wall, feeling the knots and imperfections. She could almost hear the laughter that had once echoed in the halls. She could almost see the people from those few pictures on the walls gathered around the fireplace downstairs drinking hot cocoa.

But something had gone wrong.

She hadn't meant to start snooping. Not really. Dad had asked her to check the place out, to see if anything would be salvageable "when" they built the resort. The more she'd seen, the more she wondered about Bryce, about his family. Cobwebs laced the corners of doorframes. Faded curtains hung limply together. Closed doors hinted at memories carefully tucked away to be forgotten. For all of its antique charm, the lodge shuddered with an echoing hollowness, eerie and contemplative, like a dwelling where ghosts existed. A few framed pictures on the walls depicted a vivid family life: Bryce and his mom and grandparents skiing and hiking and driving their Jeep all over those mountains outside, but inside, the lodge had died. She just couldn't figure out how.

At the top of the staircase, she detoured down yet another dim corridor. More framed pictures decorated the walls. She paused to study one. Bryce as a small child. The mischievous smile gave him away. He stood between his grandparents, hearty-looking people with gray hair and tanned faces. A younger Elsie stood on the other side, arm draped his shoulder, proud smile beaming. Even back then it was obvious Bryce had been destined to be a lady-killer. Throughout the years, he must've left quite the string of broken hearts in his macho wake, though she hadn't seen any photographic evidence of him and a girlfriend. Or a wife...

Did he have someone? She really shouldn't wonder because it was completely irrelevant to her mission there, but her traitorous mind kept circling back to that particular mystery. What was wrong with her? She'd never been so stunned by a man. The first time she'd met Logan at a charity event, they'd flirted and danced and by the end of the night, they'd been good friends. She'd been so comfortable with him, easygoing and sure of herself. But the force of Bryce's presence, the way he'd shaken her, made her unsure of anything.

Moving on...

She ambled deeper into the hallway. The air sat heavier and stale upstairs, as if no one had been up here for years. Her body tensed. She shouldn't be up here either. The last thing she needed was for Bryce to catch her snooping around.

The thought of seeing him again stoked the embers that glowed in the hollow of her stomach. She'd have to face him again, eventually, but first it might help if she knew more about him, if she could unlock some of his secrets so she could gain the advantage and figure out how she'd convince him to give this place up.

The faint sound of dishes clanging downstairs halted her progress. She crept toward the sounds until the hallway opened into a loft. Peering over the banister, she leaned over as far as she dared to catch a glimpse of the dining room, but the massive river-rock fireplace blocked her view. Maybe she should go see if dinner was ready.

Quiet. She tiptoed across the worn carpet. *Almost to the staircase...*

A ring tone blared. *Her* siren ringtone, with the volume cranked. She dashed back to the darkness of the hallway and tried the first door. It opened.

Closing it as quietly as possible, she dug out her screaming phone. Her father's picture lit up the screen.

"What do you want?" she hissed.

"Hello to you, too," he said, sounding wounded. "Forgive me for wanting to check in on my daughter."

Mmm hmmm. Right. "You know your daughter is perfectly capable of handling herself." He rarely called to check on her, even when it came to multi-million-dollar deals. Switching the phone to her other ear, she crept deeper into the room. It looked different from her guest

room downstairs. It was more of a suite, with a small
kitchen in one corner and a leather sofa set in the other
corner. On the opposite wall there was a king-sized bed
covered with what looked like a hand-sewn wedding ring
quilt. Pine wainscoting adorned the walls.

"Fine," her father conceded. "I called to see if you've
talked to Walker yet."

"Not really." She kept an eye on the door. "I'm having
dinner with him tonight." At least, he'd better be there.
Mrs. Walker hadn't mentioned Bryce on the phone, but
she'd said "we," so hopefully . . .

"What about the property?"

"I've walked around." The lodge held a simple, unique
beauty, but she couldn't deny that it showed its age.
"Nothing's salvageable." At least, not for an Edward
King-style resort.

"I figured." A swishing sound echoed in her ear. Wind.
He was probably leaving work, jogging down the sidewalk so he could meet his colleagues for their pre-dinner
whiskey sours. "We have to move forward, Avery. I heard
from the mayor. It sounds like Walker is trying to get a
loan." He half shouted the words, competing with honk-
ing horns and the swishing car sounds. "We can't lose
this. You'll have to work fast."

"Don't worry. I'm on it." Bryce might've thrown her
off her game, but she'd get it together and do what she
did best. Charm him, negotiate with him, deliver results.
Speaking of . . .

"I should go." She rose from the couch. "Can't be late
for dinner." Mrs. Walker had made it sound more like a
family dinner than a business transaction, but she still had
to make a good impression.

"All right, Aves," Dad said. "Keep me posted."

"I'll send you an e-mail tonight—"

The line clicked.

Good-bye to you, too. She slipped the phone into her back pocket and started for the door. Might be time to have another chat with Dad about how to politely end a phone call.

Crunch. The sound of cracking glass under her boot made her cringe. *Oops.* She slowly lowered her head, as if that could undo the damage, and saw a beautiful sliver picture frame, now squashed into pieces.

Damn it. Where did that thing come from? She dropped to her knees and picked it up, scattering shards of glass across the floor.

In the black and white photograph, a bride laughed, her husband's lips pressed against her cheek. Though only a profile was visible, she recognized the smile, the dark unruly hair, even though it was much shorter.

Avery blinked at the picture, seeing her own shocked reflection in the glass, and held it up to read the engraved inscription.

To Bryce,
    My love, my heart, my best friend. Love you always, Yvonne

He was married. Bryce Walker was married? She studied the woman in the picture again. Yvonne. A ring of small white daisies crowned her beautiful dark hair, which waved down around her shoulders. Deep brown eyes glistened with the joy of a woman in love. A dimple topped off her friendly smile.

Avery touched a finger to the inscription. *Huh.* Still studying the picture, she stood. She'd always been just a tad nosey, and something about it didn't seem to fit. There were no other pictures of this woman in the halls. And...her head swiveled so she could investigate the area...where had it come from? She hadn't seen the frame before she stepped on it. Maybe it'd fallen out of the closet next to her. But why would it be hidden in the closet?

Her hand moved to open the closet door—just for an innocent peek—but before she could touch it, the door to the room flew open.

Uh oh... She looked around for a place to stash the picture, but it was too late.

Bryce strode into the room. First he glared at the broken picture in her hands, then his narrowed, dangerous eyes moved to her face.

He looked different. Good different. *Really* good different. Maybe it was the shirt, a faded green cotton Henley that pulled tighter across his chest. Or it could've been the way his dark hair glistened with evidence of a shower. Yes indeedy, he looked mighty good, but he definitely did not look happy.

"Hi!" she squealed, then inwardly winced. With that kind of greeting, he probably expected her to belt out a cheer. *Give me a B!*

His tight glare tempted her to go through with it, along with the arm motions and everything, just to see if she could get a smile out of him.

"What're you doing?" he asked, eyes flashing with suspicion.

"I was just on my way down for dinner." She broke

the thick chill that iced the air between them and pasted on her brightest smile. Suddenly, the five-by-seven picture frame felt like it weighed two hundred pounds. She held it out to him. "Um...I accidentally stepped on this." Lame. She sounded so lame. "I'd be happy to pay for it. Just let me know—"

"That's not necessary." He snatched it away from her and set it on the nearby counter carefully, reverently. Then he turned back to her, his face as hard as stone. "I meant what're you doing *up here*?"

The intensity radiating from his eyes, from his voice, reduced her breaths to gasps, but she tried to hide them behind a smile. "I was...um...looking around your beautiful lodge." When all else failed, there was always flattery. "The craftsmanship is remarkable."

His rigid stance made it clear he didn't buy the act. "This room is private. You shouldn't be in here."

"I'm sorry." *So, so, so sorry.* Because now that he stood so close, she could see his left hand, his left ring finger where a gold band should be. Instead, it was bare. He wasn't married, not anymore. The raw pain in his eyes confirmed it. She gambled with a step closer to him and peered up at his face, which was smooth with a fresh shave. "I'm sorry," she said again, hoping he knew she meant it. "I didn't mean to intrude."

A subtle flinch steered his gaze away from hers. "You scared Mom. She heard something. Thought we had another raccoon."

Another raccoon? She glanced around the room and tried not to shiver at the thought of critters skittering around the attic right above her head. "I didn't mean to scare anyone." She hadn't meant to hurt anyone, either.

Without thinking, she rested her hand on his arm. "I won't wander anymore. I promise."

He jerked his arm away and bolted out the door. "Dinner's been on the table for ten minutes." The words trailed behind him.

"Sorry about that, too," she called. "I lost track of time."

He didn't respond, and by the time she'd made it into the hallway, Bryce was gone.

CHAPTER FIVE

Okay, so she wasn't exactly winning the man over. Avery's cheeks flamed as she hurried down the steps in a rare walk of shame. What was the matter with her? She always maintained the highest level of professionalism, the strictest discretion, but so far in her brief encounters with Bryce she'd managed to make herself look both green and duplicitous—getting so flustered, sneaking around his house and discovering things he obviously wanted to keep hidden.

The look on his face when he'd seen her holding that picture frame branded her heart with regret. She'd already lost his trust and something told her that wouldn't be an easy thing to recover.

On the main level, the lodge opened up into a great room with that epic fireplace towering in the center. Bookshelves lined almost every wall, stuffed with colorful hardbacks of every size. Plush wingback chairs and antique Victorian sofas clustered throughout the room like ancient ladies and gentlemen mingling at a formal affair. Handmade log coffee and end tables accented each group with rustic elegance.

All along the back wall, gigantic picture windows framed chiseled mountain peaks powdered with snow. Changing aspen leaves blazed a gold path to the tree line. A weary sun hovered low, breathing a pink glow high into the sky.

Avery paused to admire the view, then looked around for Bryce. He couldn't have gotten far...

"Welcome! Welcome!" A woman dashed through a door on the other side of the room. She was short and plump, but moved as gracefully as a ballerina on toe shoes. Her familiar green eyes glistened and her face radiated an openhearted smile. "You must be Avery. I've been waiting to meet you."

"Yes, hi." She reached out a hand for the customary shake, but Mrs. Walker stretched her arms wide and gathered her in for a hug.

"Oh!" At first she wasn't sure what to do—she'd never been hugged by a complete stranger before—but then she inhaled the calming scent of cinnamon and yeast, and returned the embrace. "It's nice to meet you, Mrs. Walker." She'd seen so many pictures of the woman's kind smile she felt like she already knew her. Well, that and Mrs. Walker had one of those familiar faces—plump rosy cheeks, wrinkles that revealed her propensity to enjoy a good laugh. At least she knew they had one thing in common.

The woman pulled back. "The pleasure is all mine, dear."

The words were so genuine that she felt some of her guilt at the scene upstairs fade away. Something told her Mrs. Walker was a lot more forgiving than her son. Avery smiled back at her. "Sorry I'm late. I was exploring your beautiful lodge."

"No need to be sorry." The woman gave her arm a friendly squeeze and led her to the other side of the dining room table. It could have easily seated twenty, but there were only three place settings.

Three. That was good. That meant Bryce would join them, if she hadn't driven him away.

Mrs. Walker wiggled a chair away from the table and gestured for her to sit. "You get comfy, dear. Don't worry about a thing."

Don't worry? Too late for that. Worry had plunged into her stomach like a stone, solid and heavy. She sat down and glanced at the empty setting across from her.

"Bryce should be back any minute." Mrs. Walker leaned over and filled her water glass. "He went to check on something upstairs."

Uh oh. She looked down and studied the delicate flower pattern on the china, but there was no way she could pretend she hadn't seen him. The woman was bound to find out, eventually. "Actually...I ran into him up there."

Elsie scooted herself into the chair across the table. "Oh. Wonderful. Well, where is he, then?"

"I don't know." She forced herself to meet the woman's eyes, even though it was as hard as staring at a priest during confession. "I was looking around upstairs, and..." How could she say this without sounding like a criminal? "I ducked into a room to answer my phone."

Now that she'd said it, it sounded innocent enough. It wasn't like she'd tried to break that frame, like she'd pulled it out of the closet and stomped her heel into it or something. "There was a picture," she said, scrapping the unnecessary details. "When Bryce saw me looking at it, he took off."

"I see." His mother's cheerful expression collapsed into a sad, soft smile. "I assume it was a picture of Yvonne, then."

"A wedding picture. She'd engraved the frame."

Mrs. Walker nodded as if she knew it well. "She gave it to him for their third anniversary."

So they'd been married at least three years, but then what? She bit her lip to keep from blurting out the question. Technically, it was none of her business, but she couldn't erase the memory of Bryce's wounded look when he'd taken the picture out of her hands.

The regret made a comeback, this time manifesting as an uncomfortable pressure in her chest. "I didn't mean to upset him."

"Of course you didn't mean to upset him, dear." Mrs. Walker reached across the table and gave her hand a firm pat. "How could you have known? Don't feel bad, Avery. He'll be fine."

He sure hadn't looked fine. "His wife is beautiful." Yes, the question was a shameless fishing expedition, but that wasn't as taboo as blurting.

"Yvonne was killed in an accident," Elsie murmured, her eyes cast down. "Three years ago. It happened on their third anniversary."

His wife was dead.

The revelation knifed through her in a familiar, searing

pain. She'd felt it before; that same mixture of grief and sorrow she'd seen on his face. It had been so deep and cutting that it left an incurable scar. Over time, it might seem to have healed, but then something would rip it back open and the pain would come again, as excruciating as it had been fifteen years ago, the day she'd found Mom's lifeless body.

"I'm sorry." She looked into Mrs. Walker's eyes so her words wouldn't be a meaningless cliché, so the woman would know she'd earned the right to say it in a way not many people could. "That must've been so hard on all of you."

"It was harder than losing Bryce's dad," she admitted, carefully unfolding her napkin to dab at the corners of her eyes. "He was so young when his father died, he didn't know what had happened. But watching Bryce suffer after Yvonne passed...it was the closest thing to hell I can imagine." A brave smile shone through the storm in her eyes. "He's always been strong, though. He's in a much better place now."

"He must have loved her very much." Just like Dad had loved Mom. He'd lost a part of himself the day she died, and he'd never been able to find it again.

"He did," Mrs. Walker agreed. "They met in the sixth grade. Dated all through school. After college, marriage was the natural next step, of course. Yvonne was a lovely—"

Somewhere nearby, a door crashed open. Bryce plowed into the room with the poise of a UFC fighter, scowl and all.

"There you are." His mother's tone somehow balanced reprimand with pure joy. She rose from her chair and started to cart over platters and bowls from a mahogany serving credenza against the wall. The smile had returned to her eyes. "Oh, this is so much fun," she cooed. "We don't get much company around here anymore."

Not everyone looked like they were having fun. Avery kept a wary eye on Bryce, who hovered in the corner and completely ignored her presence.

His mom didn't seem to notice. "I made one of Bryce's favorite dinners. Apple butter-glazed pork chops with parmesan risotto." She set down the last dish and swatted the air. "Don't ask me to share the recipe, though. It's a family secret."

"It looks amazing." Avery gawked at the bowls and platters now scattered across the center of the table. She couldn't help it. The smells and the presentation rivaled anything at a five-star restaurant. "Thank you for going to all this trouble, Mrs. Walker."

"Elsie. Call me Elsie, dear." She heaped a huge spoonful of risotto onto Avery's plate.

"I'll take my plate to the office." Without a glance in her direction, Bryce swiped his plate off the table. "I have work to do."

"You'll do no such thing." Elsie dashed over and tugged him back to the table across from Avery. "You've been out there for hours. It's time for a break."

He sat in a huff, chin nearly touching his chest, eyes focused on the food while he drummed his fingers against the table as if counting down the minutes he would have to endure her presence.

Her face heated. Sorry. She was sorry, damn it. How many times would she have to apologize?

Elsie picked up a pair of silver tongs and presented

her with the largest pork chop on the platter. Then she perched in the chair across from her, next to Bryce, and leaned into her hands, watching, waiting for something.

Compliments. She was great at giving compliments. Avery picked up her fork and eased in a hearty bite of the risotto. "Mmmm." Covering her mouth with a hand, she hurried to chew so she could offer the praise Elsie seemed to crave. "I've never tasted better." It was the truth. The sauce was so creamy and rich. Her mouth watered for more.

Seeming satisfied with the offering, Elsie picked up her own fork. "Glad it's to your liking, dear. You always hope to get it right, especially when there's special company."

"It's perfect." She sawed into the pork chop and took another bite. The meat melted in her mouth, more juicy and seasoned than any dish at Charlie Trotters back in Chicago. Elsie had mastered the tricky art of complementing the natural flavors with sprinkles of rosemary. She inhaled the aroma. Thyme. Sage. Techniques that brought out the absolute best in the meat.

It appeared she might have the same gift with people. Her smile initiated Avery into her circle. She accepted her, wanted her there, even though she didn't know her at all.

This might not be as hard as she'd thought. Smiling as though competing for a crown, she pulled the napkin into her lap and smoothed it over her thighs. Elsie might be her "in" with Bryce. If she could win her over, maybe she could win him over, too. Maybe he'd forgive her for trespassing in his memories. That was the only way she'd ever get him to consider their offer.

"So Elsie," she said politely. "Do you live here at the ranch?"

"Oh, no, no, no," the woman bubbled. "After Bryce got mar—"

Her son's sharp look cut her off.

"Um," she glanced down and rearranged her silverware, then seemed to recover enough to smile again. "I wanted to give him some space, so I bought the cutest little Victorian in town. Two bedrooms and two baths, but that's really more space than I need."

"It sounds lovely," Avery said, relaxing against the chair. Her attention turned to Bryce. "I'd love to hear more about the ranch." She braved the glare he cast into her eyes. Now that she knew about his wife, in some ways the pressure was off. The man was appealing, there was no doubt about that. But after watching her Dad grieve Mom's death for the last sixteen years, after watching him torture himself and ruin every other relationship he'd started, she wouldn't fall for a man who couldn't fully give himself to her, who could never fully love her. There were no exceptions.

Not even for someone as tempting as Bryce Walker.

* * *

Small talk. God, how he hated small talk. What was it with women, anyway? They had to discuss every detail about every little thing, from recipes to china patterns to table linens to the latest in celebrity gossip. So far, in one half hour, Avery and his mother had covered all four. It was just his luck that he had gotten roped into eating a meal with two women who exceled in his least favorite activity. Bryce set his fork on his plate and settled in. It would be a long night.

"I just can't believe we get to serve you dinner," his mother gushed. "Avery King! At our lodge, of all places. This is wonderful!"

"Are you kidding?" Avery brandished an arm toward her like they were old friends. "I'm the one who's honored to be here."

The food in his stomach boiled. Honored his ass. She wasn't there to make friends, to get to know them over dinner. She was there for one reason. She'd proved it by snooping around upstairs. What was she looking for, anyway? Information that would give her the ammo she needed to force him into selling?

"This is the best meal I've had in a long time." The woman flashed him another smile and, yet again, he answered with a glare. She was nice to look at, though, so he couldn't glare at her too long or his eyes started to wander. Her blond hair had been pulled back into a loose ponytail so that the free curls in the front dangled around her face. And god, what a face. From what he could tell, she didn't wear much makeup. Her natural coloring was damn near perfect: smooth and creamy skin, a slight blush on the apples of her cheeks. She still wore the flowered button-up shirt that fit snug around her curves. A lacy white tank top peeked out from the V where the top buttons were left undone. He could only imagine what hid underneath...

And there he went again. *Damn it*. He shifted his gaze back to his empty plate. Avery King. She was Avery King. She'd probably left those buttons undone on purpose. Especially now that she knew about Yvonne. His traitorous mother had no doubt spilled his life history while he'd regrouped up in his apartment.

"Just wait until you try dessert," his mother said with a wink. "I'll go get it right now." Rising from her chair, she gave him a pointed look that warned him to behave. But he'd had enough behaving, enough listening politely while the woman lied her ass off about what an honor it was to stay at their ranch. He'd had enough of her.

As soon as Mom disappeared into the kitchen, he pushed away his plate and targeted Avery's wandering gaze. "What the hell do you think you're doing?" Small talk wasn't his forte. He preferred to get right to the point.

Her blue eyes went wide then lowered like the question had hurt, but she quickly seemed to rein in her shock at his rude behavior.

He battled a grin. Oh, baby. She hadn't seen rude, yet.

"I'm sorry. I don't know what you mean." To her credit, her eyes didn't shy away from his.

"Chatting up my mom…charming her over dinner… it won't change my mind. I'm not selling." He folded his arms over his chest and leaned back in the chair just in case she hadn't gotten the hint that this discussion was over. He wouldn't go there with her again.

At first, she didn't say anything. Her shoulders rose and fell with steady breaths. Then she leaned forward slightly, just enough that he could see a section of her bra. Pink. Of course it was. Probably had unicorns and hearts all over it to match her magical, charmed, entitled life.

Eyes up, he reminded himself, but it was too late. His body had already responded. What could he say? It'd been awhile since he'd seen a bra. Anyone's bra. She wasn't special.

"You'll lose it anyway, Bryce," Avery said quietly. "I know you're facing foreclosure."

He shook his head. At least she made it easy to keep himself in check. "That's none of your damn business." He leaned halfway over the table. "Mom doesn't know about the bank, so we will *not* have this discussion in front of her."

She glanced at the door, then back at him. "I can get you a check for twenty-three million dollars tomorrow," she whispered. "That's more than enough for you and your mom to do whatever you want. We're talking seven figures, Bryce." Her palm hit the table, emphasizing each syllable. "You'd be crazy to pass up that kind of money."

Crazy? She was calling *him* crazy? He pushed back from the table and stood. "This is my family's land." And it was part of him. It was his life. He strode around the table and leaned down so that his lips stopped next to her ear. Maybe not the smartest move, considering she smelled real good, so fresh...citrus-y.

He heard her swallow. She tipped up her chin and gazed at him. Those eyes...the clarity of those blue eyes...

"I'm not selling," he managed to say past the tight ache in his throat. Then he retreated back to his chair, before it was too late. Before he didn't want to.

Avery folded her hands on the table like a prim head-mistresses. "For the record, I happen to like your mom. She's she sweetest woman I've ever met. I'm not trying to charm her."

Like hell she wasn't.

Her gaze intensified. "Think about her, Bryce. This money could take care of her for the rest of her life. It's—"

"Here we are!" His mother scurried back into the dining room with a silver tray balanced in her hands. "Warm apple pie right out of the oven." She set it on the table, and even though he wasn't hungry the sugary cinnamon scent made his mouth water.

"Wow," Avery gushed, purposely avoiding his eyes. "It smells like heaven!"

The compliment lured out Mom's brightest smile, and she placed a plate in front of Avery like she was the queen of England, a huge slice of pie topped with homemade whipped cream.

Wow. She'd pulled out all the stops. That didn't bode well for him. Mom taking a liking to Avery. That was the last thing he needed right now.

"So, what did I miss?" She slid his plate in front of him.

He opted to shovel in a hearty bite rather than answer that loaded question.

"Nothing much," Avery chirped. "I was just telling Bryce we have a very generous offer to make you."

His jaw clenched. He swallowed fire. "And I said, we're not interested," he muttered.

"Well good, then." His mom's smile attempted to build some kind of bridge between them. "We can move on to other, more interesting topics, can't we?"

They did, but he had nothing more to say to Avery King. She babbled on and on about some charity she volunteered for, about her father's fame and how hard it was to be so filthy rich, blah, blah, blah.

Finally, he couldn't take it anymore. He rose and started to stack plates. "I have to head out soon. Got a game tonight."

"That's right!" Mom jumped up and took Avery's plate. "We have a baseball team," she informed her.

"I love baseball!" Avery scrambled out of her chair and collected the rest of the plates. "What time? Where is it? I'd love to come watch."

His grip on the plates tightened until he could feel the tension in his knuckles. *Shit.*

"You can do more than watch. We're down a player tonight, isn't that right, Bryce?"

Traitor. His mother was a traitor.

"Don't think so," he lied.

"Well, of course we are! John is out of town, remember?"

"We'll be *fine*," he exaggerated the word so she'd get the hint. "We don't need a sub."

Avery swooped next to him, her eyes round with what had to be fabricated innocence. "Are you sure about that? I'm really good. I played softball in high school and college."

"Great." He made sure his tone was as flat as the napkin he held in his hand. Before she could say anything else, he headed for the kitchen.

"Oh, this'll be so fun!" She followed him and set the plates on the counter. "I'll go change. I'll be right back!"

"No hurry," he called after her, but she didn't seem to hear. That was because women like her only heard what they wanted to hear. She had no concept of reality, of what it felt like to battle through life instead of skipping merrily along Easy Street while she stopped every so often to smell the damn flowers.

He carted the dishes over to the sink and flicked on the water, squirted in the soap. Dishwasher. They needed a dishwasher. Another thing to add to his fix-it list. Fingers stinging, he scoured plate after plate until footsteps on the other side of the door warned of his mother's impending arrival.

She'd have plenty to say about dinner. Unless he missed his guess, he was in for a stern talking-to. Mom never missed a chance to lecture on manners.

Sure enough, she plowed through the door with the momentum of a wild stallion. Wouldn't surprise him if she snorted and pawed the ground before charging.

He pretended to be completely engrossed in scraping grease off her best platter, but it didn't divert her.

She marched straight to the sink. "What was that about?"

He scrubbed the china, shaped his eyebrows into innocence. "What?"

"You know perfectly well 'what,' Bryce Walker." She swiped the sponge out of his hand and tossed it in the sink. "You were downright rude to that girl. That's not like you. Not at all."

He retrieved the sponge and took his frustration out on the plate. "She's so…pushy." And oblivious to the fact that he couldn't give this place up. He couldn't turn his back on every memory he had of Yvonne, of his life here…

"She's doing her job. You can't fault her for that." Mom's disappointed frown relaxed into a softer gaze. "Besides, I happen to think Avery is lovely."

"You think everyone's lovely." He flipped on the faucet to rinse the plate and resume his dish-duty penance for bad behavior. Not that it would get him anywhere with her.

"Well, she is." She snatched a towel off the counter and stole the clean plate from his hand. "Didn't you hear what she said? She's on the board of a women's shelter." She held up the plate and inspected it, then set it on the counter. "She's obviously very compassionate."

"When the cameras are clicking, sure." *She probably rescues kittens from trees and carries grocery bags for little old ladies, too.* He kept those comments to himself. Mom had never been a fan of sarcasm. He handed her another dripping plate.

"For your information, Avery told me she hates cameras." His mother took great care mopping the plate, then set it on the clean stack. "She said she hates all of it, actually. The hullabaloo. She'd rather be left alone."

He shook his head. He couldn't help it. Sometimes the woman was too gullible for her own good. "And you believe her."

"I can tell when someone's lying." Elsie crumpled the towel on the counter. "It's all in the eyes. Hers are sincere."

Sure. Okay. He'd give her that. Avery had sincere eyes. Stunning, intense eyes. But that didn't make her a good person. He faced the sink again and washed the last of the dishes.

It got quiet. Too quiet.

When he turned back around, Mom's gaze gave him nowhere to hide. "Bryce...you don't have to stay here. You know that, don't you?" She stepped closer. "You could sell to Mr. King. You shouldn't hold onto this place for me."

"I'm not." There was a time, right after the accident that he wanted to leave, but this place had everything he needed. Simplicity, solitude, space. Not to mention his memories. How could he turn his back on all of that? "I'm holding onto it for me. It's all I have left."

"But you could build yourself a new life. Anywhere you want."

"I've been everywhere. This is where I belong."

She sniffled and dabbed at her eyes. "Yvonne would want you to be happy. To move on."

Her name. Even just the sound of her name made him flinch. Someone would say it and she'd appear in his field of vision, a shimmering mirage with her brown hair gathered up on her head the way it always was right before bed. He still saw her that way, dressed in her pajamas right before bed because those moments were some of their best times together. The nights when he wasn't out drinking. The nights when her depression wasn't so severe and they'd give themselves to each other, their bodies speaking what their mouths couldn't seem to voice...

"Bryce? Did you hear me, son?" Mom interrupted and jolted him back to the present.

He blinked to blot out the memories and eased in a breath. "I am moving on," he lied. "Fixing up this place helps." He ran his hand over the countertop's chipped tiles. "It's not much to look at now, but we'll get there. There's no way I'll let them build some fancy resort on Gramps and Gran's land."

"That's *not* moving on," his mother murmured.

Before she could lecture him on the true definition of moving on, he slung an arm around her and steered her to the door. "Come on. We don't want to be late for the game."

"Wait." She shrugged out from under his arm and glared up at him like she'd done when he was a kid.

"Don't be so hard on Avery. You be nice to her. Show her you know how to treat a lady."

The word "lady" was a stretch for Avery King, but he let it go. "All right. Fine." He eased his mother out the door. "I promise not to be a complete jerk."

Unless she deserved it.

CHAPTER SIX

Now *this* was a ball field. Avery lowered herself from Bryce's monster F-450 and wandered to the edge of the dirt parking lot. Down a small hill, on a flat section of land surrounded entirely by mountain peaks, overhead lights illuminated the baseball diamond, which had been marked off with white paint. A chain-link fence separated the field from a section of battered aluminum bleachers that had seen better days, but those mountains made up for the condition of the equipment. Who cared about the bleachers with a view like that?

"*Mmmwooofff!*"

Uh oh...she spun just in time to see Moose barreling straight for her.

"Moose!" One word from Bryce and the dog hit the brakes, stopping just short of knocking her right down the hill.

It was the first word he'd spoken since they'd left the lodge. After Elsie insisted on driving herself so she could go straight home after the game, it had been quite the silent ride over, minus good old Moose whining in the back of the truck.

She bent to pet him. "What a good doggie."

The dog licked her hand while his tail happily thumped the ground.

"So sweet, too, aren't you?" She snuck a glance at Bryce. He wasn't being sweet. He wasn't being much of anything, really. Stoic, indifferent...those seemed to be his default settings.

Her gaze lingered on him a little too long as he unpacked his gear from the back of the truck. How did he do it, anyway? She found it impossible to be indifferent when he was around. One look at him and her heart thrummed recklessly, even when he was wearing black Nike wind pants and a plain gray t-shirt. And oh, sweet mercy, the way his hair stuck up around that faded Denver Broncos ball cap. A slow heat rolled through her and awakened the longing she'd tried to stomp down when she'd learned he was a widow. Bad idea, falling for someone who was clearly still in love with someone else. She'd seen it up close for too many years. For Dad, no one would ever live up to her mother. And judging by the way he'd reacted with that picture, Bryce felt the same way about Yvonne.

He wandered over. "We should head down."

Wow! Four whole words! She fought the urge to give him a round of applause. Not that he would've seen it anyway, because he slung the duffel over his shoulder and turned his back to her, trudging down the slope like a big brother who was forced to let his annoying little sister tag along.

She jogged after him, but had a hard time catching up, what with those long strides of his and all. If she didn't know better, she'd think he was actually trying to run away from her. Good thing she knew where he lived. He could run, but he couldn't hide from her. Not forever.

At the edge of the outfield, she finally caught up with him and Moose. People were already clustered around the benches by the chain-link fence.

The two of them walked in silence, seeing as how he didn't talk much and she could hardly breathe because of the altitude. Moose trotted beside them, then must've caught some delicious scent because he bounded away in that happy-go-lucky way, ears flopping, tongue flapping in the breeze.

Bryce's tennis shoes kicked up dust with his swift pace. His face had frozen into a somber expression—eyes focused straight ahead, lips set into a frown. She had half a mind to trip him or hug him or something…anything to snap him out of whatever mood he was in. Seriously. The man really needed to lighten up, smile more. He had the best smile. At least she thought he did. It was hard to remember, seeing as how he'd only smiled once in her presence.

Lucky for him, fun was one of her specialties. She sidled up next to him. "This is gonna be great. Who're we playing?"

"Team Coors." His eyes lowered for one of his special *I'm so above you* glances, but he didn't turn his head. "They're a group from the local bar."

She checked out the opposition's bench. Sure enough,

there were a couple of twelve packs stacked near the gear. Some members of the team already held open cans in their hands. "Sweet. That'll make it easy. By the seventh inning, they won't even be able to walk the baseline, let alone run."

Bryce slowed and peered down at her.

Wait a minute. Holy smokes, Batman. Was that a smile on his face?

"We've shut 'em out the last six games." The smile grew. It grew until it lit his eyes with an intensity that sparked a burning sensation deep in her chest. She did her best to ignore it, even as the feeling spread through her. *Whew.* She fought the urge to fan herself. She'd never felt a singe like this, not even with Logan.

They made it to the bench and he slung down the bag, that bicep of his knotted and tan and hard.

Her fingertips tingled with a desperation to touch it, to crawl their way up his arm, across his shoulders, kneading and caressing until all of his tension melted away...

"Can you help me with something?"

She gulped air to steady her lungs. "Sure," she rasped, not meaning to sound all sultry, but it couldn't be helped.

He dug a clipboard out of his bag and handed it to her. "Need someone to keep the stats."

"Stats?" She glared at the clipboard and read the score-card. He wanted her to sit on the bench and take stats?

"Yeah. You do know how to take stats, don't you?" he asked as if skeptical about her vast baseball knowledge.

Despite the chill in the air, perspiration beaded on her forehead. Bryce was unbelievable. "Of course I *know* how to take stats." She tossed the clipboard onto the bench. "But if I take stats, I won't be able to play." That was exactly what he wanted, wasn't it? To stick her on the bench, out of the way. "I'll be on the bench the whole game."

He shrugged, a silent *so what?*

A smile wriggled on her lips. She'd show him so what. She'd been an All-American pitcher on her college softball team. One of the best hitters on the team. *That's right, Bryce Walker.* She had a lot to offer, and she'd prove it to him. "Your mom invited me to play."

"My mom's not in charge." He stooped and unpacked the batting helmets, as if by not looking at her he could somehow deny her existence. But she wasn't about to make it that easy.

She lowered to the ground, right next to him, and reached her hands over his to unpack the bats. "Fine, Bryce. That's fine."

His body stilled. Their eyes connected.

Pressure built inside of her, but she didn't look away. She refused to let him know he got to her. "I'll take the stats," she said with a wry smile. "And I'll play, too." She leaned close for added effect. "So make sure to put me in the batting order, Coach."

His mouth opened and his gaze lowered to her lips. Something flashed in his eyes. Desire? Intrigue?

A breath wedged in her throat, begging for release, but she couldn't. Breathe. Move. Look away.

He didn't either...

Voices drifted behind them. Bryce's green eyes opened wider as he peered past her shoulder. He scrambled to his feet, leaving her crouched—legs numb, heart thundering, echoing in her ears.

What just happened? She rose from the ground, slow

and with great awkwardness, given the way blood surged through her limbs. There was a second there, when Bryce had stared at her mouth, that his eyes had gotten all droopy and defenseless, like he'd let her in, let her see him. And she could've sworn he'd almost kissed her, right there kneeling in the dirt.

But he couldn't stand her...

"There you are, dear!" Elsie bustled over, full of the same aging elegance as Grace Kelly. "You have to meet everyone." She hooked an arm through hers and dragged her over to a woman who was tying her cleats on the bench. "Avery, meet Paige. She's been a friend of our family's forever."

Paige finished tying her shoe and stood. "Hey." What she lacked in height, she made up for with a strong voice, fierce eyes, and a cascade of wavy, sun-streaked hair. She reminded Avery of one of those roller derby girls she'd seen on TV. Minus the stockiness.

"Nice to meet you, Paige," she said, trying to reel in her brain from wandering back to the deep, murky pool of emotions Bryce had cast her into.

"You, too," the woman said with a skeptical edge, like she was being polite but hadn't yet decided if it really was nice.

"Avery's our guest at the ranch for a few days. Isn't that right, dear?" Elsie beamed.

"Right." She pasted on a smile but couldn't stop her eyes from executing a quick search for Bryce. He stood in the center of a group of his friends laughing like he didn't have any trouble at all moving on from their little moment. Had they even had a moment? Or had she imagined it?

"What's up, ladies?" A man approached them, tall and stocky, dressed in a Broncos jersey, jeans, and cowboy boots.

Interesting. She'd never seen anyone run the bases in cowboy boots.

"Shooter." Elsie latched onto the guy's arm and towed him closer. "This is Avery. She's our guest at the ranch." There was no mistaking the pride in her voice when she said the word "guest."

"Bryce and Shooter have been friends since the third grade," Elsie informed her.

He gave her hand a hearty shake, while his brown eyes made their way up and down her body. "Glad to meet you, Avery." He winked. "Let me know if you need any tips out there tonight."

Seriously? Tips from a man who was about to play baseball in cowboy boots? She gagged back a laugh. "Will do. Thanks."

Elsie escorted her toward the group Bryce stood with. It got awkwardly silent when they approached, but she made herself focus on Elsie's happy smile.

"Avery, this is Yates and Timmons." She gestured to the two lanky men standing next to Bryce. "And this is my nephew Sawyer." Elsie pointed out the third man, who had Bryce's same look—the dark hair, the tanned skin, except that his eyes were blue instead of green. "Avery is staying at the ranch for a while," the woman informed them, like it was the biggest news of the year.

"Great to meet you." Sawyer gave Avery's hand a hearty shake. "Where're you from?" he asked, and she made the mistake of glancing at Bryce.

That tight look of annoyance was all she needed to

see. He didn't want her here. Didn't want her talking to his friends and relatives. "Um." She tried to recover from the intensity of Bryce's glare. "I'm from Chicago," she finally spit out, feeling a flush spread up her neck.

"I love Chicago." Sawyer grinned and started to chat about the Cubs, but she couldn't focus because Bryce turned and drifted away.

Unease knotted her stomach. He had every right to glare at her. What was she doing here, anyway? Invading Bryce's life, pretending this was her community? When she'd heard the word "baseball" she'd gotten carried away, but now...

She scanned the crowd. They were a varied group of men and women, all different ages, dressed in different styles—a couple of hippies with dreads, a couple of gray-haired men decked out in the latest high-end sportswear. They were obviously a diverse group but all of them chatted and laughed and whacked each other on the backs like best friends.

Longing bloomed in her heart. These people had a deep connection, she could see it; the kind of family connection she'd longed for since Mom had died. But this was Bryce's community, the Walker Mountain Ranch community, and no matter how badly she wanted to be part of it, she was an outsider. She had to be. Dad had sent her here to acquire the ranch, and she couldn't forget that.

* * *

"Come on, Avery!" Paige squealed. "You've got this! Hit another triple!"

Bryce tried not to roll his eyes. Three innings. That

was exactly how long it took for Avery to win over every single person on the Walker Mountain Ranch Misfits team. Hell, he'd been working on some of them going on ten years now and they still didn't like him. But as she strutted out to home plate for her third at-bat, the women cheered her on like she was some female version of Derek Jeter, while the men checked out her ass, offering up high fives just to slow her down and get a better look.

Had to admit, it wasn't a bad view. The black yoga pants she wore fit sleek and tight across her cinched waist and over that distinctly feminine curve of her hips. The fabric showcased the toned shape of her long legs. And don't get him started on that well-worn Cubs shirt. Looked like it'd been washed so many times that it'd shrunk a few sizes, which wasn't a bad thing, considering she had plenty to show off.

Avery made it to home plate and hunched into a perfect batter's stance—hinged forward at the waist, elbows straight and wide. Couldn't deny she had some mad skills. He'd never seen a woman hit a triple before, at least not in this town. She'd nailed it low and perfect, right down the third-base line and into the field. Their fielder had been too drunk to move fast, so she'd brought in three runs.

He glanced out at the pitcher, Rollins, one of the bartenders from the dive he used to hang out at. He seemed frozen in the spotlight of Avery's glory. Bryce could relate. Shoot, just before the game, when she'd knelt so close, when he'd inhaled her citrus-y scent, he'd almost lost it, almost forgotten what her name was. She made it easy to forget, with that laugh, so carefree and easy. He could get wrapped up in that real easy. Too easy.

Out on the mound, Rollins finally got himself together enough to toss it in, slow and steady, right over home plate.

Smack! Avery connected, hit a line drive right at the guy. The poor schmuck dove to the ground, arms over his head while the ball shot out into the field again.

All around him, the bench cleared. People high-fived and cheered her on.

"Woo hoo!"

"That's it! Run, Avery!"

She sprinted for first, then second, then third, but her momentum didn't stop. Somehow, the shortstop came up with the ball and threw it home.

She wasn't gonna make it...

Just as the ball hit the catcher's mitt Avery slid like a pro—legs outstretched, foot reaching for the base. She touched it just as the catcher stepped down.

"Safe!" The ump signaled. The bench cleared in a wild pandemonium. Hell, even he was on his feet, cheering and whooping it up like another Avery King groupie.

Avery waved to the crowd, then got up and gingerly jogged over to the bench. Everyone had a turn to slap her on the shoulder and congratulate her for what just might have been the best run they'd seen in years. She made her way down the line, laughing and slapping high fives, until she got to him. She stopped, looked up from under the shade of her Cubs hat with what looked like shyness tugging at her eyelids.

Even though he knew it was a bad idea, he looked her straight in the eyes. That same sensation stirred, the one that had almost driven him to kiss her. Maybe if her lips didn't look so soft...

She raised her eyebrows at him and he knew he couldn't just keep staring at her all night without her suspecting something was up. So he smirked. "Nice hit."

She grinned, no longer shy and wondering, but full of smart-ass flare. "Told you I could play." Then she bumped past him and paraded to her spot on the bench, lighting a flame of want in his gut.

During the next few batters' turns, Avery and Paige had their heads tilted together, chatting and laughing. He wasn't close enough to hear what they were talking about. Must have been pretty interesting, though, because Paige never carried on like that. Especially with people she didn't know. He glanced over at the two of them. Something about Avery seemed to make people feel like they'd known her forever. Probably served her well working with her crook of a father. The man already had like three billion in the bank. What'd he need Bryce's ranch for, anyway?

After the third out, he got up to head to the outfield. Shooter appeared next to him and bumped his shoulder. "Damn, Walker. She's somethin'." He nodded toward Avery. "And she's single, right?"

Some weird defensive energy surged through him. Shooter was a player. The worst kind of player. The kind who macked on other women even when he was out on a date. No way did Avery belong with someone like him. He eyed him. "Nah. I think she's engaged or something."

"She's not engaged," he said, his face smug. "Logan Schwartz proposed to her during the seventh inning stretch and she said no."

He stopped in the outfield. *Wait. What?* "Logan Schwartz?"

"Yeah. Cubs' pitcher."

Holy shit. She'd dated a ballplayer? "When?" Trying to look nonchalant, he closed the gap with Shooter so she wouldn't hear them talking about her.

"Week ago or so," his friend said, eyeing Avery again. "It was ugly. She got booed out of the stadium."

Wow. How'd he miss that? "I had no idea."

"Yeah, so it looks like she's back on the market." Shooter's eyes gleamed. "I might have to take a crack at that."

"Good luck," he muttered, his defenses rising again. But why should he care if Avery went out with him? Wasn't like he could date her. Edward King's daughter. *Pshaw.* Right. That would be . . . stupid.

"Come on! This is the first out!" Avery called. She stood a ways in front of him, playing shortstop. Great. He'd have to stand there and look at her backside for the next half hour. Just what he needed to convince himself she was a bad idea.

He pulled the bill of his cap lower over his eyes. Fine. That was fine. He wouldn't look. He refused to look. *Focus on the ball . . .*

His old drinking buddy, Dave, stepped up to bat. Bryce jogged backward. The man could hit. First couple of pitches, Paige threw solids strikes, but then Dave hit a pop fly and it was headed straight for him. Bryce followed the ball with his eyes, running forward, to the left . . .

Blond hair flashed right in front of him. *Shit.* He thrust out his arms, but it was too late.

Avery tumbled into him, knocking him off balance. His arms flailed in search of stability, but the momentum pitched him back. *Thud!* He hit the soft grass and Avery ended up on top of him while the ball sailed over both of their heads.

She stared at him, her shimmery blue eyes wide with shock, lips formed in an O inches away from his.

So close. Too close. Her curves fit against him, reminding him how it felt to pull a woman close enough to feel her best features. His chest locked up.

Off in the distance, his teammates snickered like a group of junior high boys.

"Get a room!" someone called.

Avery's expression went from shock to a feisty smirk. She balanced her elbow on his chest and propped her chin on her fist. "Jeez, Bryce. If you wanted it that bad, you could've just asked," she said.

Nice. He shook his head at her, but couldn't fight off a smile. "You done, Slugger? 'Cause I know I am." Carefully, he wrapped his arms around her in a tight embrace.

She flinched and that shocked look made a strong comeback.

Ha. Two can play this game. He rolled her off of him so that her back was against the grass and he was the one looking down at her. "*If* I wanted it, I wouldn't have to ask."

Her mischievous expression dared him to prove it.

He laughed to add to the show. Instead of indulging her boldness, he let her go, pushed off the ground, and trotted back to his spot a safe distance away.

Space. He needed space. When Avery got too close, when he touched her, his memories of Yvonne faded into obscurity. She made him forget. She made him betray his wife and want something he never thought he'd want again.

And he wasn't ready to let go.

CHAPTER SEVEN

Reveling in the aftereffects of one of the best games of her life, Avery meandered through the cluster of Bryce's friends, who'd gathered around the bench to enjoy a post-game snack courtesy of Elsie. She inhaled the scent of crisp chocolate. Brownies. Gooey brownies that still smelled warm. And boy, was she hungry. She picked one up and shoved the entire thing in her mouth, her face still stinging with the thrill of physical exertion.

Nothing felt better than a win like that. They'd given the other team a good trouncing. She'd stopped keeping the score at 18-4.

"Hey, Avery. Good game." Paige thwacked her on the back and she tried not to wince. As petite as she was, the woman packed a punch.

"You rocked the hits tonight." Shooter nudged her shoulder and cozied up beside her.

"Thanks," she said around the mouthful of brownie,

then discreetly shuffled sideways because, well, Shooter wasn't exactly subtle.

"Outstanding performance!" Elsie shoved her fingers in her mouth and gave a shrill whistle. "Someone get this girl an MVP trophy!"

Waving a hand through the air, she laughed like it was nothing, but their praise went straight to her heart. This was better than when she'd earned All-American in college! "Thanks, everyone," she said, then plucked another brownie out of Elsie's magical basket.

Paige helped herself to one, too. "Hey, girl," she uttered between bites. "We're all heading out to Moe's for a more adult-style post-game celebration."

"Moe's?" She gave Paige a blank look.

The woman laughed like she'd forgotten that Avery wasn't part of their crowd. "It's a bar. The local hangout. You've *got* to come. After that performance, your drinks are on me."

She grinned. She couldn't help it. These people were so nice! She'd never had so much fun with a group of strangers before.

"So, are you in or what?" Paige demanded in that endearing, intimidating way of hers.

"Um." She looked around for Bryce. He stood on the outskirts of the group, expression locked into the same scowl he'd worn since she'd met him, his arms crossed like he couldn't wait to get out of there.

He definitely didn't look like he was in the mood to party. She slung her backpack over her shoulder. "I should probably check with Bryce. We rode together."

"Really?" The woman drew out the word into an innuendo. "Interesting."

Heat rose to her face. She hadn't intended to imply anything, but Paige seemed to think that meant something. "Actually it wasn't that interesting," she informed her before she got any ideas. "He didn't say a word to me." His mommy had made him include her, and he'd spent most of the evening avoiding her—except for those few moments before the game, and then when she'd ended up on top of him. Talk about a shocker. She could still feel the sturdiness of his body beneath hers, the strength of his arms around her...

Okay, that wasn't helping the blushing problem.

Paige gave her a funny smirk. "Don't worry about Bryce. I'll ask him," she called, already jogging away.

Wait! What would she say to him? Something told her it wouldn't be good. "Paige!" Avery took off after her.

Bryce stared as she approached. His expression remained neutral, unreadable.

"We're all heading to Moe's," Paige announced before Avery could stop her. "You in?"

"Nope," he said, face suddenly drawn with determination.

Huh. Avery studied him. Why'd he seem so uncomfortable?

Bryce looked away from her and reached down to pet Moose, who inched his head up higher, like he wanted a better scratch.

"Didn't think you'd join us," Paige said with a wry smile. "But your *friend* Avery's coming with me, then. Okay by you, boss?"

She watched his reaction to Paige. He actually made eye contact with the woman, but not with her. His gaze didn't go anywhere near her eyes. What was his problem? Was he mad she'd played so well?

"She's not my friend," he said to Paige, patting the dog's head. "She can do whatever she wants."

Humph. Avery turned away so she didn't have to look at him. The rosy glow on her cheeks was no longer related to his hotness.

"Come on, Moose. Let's go home."

As Bryce walked away in that lazy gait of his, the sting of her humiliation subsided. What had she done to piss him off now?

"Don't mind him," Paige said. "He's moody. He's been through some tough shit. You can't take it personally."

"I know." Except his moodiness hadn't seemed to be a problem when he was surrounded by his friends. Only when she got near him. He obviously didn't want her around, but she was here to help him.

If he understood that, if he saw who she really was, then maybe he'd listen to her. Maybe he'd let her help him move on with his life.

Paige gathered up her bag and dug out car keys. "Ready?"

Avery looked longingly at the group now drifting toward the parking lot. They'd accepted her, high-fived her, complimented her skills, but she hadn't come to make new friends. She smiled at Paige. "Thanks for the invite, but I just remembered I have some work to do. I should go back to the lodge with Bryce."

The woman gave her a skeptical look. "Work?"

"Yes." It was true. She had plenty of work to do. Starting with presenting their offer to Bryce in a more formal manner.

"Suit yourself," Paige finally said. "If you're still around, we have another game Sunday. We could use you out there again."

"Thanks," she called as her new friend walked away. "I had a great time!" The best time. She glanced up at the parking lot. Something told her the ride home wouldn't be nearly as fun as the game had been. Even so, she hurried to catch up with Bryce. Unfortunately, by the time she'd made it to the parking lot, she was completely winded. How did all of these people survive on such little oxygen? By the time she caught her breath, he'd almost reached the truck.

"Hey!" she gasped, panting.

He stopped. Turned.

She could've sworn his face tensed into an irritated expression. She tried to take Paige's advice. *Don't take it personally.* If her heart didn't inexplicably swell and pound whenever she saw him, that'd be a lot easier.

Mustering courage, she forced a peppy smile. "Turns out I'm pretty tired. Is it okay if I catch a ride back with you?"

He shrugged and turned around, lowering the truck's lift gate for Moose. "In you go, boy," he said in that firm gentle tone that made her quiver. She'd give anything to hear him talk to her like that.

Don't count on it. He had one decimal when he talked to her and it wasn't anywhere in the vicinity of gentle. But she could handle it. She wasn't afraid of Bryce Walker. They'd gotten off on the wrong foot, that was all. He hadn't seen how charming she could be, how fun, how sincere. She'd never met a business acquaintance she couldn't charm. She'd win Bryce over eventually. Damn it.

Her tight stomach remained unconvinced, but she stomped over to the passenger's side of the truck anyway.

Just as she went to open the door, her cell rang. Dad's face lit up the screen.

Bryce glanced over.

Was he in a hurry to leave? She held up her phone in a silent question.

He waved a hand toward her as if they were playing a game of charades. What was he trying to say?

Go ahead and take it?

Take your time?

Answer it over there so I don't have to listen to you talk?

A smile snuck past her better judgment as she answered him with a series of wild arm gestures, because he sure didn't seem to get along well with actual words.

He only stared back at her with that blank indifference. Yet another joke wasted on him.

Opting for space and privacy, she trotted to the edge of the parking lot before swiping the screen and holding it against her ear.

"Hey, Dad. Now's not a good time."

"You haven't checked in," he answered in his brisk, *I want an update and I want it now* tone.

She lowered her voice. "I've been busy. You sent me out here to work, remember?" The sight of her dusty yoga pants and Cubbies shirt mocked her. Yeah. Work.

"You've been busy negotiating, I hope. When can I expect a signed commitment?"

The question made her queasy. She snuck a quick glance at Bryce over her shoulder. "We haven't gotten that far."

"How far have you gotten?" Her father demanded.

"Um. Well…"

"He hasn't budged, has he?" he grumbled. "Stubborn son of a bitch. It's time to play hardball."

"No!" The last thing Bryce needed was Edward King playing hardball. She'd seen her father do whatever it took to get a property he had his eye on. He always managed to get his way, and he didn't care what it cost or who it hurt. But she did, especially knowing that Bryce was a widower. "He'll budge. Trust me. I need more time with him. A couple of days."

"Fine." Her father conceded with a sigh. Luckily, he'd always hated telling her no. "You work it from your angle. I'll work it from mine."

"That won't be necessary." She'd make sure. His angle meant using his name to bully his way through the process and coerce people into making exceptions.

"I expect an update as soon as possible," Dad said. "We'll talk soon."

The line went dead. She slipped it back into her bag and trotted over to Bryce, attempting to channel the inner professional who'd seemed so displaced since she'd arrived in Aspen. Time was running out. If Bryce would quit being so stubborn, she could help him understand that it would be best for everyone if he sold to her father. For him. For Elsie. They could go anywhere, do anything they wanted. If he'd stop looking at her like an enemy for five minutes, she could show him she was actually trying to help. She understood how it felt to have the pain of the past hold you back.

But it was time for Bryce to move on.

* * *

Bryce drummed his fingers against the steering wheel. *Okay. Any day now.*

Across the parking lot, Avery had finally slipped her phone back into her bag. Whoever she was talking to, she obviously hadn't wanted him to hear. She'd drifted out of earshot right when she looked at her cell phone screen. Fifty bucks said it was her daddy. Probably calling to see if she'd brokered the deal of the century yet. A smile twitched. As much as she annoyed him, there was some satisfaction in not giving her what she wanted like everyone else seemed to. He had to admit, she had a talent for making people like her, for making people think she liked them.

But he wasn't easily fooled.

Avery climbed into the truck, tucking those long legs into the passenger side.

And damn if the sight of them didn't send a hot throbbing all through him. A purely physical reaction, that was all. Ever since she'd taken him down on the field and he'd felt her curves pressed against him, warm and right and satisfying, his imagination had started to wander into enemy territory...

"Sorry about that," she said, interrupting a traitorous fantasy that involved him taking her back to the grass. A warning flared in his gut. He didn't look at her.

"No problem." Starting the engine, he glanced over his shoulder to make sure Moose was lying down, then backed out of the parking spot.

"So that was a great game, huh?" she remarked in that animated melody she'd used on his friends all night.

"Yep." One-word answers. He'd stick to the one-word answers. Things were safer that way. She had this crazy ability to open people up, to make them talk, to say things they didn't usually tell people. During the fourth inning, he'd heard Paige spill the whole story about being the black sheep of her family, about how she wished she had a better relationship with her parents. She didn't even talk to *him* about that stuff.

That's why he had to steer clear. Avery pried too deep and he couldn't go there with a woman. Not right now. Look at what had happened to him after Yvonne died. He'd lost himself for three years. He'd wandered around like he didn't know who he was without her. Hell, he was still trying to figure it out.

"Bryce?" Avery asked in that sugary sweet voice. "Is everything okay?"

"Sure." He followed the road. Ten minutes. It'd be a quick ten-minute ride back to the ranch. Surely he could wait her out for ten minutes.

"Are you sure?" Her hands fidgeted nervously with the hair spilling down over her shoulders. "Because it feels like you're upset with me or something."

Ah, hell. Not this. What was it with women, anyway? Why'd they have this burning desire to get to the bottom of absolutely every feeling they had? Why couldn't they sit in silence, enjoy the scenery? "I don't know you well enough to be upset with you," he finally said, increasing his pressure on the gas pedal. The cops were notorious for pulling over speeders on this section through town, but tonight he was willing to risk it.

"Look." Avery's hands sliced the air in front of her. "I understand why you don't want to sell. Trust me. I get it."

Ha. Trust her. He didn't trust her any more than he trusted her father. At the end of the day, she worked for the infamous Edward King. She might be smokin' hot and nice, and, like she insisted, a good person, but she still had a job to do. He wouldn't forget that.

Instead of answering, he leaned over and flicked on the radio. Nothing like a little Brad Paisley to tune out a woman.

Avery shot him a fiery look, topaz eyes blazing, lips thinned into a warning that tempted him to test her.

That didn't help things. She looked even better when she got mad. His grip on the wheel tightened until his knuckles ached. Mom was right. He had to get out more. Start dating again. Any woman besides Avery King...

She hunched forward and fiddled with the radio until he could hardly hear Paisley. *Fine*. That was fine. Five more minutes and they'd be back at the ranch anyway. He'd be free of her.

"You need to listen to me, Bryce. Please." She launched into yet another impassioned monologue about how selling the ranch could change his life.

Yeah, well. He'd had enough changes in his life over the last few years. So sue him if he wasn't interested. She didn't seem to pick up on his lack of concentration, though. She went on and on until he pulled the truck into the driveway and parked in front of the office.

"Are you listening to me?" She leaned over the console between them and got in his face, close enough that he could smell oranges, that he could trace the sexy curve of her upper lip with his tongue if he'd wanted to.

"Have you heard anything I've said?"

The throb started again, deep in his chest, invading his body until it occupied all of him.

"Seriously, Bryce this is—"

Screw it. He cupped his hand around the back of her head and roughly brought her lips to his, totally unprepared for the impact it would have. Shock waves coursed through him, unleashing a craving stronger than he'd ever felt.

Avery squeaked in surprise but he didn't let up. Need thundered through him and it was a helluva lot louder than the logic he'd spent the last several hours beating into his thick skull. Her lips were soft and moist and everything he'd hungered for during the last three lonely years. He gentled a hand up into her hair. It felt like silk against his skin.

A small moan purred in her throat and her upper body relaxed, lips melding to his in a pulsating heat. She ran her hands up his chest, and that was all he needed. He bent forward, halfway over the console, gathering her closer, kissing her harder, deeper. If it wasn't for that console, he'd pull her right into his lap...

"Wow. Just...wow," she whispered against his lips.

He answered by parting her lips with his tongue. There. That'd take care of her chatting problem.

Avery gasped a sharp intake of air, her chest rising against his.

Taking it as an invitation, he commanded her with his lips, opening and closing them in a sensual rhythm. A dull ache resounded in his chest. God, he'd forgotten the depth of a kiss...

He shifted to get a better angle, more access, but that console...

She pulled back with a small smile, lips grazing his in a tease, then she pressed in again and proved that she could make out as well as she could talk.

A scratching sound scraped the window. Moose whined, then barked.

Great timing, as usual.

Avery pulled away, eyes sparkling with a look of happy surprise. "Um…" Her tongue ran over her lips and her eyes peered up into his. "We should talk about this."

No. Oh, hell, no. As far as he was concerned, there wasn't much to say. She tasted good. Real good. But now that he was breathing in the fresh, mountain air, instead of her intoxicating scent, he remembered. Yvonne. Her face haunted him, and that kiss…it was intense and real and it felt exactly like a betrayal.

"Bryce…" Avery collected his hand in hers. "That was…really something. I'm just not sure—"

"Sorry." He yanked his hand out of hers. Time to go. "Good night, Avery." Air pounded for release in his lungs as escaped from the truck. Without looking back, he jogged into the office, the burn of want still torturing him.

Once inside, he slumped into the chair behind the desk and stared blankly at the wall. Holy hell. He'd kissed her. He'd kissed Avery King.

Well. That ought to shut her up.

CHAPTER EIGHT

Four days. Bryce had managed to avoid her for four flipping days. Avery left her guest suite and marched down the hall to the Walker Mountain Ranch dining room, like she did every morning. It had become something of a routine. Over breakfast, she'd ask Elsie when she could expect to see him, and each day the woman apologized and made excuses.

"Sorry, dear. He's helping Sawyer install a patio today."

"He took an overnight trip to Denver for some supplies."

"He's rock climbing with Shooter."

If his mother knew about the kiss, she didn't let on, but she obviously felt bad that Bryce was clearly avoiding her, profusely apologizing on her son's behalf and making Avery a gourmet breakfast every morning as a peace offering. Quite effective, the way that woman could cook.

For the most part, Avery had managed to put on a good performance and act like Bryce's absence didn't matter. But it made it impossible for her to do her job. Not to mention...how could he kiss her like that? Like she was water and he was half-dead with thirst—then avoid her like nothing had happened? She wasn't sure if she should be humiliated, angry, or completely infatuated with the man. Her brain, her body, and her heart had been battling it out, and so far her body seemed to be winning, quaking with sheer elation every time she pictured his face.

Warding off another internal earthquake, she rounded the corner into the great room and was greeted with the scent of strong coffee. It reminded her of her father. He preferred his coffee like motor oil and always drank it black. That smell was all it took to wake her up.

Today. She had to talk to Bryce today. Over the last three days, Dad had left her twelve messages. She'd texted him and claimed that things were moving forward, but that her cell reception was bad. She'd promised to have an answer for him by today. Therefore, it didn't matter if Bryce was hiding in Denver again. She'd track him down, force him to face her, and make one closing argument for why it would be better for him to sell for millions than to lose it all to the bank.

"Good morning!" Elsie swooped across the dining room and wrapped her in a customary hug.

"Morning." She hugged her back, always calmed by the woman's soft and friendly presence.

Elsie pulled away, a special glimmer in her eyes. "I hope you don't mind, dear. But I've packed a 'to go' breakfast for you today." She gestured to the table, where a small picnic basket sat, almost overflowing with goodies.

To go? Avery walked over and peeked inside. Muffins, granola bars, plump red grapes and a Tupperware container of fancy sliced cheeses. "Wow." For the first time in quite awhile, a grin stretched her mouth. "So where am I going?"

"Well..." Elsie clasped her hands like she was trying to quell her excitement. "Bryce has to work in the stables today. I thought I'd send you out there to share with him."

Sure enough, the traitorous tremble worked its way up her body and ended in a heated flush on her face. She had Mom's Scandinavian complexion to thank for that.

"Besides,"—Elsie murmured with a sly expression— "the horses need to get out. It's been weeks, and it's a beautiful morning for a ride."

She couldn't argue with that. Outside the dining room windows, the flawless blue sky stretched out, clear and glassy, as serene as a lake on a still evening. Despite the fact that she'd once had a bad experience on a horse, it was the perfect scenario. A ride would give her extra time with Bryce. He wouldn't be able to avoid her. That alone made it worth risking her life.

"So what do you say, dear?" Elsie asked with a hopeful smile. "Will you take breakfast out to Bryce?"

"Of course," she answered quickly to ward off any suspicions the woman had about what had happened between them.

Yeah, right. His mom's knowing glance proved it was too late for that.

"Wonderful," the woman purred. "Out you go now." She carefully placed the basket in Avery's hands and shooed her to the back door. "You tell him I said those horses need to get out today, you hear? If he tries to argue, send him in here to me."

Despite the apprehension building in her stomach, Avery laughed. "I'll tell him." Not that it would do any good. Once he saw her, he might take off before she could say a word.

On the back concrete stoop, Elsie gently patted her shoulder. "Have fun, dear. The stables are just down that path." She pointed to a strip of dirt that had been worn into the tall grasses behind the lodge. "Good luck!"

Yeah. Luck. Her legs wobbled as she made her way down the steps. Something told her she'd need more than luck to get through to Bryce.

* * *

The stables sat in a clearing next to a narrow brook that gushed in a shallow crevasse of the land. With her feet scuffing the dirt, Avery ambled toward the log-sided building about twenty yards ahead. It resembled the lodge, constructed with the same log beams, that were now cracked and peeling. Three wide stalls opened in the front, and a horse whinnied from somewhere inside.

All around her, the outside world was still waking up. Pinkish streaks looped and whirled across an opalescent sky. Stillness smothered everything underneath an awestruck blanket. Not even a bird chirped. She breathed in the slight honeyed scent of wet grass, hoping it would calm her.

It didn't.

Anticipation closed in on her, making her breaths

shallow and her heart pound harder. She couldn't seem to stop thinking about the way Bryce had touched her in the truck, about the way his lips had catapulted her into a new realm of awareness she'd never before experienced. If he hadn't pulled away and left her sitting there, she was pretty sure she would have gone anywhere with him...

No, no. She couldn't think that way. Not right now. Not when she was about to spend the morning with him. She had to handle him just like she'd handled Tommy Atchison when he'd threatened to pull out of the London project, just like she'd handled Larrisa Payne when she'd waffled on the merger. He was a business associate, nothing more. A potential partner. At least that was how she looked at anyone who sat on the other side of the negotiation table.

Approaching the stables, her feet tread carefully. Just outside the doors, she stopped and peered into the dimness.

Bryce had his back to her. He stood next to a glossy brown horse, hands working to secure a bridle around its muzzle. His movements were calm and gentle, not like they'd been with her in the truck: desperate and commanding and powerful.

She gathered a breath, then let it out slowly, taking the opportunity to study him. In the dim light his profile looked softer. His dark hair curled down over his ears, carefree but somehow right. She watched him smooth his worn hands down the horse's neck. They were careful and precise.

"Ahem." She cleared her throat to announce her presence because standing there watching him would not help her maintain a strict level of professionalism. Already, her heart had started that slow melt in her chest.

Bryce glanced over and instantly pulled his features into that hardened mask he'd worn the first time she met him. "What're you doing here?" He turned back to the horse like he was afraid to look at her.

She was afraid, too. There. She admitted it. She feared him. Feared what he had made her feel with one kiss. Feared what he made her want.

But she refused to hide from him the way he'd hidden from her. He obviously didn't want to discuss the kiss. That was fine. They didn't have to. She didn't plan to mention it. Only one topic of conversation mattered. So she strode over to him and set the picnic basket on a nearby chair, feigning confidence and authority, praying he wouldn't see through it. "We're going on a ride, apparently," she said with a smirk. "Elsie's orders."

His hand paused on the horse's wide girth. "Excuse me?"

"Your mom said the horses need to get out. And I've been dying to see the view she keeps talking about." Her heart quaked. "She said you'd take me riding."

"She did, huh?" The words were strained, as if he had a hard time relaxing his jaw. He turned to face her, took his time looking her up and down. "Have you ridden much?" he asked with a glimmer of amusement in those dark green eyes.

She tipped up her chin. "Sure. I've ridden." *Once.* Probably not a good idea to tell him that the one horse she'd ridden in her life had bucked her off. She'd landed smack dab in the middle of a mud puddle and cracked her tailbone. Guess who'd had to walk around with an

inflated donut for the rest of summer camp? Her gaze
darted toward the horses. They were huge. Bulky. Unpredictable. A sudden case of heartburn nearly gagged her.
Maybe this wasn't such a good idea.

"I guess they could use a ride. Just a quick one. Up the
ridge and back." Bryce swiped his hands down the sides
of his worn jeans, and she couldn't help but notice how
perfectly they fit his sturdy form.

Look up, she commanded herself, *before he catches
you checking out his body*. By the time her eyes found his,
she knew it was too late.

The beginnings of a smile softened his jaw. "You can
ride Buttercup." He strode to the other horse, a grayish
Appaloosa mottled with brown spots. Stray whiskers
sprouted around the mare's mouth like an old man's
beard. She seemed content to stand statue-still and stare
outside. Her tail swooshed and scattered a colony of flies.

"She's still young, but she'll do okay." He swept his
hand down her mane and patted her withers.

Buttercup snorted and nuzzled his shoulder, as if begging for another gentle touch.

The smile that altered Bryce's face tempted her to cozy
up next to him, too. He had the best smile—straight white
teeth and those curved, skilled lips...

"What'd she send for breakfast?" Bryce asked, looking
over at the picnic basket.

"An assortment of yummy things." Grateful for a much
needed distraction, she walked over to the basket and
picked it up. Elsie's "to go" breakfast looked more like a
five-star buffet spread, but nerves already filled her stomach to the point of slight discomfort. There'd be no room
for anything else as long as she was with Bryce.

"Here." He tossed her a canvas bag with a long strap. "Pack it all in the saddlebag. We'll eat at the top."

"Sounds good." She strained her throat to keep her voice even and professional. She was a professional, and this was a business meeting, not a romantic picnic on the top of a mountain. That would be a date.

And she could not go on a date with Bryce Walker.

While she packed the food, Bryce readied Buttercup. She caught sight of his strong arms, hoisting and fastening down the saddle, right as he looked over. Great. He was going to think she couldn't keep her eyes off of him.

"All finished?" He approached and held out his hands.

"Yep." She placed the bag in his grasp, taking extra care not to let her skin graze his, then drifted toward Buttercup in order to maintain a healthy distance between them.

"I'll lead on Hooligan." He patted the brown horse's rump. "Buttercup usually follows him around. Should be an easy ride."

Right. Sure. Easy. She examined the worn leather saddle while Bryce hopped onto Hooligan's back like Evel Knievel mounting a motorcycle.

Show off.

He glanced over his shoulder. "Ready?"

Her gaze shifted back to the saddle. How was she supposed to get on that thing? "Sure. Yeah. I'm ready." She hoisted her foot into the stirrup and gripped the saddle horn, but her hand slipped. "Whoa." The stirrup trapped her foot. She hopped to maintain her balance, tugging on her knee in an attempt to free her boot. It must've looked like some crazy Yoga move.

"Need some help?" Clearly enjoying her predicament, Bryce dismounted.

"No. I'm fine." A couple more hops, then she clawed her way up on that saddle before he could touch her. "There. See?" Perspiration stung her forehead. "I'm good." She pasted on a smile, but a jolt of fear bolted her legs down around Buttercup's large middle. She was so high, so out of control. Gripping the saddle horn, she tried not to look down. Didn't they say that horses could sense things? Like danger? And a change in the weather? And extreme terror? She breathed deeply but the mountains didn't have nearly enough oxygen. *Hold it together.*

As if sensing her hesitation, Bryce placed the reins in her hands.

His touch *zing*ed through her. *Perfect.* Just what she needed when she was supposed to be concentrating.

His hand closed around hers and made her spine go limp.

"Hold 'em loose. She'll do most of the work." Still watching her, he backed away.

"Got it." Somehow she formed her lips into another convincing smile, but the manufactured confidence didn't reach deep inside. The whole summer camp incident was apparently still too fresh.

"Don't worry. We'll take it easy." He jammed his foot into Hooligan's stirrup and swung his leg over like it was nothing. "All right, Hoolie, let's go." He clicked his tongue and glanced back.

Buttercup didn't budge. So much for following Hooligan around.

"Nudge her with your heels."

She eased her heels into the horse's ribs. "Come on, sweetie. Let's go."

Nothing.

"Buttercup. Go." She punctuated the command with a sharper clip of her heels.

With an annoyed whinny, Buttercup toddled forward, her hooves clomping the packed dirt in a granny's rhythm.

"Are you sure she's young?" Because she moved like her hips were inflamed.

"I'm sure. Sometimes she gets stiff. I rescued her from a shady breeder out near Carbondale," he answered, wielding the reins like a pro.

Of course he rescued animals. Just when she thought he couldn't get any more amazing...

Buttercup ambled after Hooligan out of the stables, through an aspen grove, and up to a narrow, rutted road at the back of the lodge.

Avery held the reins in both hands, somehow still maintaining a healthy grip on the saddle horn. Her body rocked with Buttercup's lazy swagger. *Okay. I can do this.* Like Bryce had said, Buttercup would do most of the work. She just had to focus on not falling off. And on that other thing she was supposed to do. Close the deal.

"Come on, Buttercup." She encouraged the horse with another prod to the ribs. Buttercup jerked her head and gave Avery what she swore was a dirty look, but picked up the pace until they'd caught up to Hooligan. Bryce peered over his shoulder. "Everything okay back there?"

She pasted on a smile. "Yeah. Of course. We're great, aren't we, Buttercup?" She reached down and patted her neck. "Best buddies."

The horse tossed her head and snorted.

"Obviously." He turned back around and prodded Hooligan up the trail.

Wait a minute. Was he laughing at her?

He was. He was laughing so hard his shoulders shook. Well, she'd show him. With another nudge of her heels, she attempted to remind Buttercup who was boss. Reluctantly, the horse followed Hooligan up a series of switchbacks.

They climbed higher, a strong wind biting at Avery's cheeks. As they crested the rise, three mountains poked up over the distant horizon, their razor-sharp granite peaks dusted with a light powdery snow. Against their dark outline, the sky brightened into a flawless sea of sapphires, the sun glinting and sparkling with a priceless radiance. "Whoa. Whoa, girl," she whispered, tugging Buttercup to a stop. The view was so perfect it looked like a postcard.

"It's even better at the top." Bryce's comment startled her.

At some point, he'd stopped Hooligan to wait for her.

Their eyes locked and Avery's heart felt light and free, like it might float away. *Say something.* She inhaled until her heart settled back into place. "Yeah. Wow." *Lame.* That sounded so lame. She fluffed the reins until Buttercup stuttered up to Hooligan's side and tried again. "It must've been amazing to grow up in a place like this."

"It was." He directed his gaze to the horizon and clipped his heels into Hooligan's sides.

Buttercup lowered her head and clomped after Bryce's horse. Avery blew out an exasperated sigh for both of them. Why did he do that? Constantly retreat from her, from a real conversation?

"Come on, Buttercup," she muttered through clenched teeth. She wasn't about to let him off that easy. The horse must've realized she meant business because her trusty steed chugged up to Hooligan's side and fell in stride. She peered over at Bryce. "I can't imagine that kind of childhood. I grew up in the city."

"Huh."

The half-hearted grunt only made her more determined. "Have you ever lived anywhere else?"

Eyes still focused on some unseen horizon, Bryce reached down and patted Hooligan's neck. "Nah. I've traveled a lot. Lived in Boulder while I went to CU. But this has always been home."

She took in the view again. With a vista like that, she couldn't blame him for never leaving. "So what did you study? In school?"

"Business management."

That made sense. Especially if he planned to run his grandparents' ranch. She wanted to ask more questions, but Buttercup stumbled over a rock, knocking her off balance. She clamped her hands back to the saddle horn. "Whoa, girl."

Bryce tugged the reins. "Easy, Hooligan." Both horses slowed. "It gets steep up here. Hold on tight. She'll work out her footing."

Avery's gaze lowered to the rocky, uneven ground beneath Buttercup's hooves. She wanted to steer the horse like Bryce guided Hooligan, but she had no idea how. Not to mention...every time she looked down, a wave of dizziness crashed her focus. The ground seemed awfully far away. All it would take was one swift movement from Buttercup and she'd be back on a donut.

In front of her, Hooligan crisscrossed a path up the rutted incline.

Buttercup stumbled again, horseshoes clanging against rock. Avery squeezed tighter. Tried to keep the grimace off her face.

As soon as the road leveled, she prodded Buttercup back up to Hooligan's side. "So after school, you came back here?" *And got married?* She didn't have the guts to say it.

"Yeah. By that time, Gramps and Gran were ready to retire." Maybe it was the vast openness surrounding them, or the fact that he seemed so comfortable on the horse, but something in his demeanor had changed. He looked at her more, and his words were less guarded.

"They took off to Florida and left it all to me."

The horses snorted and chugged, pulling their way up another incline, but Buttercup fell behind again. *Lovely.* He'd finally started to tell her his story, and she couldn't keep up with him.

"Okay, girl." She rubbed a hand up and down the horse's neck like she'd seen Bryce do. "Let's get moving. Work with me here." She squeezed Buttercup's ribs with her heels.

The horse trotted up to Hooligan. They ambled side by side under a canopy of golden aspen leaves backlit by the sun. A breeze trembled through the trees, shimmering the leaves into a dance. Then the wind picked up and set them free. They fluttered down in a gentle rain.

"Wow," she whispered, holding out her palm.

"We should keep going," Bryce mumbled.

Avery closed her hand around an aspen leaf and studied him. Something haunted him. She knew because she'd mirrored that same look, hollow and unseeing. It was the look of a survivalist who'd drawn an invisible curtain over a deep pain.

Warmth webbed across her chest. She held tight to the reins though they were useless in her hands. What she really wanted to do was touch him, to ease the turmoil that crept into his eyes so often.

She wanted to set him free.

Except she knew from years of watching her father that Bryce would have to choose that path himself. It couldn't be forced on him. As much as she wanted to, she couldn't make him a whole person again.

She had to do the only thing she could for him: help him start over. Give him the money he needed to make his dreams come true.

Horse hooves pounded through the quiet. *Clomp, clomp clomp.* Again, she eased Buttercup to Bryce's side. "Hey. I know you're sick of hearing me talk about our offer."

He gave her a stern look of confirmation, which she ignored. She had to.

"But, Bryce, think of what—"

A siren sounded, loud and piercing.

Her phone!

Buttercup jolted to a stop. The horse stood eerily still for a minute, then staggered back, back, back.

Back?

The siren ringtone blared in a relentless screech.

Bryce jerked Hooligan to a stop and turned. "What the hell is that noise?"

"My phone. It's in my backpack." She tried to shimmy out of the straps but almost lost her balance and had to steady herself against the horse's back.

After a pause, the siren wailed again.

Buttercup snorted. Her front hooves pawed the ground.

Avery jiggled the reins, like she was some small kitchen appliance that had quit working. "What's up with her?"

"Shut that thing off!" Bryce eased Hooligan closer and reached out a hand. "Whoa. Whoa, girl."

Buttercup continued her agitated dance.

Her heart plummeted. "What's wrong with her? What's going on?" Despite her best attempt to remain calm, her voice shrilled.

His lips tightened. "Take it easy. She'll sense your fear."

"Take it easy? That'd be a lot easier if she'd stand still!" She jerked back the reins.

Buttercup tossed her head and whinnied.

"Stop!" Bryce guided Hooligan toward them. "Easy, Buttercup. Easy."

Despite his soothing tone, her heart raced. The *swoosh* pounded in her ears.

Deadly cold, she shivered, gripped the reins in tight fists. "Bryce...what should I—"

The phone went off again.

Buttercup reared up. Gravity yanked Avery back. She clawed at the saddle horn, but her sweat-caked palms slipped.

A violent lurch thrust her head forward. Buttercup launched into a canter. *Oh God, oh dear God!* She hunched over and squeezed her eyes shut. This was it. She was going to die. Bile rose in the back of her throat.

"Pull back! Pull back!" Somewhere behind her, another set of hooves pounded. "You have to pull back!"

She wrestled with the reins. "It's not working!"

With massive thrusts, Buttercup arched her back. She popped out of the saddle, then hurled herself into the horse's mane and threw her arms around Buttercup's neck. Avery's face collided with the back of the horse's head. Something seared her forehead. The metallic taste of blood flooded her mouth.

"Damn it, Avery! Pull back!"

"I can't!" *Oh, God! Please!*

"Hold on! I'm coming!"

The horror continued—Buttercup chugging breaths through her nose. Hooves leaping and gnashing. *Hold on, just hold on.*

"Get the reins!"

Where are they? The world reeled out of control. Trees whizzed past. Colors blurred.

Another buck loosened her hands and propelled her into the air.

Flying…

Falling…

Thud! Her body collided with the hard ground. Pain exploded in her head and the world went dim.

CHAPTER NINE

"Avery!" Bryce hurled himself off Hooligan's back and froze next to her sprawled body. The second he released the horse, Hooligan galloped away in the direction Buttercup had fled.

Adrenaline lit his skin on fire. The flames of fear roared through him and burned him up. "Shit. Oh, shit." He hit his knees next to her. The back of her head was jammed against a rock. Blood and bruises stained her face. "Avery?" The rising tide of fear made him feel like he was drowning. "Can you hear me?"

Her chest rose and fell.

Breathing. Thank God she was breathing. "Avery." He touched her forehead and flashbacked to the kiss, to how he'd cradled her cheeks in his hands. Painful breaths shot in and out of his lungs. "Open your eyes." What if she didn't? More flashbacks. The same ones that used to drive him straight to the bottle. Yvonne's face. Blood. So much blood. His useless, helpless hands...

His body shuddered with an onslaught of panic that'd come in waves ever since the accident. He hunched over her and fought the encroaching dizziness, wrestled to get solid breaths. He couldn't panic. She needed him.

A groan eased through her lips and lurched him into action.

He tore off the hem of his shirt and wadded it up, blotted the blood that oozed from a cut across her forehead. A good-sized bruise had already formed down her temple and around her eye. "Avery? Can you hear me?" His hands palpitated her arms, her legs. Didn't look like anything was broken, but her head...

"Ow. Oh. Ow." Her face scrunched in pain. Those glacial eyes fluttered open. She squinted up at him as if the light was too bright. "Bryce?"

Relief ached in his lungs. She knew his name. That was a good sign. "What hurts?" His hands hovered over her, no longer trembling but ready to help, ready to do whatever she needed him to do.

She pushed up on her elbows and looked around, eyes glassy as though she were dazed. "I have a headache."

Ignoring the painful knot that had formed in his throat, he leaned over her and smoothed his hand down her hair. The blank look on her face gutted him.

"You're okay," he said, somehow harnessing a calm reassurance into his tone. She had to be okay. He had to make her okay. "Can you move your legs? Your arms?" Before they did anything else, he had to make sure she hadn't injured her spine.

"Of course I can move my legs." Looking at him like

he'd lost it, she bent her knees, opened and closed her fists, wiggled her feet. "See?" she said. "Everything moves."

The revelation lowered his pulse and pumped strength into his body. He leaned over her, keeping his eyes connected to hers, feeling that raw hunger she'd managed to let loose in him that night in his truck. "I'll help you sit up. Slow and easy." Sliding his arms around her, he gently lifted.

She grimaced. "Ow. My head..."

"You've got a bad cut," he murmured. He wouldn't mention the bruising. Internal bleeding? The acute possibilities reignited his internal firestorm. His hands shook. This was his fault. Avery was lying on the ground with a head injury because he'd agreed to take her riding when he could see full well she had no idea what she was doing...

Her hand lifted to shade her eyes from the sun. "What happened?"

Everything pulsed—the tips of his fingers, the vein in his neck, his temples. She didn't remember. Not a good sign. She had to have a serious concussion, at the very least. He shifted and dug his phone out of his pocket, battling his body's desire to hyperventilate, trying to stay in control. "Your phone spooked Buttercup. She threw you."

"Right." Her eyes squeezed shut. "So I guess it's time for me to fess up that I actually don't ride."

He knew that. He knew and he'd let her anyway. "I'm sorry, Avery. I'm so sorry."

She studied him, head tilted to the side, eyes probing his.

For once, he didn't look away from her. He let his eyes

make a promise. "I'm gonna get you help, okay? Everything'll be fine." Everything had to be fine. "I'll call for help."

"Help?" She grinned. "That's *so* not necessary. I'm fine. Just get me some Advil and I'll get right back on that horse."

She'd obviously meant it as a joke, but he felt sick. "I'm calling an ambulance," he informed her. "You were unconscious. God, Avery, you were lying there bleeding!"

She waved him off. "I probably just passed out from extreme fear." Another easy laugh cranked his neck muscles tight. "Seriously, Bryce. I'm fine. You're overreacting."

Overreacting? Good God. He started to dial, but Avery grabbed for his phone. "Don't call my father. Please."

He tried to read the look on her face. Was it fear? "Why not?"

Her eyes closed. "Don't call him. Please, Bryce. Don't call him."

He shifted to his knees. "Fine. I won't." *Yet.* "But I *am* calling an ambulance." Because he wasn't enough. He couldn't protect her. Just like he hadn't been able to protect his wife. His chest heaved, but he kept his eyes on Avery's. Something about the way she looked at him— like she trusted him—clarified his thoughts, gave him the ammo he needed to fight the panic. He stroked her dirty face, felt the peaceful smoothness of her skin.

Her mouth opened.

"I have to make sure you're okay," he told her gently, then focused on his phone and dialed the numbers.

"911, what's your emergency?"

Shaking her head, Avery huffed out an exasperated groan.

He ignored her. "This is Bryce Walker. I'm up at Walker Mountain Ranch Road, near the intersection with Valley View. My friend got thrown off a horse. Looks like a head injury."

He fired off answers to the dispatcher's questions as quickly as he could. When he finally hung up, Avery was curled up against him, snoring softly.

Damn it. "Avery?" He patted her cheek. "You have to wake up now. You have to stay awake."

Her eyes opened halfway. "Jeez, Bryce. I'm just tired," she grumbled. Blood had crusted over the cut across her forehead and smudged down the side of her face. Even with the attitude, somehow her looks still managed to stun him. She was appealing without even trying to be.

"We have to get down to the road. The ambulance will meet us there."

"Fine." She shot him an irritated glare. "But they're going to take one look at me and tell you I'm as healthy as a horse." Laughing at her own joke, she scrambled to her feet.

"Hey, wait. Take it easy." He reached out to steady her, but she swayed.

Her hands cradled her head, and she groaned in frustration.

"You're not walking." He picked up her backpack and slipped it on, then darted in front of her and swept her into his arms *Gone With the Wind*–style.

She yelped in his ear. "Put me down!" Her legs swung. "Damn it, Bryce. Stop freaking out!"

"We can't take any chances with a head injury." He

knew that too well, and he wasn't about to risk making it worse. With slow steps, he started the painstaking journey down the slope.

Avery crossed her arms over her chest and scowled like a pouting preteen. "This is ridiculous. I am perfectly capable of walking down to the road."

Blood surged through his arms. He tightened his hold on her. "Capable or not, I'm carrying you. So you might as well shut the hell up and let me take care of you."

Her head tilted and she studied his face.

For the first time, he noticed the flecks of gray in her eyes, a faint constellation of freckles across her nose, the curve of her high cheekbones. Man, she was gorgeous.

"Why did you kiss me, Bryce?" she demanded.

He glared past her, dodging the fallen trees and rocks that littered the ground.

Avery slipped her hand under his chin and forced his eyes back to hers. "Was it because you wanted to get rid of me? Scare me away?"

He stopped. *Yes.* He should tell her yes. It had meant nothing. It was all part of his plan to run her off. Except that would be a lie. The way his heart thundered with her in his arms only proved that he'd kissed her because he had to. He couldn't stop himself. He loved her fire, her warmth, her easy laugh. Why was it so hard to tell her the truth?

"Don't get me wrong." She smirked at him. "I'm not complaining or anything. I just want to know why."

And there it was again, that overwhelming desire to touch her, to fit his lips against hers. Inhaling courage, he traced her cheek with his thumb and smiled. "I kissed you because you made me feel something I haven't felt in a long time." In an eternity.

Instead of smiling back, her face paled. "Bryce?" It was barely a whisper.

"Yeah?"

"I don't feel so good," she whimpered.

Shit. He started moving again, slow and easy, trying not to jostle her around too much. "Okay, honey," he soothed. "You'll be okay. We're almost there."

"I think I'm gonna be sick."

"Don't worry about that." It didn't matter if she threw up all over him. He couldn't stop. They couldn't let the head injury gain momentum. "I'll take care of you, Avery. I swear." He'd do his best.

A small smile pulled at the corners of her mouth. "You're not as mean as you want everyone to think, are you?"

A warm flush crept up his neck. "And you're not as tough."

She closed her eyes and inhaled deeply, then wrapped an arm around her middle.

"Almost there," he breathed into her ear. Holding her tighter against him, he jogged down the last incline. "Stay awake, Avery," he reminded her.

"I'm awake," she whispered. But she obviously wasn't feeling well.

"Don't make me kiss you right now. Because I will," he said, voice hoarse with fear. Yvonne had fallen asleep and she'd never woken up...

The shards of sorrow and regret and guilt sliced through him again. He'd give anything to go back. He could've gotten her out faster, could've saved her if only he'd known...

"You can kiss me anytime you want," Avery murmured

with a lopsided smile. "You're pretty good at it, you know."

If his blood wasn't pumping so hard, he would've laughed. She was good at that. Making him smile, laugh. It'd been a long time since he'd felt like laughing.

They broke through the trees into the clearing.

"Thank you." Her breath wisped against his neck. "For carrying me."

Still holding her against him, he kneeled to wait for the ambulance and pulled her closer, stroking her silky hair, feeling this overpowering urge to help her, to ease her pain, to save her the way he hadn't been able to save Yvonne. The emotions had been buried so deep for so long. They were raw and painful—but holding her so close, feeling her warm body in his arms, fighting for someone else again...it brought him back to life. "Thank you," he whispered over her, "for waking me up."

She'd managed to break through every wall he'd built since Yvonne's death, and he wouldn't be able to ignore her.

Not anymore.

* * *

Sirens. Loud. Piercingly loud. Avery stuffed her hands over her ears. *Ohhhh. Ow...* Nausea spun the sky into blue swirls. *No. No.—*

She tore herself away from Bryce and hunched over on her knees in time to throw up all over a mound of innocent purple and white columbines.

Warmth radiated into her back. Bryce's hand slowly massaged her shoulders. "Hang in there."

She wanted to turn and smile at him, or at least mumble thanks, but her body had a different agenda.

Bryce gathered her hair in a ponytail and held it away from her face. His hand drew concentric circles in the middle of her back. "Want water or something?"

It wasn't safe to open her mouth and speak. Instead, she shook her head and shifted so she could sink against him. Her eyelids felt like lead. She closed them. For a minute. Only for a minute...

"Avery!" Bryce rubbed her cheek. "Come on. They're here."

She forced up the steel curtains over her eyes. On the shoulder of the dirt road, a police car skidded to a stop. Red and blue lights gyrated across everything like strobe lights.

"Here we go." Bryce steadied her while he scrambled off the ground. Then he slid his arms around her and pulled her to her feet. Everything swayed—the trees, the ground. "Ugh." Gravity threatened to take her down. She clawed at him, clutched his bicep.

His arms enclosed her. "I've got you." He breathed the words close to her ear.

Wrapped tightly in his strong arms, inhaling his pine scent, her whole body relaxed. She let him lead her closer to the lights.

"Bryce!" A policeman approached them and she blinked hard because he looked so much like Bryce—tall and sturdy, shorter dark hair, walnut-shaped eyes...

Wait a minute. She'd met him at the game. He was Bryce's cousin. What was his name, again? Sam? Seth? Skyler?

"What the hell happened?" He bent to examine her face.

"Her phone went off and spooked Buttercup." Bryce's words were rough and winded.

She slipped her hand into his and squeezed because she didn't want him to be afraid. She hadn't meant to scare him like that. Not after everything he'd been through.

"I'll be fine," she murmured.

"EMTs are on the way. They'll be here any minute," Bryce's cousin said, with a worried glance at her face.

She must look worse than she thought.

Bryce kept his arms around her, but he leaned over and said something to his officer. Cousin. His cousin. Skyler. *Whoa . . .* the world moved in shimmering waves. She fought against the dizziness so she could hear what they were saying, but the conversation only came in snippets.

"Unconscious."

"How long?"

She couldn't make out Bryce's response.

Officer Skyler ran to his car and leaned in through the open window. He yelled something into the crackling radio, then jogged back. "ETA is two minutes."

"Thanks, Sawyer," Bryce breathed.

Sawyer! Not Skyler. Sawyer.

"Hang on, Avery," Sawyer said, rubbing a sympathetic hand up and down her arm. "They're almost here."

Aww. He was so nice. Like Bryce. Must run in Elsie's family blood. "Thanks for—" She clamped her mouth shut before another wave of nausea targeted Bryce's cousin. Probably shouldn't throw up all over his crisp, blue uniform.

More sirens whined and not a moment too soon, because she really did not want to stand anymore.

The ambulance arrived in a dust storm, rocks pinging metal, dirt flying.

Doors opened. People shouted. But she leaned against Bryce and held on. The nausea started to subside.

"... getting worse." Bryce was saying something, but she couldn't focus. A high-pitched ringing screamed in her ears.

She burrowed her head deeper into him, but hands pulled her away and stood her up straight.

No. Not away. Don't take me away from him.

"Miss King?" A paramedic dressed in a stiff, blue uniform looked into her eyes. "I'm Justin. This is Lena." He gestured to a woman with cropped hair. "We're gonna check out that bump on your head."

"I already told you. I'm *fine*," she insisted.

"Let's get her on the stretcher." The EMT pushed a yellow gurney toward them. Bryce lifted her like she weighed nothing and lowered her to the foam pad. He turned and started to walk away.

"Wait." She reached for his hand. "You're not leaving?"

"Oh. No. I won't leave." He stood over her and rested a hand on her arm.

The touch sped up her heart.

"I've got to take off, though." Sawyer appeared next to her. "Another call just came through." He squeezed her hand. "Hope you feel better. I'll call and check on you later."

"Thank you." Tears pooled in her eyes. She hardly knew Sawyer and he'd been so kind to her. Just like all of Bryce's other friends. They'd been so accepting, so gracious.

"We need to take your vitals." Paramedic man butted into her moment, fit a brace around her neck and buckled her to the stretcher, while Lena checked her pulse and took her blood pressure. Then she shined a bright light right into Avery's eyes.

She blinked hard. *Ow.* "Can I just rest? Everything'll feel better if I rest."

"Sorry. No resting," the EMT said as he fished a clipboard out of a gray bag.

"So how'd you fall off the horse?"

"Her phone went off and spooked it," Bryce cut in before she could answer. He kept his hand on her, protective and concerned.

Swept up in all of Bryce's unnecessary concern, she'd forgotten that her phone had rang. Who'd called? Dad? Barely able to move, she stretched her arms down her sides as far as she could and patted her pockets. They were flat. No phone.

As if reading her mind, Bryce held up her backpack. "It's in here. I'll take care of it."

"Okay." But her fingers itched to hit the keys, check her messages, her texts. What if her father couldn't get a hold of her? Would he send in the cavalry? Would he find out she hadn't closed the deal yet?

The paramedic turned to Bryce. "How long was she unconscious?"

"A minute or two." He shifted his weight and stuffed his hands in his pockets. "No blood in her ears, but her pupils were definitely dilated."

Blood in the ears? Dilated pupils? How did he know so much about a head injury?

The EMT finished scribbling something on the clipboard. He shoved it back into a bag and shouldered it. "All right, Miss King. We'll get you back to the ER."

Hospital? Nuh uh. No way. "No hospital." She tried to sit up, but the ties roped her down. "Can't I just go back to the lodge? I'm sure I'll be fine." She shot a begging look in Bryce's direction. They didn't understand what would happen if she got carted into the ER, if Dad found out she'd been injured. He'd fly his jet straight out and make a huge scene like he always did.

"I'd rather not go." She could handle this herself. She didn't need him to rescue her.

"Sorry," EMT man said in a flat tone. "We have to take you in."

"What if I refuse? Can't I sign something and refuse treatment?"

The paramedics looked at each other.

"No." Bryce said sternly. "You're going to the hospital."

"Excuse me?" Again, her muscles fought the restraints. She squirmed and wriggled, but those suckers were tight. Finally, she gave up, but made her point with a dirty look. "That's not your decision."

He turned away from her and faced the medic. "She's not thinking clearly. She needs a hospital."

Frustration hurtled out of her windpipe in a groan. "He's not in charge of me," she growled at them, fully aware that she sounded like a sullen teenager. Why couldn't she calm down? Think rationally? Talk them into her point of view like she always did at work? Emotions clashed, gathering like dark thunderheads on the verge of letting loose.

Bryce backed away. "Take her."

"You got it." The paramedics positioned themselves on either side of emt and hoisted the stretcher into the back of the ambulance.

Through the open doors, Bryce squeezed her hiking boot. "This is best, Avery. Trust me."

Her eyes stung. She sucked in a horrified breath. *No crying!* She sniffed back the emotion. "I don't trust you. Not at all."

"You don't have to. I'm still doing what's best for you."

"Don't bother." She rolled her eyes up to stare at the ceiling. "Like you care, anyway."

"I do." His voice was so low and quiet that she had to search his face.

He stood there a second longer, staring at her like he wanted to say something else, but the EMT leaned forward and slammed the door shut.

Her eyes closed as she thought about the way Bryce had cradled her in his arms, how he'd taken care of her. He was just being nice, doing what anyone would've done in the situation, but to her it had felt like so much more.

It would look like so much more, too. The second Dad found out she'd been in an accident, he'd drop everything and get out there. And it wouldn't take him long to see that she'd broken his number one rule: never, ever, under any circumstances get emotionally involved in a business transaction.

Yeah. It was a little too late for that.

CHAPTER TEN

Bryce jammed the truck into gear and punched the accelerator. Gravel and twigs pinged the undercarriage and made it sound like he was riding out a hailstorm. He gripped the wheel with one hand and fished for his cell with the other.

Come on. Finally, he ripped the phone from his pocket and hit number one on speed dial.

Pick up, Mom. It'd taken him fifteen minutes to sprint back to the lodge, enough time for fear to root itself deep inside and entangle him in the same nightmares he'd once drank to battle. Did she make it to the hospital? Was there bleeding in her brain? His head was a mess. She was fine. She'd be fine.

Except he'd made that same promise to himself three years ago, and now he knew better. He knew life was fragile. He knew bad things happened to good people.

Yvonne was so good, a much better person than he'd ever be. She could've offered the world so much more, and she'd been the one to die.

A familiar hollowness spread through him, but he couldn't let it swallow him, couldn't let the memories paralyze him. Not now. Avery needed him. It'd been a damn long time since someone had needed him…

The phone continued to ring against his ear. Where was she? Stomping his boot onto the gas pedal, he tore out onto the highway, a cloud of dust rising behind him like a bad omen.

Finally, the line clicked. "Bryce? Is that you?"

"Yeah." He veered into the left lane to pass a sports car.

"You finished your ride already?" Disappointment laced her voice. She probably thought he'd run Avery off. If only that was the problem instead of the fact that he'd taken her someplace she had no business being, and now she was lying in a hospital bed in pain and alone.

"Mom, listen." He raised his voice over the roar of the engine. "There was an accident."

"An accident?" she gasped. "What happened?"

He switched lanes to veer right in the turnabout, and filled Mom in.

"The poor dear! Is she all right?"

"I don't know." Rising anxiety caught in his throat. "I'm on my way to the hospital now."

Movement scratched across the line. It sounded as if she'd already started running to her truck. "What can I do? How can I help?"

He sped around another slow car, watched the odometer inch up, and scanned the road for cops. "I need you to go to the lodge. Wait for Hooligan and Buttercup to come back." If they weren't back already. Those horses knew the woods better than he did.

"I'm leaving right now," Mom said, already out of breath.

"And call Edward King. Tell him what happened." Despite what Avery said, he had to tell her father before he found out another way. "Tell him she's okay, but we're getting her checked out." That was all he needed to know for now. His mother could sweet talk anyone into believing everything was fine.

"Yes. Of course. I'll find the number right away."

The wheels screeched as he careened into the hospital parking lot. "Thanks."

"Call me back as soon as you know anything, dear."

"I will." Eyes scanning the lot, he clicked off the phone and squeezed the truck into a parking spot near the ER entrance. Lungs burning, he raced through the doors. The waiting area sat empty, minus the receptionist lady sitting behind the counter.

The woman glanced up and slipped on her bifocals. "How can I help you?"

He braced his hands against the counter and tried to breathe like a normal human. "Avery King? They just brought her in."

She blinked slowly, almost like she was batting her eyelashes. "And what's your name, doll?"

"Bryce Walker."

"Oh, right. They told me to expect you. Now what room is she in, again?" The woman trailed her shiny red fingernail all the way down a chart, taking her sweet time to mouth every name on the list. "Ah ha! Avery King. Here we go. She's in Room 6, honey."

"Thanks," he called, already halfway down the hall. He busted through the double doors and watched the numbers pass by. *Four...five...*

Six.

The door opened with a *whoosh*. The face that stared back at him didn't fit. "Meg?"

Perfect. Just his luck that Meg was on duty. The woman had always loved prying into everyone's business. Now she'd find out he'd been with Avery King. Voluntarily. She'd never let him hear the end of this. He reached up to knead his forehead. *This day keeps getting better and better.*

"Hey there, Bryce." Meg closed Avery's door and braced a clipboard against her chest. "Avery told me all about your little ride this morning."

He ignored the implication in her singsongy tone. "Is she okay?"

"She has a mild concussion. And a touch of altitude sickness, which is what caused the nausea." Even the doctor speak didn't wipe that inquisitive smirk off her face. "Didn't you remind her to stay hydrated on your little date?"

He ignored the date comment. "You're sure she's okay, right?" he asked, straining for a neutral expression so she couldn't read the panic on his face.

Meg obviously didn't buy it. "So...you and Avery King, huh?" She winked. "Come on, Walker. Don't hold out on me."

He looked her square in the face. "It's nothing." At least nothing he cared to tell Meg about. He held his uninterested frown steady and prepped for more questions.

"Don't lie to me. How'd you meet her?"

"She's staying at the lodge. Trying to convince me to sell the place to her dad."

"Mmmmm..." Meg seemed to savor the tidbit like it was a piece of that dark chocolate she was always popping into her mouth. "Just how hard is she trying?"

He made a show of rolling his eyes. "Come on, Meg. It's not like that. I just want to make sure there's no permanent damage. So her asshole father doesn't slap me with a lawsuit." He did his best to look sincere. "So, how bad is it?"

"She'll be *fine*," Meg said with a reassuring smile. "We're rehydrating her and I told her to take it easy for a few days."

His heart finally slipped back into a safe rhythm and gave his lungs more space to breathe. But...doubts crowded into his gut. "Maybe you should order a CT scan. Just to be safe."

Meg's eyes got all sad like they did whenever she talked about Yvonne. "Of course. I'll do that." Her gaze flickered back to his, but before she could fire off more questions, he sidestepped her and opened Avery's door. "Thanks. See you around."

"Walker, wait."

His hand paused on the doorknob.

"She seems pretty great." Meg backed away, face softened with a sentimental smile. "I know you said she's only a guest at the ranch, but if it turned out to be more than that, I'd be happy for you. You deserve someone who's pretty great."

"Thanks." That meant a lot, coming from her. Of everyone in their group, she'd been Yvonne's closest friend.

"Tell Avery someone'll be down to escort her to radiology as soon as there's a commercial break." She shook her head and rolled her eyes. "You know how those orderlies are with their soaps..."

He laughed. "I'll tell her."

"See you around, Walker." Her white clogs squeaked down the hall and he finally opened the door, hands all tense and fisted because it was true. Avery was pretty great and he kind of couldn't wait to see her.

She looked smaller in the bed, propped up on three pillows, white sheets pulled up to her waist. The sight of the blood still crusted in her blond hair gave him a hard punch of sympathy right under his ribs. He drew closer to her, but she turned her head and glared at him.

"Get out," she snapped.

He checked over his shoulder to make sure she wasn't talking to someone else. *Nope. Okay.* So between the time he'd helped load her into the ambulance and now, something had royally pissed her off. Moving closer, he tried to decode that fierce expression on her face. "Is there a problem?"

"This is all your fault." She brandished her pointer finger at him.

Her anger pushed him back a step. "*What?*"

"You made me ride that horse," she grumbled. "You did this on purpose."

He opened his mouth, but there were no words. Didn't she realize how crazy that sounded? "You think I *wanted* Buttercup to buck you?" He threw up his hands. "What, you think I paid her off or something?"

"This isn't a joke." She shimmied her back up against the pillows and crossed her arms like a pouting three-year-old.

He gaped at her. One hour ago she'd clung to him, crying, and thanked him for saving her. Now this? "You told me you knew how to ride," he reminded her.

She answered with a frustrated grunt and stared out the window.

Despite the risk of setting her off, he grinned. She sure was cute when she got angry. Instead of retreating like she obviously wanted him to, he sat on the edge of the bed. "I'm sorry."

Her head turned slowly. When their eyes connected her rigid lips went slack.

"Really. I feel awful about this." He wagered with a touch, just a light brush of his hand on her arm, but it was enough to dry out his mouth. What was he doing? What the hell was he doing?

Avery seemed to wonder the same thing. Her eyes analyzed his as if searching for hidden motives.

She wouldn't find any, though. He'd touched her because he had to, because it was the only way to ease that growing ache inside of him. She was close enough that he could smell her, the orange blossom scent that reminded him of the orange tree outside of Gramps and Gran's condo in Florida. She was close enough that if he leaned forward, he could taste her again...

"It wasn't your fault," she whispered, looking down at the bed like she didn't know where to focus. "You're right. I might've *implied* I knew what I was doing." A small laugh squeaked out but it sounded off-pitch and nervous.

He could relate. The incessant buzzing of his body made him feel like a kid who wanted something he knew was off-limits.

"Bryce..." Avery closed those lovely lips.

He inched closer. Off-limits had never stopped him before.

A click resounded in the room. The door opened and he shot off the bed in case it was Meg. As nice as she'd been about everything out there, she didn't need any fodder for gossip.

Instead of a blond, nosy doctor, an orderly rushed in. He looked to be in his mid-twenties, had that signature sunglasses tan that gave him away as an avid outdoorsman. "Miss King? Time to head up for the CT scan."

She blinked, tore her gaze away from Bryce and pulled the covers up to her chest. "Right. Great timing," she mumbled.

The orderly made some adjustments to the gurney, then started to wheel her out the door.

She glanced back at Bryce, her face flushed. "You'll be around when I get back?"

"Of course." He'd be around as long as she needed him. As long as she wanted him. She did want him, right? He wasn't misreading that, was he?

Her gaze stayed with his as the orderly wheeled her out the door.

Nope. Her smile was all the confirmation he needed.

* * *

Avery pried her eyes open and forced them to focus past the unrelenting pulse in her head. It was starting to feel more like a never-ending hangover, complete with that sinking feeling of regret. She never should've gotten on that horse. Now she was stuck in a hospital bed instead of going over the offer with Bryce. Scooting herself up on the bed, she reached for the water glass to end the drought in her throat.

The hospital room still sat pathetically empty and quiet. Dim, too. At some point, one of the nurses must've pulled the shades closed. She squinted to see the clock on the wall. She'd slept for over two hours and still there was no sign of Bryce. He'd promised he would be there when she got back from the scan, but he must've gotten tired of waiting and gone home.

She shimmied her back up against the pillows and closed her eyes, but her phone chimed and bounced on the bedside table. She snatched it up and clicked it on. Incoming text from Edward.

Fabulous.

Where the hell are you? Is the contract signed?

Anger welled, brimming over in the form of perspiration, shaky fingers. *Sure, Dad. I'm stuck in a hospital bed, but I'll get the deal signed ASAP.* She couldn't type the words. He'd kill her if he knew what had happened, if he realized she'd been out riding with Bryce instead of acquiring his land...

Across the room, the door cracked open.

She shoved the phone back on the table. "Hello? Anyone there?" *Like maybe a doctor to tell me everything's fine so I can get out of here, already?*

The door opened wider and Bryce peeked in.

That got her blood pumping again, hard and fast through her body. Her spine went straight. She combed her fingers through her ratty hair. *Yeah.* Like that would help. "Hey there!" Her words came out overly enthusiastic and shrill.

"Hey." He shot her a sexy smile, one that quirked the right side of his lips. "Hope I didn't wake you." He eased in through the doorway, and yes, he had changed. He wore a short-sleeved blue button-up, looking almost clean cut. Even his hair had been combed.

Her face broke out in a sweat, but this time it had nothing to do with nausea. It was the sight of his arms, so strong and sure. One look at those muscles brought her back to the mountain, when he'd cradled her, held her close. Breaths came out in mere puffs of steam. Blood rushed to her face at the memory of him setting her down on the ground and securing his arms around her. The images had blurred in her injured brain, but she couldn't seem to forget the warmth of his body against hers.

Ahem. Pull it together, Avery. She peeled her gaze away from his hot body and smiled.

He shoved his hands into the pockets of his khaki Carhartts. "Have you gotten the test results yet?"

"No." She let her head fall back to the pillow for dramatic effect. "It's taking forever."

"I'm sure the doc'll be back soon." He turned to the door.

No, don't leave again. Five seconds ago, the room had been filled with that dim, cold loneliness, but then she saw him and the air had changed. It felt warm and welcoming.

"Where are you going?" She sat up and wriggled to the side of the bed, keeping her bare legs concealed under the sheets. There was nothing flattering about hospital gowns.

"Just a sec." He propped open the door. Wheels squeaked. "Thought you could use a few things." Bryce pushed a cart into the room. It was piled high with... stuff. Not a few things. A whole lot of things. A stack of magazines and a huge teddy bear and a vase full of the most beautiful, colorful wildflowers. Then there was a whole selection of food from the cafeteria—a delicious-looking salad and some kind of grilled panini and a basket of French fries and a bowl of rich potato soup with bits of bacon on top.

Her chest hurt and she realized she hadn't breathed in a while. Slowly, she exhaled the disbelief. He got all of that? For her?

"Didn't know what you felt like eating," Bryce explained when she glanced up at him. He shrugged like it was nothing, like bringing her this cart of gifts and food wasn't one of the most thoughtful things anyone had ever done for her.

Tears welled but she fought them with a blink. Emotion, yet another side effect of her headache. At least that's what she'd keep telling herself.

"Hope you like it?" His inflection formed a question, as though the obvious moisture in her eyes concerned him.

She swallowed the mountain in her throat and smiled up at him. "Like it? Bryce, I love it. All of it. You didn't have to do this." *Don't cry. For the love of God, don't cry.*

His shoulders seemed to relax. He walked to the bed and looked down at her with a softness she'd never seen on his face. "It's the least I can do."

Her heart acknowledged his closeness, his pine scent, with a leap. Did he feel that same *zing* when he looked at her? Damn that poker face of his. She couldn't tell.

"I'm glad you weren't hurt worse," he said quietly.

She stared at her hands and tried to think of something intelligent to say. *Hmmm.* Why did everything go blank when he was around?

He reached down and brushed her bangs away from the bandage across her forehead. "Looks pretty painful."

An electrical charge surged all the way down to her toes. She couldn't even swallow. "Um, actually it's not too—"

Her phone wailed.

Bryce pulled back. "Still haven't changed that awesome ringtone, huh?"

She laughed but her heart buckled. Why another interruption? Why now? "Give me a sec." She picked up her phone and checked the screen.

Vanessa?

Holding up a finger in Bryce's direction, she brought the phone to her ear. "Hey, what's up?"

"Avery." Panic screeched across the line. "I'm so sorry."

Bryce stood over her, watching.

She forced her shoulders to slouch with ease, even though her pulse throbbed in her temples. "Why? What's going on?"

"Your father's on his way out there. I just found out. He's going to check on you."

An icy sensation prickled her throat, but she smiled for Bryce's sake. "What do you mean?"

"Someone named Elsie called and told me about your accident. A few hours ago, I left Edward a message. He just called me from Aspen! He'll be there any minute."

Swallow. She couldn't swallow. And her smile was so forced her lips started to go numb.

"Avery? Did you hear me?" Vanessa asked. "He was pretty pissed off."

She deflected Bryce's curious gaze with a smile. "Um. Wow. That's not good. Really not good."

"What's up?" Concern rimmed Bryce's eyes.

"Sorry," Vanessa said. "I wanted to warn you."

"Thanks," she croaked. "I should go."

"Gotcha. Good luck, girl."

Good luck? She'd need more than luck to explain this mess to her father. She'd need a plan...

"Hey." Bryce eased onto the edge of the bed and studied her. "Anything I can do?"

She couldn't answer. What was she supposed to say? That she wanted to run away so she didn't have to face her father?

Yes!

That was exactly what she had to say. She didn't have a choice. She flung the covers to the floor and scooted off the bed. "We have to get out of here."

Bryce shot to his feet. "What? Why?"

Her clothes. Where were her clothes? She pulled open the drawers on a built-in cabinet. "Please. We have to go. Right now."

"Go where?"

"Back to the lodge." *There!* They were crumpled in a pile on the counter next to the sink. She flew to the other side of the room, hospital gown flapping behind her. But who cared? If she didn't get out of there, things would be a lot worse than Bryce getting a glimpse of her lacy black thong.

Bryce didn't mention the view, but he followed behind her. "Whoa. Slow down there, slugger. You can't leave the hospital."

Shaking the wrinkles out of her hiking pants and thermal shirt, she twirled to face him. Her head pounded. "We can sneak out. It's not like anyone's guarding the door."

His arms folded over his chest like he'd taken it upon himself to be her personal bouncer. "Who was on the phone? What's going on?"

She snuck past him and headed for the bathroom. "I don't have time to explain. I'll get dressed, then we have to go."

His strong hands grabbed her shoulders and turned her around. The bundle of clothes fell to the floor.

Bryce looked down at her, his eyes blazing. A slight tremble ran through his hands. "Take it easy."

He stood close, his hands still on her body. Her gaze ran over his lips, smooth and curved, then up to his eyes. And oh wow, he had amazing eyes. As green as spring leaves after a rainstorm. She couldn't look away.

He didn't either.

Did he feel it? That crackle of electricity in the air between them?

"Bryce," she whispered, but she didn't know what else to say. What did she want from him?

Eyes locked on hers, he wrapped a hand around the back of her neck in a gentle caress.

Every hypersensitive nerve in her body submitted to the touch. Her mouth went slack. Eyes closed. They met somewhere in the blind middle. His lips grazed hers carefully, like he was afraid to hurt her. But he wouldn't.

Couldn't. Locked in his embrace, raw desire flooded through her and carried out the pain.

She molded her lips to his and savored the sweet heat of his mouth. Her palms slid up his chest, feeling every ripple and ridge.

"You're so stunning, Avery," he whispered.

The hunger in his voice lured her back to his lips. She kissed him harder. He wrapped his arms around her waist and pulled her against him. The room whirled in a glorious blur of colors. He tasted so good, like wintergreen with a spice she couldn't name.

This. This is what she'd wanted since the day she'd walked into his office, to feel those strong arms holding her, to feel the delicious pressure of his lips against hers.

His warm hands slipped into the opening at the back of hospital gown and stroked the sensitive skin on her lower back. The light touch radiated all the way down her legs, weakening them to the point she had to hold onto him to stand.

Bryce pulled away, holding her tightly, keeping her upright. "Sorry." His gaze fell to the floor. "I'm sorry. I wasn't thinking."

Exactly. Neither one of them had thought at all. That was why it had been so perfect. "Don't be sorry." Her voice was as weak as her legs. She wasn't sorry. She *so* wasn't sorry. One thing Bryce Walker shouldn't apologize for was for the way he kissed because he had some serious skills in that area. His lips were firm but careful and so…tender. "I'm not sorry. That was—"

A hollow knock echoed through the room and cut her off.

"Avery?"

Her body iced over. Her father. Right outside her hospital room.

Bryce's hands stroked her arms like he didn't care who walked in and saw them kissing, but she did.

"I'm sorry," she whispered, then pushed him away just as her father walked into the room.

With Logan right behind him.

CHAPTER ELEVEN

Two men walked into a hospital room.

It had all the beginnings of a bad joke. A joke on him.

The way Avery practically leapt back to her hospital bed proved what Bryce should've already known. She didn't want to be caught in his arms. Hell, she didn't even want to be caught standing next to him.

In case he'd forgotten who she was—which he had—the two men now standing in her room slammed him with a reminder. It was clear the man in the slick gray suit was Edward King. His white hair was sculpted back from his tan face with gel. The guy's steel gray eyes honed in on him.

Bryce ignored King's angry glare and assessed the man who stood next to him. Had to be Avery's ex. Who else would dress head to toe in Chicago Cubs apparel? The ensemble read like a walking advertisement that he played professional ball.

Sure enough, Schwartz rushed to Avery's bedside. "Avery...God, are you okay?" He touched her face and Bryce had to turn away. Two minutes ago, the world had tipped on its axis and he'd been the one kissing her, enjoying the warmth of her body against his, feeling that burn of hunger for more. But now everything was as it should be. Daddy and the rich, famous boyfriend coming to the rescue.

"I'm fine," Avery said quietly, eyes carefully avoiding her ex.

Yeah. She was fine. But he wasn't. The residual effects of that kiss still pounded through him in a mocking reminder.

"What the hell is going on here?" Avery's father addressed Bryce as if he was a kid who'd just gotten caught in his daughter's bedroom.

"Nothing," Avery squeaked from her bed. "Nothing's going on."

King pivoted and posted his hands on his hips, assuming that imposing-father stance. "You could've been killed," he growled, then pointed at him. "And I hold you responsible, Walker."

Bryce had a hard time not rolling his eyes. How had he let himself get wrapped up in this? In her? This was exactly the kind of complication he didn't need right now. Not when he was trying to get his life back together. A long inhale curbed the rising irritation. "I get why you're upset—"

"It wasn't Bryce's fault," Avery interrupted. "It was mine. I asked him to take me riding."

Bryce shot her a look. He could talk for himself, thank you very much. He didn't need her sticking up for him.

Especially when her ex sat on her hospital bed gazing at her like a lovesick puppy.

"Why would you go riding?" Edward demanded.

"I wanted to see the scenery," she mumbled. "It was all my idea. Mr. Walker had nothing to do with it."

He flinched at the way she said his name, all formal and indifferent. What, was she afraid her father would see something between the two of them? So what if he did? She might be tempted to play like nothing had happened between them, like that kiss didn't affect her, but he knew better. He'd felt her legs give. He'd felt her clutch at his shirt. He'd felt her draw closer to him when she could've pulled away.

"For God's sakes. I am going to take care of this right now." King rifled through an outside pocket of a leather briefcase that was slung over his shoulder. He pulled out a paper and waved it in front of Bryce. "This contract, Mr. Walker, will change your life." The paper fluttered in his hand. "Twenty-three million dollars. And I know that's generous based on what I've heard about your property."

What he'd heard? From whom?

Avery's steady glance out the window gave her away. *Great.* That was great. That's why he'd caught her snooping around upstairs. She was reporting back to her father on what a hellhole his ranch was. Well, screw her.

Bryce bounced his gaze back and forth between them. It was almost amusing how they thought he was just gonna roll over when they said 23 million dollars. He could give a damn about 23 million dollars, and he didn't have a problem saying so. Fighting a smile, he shrugged. "No thanks."

King's face turned a dangerous shade of red. These

people obviously weren't used to hearing the word "no," but it happened to be one of his favorites.

The man shuffled a step closer. "What'll it take, Walker? What do you want for it?"

"Nothing. It's not for sale."

"There must be something that would help you part with it." His voice was insanely controlled and quiet. Bryce recognized the tone. The calm before a storm.

Blood pumped into his arms just like it had before those bar brawls. He could feel it, hot and fierce and prepping him to fight. But he didn't drink anymore. He knew when to walk away. "I should go. Now that someone's here to help her. I've got work to do."

"Wait." Avery swung her legs over the side of the bed. Her ex gaped at her.

King narrowed his gaze into a silent question.

"I just…" Her hands clasped together. "I mean, if you leave, how will I get back to the lodge?"

The look on her father's face tempted him to double over with laughter. He suspected something was up, all right.

He focused on Avery. "I assumed you'd be leaving." She should leave. There was no reason for her to stay. When he wanted something, he went for it. He didn't intend to play games, sneak around. Even if he took her back to the lodge, they weren't free to explore what was behind the kiss. Not when she obviously thought hanging out with him was slumming it. Why else would she be so afraid of what her father thought?

In a sudden, swift movement, King stepped aside, his rigid face almost relaxed. Bryce eyed him. Why the sudden change in demeanor? Why wasn't he shoving the offer in his face again?

"You can go, Mr. Walker." King smiled. He actually smiled. "I'll bring her to collect her luggage after we take care of things here."

Goody. That should be fun. After a formal nod to Avery, he stormed out of there.

Edward King was probably formulating some sort of strategy to entice him to sell. But it wouldn't work.

Like he'd said, the ranch wasn't for sale. To him, it was priceless.

* * *

This was wrong. All wrong.

Avery looked down at Logan's hand, which was still entwined with hers. His concerned expression heaped on the guilt. While Logan sat there holding her hand, the memory of Bryce's kiss tingled on her lips, still very much alive.

She couldn't deny it. Instead of using her negotiating prowess to convince Bryce to sell his land, she'd fallen for him. Hard.

Though her father stood over her, lecturing her about the dangers of horseback riding, thoughts of Bryce swirled in her mind. She wanted to explore why he gave her that jittery, overly-caffeinated feeling. She wanted to know what he'd been through that had made him so intense and deliberate and strong. She wanted him, period.

"Are you listening to me?" Dad asked in his dramatic way, arms outstretched, palms tilted up.

"Of course," she lied.

Logan let go of her hand. "You seem tired." He leaned in and inspected the bandage on her forehead. "Are you sure they didn't see anything on the CT scan? Concussions are dangerous."

Pressure built inside of her until she had to scoot away from him. *Enough.* She'd had enough. Even though she appreciated the concern, Logan shouldn't be there. Her father, either. She could handle this. Bryce had started to trust her and she could convince him to sell, but it had to be her way. Which meant she had to remove the distractions, one by one.

"Dad?" Avery edged off the bed and faced her father. "Can you give us a minute?"

"Why would you need—?"

"Out in the hall. Please." Holding the flimsy hospital gown together, she strode to the door and opened it for him, leaving no room for him to talk her out of it.

"Fine. But this is not over, Avery." His loafers thunked the floor in heavy, irritated steps, but after shooting one more stern glance over his shoulder he finally walked out.

The second the door clicked, Logan approached her. "Sorry I never returned your calls," he said before she could ask him what he was doing there.

Hadn't she made it clear they'd broken up? "Logan—"

"I needed time to think." He led her back to the hospital bed. They sat down, side by side. "It was stupid, proposing to you like that."

"No it wasn't." She nudged his shoulder. "It was sweet. Really. I just…" How could she say it without hurting him? "I don't love you that way." Passionately. Wholeheartedly. They'd never had that kind of chemistry…

"I get it." Those brown, calming eyes met hers, and she knew. He wasn't mad at her. He didn't hold any of it against her.

"You're one of my best friends, Aves." He turned to her with a shrug. "I thought we could make it more, you know? But you're right. It would've been a bad idea."

Her shoulders relaxed, loosening the knots of apprehension that had pulled her stomach tight when he'd walked into the room. "You're one of my best friends, too. I hate that I humiliated you in front of the world."

Logan grinned. "I take full responsibility. You know how I get carried away. I never should've put you in that position." He slung an arm around her. "And I could give a shit what the fans are saying. I'll always want you in my life. That's why I came out here. To make sure we're still friends."

"Always." A happy peace settled over her headache. "You deserve the best." She meant it. He'd find the person he couldn't live without. By tomorrow, he'd probably have a thousand potential wives lined up outside the stadium.

"You do, too, Avery. I hope you find what you're looking for."

A picture of Bryce flashed in her mind. He wasn't what she'd been looking for. Not at all, but...she seemed to have found him anyway. Her face got all hot and steamy. The sensation traveled lower until it engulfed her body.

Logan didn't seem to notice. "Guess I should head back to the airport. We've got a team meeting tonight." He stood and took her hand, helped her up. "Take care of yourself. No more horseback riding. Got it?"

She hugged him. "Got it."

He let her go and sauntered out the door.

As she watched him walk away, a pang of loss stabbed

her, but there was also a release—a glimpse of freedom. The only way to figure out what she wanted, where she belonged, was to let go of the things that didn't make her feel alive.

Then she had to be brave enough to embrace the things that did.

CHAPTER TWELVE

Bryce swung the ax high enough to obscure the royal blue sky. Early morning sunlight glinted off the blade. Gritting his teeth, he slammed it down. The contact made a clean cut straight through the log and released the scent of wet wood into the air.

Sweat poured from his face, even though the temperature couldn't have been more than seventy.

He flung the split logs onto the pile. It'd grown as tall as a bale of hay. After the scene at the hospital, he'd hit the ground chopping. At this rate, he'd have enough firewood to last him three winters.

The thermal shirt he'd pulled on earlier clung to him. He peeled it off and threw it on the ground. For an hour and a half he'd been chopping wood, but the tension hadn't even begun to work itself out of his shoulders, his neck. After what had happened with Avery, he could've chopped for a week and still not have worked out the frustration.

But he could try.

He positioned another innocent log on the chopping block and swung.

Crack! There was something satisfying about that sound, clean and ear-splitting.

Sweat dripped into his eyes. He swiped an arm across his forehead. He hated to admit it, but having Avery around brought back memories of the ranch during a different time. A time when guests had lounged at the breakfast table listening to Mom's wildly spun stories, that seemed to inflate with each telling. Mom had been glowing with happiness the night before when she'd made them dinner. Like she was finally back to doing what she was born to do—serving whoever walked through her door.

Avery had brought life into the place. Warmth.

It still smoldered in his chest, just like it had when he'd kissed her.

He brought the ax down again, harder this time. The split logs fell to the ground.

Didn't matter, really. Couldn't matter.

She was about to come back and pack up her stuff, then disappear from his life. And good riddance. She'd distracted him, but it was time to refocus. He still had the ranch, at least for now, and he wouldn't let it go. He'd fight anyone, everyone, who tried to take it away from him. Including the King family. Which was why he'd called in the big guns.

A dust cloud rose down the road. He balanced the blade of the ax on the ground and watched a black Jeep Wrangler roll into the driveway, the images of aspen and pine trees reflected in the shiny paint.

The Jeep jerked to a stop just down the hill. Grinning, he leaned the ax against the chopping block. *Right on time.*

Ben Noble catapulted himself over the side of the Jeep *Dukes of Hazzard*-style, and he looked the part, complete with the cowboy boots and those snug jeans Bryce had been giving him shit about since they'd met in college.

"Well, look who it is," he called as he pulled on his shirt.

"Walker! How's it goin'?" Ben strode up the hill and Bryce met him halfway.

"Good to see you." He whacked his old frat buddy on the shoulder. "I feel honored." He was only half kidding. Benjamin Hunter Noble III was in high demand these days. He hailed from the infamous Noble dynasty down in Texas. Most of his male relatives had been faithful servants of the U.S. government at one time or another and last he'd heard, Ben was following suit. Pursuing the same senatorial seat his father'd once held. The Nobles were an oil and cattle ranch family, about as rich as Edward King, but Bryce didn't care about the money because Ben was the most down-to-earth guy he'd ever met, easygoing and funny as hell.

"You should feel honored." Ben cocked a grin. "When you called, I was just headin' out. Caught me just in time."

He wasn't surprised. Ben never stayed in the same place too long. When he'd heard he was in town this week checking out some land for his grandfather, Bryce had gotten an idea. But there was no reason to rush the discussion. "How about a drink? Mom made a fresh batch of sweet tea yesterday." A year ago, he would've offered him a beer, but these days, tea was the best he could do. He still couldn't even watch someone drink a beer without the craving taking over.

"Hell yeah," Ben said, following him down the hill. "Your momma's the only one in this town who knows how to make sweet tea. Trust me."

They ambled across to the porch.

"So it's been awhile." Bryce held open the back kitchen door for Ben. The last time he'd seen him was at Ben Noble, Sr.'s funeral about six months ago. "How're things? How's your mom holding up?"

"You know her." Ben waved him off. "She's Gracie Hunter Noble. Nothing fazes her."

He laughed. "What about you? How're the campaign plans coming?"

"Good, as far as I know." Ben pulled out a stool at the kitchen island. "My campaign manager is taking care of it." Something in his voice dulled, but before Bryce could mention it, Ben pointed at the freshly baked pie sitting on the counter. "You expecting company or what?"

"Nah. You know Mom. She's always ready." She'd probably force him into another dinner with Avery tonight. Not that he wanted to talk about that. So he changed the subject. "How long are you in town?"

"About a week. Somehow I got elected to take care of some family business." He grinned. "I figured it'd be the perfect opportunity to finally get my paragliding certification."

Of course he did. Because climbing Mt. Rainer, skydiving in South America, and racing motorcycles in Spain wasn't enough for him. And all that was just what he'd done in the last six months. That was one thing about

Ben. He was always chasing some big adventure. "Glad you could make time to stop in." Bryce poured them each a glass of tea, and yes, he was procrastinating about revealing the real reason he'd asked Noble to come.

"Yeah, well. All I've been doin' is research." Ben raised his glass and took a gulp. "Granddad's got this harebrained idea that he wants to franchise the ranch."

"What do you think?" he asked, even though he could read the answer in Ben's skeptical expression.

"I don't know. Hell, I'd love to live in Aspen. Who wouldn't? But starting a new operation? Too much work. You want my opinion, I think he's bored."

It hit Bryce like a punch to the gut. What would that be like? To have so much money you're bored?

"Hey, after I check out the land, I'm headed up the mountain for my first jump." Ben took another sip. "You in?"

"Nah. I can't take that on right now." Too much to deal with at the ranch. Besides that, he didn't care much for paragliding. He preferred the feeling of both feet on the ground. "I've got a crisis to take care of. Can't afford to pay someone to teach me how to jump off a cliff."

Ben took the jab in stride. "What's up, Walker? What's the crisis?"

He preferred not to hang his dirty laundry out there for everyone to see, but Ben would get it. His ranch in Texas had been in the family since the late 1800s. He knew the value of family, the value of keeping those connections with your history. He heaved a deep breath. There was no pretty way to spin it. "You know the King family?"

"Sure. I've heard of Edward King. Who hasn't?"

"He's after my ranch," Bryce said. The words lit a fuse

on his temper. "He sent his daughter out here to make me an offer."

"You turned 'em down, right?" Ben asked. "This is your family's place. You can't let it go."

"Yeah. I turned him down. Not that it'll stop him." It wouldn't stop Avery, either. He had a feeling the forbidden fruit didn't fall too far from the tree.

"Sure it'll stop him. Not like he can take it from you."

"Well…" Bryce hesitated, trying to find the right words. This was harder than he'd thought it would be. "Things have been tough. I'm way behind on the mortgage."

"Shit, Walker. Why didn't you tell me?"

Because he'd thought he could take care of it. And he would. He'd find a way. But he might not be able to do it alone. "I've been meeting with banks, trying to get a loan, but so far no one's interested."

Ben glanced around the kitchen with that honed, businesslike glare. "I thought your grandparents paid the place off."

Yeah. They did once. But people who traveled to Aspen had high expectations. "They took out a new loan about fifteen years ago. Had to dig a new well, put in a new septic. Then they did some remodeling, bought new furniture." Not that it had helped business. "After that the economy tanked." Truth was, it'd been tanking for a long time. Especially with all the high-end resorts taking over. So they'd taken out a few more loans, which left him with a hefty mortgage. "Most people who come to Aspen like to drop a grand on one night in a five-star hotel."

"How much are we talking?" Ben asked before draining the rest of his tea.

"I don't know." Too much.

"Ballpark it for me."

His face heated. "We're a good five million in the red. Soon to be more." If none of the loan applications came through.

His friend nodded with a carefree wave, as if that was pocket change. Which, for the Nobles, it probably was.

"I might be able to help you out."

"Nope." He sipped his own tea. "That's not why I asked you here. I don't want you to give me the money." He'd never take money from Ben. Too messy. "I just wondered if you had any contacts, potential investors."

"Sure," Ben said without a pause. "I'll ask around. Land in Aspen is at a premium. It's a good investment. I'm sure I can drum up some interest."

"The Notice of Election and Demand gave me a hundred and twenty days to catch up." Before the bank earned the right to auction off his life. His arms itched to go outside and split another log in half. "That'll be up next week."

"That's not gonna happen, Walker," Ben said in that laid-back twang. "Banks take forever with that kind of stuff. Trust me. You've got time."

Maybe so, but he didn't want to chance it. "Let me know what you hear."

"I'm on it," his friend assured him, flicking a glance at his watch. "I should head out. Let's hang while I'm in town. We can grab dinner or somethin'."

"Sure. Let me know what works." Bryce followed him outside and headed straight for the log pile.

Ben opened the Jeep door. "I'll make some calls tonight, let you know what I hear."

"Thanks man," he called, then lined up another log.

Watching Ben drive away, he snatched up the ax and raised it high in the air. This time his arms were lighter, his shoulders looser. He brought the blade down hard enough to split the log in two on the first shot. With ease, he tossed the halves onto the growing pile and welcomed the first hint of relief he'd felt in years.

At least if everything else fell through, he had options, an even playing field with the Kings.

Now it was two against two.

* * *

"Let me get this straight," Dad said for about the hundredth time in a half hour. "You went riding with Mr. Walker so you could *talk* to him?"

Avery sighed and turned the page in the travel magazine Bryce had brought her. So thoughtful. She hadn't pegged him for the thoughtful type, but then again, Bryce Walker seemed full of surprises.

"I don't understand." That'd been another of Dad's favorite phrases during the last hour. He'd started to sound like a skipping CD. He'd probably said it ten times alone when she'd told him she and Logan were just going to be friends. Lucky Logan. He'd left over an hour ago and was on his way back to Chicago, while she was stuck here with Mr. 20 Questions.

"I thought a horseback ride would give me a chance to get to know him." She let that sink in while she lazily scanned an article on Belize, thinking about how nice Mr. Walker would look in a pair of swimming trunks.

"Why would you *want* to get to know him?"

Avery glanced at the door. How hard was it to draft up discharge papers anyway? Dr. Carlson had promised she'd be out of there "as soon as possible."

"There's no reason to get to know him." Dad squeezed his eyes shut and probably did that silent countdown his therapist had recommended for restraining his temper. "I mean, you had one job, Avery. Get him to sign the contract. You know how much this means to me."

She tossed the magazine aside and looked at Dad. His eyes had dulled like they did every time he thought of Mom. Shoulders slumping with defeat, she reached across and patted his forearm. "I do. I know how much this means to you." She'd always known. "But she wouldn't blame you for what happened." She was sick. He hadn't made her sick. Why couldn't he believe that?

He looked down, that grieved expression hollowing his cheeks. "Being here . . . I just see her everywhere. We were happy here. *She* was happy here. Don't you remember?"

"I remember." She sighed, because she'd never forget that trip. She'd never forget the way Mom had gasped at every vista, how she'd told them to pause while she dug out the camera, yet again. They'd taken over three hundred pictures that week, and in every one of them, Mom's radiant smile had outshined them both.

"This is how we can honor her memory, Aves," Dad proclaimed in his impassioned monologue tone, which was normally reserved for the board of trustees. "This is how she can live on."

Tightening her lips, she held back the words she wanted to say. What was it with men? Always having to *do* something, to fix things in some external realm so they never had to deal with their real feelings? Mom lived on in so many other ways. But she'd tried reminding him of that for years and it had gotten her nowhere. Maybe if Dad understood the situation, he'd see things differently. "Bryce lost his wife," she told him. "He's a widower. He feels like the ranch is all he has left of Yvonne and his family."

"I see." Dad's head slanted with a thoughtful and somewhat impressed look.

That's right. She pretty much had Bryce figured out, and truth be told, he wasn't that different from the man sitting across from her. In his flawed thinking, Dad seemed to believe this resort would right every wrong, release him from the guilt he carried. It was his offering, and no matter how many times she tried to tell him that it wasn't his fault, that Mom had known he loved her, he couldn't accept it.

She thought back to both times Bryce had kissed her. He'd apologized. *I'm sorry.* But he wasn't apologizing to her. He was apologizing to his dead wife. Which meant, she couldn't let him kiss her again. Because the more he did that, the more she forgot he was still in love with another woman. And she couldn't afford to forget that.

Bryce couldn't give her more. Just like her father had never been able to give himself to anyone but Mom. He needed the resort the way Bryce needed a new start. And she was in a position to help them both.

But she had to put it in a way Dad would understand. "Bryce needs someone to help him see that he *can* move on. I was trying to be a friend. A good listener. You know, show him that I actually cared about *him*, not his land?" He ought to try it sometime instead of steamrolling people. Most of the time empathy got much better results.

"I misjudged you, Avery," her father said, a hint of a smile edging into his mouth. "Walker likes you. It's perfect."

"Oh…" It came out in a *whoosh.* "No." How could he have possibly misunderstood what she meant? "No, he doesn't *like* me." It wasn't like Dad thought. She wasn't trying to seduce the man on purpose!

"The hell he doesn't." He clapped her on the back. "Sorry I misunderstood the situation."

Sorry? *Oh, boy. Oh, no.* Her stomach churned. "Are you kidding me? I wasn't trying to manipulate him."

"Of course not." Dad stood. "But we can use this to our advantage. It might be our only shot."

"Use it?" She stood, too, and fought a building urge to shake the man's shoulders until he realized how callous he sounded.

"Yes. Use it. You know, you can pretend to like him, too. Then get him to sign the contract. You *are* staying at the ranch, after all. It shouldn't be hard."

"No. No way." That wasn't how she worked. She could get Bryce to sell, but she wouldn't seduce him. That's not what the kiss was about. "He's a reasonable guy. I can talk him into it." Without pretending to have feelings for him. She wouldn't have to pretend. They were there. She just couldn't use them. She had to forget about them so she could do what she did best: work.

"We're in this together, Avery," Dad said in the sad tone that never failed to get to her. "I need you to come through for me."

Damn him.

For the thousandth time, she groped her memory for the image that bound Dad and her together, the one that prompted her to keep trying, to remain loyal even when he asked too much of her. It had happened less than a week after Mom had died. She still sat by the window of their brownstone every evening, watching, praying that they'd made a mistake and her mom hadn't really died, hoping she'd waltz through the door in one of her twirly skirts that swished so elegantly around her legs.

That night, she'd fallen asleep. She woke to her father lifting her into his arms. He rarely held her, never carried her to bed. That was her nanny's job. But that night was different. He'd been drinking heavily. She recognized the overpowering scent of whiskey she'd always smelled when Mom held her close. When she'd looked into her daddy's eyes, she saw his pain. He let her see it. "I'll never leave you, Avery. I promise," he whispered. And he hadn't. He hadn't left her. He hadn't sent her away. Though plenty of her friends had attended boarding schools, Dad had always kept her close, at home. That was what tethered her to him, what entangled them in such a complicated relationship. In some ways her mom's death broke them both, but somehow they seemed more whole together.

Weariness settled on her eyes. She surrendered with a heavy sigh. "He'll sign the contract. I'll make sure."

She'd never failed her father, and she wouldn't start now.

CHAPTER THIRTEEN

Avery glanced out the window of her father's limousine, watching the Walker Mountain Ranch sign grow closer and closer until she could read the etched words, see the striations in the weathered wood sign.

A gagging sensation tangled her throat as the driver slowed and carefully turned onto the gravel road. She hadn't been this nervous since Charlie Stanton had taken her to prom her junior year. He'd been one of the best-looking boys at her private school, and not stuck up like most of them. He was there on a scholarship to play basketball. He lived with his single mom in an apartment, which Avery had thought was wildly exotic at the time, compared to the other boys who lounged in their parents' mansions, destined to remain eighteen well into their thirties. Charlie had this rawness, this real-ness that'd made him as unpredictable as a Midwestern spring—sometimes violently stormy, sometimes bright and sunny, other times as cold and distant as a late-season blizzard.

And Charlie had nothing on Bryce Walker.

"You're sure you want to stay in this junkyard?" Her father asked, lowering his head to get a look at their surroundings. A look of disdain curled his lips.

"It's not a junkyard," she snapped, that fluttery, nervous feeling from her chest bubbling into her throat. "It's old, that's all." Her gaze drifted to the window, to the homey log structure that brimmed over with Elsie's warmth and authenticity. It had such a history of love and togetherness. "It's still a beautiful place." Maybe even more so because of the memories that had been made there...

"It will be *more beautiful* when it's a five-star resort," he grumbled, then waggled a finger in front of her face. "Do not lose your edge, Aves. Not now. I need you on this."

Ignoring him, she continued to focus on the world outside, on the intricate shadows cast down by the trembling aspen leaves, on the charming little office building next to the lodge, on the clearing up a small hill where there was a pile of wood—

Oh, wow. She blinked to make sure it wasn't some kind of dreamy mirage. Nope. When she opened her eyes, Bryce still stood there, and yes, ladies and gentlemen, he was shirtless, muscles tensed and hard as he raised a thick, gleaming ax to the sky. His powerful arms brought it down in one quick slice through the wood, and, yes, she trembled in that yearning way. What could she say? She was only human.

The car stopped in front of the office.

"I'm staying at The Knightley," her father informed her.

That snapped her out of her reverie. "What do you mean you're staying? Why aren't you going back to Chicago?" She had to work on Bryce her way, continue to build trust with him, and the last thing she needed was Dad around to complicate things.

"I'm concerned about you," he said in a placating tone that she saw right through. He wasn't concerned about her. He was concerned about his deal falling through.

The driver opened the door. Her head ached. The pain meds were starting to wear off.

"Get this done, Avery. Let me know if you need me to take over." Her father waved her away. "After the contract is signed, you can join me at The Knightley. I'll send someone to pick up that pathetic rental car you have. Use the car service instead."

"I don't need your help. It's under control." She scooted out of the limo and found her footing on the ground, fighting the dizziness that delayed her movements. She wouldn't need anything from him. She could handle this. She could manage Bryce Walker. "See you later," she mumbled to her father.

The driver nodded at her, slammed the door, and drove away in a cloud of dust while she slowly made her way to the hill, where she could still hear the sounds of the ax reverberating.

If he was aware that she'd found him, he didn't let on. Bryce kept his muscular back to her as he positioned another log on the stump in front of him. She tried not to stare. Tried, but wow. His sweat-slicked body was so broad, tanned, and defined. This definitely wasn't his first wood-chopping rodeo.

As she got closer, she made sure to drag her feet to make some noise, but he still didn't turn around.

He knew she was there. He had to know. He must've heard the limo. She cleared her throat extra loud, feeling the scrape all the way down her windpipe.

Bryce shifted to throw the freshly cut wood on the pile and looked right through her.

"Hey," she squeaked, the bandage on her forehead itching with a sudden onset of perspiration.

A silent nod returned the greeting, then he turned back to the stump.

"Sorry about what happened at the hospital," she tried again because, damn it, she had to do this. Not only for her father, but also for Bryce. For Elsie. Even for herself. She knew all about letting the past hold her in its fierce grip, making her a slave to things she didn't want to serve. If she got him to sell, maybe she could help set him free.

Bryce's shoulders slumped. He rested the blade of the ax on the ground and turned, those eyes blazing with something much stronger than irritation. "What d'you want?"

That was one loaded question. And unfair to ask when he wasn't fully clothed. She steadied a hand against the chalky white trunk of an aspen tree. "To apologize," she answered, making sure to sound wounded. "My father can be pretty intense. But I managed to convince him you weren't trying to kill me."

He balanced the ax against a tree trunk and stomped over to her. "I didn't mean what you want right now. I meant what do you want from me?" The intensity of his glare robbed her of every word. Even breathing became difficult...

"You shouldn't be here." His head shook and his unruly, glistening black hair dropped in front of his eyes. He raised his hand and pushed it back. "You were spying on me." He lowered his head to hers. "Taking notes on what a dump my home was and passing them off to your dad." He turned back around and ripped the ax off the ground. "You can't stay here. Not anymore."

Okay. He was mad. He had every right to be mad. Yes, she could understand how it had sounded when Dad had said, *From what I hear...* That hadn't made her look good, especially when she was flirting with the man— kissing the man.

He was right. She shouldn't stay, especially when he affected her this way.

She should go. But something told her he needed to feel her touch, to prove to him that she hadn't been pretending or leading him on. The things he made her feel were real; she just couldn't give in to them.

Even so, she crept closer and placed her hand on his shoulder.

The touch seemed to shock him into a rigid stillness. He gazed at her.

"I want what's best for you. That's all," she murmured past the throb in her throat.

He didn't respond, but he didn't move or look away, either. That was an improvement.

"I happen to love your ranch." The palm of her hand flamed. She let it fall to her side. Risky business, this touching stuff. "I love that you have a connection to it, that it runs in your blood." They'd moved around so much with her father's ambitions that she'd never had a place that felt like home. Except for Wrigley Field, but it wasn't like she could live there. "I envy that."

Bryce faced her fully, his gaze slowly taking her in.

She loved when he looked at her like that. Carefully, like the details mattered.

"I lost my mom." She didn't know exactly why she told him. Maybe so he'd know she'd lost a part of herself, too.

A look of surprise widened his eyes and parted his lips.

"She died when I was twelve." Those same unresolved emotions surged, still raw, almost as strong as they'd been that day.

"How?" His eyes lowered to hers.

She held her breath until the sting in her throat subsided. "She was an alcoholic. She drank herself to death."

His face softened. "I didn't know. I'm sorry."

"Thanks." Coming from him the words didn't sound trite at all. "Since I lost her, my life has always felt incomplete. Like I lost part of myself I can't get back."

"Then you should understand why I won't sell." He said it with such quiet, she couldn't argue. "I don't want to lose any more of myself, Avery."

She understood. Really. She did. But she also knew what would happen when the bank foreclosed. Working under her father, she'd seen it a hundred times. He had a knack for flipping properties like Bryce's, for taking some rundown building and turning it into luxury apartments.

If the bank foreclosed, Bryce would lose everything. His home. His credit. It would take years for him to dig out from the financial ruin. As much as he loved this place, he wouldn't be able to keep his ranch.

She just had to figure out how to tell him that.

* * *

Why'd she have to come back? No. He should rephrase that. Why'd she have to come back looking so fragile and hurt, with that bandage across her forehead? Why'd she have to touch him and spark the reminder of how it'd felt to gather her into his arms and kiss the breath out of her? Why'd she have to go and change everything by telling him she'd lost someone, too? Her life hadn't been all fairy tales and unicorns like he'd thought.

Avery gazed up at him, still looking so perfect, even with those wounds, maybe more so because of those wounds. Her fitted long john shirt stretched over her lovely curves, dirty and torn at the edges.

Bryce closed his eyes and massaged his pounding forehead. Other parts of him pounded, too, but he tried to ignore them, because how would it look if he dropped everything to kiss her right there? Again?

So they only stared, both of them waiting, he assumed, for the other to make a move...

"There you are, dears!"

He broke their stare and turned to watch Mom rush across the porch like she was afraid she was missing out on something important. She'd always had impeccable timing.

"I've been so worried!" She charged up the hill at a speed much faster than Bryce thought a sixty-seven-year-old should be capable of.

He looked down at Avery again. Her expression had changed. It wasn't so sad anymore.

God, he loved the way her lips smiled...

"Avery!" Mom hugged her gingerly then held her at arm's length to look her over. "Dear me, you must be hurting! Look at those bruises."

"It's not so bad," she insisted bravely.

Come to think of it, she'd been pretty brave through the whole thing.

Bryce stepped aside; his presence obviously wasn't required for this conversation. Or for any other conversation those two had...

"I'm so sorry, dear," his mom clucked. "I just can't believe it. Thank the lord it wasn't worse!"

"I'm fine, Elsie. Really." She gave him a look that revealed just how much she loved Mom.

Yeah. Join the club.

"I should go take a shower or something." Avery laughed. "I'm sure I look much worse than I feel." She patted her hair self-consciously.

"Nonsense. You're lovely." Mom elbowed him in the gut. "Isn't that right, Bryce? Doesn't Avery look lovely?"

Yes. The woman had no idea how stunning she was. But it was best not to touch that one. He ignored his mother's probing gaze and focused on Avery. "So you're staying?" He hadn't meant to sound so hopeful, but damn it, she brought out that heart-raising desire in him. Mom was right. He hadn't let go of Yvonne. He still dragged the memories of her along with him every day. They were heavy and cumbersome and Avery made him want to let them rest in the past where they belonged.

"I'd like to stay. If that's all right." She gave him a

tentative smile. "I mean, I'm stuck here for a few days, anyway, because of work, and I enjoy it so much…"

"Don't be silly, dear. Of course you'll stay here!" Mom gave Bryce a stern look. "Why wouldn't you?"

Because he had a hard time being practical when Avery was around and he did stupid stuff like kiss her when she stood too close to him…

"Thank you, Elsie." She knew better than to thank him.

"Of course, of course. You're welcome here anytime. You must be absolutely exhausted." Mom took her arm and started to guide her down the hill. He trailed behind them like the outsider.

"You should rest. Then I hope you'll come to the game this afternoon."

Avery stopped so fast he almost rammed into her back. *Here we go…*

"Game?" she asked.

"Yes," Mom answered before he could remind her that concussions required rest, which meant she wouldn't play. Not on his watch.

"We have a game at five. Isn't that right, Bryce?"

"Yup." Not like he could lie about it now.

"I'd love to come!" Avery's eyes went wide. You never would've known she had a head injury if it weren't for that bandage on her forehead.

"Wonderful," Mom gushed, "and I hope you'll join us for dinner afterward."

"Really? Are you sure? I don't want to be too much trouble."

"It's no trouble, dear. I've missed cooking for a crowd. We'll plan to eat at seven. That is, if you're not too tired. You've had one humdinger of a day."

"Seven would be great." Avery broke away from them and started to jog.

Seriously? She was jogging? "Hey!" he called after her. "Take it easy. You still have a concussion, you know."

"Okay! I will!" she sang, but she sure as hell didn't slow down.

Stubborn. The woman was more stubborn than a mule.

"I'll go get cleaned up and meet you outside in a half hour," she yelled before disappearing into the lodge.

He shook his head while Mom shot him a knowing smirk. "Such a nice girl."

It was getting much harder to deny that.

But she was Edward King's daughter. In other words, off limits.

Better keep reminding himself of that until she left Aspen and he could get his life back to normal.

CHAPTER FOURTEEN

Avery popped some ibuprofen and checked the mirror that hung over the antique log dresser. The white bandage square in the center of her forehead might as well have been a neon sign news-flashing her clumsiness to the world.

She sighed and pulled her long hair into a single braid at the back. Not a pretty sight, but it couldn't be helped. She couldn't erase the bruise on her forehead or conceal the stiches that gathered her skin at the edges of that bandage. At least Bryce hadn't seemed too repulsed by her. When he'd first seen her lying in the hospital bed he'd winced, but he'd looked more empathetic than disgusted, and since then he'd been nothing but sweet. Well, mostly.

Ah, Bryce. She had a vague memory of him whispering something over her when he carried her down the mountain. *You made me feel something I haven't felt in a long time.* Or had she imagined that? She'd always excelled at wishful thinking. Irrational optimism, her father called it, but it served her well. It made her think differently, in terms of possibilities instead of concrete ideas.

And when it came to Bryce, there were so many possibilities. So many wonderful, amazing, beautiful possibilities. Her skin flushed with a lazy warmth that made her feel the slightest bit tipsy.

But no, she couldn't be tipsy. Not right now. Not with her father in town, figuratively breathing down her neck. After this was over, though...after she'd convinced Bryce he needed to sell and get a fresh start somewhere else, who knew what could happen? The whole horse riding accident had brought out another side of him, a side she wouldn't mind getting to know better, and if he walked away from the ranch, maybe he'd be ready to walk into something new. With someone new...

Unable to confine a smile, she reached for her ball cap and gingerly plunked it on her head, tugging it down as far as she could to keep the bandage in the shadow beneath the cap's bill. *There.* That helped a little. After slinging her backpack on one shoulder, she opened the door.

"Whoa." Bryce stood right in front of her, hand raised as if he'd been about to knock.

"Hi!" Her voice went all high and breathy like it always did when he caught her off guard. Somehow he managed to catch her off guard every time she saw him, though, even just wearing gray sweats and a dark t-shirt. It was probably because he stood a full head taller than she, and her eyes happened to be at the same level as his impressive chest, those sturdy shoulders...

"Hey," he said in that deep lullaby tone. "Just wanted to check on you."

Awww. Seriously? She glanced up. She'd get trapped in those mesmerizing green eyes of his if she wasn't careful...

"Still up for the game?" he asked.

"Of course." She slipped out the door and stood close enough to feel the heat emanating from his body. Or maybe that was her body, smoldering from the memory of being crushed against him, those lips on hers...

"You okay?" he asked slowly, sounding concerned.

Nothing to be concerned about. She was just checking him out again. Couldn't tell him that, though. So she simply smiled. "Why wouldn't I be okay?"

His lips quirked with amusement and he leaned one shoulder against the wall. "No reason." He pointed at her backpack. "What's in there?"

"My glove."

"Your glove?"

Embarrassment prickled across her skin. "Yes. I picked one up earlier this week," she muttered. "You know, just in case." In case she got to play again. She couldn't help herself. A few days ago, she'd been walking around town and happened to saunter past the local sports shop. In the window she'd spotted this amazing Minuzo Classic—throwback leather, rugged and rich—pre-oiled, even!

She swore it had glowed in a ray of light cast straight from heaven. It was probably the same feeling other women had when they saw a pair of designer shoes—helpless, stuck under some kind of spell. Then, before you know what's happened, you're handing over your credit card and in a distant reality hearing the cashier say, "That'll be two hundred dollars, please."

The dark look on Bryce's face only proved he wouldn't understand. He stood upright and posted his hands on his hips, the muscles in his arms tensing. "You do realize you're not playing today, right?"

Suddenly, she felt like a little girl about to receive a stern lecture from her father. She should know. She'd endured plenty of them. Only, Bryce was not her father. "Of course I'm playing."

He lowered his head so they were eyes to eyes, nose to nose. "You have a concussion. You have to take it easy."

Dangerous. Having his lips so close was downright dangerous. "I will take it easy," she said, forcing herself to stay put even though she wanted to step back and inch some safe distance between them. "I can play the outfield." Lord knew not many people around here could hit it all the way to the grass, but at least she'd be out there. At least she'd be part of the team.

His frown softened into amusement. "Avery."

Her joints melted at the affectionate way he said her name. Oh, heaven help her. He'd used his Moose voice.

His eyes took on a gentle sheen as he gazed down at her. "I'm sorry. I can't let you play."

But... She felt the weight of the new glove in her backpack. She had to use it. She had to put it on and test it out. "I feel great." She danced a quick version of the electric slide to prove it. "See? Nothing hurts. No pain at all."

Bryce's lips folded like he was trying not to laugh. "You can come and watch. But you're not playing. Got it?"

"I hate watching," she whined.

He took her shoulders in those powerful hands and

tugged her closer until their eyes connected. The amusement that had lifted his facial features only seconds before fell flat. "I can't let anything happen to you. You can't risk it with a head injury."

His tone was too weighted for her to argue. It sounded too much like fear. Real, deep fear.

"Fine," she huffed. "I'll watch, then."

"You can take stats for me," he offered with a consoling smile.

"Great. That's way more fun than being out on the field." But the little sparkles dancing in her chest made it hard to sound grumpy. He was worried about her. Which meant he cared, right? At least he wasn't benching her because he didn't want her around this time.

Still feigning a good pout, she scooted down the hall. Bryce hovered one step behind her, all tense and protective, like he was afraid she might fall over backward. She bunched her lips to ward off a smile. Maybe she should—*accidentally* tip over and land right in his arms.

Except, judging from his uptight attitude about head injuries, he would miss the humor, yet again.

They crossed the foyer. He slipped in front of her, opened the front door, and lightly touched his hand to the small of her back. The warmth from his palm radiated through her and heightened her senses. He smelled like freedom, like the freshness of the woods outside.

"Take it easy. These steps are loose." His hand pressed into her back and started the palpitations again. *Hmmm.* She could easily stumble and land right on him again...

But his hands supported her as he guided her down the porch steps and over to the truck.

"*Mmmmwufff.*" Moose vaulted out of the forest and

galloped toward them in his enthusiastic *you're-my-two-favorite-people-in-the-entire-universe!!!!* way.

Bryce secured an arm around her like he was preparing for impact.

Wow. She could stay like that forever, pressed up against him, *feeling* those solid muscles instead of gawking at them.

Sure enough, Moose's head collided with their legs, but the impact didn't faze her. Not at all.

Laughing, Bryce kept her upright. "Sorry about that. Not much I can do. He likes you."

"I like him, too." She lowered her hand, fluffed Moose's ears, and was rewarded with a big ol' lick all the way up her forearm.

"All right, boy." Nudging Moose out of their way, Bryce led her around to the passenger side of the truck. He opened the door for her, took her hand in a tight grip, and helped her climb in.

"You good?" he asked.

"Yes." She laughed. "Good God. You must really think I'm a klutz."

His head tilted and his eyes met hers in a meaningful gaze. "I think a lot of things when I see you. But that's not one of them."

She resisted the urge to fan herself. Whew. Hot flash. Someone roll down a window...

Bryce slammed the door shut, leaving her to sit there and simmer while he got Moose settled in the back.

Finally, he climbed into the driver's seat and started the engine. "What d'you like to listen to?" He flicked on the radio, but she was too shocked to answer. He was acting like a boyfriend, and it all felt so intimate. The way he was watching out for her, helping her, caring about her . . .

He looked over, waiting.

"Whatever you like," was all she could get out. She'd never been picky about music, although the way Bryce was making her feel, she could've easily gone for something in the Barry White genre.

With a shrug, he flicked on the country music station he'd had on the other night. She didn't recognize the song, but it felt right, sitting next to this man with tousled, carefree hair in his big, bad truck listening to a woman twang about her lost love.

Except it wasn't right. She'd started to care about him. *Really* care about him. She wanted to spend time with him, to let him know her, to know him—but what about him? She peered over at Bryce. He watched the road intently, took the curves slower than he had the last time she'd ridden with him, like he was afraid to jostle her.

Suddenly, her shoulders felt heavy.

The truck slowed and Bryce looked over. "Everything okay?"

"I'm not sure." Because she didn't know how to do this, how to let him touch her and be sweet to her and protect her without letting herself fall for him. She was teetering on the edge, held back by the knowledge of his unresolved pain, but also inching forward to think about the possibility of a future. And if she were to let go, what if the landing hurt too much?

Her stomach fluttered. Just her luck that the nerves always hit there first. But she had to know. She had to ask him before this momentum between them pushed her off the cliff. "Bryce," she said quietly enough to get his full attention.

"Yeah?" He bounced his gaze between her and the road. "What is it? Are you in pain?"

She shook her head, her hands gripping her knees. Forcing herself to look at him, she inhaled and held her breath until she felt strong enough to ask. "Are you still in love with Yvonne?"

He didn't answer. He didn't have to. A familiar expression of guilt tightened his lips. He stared straight out the windshield, hands gripping the wheel tightly, steering to follow the curve of the road.

She turned away from him and gazed out the window, but the trees and the lovely Victorian houses that lined the highway all blurred together. "I shouldn't have asked you that. I'm sorry," she said. And she was. Sorry for both of them.

He'd shut down again, and that was the only answer she needed.

* * *

Bryce eased off the gas and let the truck crawl across the parking lot, but that still didn't give him enough time to figure out how to answer Avery's question.

Why'd she have to ask?

He silently cursed himself. He knew good and well why she had to ask. Because for the last half hour, he'd been treating her like they were on a date. He couldn't help himself, not when it came to her.

She did things to him. Things no one else had ever done, not even Yvonne. There. He'd said it. Guilt rose up in that familiar way, tightening his chest, making it hard to breathe.

He looked over at Avery and got a perfect view of the back of her head. Like the scenery in the parking lot was really fascinating. *Damn it.* What did she want him to say? He didn't know. That was the truth. He just didn't know. For as long as he could remember, it had been Yvonne. She was his best friend, his first love, so much a part of him that he still hardly recognized himself without her.

How could he say he wasn't in love with her?

He pulled into a parking spot at the edge of the lot, but let the truck run.

Avery didn't look at him. "I'll see you down there," she said like she was talking to one of her colleagues. Then she scooted out of the truck and slammed the door.

He cut the engine, but instead of getting out he sat and watched her walk away. He wanted to say yes. God, he wanted to say yes. She was worth a yes...

Outside his door, Moose barked and turned in circles. The dog couldn't wait to tear down to the field to greet everyone, but Moose would never go without him. Guess that meant he'd have to get down there and face Avery.

He took his time unpacking the bat bags and extra water bottles for the yahoos who'd inevitably forgotten theirs, then schlepped it all down the hill. Avery already had a crowd of his best friends gathered around her. As he neared the bench, he caught snippets of their conversation.

"O.M.G., Avery!" Paige exclaimed. "What happened to your face? It looks horrible!"

He shook his head. Paige was always so subtle.

"Horseback riding accident," Avery said and waved it off like it was nothing.

His fist clenched around the handle of the bag he was carrying. How could she be so flippant? Didn't she understand the potential dangers of a head injury?

"That sucks." Paige slumped on the bench next to her.

Avery wouldn't look at him, but that was fine. Someone had to watch out for her. What if she got beaned in the head? Or what if she collided with someone again? He dug out his glove and snatched a ball, then trotted to the outfield to warm up.

"You acted like you knew nothing about her." Shooter's coarse voice trailed behind him.

He stopped and turned around, faking ignorance. "What?"

"Don't play dumb, Walker. You expect me to believe you don't know her that well? You were out riding with her this morning."

Instead of answering, he jogged backward and tossed the ball at Shooter. "We should warm up."

"But I can't see her legs from here," Shooter complained.

Bryce fought the urge to deck him. "We're not here to stare at her legs." His gaze wandered over to her. He couldn't deny that it was a nice view, especially in those tight black pants…

"See?" Shooter jogged over to him and nudged his shoulder. "You can't take your eyes off of her."

"Sure I can." He looked toward the outfield where Yates was trying to flirt with some woman on the other team, the poor jerk. He must've said something stupid because she flipped him off.

"Come on, Walker," Shooter persisted. "I've seen that look before. You want her."

His face started that burning flush, so he backed away and tossed the ball to Shooter again.

"Wait a minute." His friend cocked his head and narrowed his eyes. "You already had her, didn't you?"

"Had who?" Sawyer chimed in, jogging over. "Avery?" He didn't wait for a response. "You and Avery, huh?" His cousin's sly grin heckled him. "She's way too good for you, bro." *Yep.* Typical Sawyer. Since they'd grown up two miles away from each other, Sawyer had always felt like a brother. Most days he felt like an older brother who made fun of Bryce whenever he got the chance.

He shook his head. "You guys are nuts. You know that?" He held up his glove. "And you throw like a bunch of pansies."

Even an insult didn't distract them.

"You're holding out on us." Shooter stomped over and stabbed a pointer finger into Bryce's chest. "You don't look at a woman like that unless—"

"Unless you've done the deed," Sawyer cut in with a solid shot to his shoulder. "What'd you do, Walker? Seduce her in the hospital?"

"You're sick." And alarmingly observant. He swiped the sweat from his forehead. Was it humid out tonight?

"So you wouldn't care if I walked over there and grabbed her ass, then." Shooter took a threatening step toward the bench. "Is that what you're telling me?"

Sawyer's eyes widened into a warning. They both knew Shooter did stupid shit like that every day.

Bryce dodged in front of him. "I wouldn't do that if I were you. She's tougher than she looks." And he might have to throw a punch if Shooter made good on that threat.

"I'm willing to chance it." He took a few more steps.

Bryce chased him while Sawyer laughed his ass off.

"Fine. I like her. Is that what you want to hear?"

"Like her or want to hook up with her?" Shooter demanded.

He pounded the ball into his glove. These two were the last ones he wanted to discuss this with. Sawyer, who was madly in love with his new wife and Shooter, who was madly in love with every woman who walked past him. But it wasn't like they were giving him much of a choice. "I like her. I'm interested, okay?"

"No offense, man." Sawyer clapped a hand on his shoulder. "But she doesn't seem too interested in you."

"Yeah, well it's been awhile since I've played the game." He'd blown her off in the truck. That definitely didn't score him any points. But before that, she'd gotten all red and flushed whenever he'd touched her...

"You should go for it, Walker." Shooter's smug expression relaxed into thoughtfulness.

His cousin glanced over at Avery and grinned at him. "Shooter's right. It's time. This is your chance to get back in the game, buddy."

If only it was that easy.

CHAPTER FIFTEEN

Avery slipped the Minuzo Classic baseball glove on her hand, inhaling the musty scent of oiled leather. It fit her perfectly, snug and soft against her skin.

Squinting into the late afternoon sun, she analyzed the team's lineup for the field. Paige stood on the pitcher's mound again, right where she belonged. The woman threw quite the impressive curveball for someone who'd never played on a real team.

Shooter had been exiled to the outfield along with the other two maintenance workers. In her humble opinion, he belonged on first. For being such an oaf, he had quick reflexes. Instead, Sawyer stood near first base ogling his wife, who'd been assigned to second, which was actually pretty sweet, even if Sawyer seemed better suited to catcher.

Not that Bryce had asked her opinion on the team lineup. Hard to ask when someone won't talk to you.

Her question had shut him down faster than a hard-drive crash. Since he'd sauntered down to the field, he'd looked over her, past her, and through her. Never right at her. That didn't stop her from looking at him, though. Her eyes had followed him around all night. At present, he stood between second and third base, playing one of the most important positions on the field: shortstop.

And she was stuck on the bench.

Leaning over, she snatched a ball off the ground and stuffed it into the glove. Wow. What a grip. With that glove on her hand, she'd be able to make any catch—high, low, wild...She pulled off the glove and ran her fingers over the soft leather. Not like she'd even get a chance to use it. After tonight, she wouldn't go to any more of the Walker Mountain Ranch baseball games. She wouldn't hang out with Bryce. She couldn't. He messed with her head too much, which was bad enough, but he'd also started to mess with her heart...touching her, kissing her, being so protective. But Bryce could never be with anyone. Not really. His heart belonged to someone else, and she wanted more than being someone's second best.

A beefy man from the other team—some insurance agency, judging by the sound of their name—strutted up to the plate.

Out on the mound, Paige wedged her toe into the dirt and assumed the pitcher's stance. Avery couldn't help but smile. She could relate to that competitive streak.

"You ready for this, Collins?" Paige called. "I'd hate to embarrass you like I did last year."

"Shut up, Harper," the man shot back. "Just toss the damn ball."

"You got it." She wound up and hurled it in fast and hard, so that it curved slightly just as it sailed over home plate.

Collins swung low but still connected, launching a pop fly that headed straight for Bryce. An easy jog toward third, and Bryce raised his glove to snag the ball, giving the team their first out. Everyone gathered around to congratulate him, give him a good whack on the back, while Bryce's face lit with the wry smile she'd only seen when he hung out with his friends.

A heavy sigh welled up as she watched them out there. It reminded her of a scene out of one of those quaint Hallmark movies she'd secretly watched after a tough day at the office. The small-town community knit together by a connection to each other and to the place they called home. They obviously had a history, a bond.

And she was stuck on the bench.

Everyone jogged back to their zones and Paige struck out another man, who stomped back to his team's dugout.

The team cheered again. Shooter plowed over and lifted Paige off the ground, hoisting her onto his shoulders and parading in a circle around the mound while she beat him with her fists and demanded he put her down.

Avery mustered a smile to cover up a yawning hollow feeling. Watching them only amplified the emptiness of her own life. She lived on the fringes of relationships, working nonstop—for what? For her father?

Sure, she had friends. People liked her. She was good at her job. And she'd dated some great guys, but it never went anywhere because she never let it. She preferred things less complicated, especially after watching Dad's heart slowly die over the years.

But staying at the ranch had made it painfully obvious that her life was missing something.

Significance was only found in relationships. As much hell as Bryce had lived through, he had real relationships, solid friendships.

And what did she have?

She slipped the glove back on her hand. Best not to dwell on that question too long...

Gravel crunched behind her, thank goodness. She needed a serious distraction.

Elsie bustled over to the bench, balancing a woven basket in her arms. The sight of her tugged at Avery's heart and made her miss her own mother in a way she hadn't for years.

"Avery!" Elsie set down the basket and greeted her with a hug. "I'm so happy you're here," she gushed as she settled herself on the bench next to her.

"Me, too." She was. Even if it hurt to know she wouldn't be there much longer. "I'd be happier if I was out there, though," she said, gesturing to the field, where Bryce had just caught another ball.

He was so athletic, lean but built, tall...

"I know, dear. But Bryce is cautious." Elsie nudged the basket closer to her. "He's only trying to protect you." The older woman's smile implied that there was more behind his desire to protect her.

There wasn't. Avery already knew that for a fact.

"I get it." She leaned over and peered into the basket so Elsie couldn't see her face, and almost drooled at the sight of the biggest, fattest chocolate chip cookies she'd ever seen. "One of those babies might make up for being benched."

"Well, then..." Leaning over the basket, Elsie took her time choosing the best one. Finally, she plucked one out of the batch and handed it to Avery, along with a heart-shaped napkin. Then she unwrapped one for herself and nibbled on the edge. "No need to worry, dear. We have another game on Wednesday night. By then, you'll be as good as new."

A sense of sorrow pinged again before deepening into an ache. She wouldn't be there Wednesday night. She couldn't stay. Tonight at dinner, she'd get his damn signature on the contract, then she'd walk away before it got any harder to stay.

She peeked over at the woman who'd made her breakfast every morning, who'd been so open and welcoming. How could she tell Elsie she was leaving?

"Um..." Shifting to a more comfortable position, Avery stared out at the field so she didn't have to face the woman's kind eyes. "Actually, I have to leave in the morning."

"Leave? Whatever do you mean, dear? Why?"

What could she say? *I have feelings for your son... feelings he could never reciprocate?* She bunched her shoulders into a slightly painful shrug, given the tension in her neck. "I have to get back to work. There's a lot to do."

Elsie clucked at her. "Work. *Pshaw,*" she muttered, biting into her cookie. She covered her mouth with her hand as she chewed, then dabbed her lips with a napkin. "It seems to me you need a vacation, dear. A real vacation. Why don't you stay another week? Enjoy some rest in the mountains?"

Elsie was as bad as Bryce in the temptation department. She looked past the field and out to the mountains that surrounded it, and for the first time in her life, she understood what "Purple Mountains Majesty" meant. The granite peaks gleamed with a royal glow, solid rock plunging so high into the sky's blue depths they almost looked purple.

Even with the sounds of cheering and heckling coming from the field, the space around her echoed with a peaceful stillness that had started to influence her. Things were slower in the mountains, quieter. There was space to think, to feel, to be. Back in Chicago, she lived in a hurry, stilettos pounding the pavement to and from work, to and from meetings, to and from dinners with Dad...

A real vacation. Yes. It was tempting. When was the last time she'd taken a vacation? There'd been the week in Barbados last year, but that was for the opening of their resort, which had demanded that she work and attend meetings from eight o'clock in the morning until well past eleven o'clock at night. She'd never even had the chance to put on the bikini she'd bought.

"You're welcome to stay as long as you want." Elsie leaned close, brushing her shoulder against Avery's. "You know that, right?"

"I know." She'd never felt so welcome anywhere in her life.

"It's been wonderful to have you," the woman murmured and Avery could've sworn tears gathered in her eyes. "Things have been lonely since Yvonne passed. If you want the truth, I was starting to lose hope. I didn't think we'd ever welcome another guest."

A guest. That was exactly how Elsie had treated her, even though she'd been up front about her agenda from the beginning.

"I was thinking we could have a barbeque this weekend." Elsie polished off her cookie and brushed the crumbs from her fingers. "We'll invite the whole team. Why, you can give everyone tips on batting. Lord knows some of them could use the help." Her lips lifted in a hopeful look that sent Avery's resolve spiraling. This was so hard.

"I'm sorry." She wrapped her cookie in the napkin and set it next to her on the bench. "I can't stay."

"Whyever not?" The woman eyed the cookie on the bench, obviously concerned that Avery hadn't finished it.

She couldn't, though. Sadness had ruined the taste. "Because Bryce and I have..." *Hmmm.* How could she best phrase their complicated relationship? "We've gotten close."

"Mmm hmmm," Elsie murmured, eyes wide with interest, inviting her to continue.

Even though she'd rather not, she felt she owed Bryce's mother an explanation, especially after everything she'd done for her. "But he's still in love with Yvonne, and I know how hard that is. After my mom died, my father wasn't capable of loving anyone. He's still not."

"I see." Elsie gazed out at the field, her face softened into a thoughtful expression.

"I'm grateful for everything you've done." Avery tried to make light of the heaviness between them with a laugh. "I'm pretty sure I've gained about fifteen pounds eating all of your wonderful cooking. I'll probably have to buy a whole new wardrobe when I get home."

But Elsie wasn't easily distracted by a joke. She didn't even seem to hear it.

"You know, dear," she said in her sweet, motherly tone,

"I lost Bryce's dad a long time ago. He had a heart attack when he was only thirty."

So Bryce had never known his father? She watched him out there on the field, laughing at something Shooter said. "That must've been so hard."

"Oh, my, yes." Emotion quieted her voice. "I was angry and lost. But I loved Bryce too much to let myself stay that way."

"You never moved on? Never got remarried?" That seemed impossible. There was something about Elsie that drew you in, that made you want to know her. She was so different from Dad. There wasn't one hint of bitterness or guilt anywhere in her. She seemed so free.

"I didn't have to remarry. I already had the love of life with me every day." She glanced in Bryce's direction, and her smile held so much—a blend of pride and joy and hope. Her wise blue eyes met Avery's. "Real love is the only thing in this world that can make you free, dear. It's the only thing that can help you heal." She squeezed her shoulder. "But you have to choose it. I can't say what Bryce will choose. He knows how to love. Trust me. He's a bit fierce but once he gives his heart to someone, they have it forever."

That was exactly what she was worried about. He'd already given his heart away. If she chose Bryce, she'd always live in the shadow of that knowledge.

Out on the field, Sawyer managed to tag someone out on first.

"Three! That's three!" Paige yelled, and the Walker Mountain Ranch Misfits ran for the bench.

"You're still planning to join us for dinner tonight, aren't you?" Elsie stood and collected her basket.

"Are you kidding?" Avery grinned up at her. "I wouldn't miss it."

She couldn't miss it. Tonight, she'd end this. She'd get his signature and deliver the signed contract to her father.

Then she'd hop on the first flight back to Chicago before it got any harder to leave.

* * *

Another day, another victory.

Bryce high-fived Sawyer and Timmons as they dashed toward the bench for their post-game snacks, courtesy of Mom. He'd tried telling her he wasn't in Little League anymore, but she still had a hard time coming to a game empty-handed. Not that anyone complained. In fact, Elsie Walker's baked goods had earned quite the reputation. Those cookies she was currently handing out were known to draw plenty of fans from town who'd figured out she always brought extras for the people in the stands who cheered for her team. If you happened to like the opponents, though, forget it. No cookie for you.

No cookie for him, either. Because Mom happened to be standing right next to Avery, and he still hadn't figured out how to answer her question. Not that she seemed to care. Every time he'd gotten near her, she'd managed to concentrate pretty hard on those stats. She seemed to have plenty to say to Mom, though. They'd spent the entire inning with their heads tilted together, and it hadn't looked like they were chatting about the weather.

Damn. He'd never been good at this. When Yvonne used to mention his drinking, he'd blow her off exactly the way he did Avery in the car. Never knew how to bring up her depression, either. Those weeks she'd curl up in bed, too weary to do much of anything, he'd avoid her, avoid it all, and practically move into the bar. He'd had a problem even then, never knew when to quit. But he never wanted to talk about it. Never wanted to talk about anything.

Nope. He was more of a doer. So instead of heading to the bench where everyone celebrated, he jogged the bases, picking up each one so he could store them in the truck until the next game. He'd made it to third when Shooter lumbered over, munching on a cookie.

"Dude, you gonna go over there or what?"

He knelt to collect the base . . . and so he wouldn't have to face his friend. "Pardon?"

"How do you expect to get back in the game if you don't even talk to her?"

How did Shooter expect him to pick up home base when he wouldn't get out of his way? He stood. "I have no idea what you're talking about," he lied. Because the last person he'd ever discuss Avery with was Shooter.

His friend spread his arms like Bryce was stupid. "You wanna get in her pants, you gotta talk to her. Even I know that."

It was hard to take him seriously with that smear of chocolate down his chin. Some guys never left Little League. He bumped his shoulder on his way past him. "Sue me if I'd rather not take dating advice from you." Shooter's longest relationship had been with a foreign exchange student from France who didn't know much English. After being in the country for three months, she learned enough to dump his ass.

"Shooter's right, moron." Paige came up behind him.

"You've been staring at her all night. Here." She yanked her sleeve down and dabbed his chin. "Let me get that drool for you."

He jerked away from her and darted a glance at Avery to make sure she hadn't seen his friends razzing him. That was all he needed.

"See?" Paige taunted. "You can't even keep your eyes off of her for five seconds."

He bent to the ground and ripped up the base, tucked it under his arm. No use denying it. They knew him too well.

"Come on, Walker." Paige barricaded him against the chain-link backdrop.

Shooter lined up next to her. "What happened? You two were all cutesy last time we played. Now she won't even look at you."

There was no way out of it. If he tried to walk away, these two yahoos would make a scene. He tossed the bases down in a pile. "We had a…" Problem? Fight? He didn't even know what to call it. "…*thing* on the way over."

"A thing," Paige repeated, her brows peaked in a question.

"Yeah. She asked me a question about Yvonne and I blew her off."

"This is shocking." Paige slapped a hand over her mouth in mock astonishment.

He glared at her. Not helpful. "It caught me off guard. I wasn't expecting it."

"I get it, man." Shooter gave Avery a once-over with his eyes. "Her hot body catches me off guard every time I—"

"Hush." Paige clasped her hand over Shooter's mouth

until he shrugged away from her. The scowl on her face dared either one of them to interrupt her. "You know I love you and everything, and that's the only reason I can say this."

He shot her a desperate look. Did she have to be so loud?

"It's time to stop playing the martyr," she announced, and it was a damn good thing Avery was busy talking to Sawyer and Kaylee.

"Yvonne died. It sucks. Shit happens every single day."

His heart thudded until he reminded himself that she'd earned the right to say that.

"We all miss Yvonne. We loved her, too." The hard edge in her tone softened. "But Avery's into you. Trust me. I can tell. And if you don't go over there right now, you'll miss your chance."

He drew in a breath but his chest was so tight it felt like he'd inhaled glass. Maybe he didn't deserve another chance; had Paige thought of that? Maybe Yvonne had been taken away from him because he'd taken her— everything—for granted. Maybe if he'd been a better man for her, she'd still be alive. "I don't even know what to say."

"I can think of a few things." Shooter snickered like a kid looking at a dirty magazine in church, but Paige gutted him with her elbow.

"Start with hi," she said with a smirk. "It's a conversation, not a marriage proposal." Spreading her feet, she kicked out her hip and stacked her shoulders into some kind of really bad impersonation of him. "Hi Avery. How's it going? Sorry I bit off your head earlier."

Her interpretation of a man's voice almost made him laugh.

Silencing him with her hand, Paige continued. "Obviously, I have some issues to work through, but I'd like to take you out so I can answer your question over a nice, expensive dinner." Her hands spread in a silent *ta-da*. "See? Nothing to it. Trust me. You'll have her at 'expensive dinner.'"

"I don't want to bribe her." But Paige was right. He did owe her an apology. That much he could do. He'd gotten pretty good at apologizing over the last couple of years.

"Oh! Hurry up and get over there." Paige prodded his shoulder. "She's alone."

He gave her a gentle shove in the opposite direction. Didn't need an audience for this. "Thanks. I think I can take it from here."

"You got it, chief." After saluting him, she stooped to grab the bases he'd dropped on the ground. "Shooter and I'll just get these loaded in your truck." She stabbed her pointer finger into his friend's back and forced him up the hill toward the parking lot.

As soon as they were out of sight, Bryce sauntered over to the bench, hopefully looking more relaxed than he felt.

Avery sat at the edge, head down, eyes focused on the stats clipboard. Even with the sound of his footfalls against the gravel, she didn't look up.

"Hey." He plopped down next to her. "How's the head?"

"Great."

A one-word answer? From Avery King? That wasn't good. He tried again. "I'm sorry about earlier."

She blinked a beat too long before looking up. Her lips eased into a smile, but her expression was guarded in a way it hadn't been before. "I'm the one who should apologize. I shouldn't have asked you that. It was a silly question."

"No. It wasn't." He'd been all over her. He'd kissed her. But he wouldn't talk to her about anything important. No wonder she seemed confused. "You had every right to ask. I wasn't sure how to answer."

"You don't have to," she insisted, standing up. "Let's forget it, okay?"

"I don't want to." He owed her an explanation. If she knew how Yvonne had died, maybe she'd understand why it was such a loaded question. Why he still carried her with him. "Let's talk on the way back to the lodge."

"Actually, Paige said she'd take me back to the lodge."

"Paige?" He looked up the hill but couldn't see her. *Great.* She was the one who'd insisted he talk to Avery and now she'd ruined his opportunity.

"She said she wanted to swing by her apartment and show me her kayak collection."

Her kayak collection? What, were they best friends now? "Have you ever been kayaking?"

"Well…" Her eyes darted to the side. "No. But she was so excited about it. And it looks like fun. Maybe I'll learn someday."

Or maybe she wanted to escape from him.

She handed over the clipboard. "Here are the stats. I think I got everything."

"Thanks." He wanted to reach for her, to slow her down and make her look him in the eyes.

But she backed away. "I guess I'll see you later."

His arms hung heavy at his sides. *Yeah.* She was definitely avoiding him. "You'll be back for dinner?" he asked, letting hope flicker in the words.

Her smile picked up and gathered in the corners of her eyes. "Wouldn't miss it," she said briskly, then left him standing there.

Alone.

CHAPTER SIXTEEN

There had to be something she could wear.

Avery kicked through the pile of clothes strewn across the floor of her small suite. This was it. Her closing argument to Bryce and Elsie. She needed something professional, yet casual. Something that said, *listen to me! I'm trying to help you! I know what I'm talking about!*

It was time to get down to business, do what Dad taught her. Get in. Sign the deal. Get out. No emotions involved. As he said, emotions only complicated things, and the scene at the ballpark had proven it.

The truth was, she'd asked Paige to drive her back to the lodge so Bryce wouldn't feel awkward. Somehow she'd gotten derailed in her mission here. Blame the thin mountain air or the concussion, but whatever had caused it, she had to take back control.

No...

She kicked a pair of jeans.　.

More...

She knelt and plucked a soft, navy tunic off the floor. The hand-embroidered V-neck hit just the right spot—not too low, but still attractive. Elegant.

Swooning over those green eyes, bulky arms, and unkempt hair. Enough was enough. He'd made it clear that she wouldn't fit into his life, though he'd seemed to regret saying so later, but he was right. Her father wanted the man's land and Edward King usually got exactly what he wanted, one way or another. That made her mission even more critical. Bryce had to sell before Dad found a way to work his angle. She didn't even want to think about what that would look like. She'd seen him pay off banks to accelerate foreclosures before. This wouldn't be the first time.

She yanked the tunic over her head and fluffed up her hair. Next, she traded her comfy yoga pants for a sensible pair of dark, professional skinny jeans.

There. Add a pair of Uggs and she was ready to attend a casual business meeting. Fully platonic. No more quivery muscles when she noticed how Bryce's shirt pulled tight across his shoulders...

Face blazing, she rifled through her backpack and located the offer package, went over the details one more time. *Focus on the job.* Not on the way he'd started to look at her. Not the way he'd kissed her...

Ahem. Twenty-three million dollars. That would be enough to convince anyone to sell an old rundown ranch. He'd be crazy not to take it and run to the nearest beach. She carefully folded the printout and slipped it into her handbag.

At approximately 5:55 p.m., she took one last look in the mirror, plucked three fuzzies off her tunic, and pranced down the hall with the elegance of Grace Kelly, if she did say so herself.

In the entryway she looked up and there he was, bounding around the corner.

One look at him and *poof* her little pep talk vanished in a cloud of longing. He wore a plaid shirt with the sleeves rolled up. Dark carpenter jeans that fit him just right. Heavy work boots. His dark hair framed his face in typical disarray. He could've just stepped out of the pages of an REI catalog.

Despite a mounting protest from her practical side, her eyes lingered on him. Why was how he dressed so much sexier than the preppy look?

He didn't seem to see her until the last second, when he almost ran her over. "Whoa. Sorry about that." He caught her shoulders in his hands. "Have you seen my mom?"

The warmth of his fingertips melted into her skin. She breathed in some kind of subtle pine scent that made her want to lean into him and snuggle into the curve of his neck. "Uh...no." His closeness made her throat ache. What was all that mumbo jumbo about keeping her distance again? "Haven't seen her."

His hands opened as if he'd just realized he held onto her too long. Stepping back, he lowered a blatant gaze down her body. "Wow. You look...wow."

The compliment muted her annoying inner professional and made her heart prance. What was with that killjoy, anyway? It didn't hurt to flirt with him, did it? "You don't look so bad yourself," she shot back before she could overthink anything. Battling temptation had never been her strong suit.

"Don't know about that." He looked down at his attire as though trying to make a judgment call. "I've been out baling hay in the meadow."

Baling hay? Bummer she'd missed it. Did he do that shirtless, too?

"Mom said she'd call when dinner was ready," he said with a worried frown. "But I haven't heard from her."

"Maybe she's in the kitchen," Avery suggested. She took the lead across the sitting room and curved around the double-sided fireplace, which blazed with a roaring fire.

"That's weird." Bryce angled his head toward the glow. "Why'd she start a fire? It's so warm out."

So warm. So very, very warm. She tugged on the tunic to release the building steam. *Suffocatingly warm.*

Past the fireplace, he stopped cold. "What—?"

Forcing her gaze away from his exquisite backside, she glanced up. The dining room table had been transformed into a setting that would rival any five-star restaurant's. The red tablecloth contrasted beautifully with the white platters and bowls and plates. She stepped closer. The china had to be expensive, possibly antique. One place setting flanked each side of the table. Two red candles flickered between them. Golden aspen leaves lay scattered across the surface like rose petals.

The sight pounded alarm bells into her heart. *Retreat! Retreat!* Elsie had set up a romantic dinner for two. Not a business meeting. Well…unless you were in *that* kind of business. Which she was not. She *so* was not.

Flirting was one thing, but dinner? Alone? That was asking for trouble.

A folded note card sat on the plate closest to her. She snatched it up and handed it to Bryce.

He unfolded it and shook his head before he handed it back.

Enjoy you two! Love, Elsie

"Well." Bryce looked around the room. "She's subtle, huh?"

Oh boy. This wasn't what she'd planned for. She thought they'd have Elsie to be the buffer, to calm the palpitating chemistry that seemed to flare between them when they were alone.

"Uh…" She did a two-step in the direction of the entryway. "I can eat in my room, if you want. I have work to do, anyway."

He caught her elbow and gently tugged her back to the table. "That's okay." His eyebrows raised hopefully. "I mean, I'm fine with it if you are." He let go and looked into her eyes.

His were so steady and clear. Uncomplicated. Why did she have to be such a mess? "I'm fine with it, too." The squeak in her voice exposed the blatant lie.

"I guess we should sit, then." He stood behind his chair and waited.

She pulled out the chair in front of her and sat as stiffly as one of those log beams that held up the ceiling.

Bryce slouched across from her, completely calm, and dished up a helping of the perfectly seared scallops and strawberry spinach salad. "Looks like she went all out."

"She sure did." Why? Why would Elsie do something

like this when she knew where Avery stood? When she knew Avery didn't want to be someone's second best?

Bryce seemed oblivious to the questions that crowded her thoughts. His eyes were focused on the food, of course. *Typical man.*

A curl dipped down over his forehead. His button-down pulled tight across his broad shoulders. He was good-looking in a "rugged outdoorsman" way, but that wasn't what made him so appealing. No. There was something else, something deeper.

"You look better." Bryce set his fork down and gave her that bold stare again, the one where his eyes wandered slowly down then back up, like he wanted to focus on all of her. "I mean, your color's back. You look like you feel better."

"I do." Suddenly too aware of her appearance, she smoothed her hair back. She knew how to navigate a date—with Logan, and before him, with the other high-society eligible bachelors Dad had sent her way. But sitting across from Bryce felt so different. He didn't fill the air with meaningless small talk. He made his words count. He didn't act like silence made him uncomfortable. He seemed to enjoy it. How could she hold onto her boundaries when she had no idea what to expect from him?

"You tried this yet?" He took another hearty bite of scallop as if he was actually enjoying himself—the date, the food, even the company.

"Um. No. Not yet." She wished her heart would stop beating so hard. That would make it easier to think.

"It's really good."

She didn't look at him. Couldn't. His eyes would've

trapped her and she never would've found herself again. That didn't seem to stop him from looking at her, though. He gazed across the table like she was the only thing in the room he wanted to see. After a few minutes of her squirming and his staring, he set down his fork. "I'm really glad you're here. That we have a chance to talk."

"Mmm hmmm," she hummed, feeling the heat from the fire spread across her face.

"The answer to your earlier question is yes." A long inhale raised Bryce's shoulders. "I'm still in love with Yvonne. I knew her most of my life."

She gripped her fork harder. "Of course you are. Like I said, it was a silly question. You don't owe me—"

"We were in a Jeep accident." His eyes widened as if he were still in shock. "On our third anniversary."

Even though her face still flamed, her body felt cold, like somehow the chilly mountain air was seeping through the walls. "I'm sorry," she whispered. Sorry that it had happened, but even more sorry she had forced him to relive a nightmare that still seemed to haunt him.

"We were about fifteen miles back toward the Bells on an old forest service road. Half washed out. Too narrow."

A lengthy silence tempted her to speak, to say "how awful" or "it's okay, you don't have to tell me." Instead, she lifted her fork and tried to eat a few bites. The determined look on his face made it clear he had to tell her. For his own purposes.

"I don't remember how it happened. Cops told me the ground gave. We rolled, though. A hundred feet."

Avery peeked up at him.

His body remained eerily still, eyes focused on something unseen, face expressionless, hands dead at his sides.

"Yvonne was injured." A blink brought life back to his eyes. They focused on hers again, as if he'd suddenly awakened from a nightmare.

A nightmare he relived every day.

Her heart ached for him, for what he'd lost—a future with the wife he adored. Everything.

What had he been like before that had happened? Before she was taken away? Maybe he'd been the person the pictures on the walls depicted—easygoing and quick to laugh, maybe even the life of the party. "I can't imagine," she whispered.

"I knew it was bad." The words trembled through his lips. "She had a broken arm, but she said she was fine." His mouth tightened.

Avery gave in. "It's okay, Bryce. You don't have to tell me…"

His head shook, but his eyes changed again, wandered back to a dark, empty place. "I didn't have cell reception." A helpless look gouged his cheeks. "So I hiked. I went as fast as I could but it took hours. By the time I got back to the accident site, she was…gone."

It required a strength she didn't know she possessed to remain seated on her side of the table instead of rushing over to try to soothe that haunted look off his face. "How did she…?" She couldn't even bring herself to say the word. "What happened?"

"Head injury. A hemorrhage in her brain."

Well, no wonder he'd been so worried about her when Buttercup had thrown her. The poor man. His sorrow seeped into her with a cold shiver. She looked across the room and glimpsed the mountains outside. How could the world be so beautiful and so ugly at the same time?

"I never should've left her out there alone," Bryce said. "I should've stayed with her."

"You couldn't have known. There's no way." And even if he had known, he couldn't have saved her. Not out there. Not by himself. "It wasn't your fault," she said, desperate to take that burden off of him. It was too much for anyone to carry through life.

"That's what everyone tells me."

Avery straightened, lifted her head so she could beam the truth into his eyes. "You don't believe them?"

"Most days I do. Now. I've come a long way. Trust me." Pain shadowed his eyes, but they held resolve, too.

That was it, what made him so appealing—his quiet strength, his deliberate nature.

"Avery..." he hesitated, then targeted her eyes again. "You should know that I'm an alcoholic."

That word. She hated that word. When she was little, when things got bad with Mom, people had whispered that word when they didn't think she was listening. Then finally, one day, her nanny had said it to someone on the phone. She was ten, old enough to know what it meant. "She's my mom!" Avery had screamed, because people were forgetting who her beautiful mother really was, and she didn't want to forget. "She's not an alcoholic. She's my mom!"

Gulping water, she attempted to quiet her own memories.

"I just got out of rehab a few months ago. It was a long time coming," Bryce said, his face coloring. "It started in college, got worse after we were married." His stare lifted to hers, hard and intense, like he was battling the temptation to look away. "We didn't have the greatest marriage.

We were young. She struggled with depression, but we never talked things through."

"I get that," she offered. It reminded her so much of her parents, dancing around the issues that chipped away at the foundation of their family, because no one had seemed to know how to fix them.

"Three days before the accident, we had a fight." His pause stretched into a weighty silence, but she let it be. He had to do this. She could tell. He had to share it with someone.

Finally, his eyes wandered back to hers. "She confronted me about the drinking, about how I was never there for her. She was right. I wasn't."

"You were sick." Avery understood that, too, better than he could ever realize. Mom had wanted to be there for her, but she couldn't be. And that only seemed to make everything worse...

"That day, she screamed at me. I screamed at her. It was ugly, but it felt like we were finally getting somewhere, you know? Being honest?"

"Yes. I know," she murmured. Honesty might have changed everything for Mom and Dad.

"The day of the accident felt like a new start. It was our anniversary. We packed a picnic and got in the Jeep..." The words trailed off, but another pause seemed to replenish his strength. "We talked about getting her on some medication and me joining an AA group. So both of us could get healthy before we started a family." His eyes closed. "God, Avery. I wasted so much time. I wish I would've gotten sober before..."

"All that matters is that you did it," she said firmly. He had to know that proved how much he loved his wife.

"My mom never did. She drank herself to death." Until she was sick and wasted away. She'd lost her mother little by little. "You loved Yvonne enough to go, even though you couldn't be with her anymore. She'd be so proud of you, Bryce."

"I still love her." He shoved his unfinished plate to the center of the table. "I'll always love her, but I know I need to move on. That's not a clear answer to your question, but it's honest."

It was clear. At least to her. He was exactly like her father, tethered to his dead wife by guilt. He may not be committed to Yvonne anymore, but he was committed to the guilt. And that made it easier for her to remember why she sat across the table from him.

This offer, the money, could lead him away from his past. It could give him a new future. But she had to finesse it so he didn't get all defensive again. "Yvonne must've been an amazing person," she said, forcing herself to look at him with a genuine smile so he wouldn't see through her next question. "Did you two ever dream of living someplace else?"

"No." Those green eyes steeled with defiance. Never had one syllable said so much.

But she refused to accept it. Everyone had a place they dreamed about when the stress of life pressed in too hard. Mom used to dream about living in a cabin in the mountains, surrounded by beauty, away from the noise and the rush. She'd dreamed of a place exactly like the Walker Mountain Ranch, a place protected from the ugliness of the world.

Avery set down her fork. "But if you could live anywhere in the world, where would it be?" *Because I've got twenty-three million dollars in my pocket and it'll take you wherever you want to go.*

"Don't know." He rested his elbows on the table and leaned over them in a casual *I am so laid back* pose. "I traveled all over in college. Backpacked through Europe. Surfed in New Zealand. But I can't imagine *living* somewhere else."

"Come on, Bryce." She bounced her eyebrows with enticement. "Anywhere. Don't tell me that's not tempting." She knew she sounded like an overbearing big sister, but they were so close. All she had to do was encourage him to chase his dreams and the signature would be a formality.

He glanced out the windows. Something held his gaze. "I guess ... well, here's the thing. It doesn't matter where I live."

"Of course it matters. I'm talking anywhere. If price was no object. If you didn't have to work." Because he wouldn't. Not with twenty-three million dollars.

A weighted silence yawned between them, then Bryce drilled his gaze into her. "I guess I care more about who I live *with*."

The intention, the thought behind those words, stilled her to the point that she no longer heard the fire's crackles, the wind's sigh against the windowpanes. The haunted look on his face told her that he would never take another relationship for granted. He wouldn't live for thrills or beauty or luxury or quiet solitude. He would live for the people he loved. For Elsie and his friends, and maybe someday for a woman who gave him a reason to let go of his past.

Oh, Bryce. A sigh welled up and came out in a *whoosh*

of longing. That woman, the one he chose, would be the most adored woman in the world. She had no doubt. But she also knew it couldn't be her. She was not enough to make him forget. She couldn't heal that deep wound.

Avery forced herself to maintain eye contact, even though her eyes burned. "You're right. That's so much more important." A hard swallow dissolved the lump in her throat. Forward. She had to move forward. "Maybe that person is out there somewhere."

He kept his eyes trained on her. "Maybe."

The tips of her ears burned. An opportunity loomed in front of her. She had to take it now, or she'd lose the courage. "Don't you think you should look? I mean, this place is great, but doesn't it tie you down?"

His shoulders tightened and he sat straighter.

Avoiding his captivating eyes, she fished the offer out of her handbag. Because she had to. For him. For Dad. "Our offer still stands. We're prepared to give you twenty-three million dollars for this property." Hands shaking, she placed it flat on the table and pushed it across where he could read it.

The shock on his face forced her to her default setting—talk. *Say something. Anything.* "I know it might seem —"

"Did your mom leave you anything?" he asked, the hard edge in his words making him sound dangerous.

"What?" Why would he ask her that?

"Your mom. Before she died. Did she give you anything?"

Her chest tightened with a familiar grief. "This isn't about my mom. This isn't about me."

"What was it?" He demanded.

A sting shot down her neck and pierced her chest. How did he know?

"You can tell me," he said quietly. "What'd she give you?"

Her neck tensed as she prepared to shake her head in a hearty *no*, but she couldn't lie to him. "She ... gave me a necklace." A simple beaded necklace that probably cost her five dollars at Walgreens. Sixteen years later, she still had it safely zipped into the inside pocket of her purse, as if it was some priceless artifact she could never replace.

"You protect it, don't you? You keep it safe?" He watched her carefully.

She said nothing. Surely he saw the answer on her face.

"My grandparents gave me this." He glanced around. "I know it doesn't seem like much. But when you look at this place, you don't see what I see."

She couldn't argue. He probably saw memories in every scuffed wall, in every dent on the floor. But that didn't change the fact that it was about to go into foreclosure. "You'll lose everything," her professional tone slipped into a blatant pleading. "Don't you see that? The bank will take it all away."

"Avery." His eyes pinned hers down. "You don't have to worry about me. I have some potential investors."

"Investors?" Her shoulders went limp with relief. That meant she could stop pushing him. She could walk away.

"Yeah. I mean, nothing's set in stone, but—"

"You have to hurry," she interrupted. If he didn't, he'd lose the ranch. And after what he'd told her tonight, she didn't want him to lose anything else. "Don't wait."

"I won't," he promised, then fired up that heart-stirring

smile that lured her back into the land of possibilities. *No. Not possible.* Bryce was not possible. *Time to go.* Before it was too late. Her job was done, and so was she. She pushed back from the table and stood. "Thank you for dinner. For everything."

"Wait." He stood, too. "You're leaving?"

She picked up the printed offer, folding and refolding it in her trembling hands. "I should get some sleep."

"Okay..." His eyes narrowed. "Are you in pain? How's your head?"

"I'm great. Everything's great," she choked out. "I'm happy for you, Bryce. Really. I'm so glad you get to stay here." It was where he belonged. "I'll see you in the morning." She started to walk away.

"Hold on." He followed her into the sitting room. "Can I call you tonight? Every couple of hours?"

Call her? She tried to read the look on his face. "Why?"

"You have a concussion. Someone should wake you up. Make sure everything's okay."

Right. The doctor had told her that she was fine, but after hearing Bryce's story, she knew it probably wasn't best to argue with him. "That's fine." She pasted on a smile. "Sure. You can call my cell."

As quickly as possible, she gave him the number, then escaped to her room before she could change her mind.

When it came to Bryce, she couldn't trust herself. Not even a little bit.

CHAPTER SEVENTEEN

Buzzing. Incessant, mind-numbing buzzing. God, he hated that sound.

With a groan, Bryce rolled over and smacked the damn alarm. Hopefully broke it. He peeled his eyes open. Hadn't he just closed them ten minutes ago? Squinting at the clock he tried to focus. Two o'clock. In the morning. *Yeah.* He hadn't been asleep long. Tossing and turning didn't count as sleep, and after Avery's disappearing act, he hadn't been able to get comfortable.

What had gone wrong? Dinner was fine, at least in his book. He'd had a great time, learned more about her, thought maybe they'd end up sitting by the fire, and after that, who knew what could happen?

Man, had he been mistaken.

She'd spooked for some reason, then run away from him. Talk about role reversal. That'd been his M.O. since she'd arrived at the ranch, but now when he'd finally manned up and told her about Yvonne, she'd bolted and left him wondering what the hell had happened.

He groped a hand across the nightstand until he found his phone. He had to call her. Maybe he should just come out and ask her what had gone wrong so he didn't have to wonder all night.

Without bothering to raise his head from the pillow, he scrolled through, found her number, and dialed.

The phone rang. And rang. And rang.

"Great." He threw off the covers, eased to the side of the bed and tried again. No answer. What the hell? He'd told her he was going to call. "Come on, Avery. Wake up." He reached for the landline on the nightstand and dialed the extension for Room 5. Incessant ringing blared in his ears and cranked his neck tight. He slammed the receiver down and tried again.

And again.

Nothing.

Everything's fine. But the scenes he'd tried so hard to delete from his memory played for him again as clear and crisp as if the accident had happened yesterday: Yvonne's lifeless body slumped over a rock, as if she'd tried to crawl to find him, to get help. He could still smell the oil that had leaked from the Jeep, the acrid burning of the battered engine. A rising panic submerged the last shreds of sane logic. His pulse thrummed in his ears, the familiar precursor of impending panic.

He snatched his phone again, tried one more time. Avery would answer. She had to answer.

A series of lonely rings resounded in his ear.

Damn it. Why wasn't she answering? He jolted off the bed and shoved on his boots. Without bothering to grab a shirt or a coat, he shot out of his apartment above the office, down the steps, outside, and across the parking lot to the lodge. Hands unsteady, he barged through the main entrance and sprinted to Room 5.

His fist pummeled the door. "Avery?" He stilled his body, listened.

No response.

He knocked harder. "Come on, Avery! Wake up!"

Silence.

He blinked against the images that had gotten stuck on replay and gripped the doorknob, shaking the whole thing hard. The door popped open.

A scream drilled into his eardrums.

"What the—" Bryce darted into the room.

Avery was sitting up, clutching the covers against her chest. "Bryce! It's you!"

Who else would she expect? He looked around the room. "Why didn't you answer the phone?" Adrenaline taxed his lungs. He could hardly breathe.

"I didn't hear it." Her voice was wispy and high, sleep-laden.

"You didn't hear it." He tightened his hands into fists so they'd stop shaking. "I called three times."

"I'm a heavy sleeper." She swiped her phone off the nightstand and studied it. Her eyes lowered sheepishly. "My ringer was off. I'm so sorry..." She shimmied out of the covers and stood next to the bed.

Holy...

Stripped pajama shorts and a white tank top clung to her curves. Curls cascaded from her ponytail and framed her face. Even with the bruises, her features managed to stun him. Those rosy cheeks, full lips. His gaze lowered to the perfect swells of her breasts, down to the sexy curve of her hips.

He couldn't stop looking her over, every part of her. Nerve impulses fired all over his body. Hot, cold. Desire, anger. His body couldn't decide.

"Is everything okay?" she asked through a sleepy yawn.

He swiped the sweat from his forehead with the back of his arm and felt the cold shudder of shock. "You didn't answer. You didn't... I thought ..." The explanations died in his throat.

"Bryce?" She approached him slowly, her delicate hands outstretched. "What is it? What's wrong?"

He backed away before she could touch him, remnants of primal fear still squeezing a hand around his throat. "Nothing. I wanted to make sure you woke up. That's all." *Yvonne never did. She never woke up...*

His back collided with the door.

Avery crept closer, her gaze never leaving his, and damn it, he couldn't stand that look in her eyes. He didn't want her pity. He only wanted her.

"Bryce..." She reached for him.

Flinching, he stepped back. No. Not a good idea for her to touch him. Emptiness and need thundered through him, shaking the grounds of his rationality.

"It's okay." Her open hands raised to his face and cupped his cheeks. Her soft skin, the warmth of her palms, soothed that deepening ache.

His eyes closed, his jaw locked. He couldn't take what he wanted so badly, not like this, not when memories crammed his thoughts...

"I'm fine," she whispered gently.

Her thumbs stroked his skin and loosened his knees. His jaw worked, but he couldn't form words. She was too close. The memories were too close. Everything jumbled together.

"Look at me."

The blend of authority and empathy in her tone forced his eyes open. He stared into the blue depths of her eyes, concentrating on the silvery flecks that seemed to make them shimmer.

She guided his face closer to hers and stole his ability to swallow.

"I'm okay. Everything's okay."

He blinked at her, stilling himself, fighting the onslaught of desire that guided his hands to her shoulders, that curled his fingers around her bare flesh. God, she was so soft and warm and sweet with that orange blossom scent...

"I'm sorry I scared you," she breathed, then brushed her lips against his.

The heat of her breath on his mouth, the softness of her skin against his, unlocked a rush of want that swept through him and flooded out the memories. He wanted to forget. He just wanted to forget.

Her lips sunk into his again, harder this time, more sure, and he couldn't hold it off. Not anymore. He slid his hands down her back and pressed her against him, breathing her in, feeling her strength and her generous curves until he had to pull his hands back so he didn't take more than she wanted to give him.

Avery leaned away and found his hands. She pressed her palms against his, then weaved their fingers together. Gaze fused to his, she guided his hands back to her body and placed them at the swell of her hips, tempting him with a small smile that invited him to do what he wanted.

So much. He wanted so much. Too much...desire trembled through him, all the way to his hands, making them wander lower until they molded to her perfect ass and he could lift her up.

She wrapped her legs around his waist as his lips found hers. He lightly ran his tongue over her mouth and she opened hers to let him in. Her sigh ended in a moan and he felt the weight of her breaths against him. The jolt of her desire electrified the beat of his heart until his entire body pulsed.

Smiling against his mouth, taunting him with her tongue, she tangled her fingers into his hair.

"Bryce..." The breathless pant glowed against his skin. "Oh god, Bryce..."

Oh God was right. He held her tightly and kissed her harder, until the pictures from the past blurred and faded into an alternate reality. He pinned her against the wall and moved his mouth across her cheek, kissing his way down her neck...lower, lower.

She tipped back her head, giving him more access, so he kept going, kept kissing her sweet flesh all the way down to her collarbone.

Her legs tightened around him and his hands gripped her ass harder, caressing, savoring the feel of the thong through the thin fabric of her shorts.

"The bed," she gasped, and he didn't have to be told twice. Fitting his mouth to hers again, he carried her to the mattress and laid her on her back, then lowered himself down next to her.

Smiling again, she bit her bottom lip like she didn't know what to do next. But he did. It'd been a damn long time, but he hadn't forgotten.

"You're perfect." He moved his hands low on her stomach and slid them up, catching the hem of her tank top and raising it until he pulled it over her head and tossed it aside. Then he took his time letting his eyes wander over those curves, tracing a finger from the center of her chest down her to bellybutton. "Every inch of you is perfect."

Starting just below her belly button, he kissed his way up her body, straining not to rush, not to touch her flawless breasts until she wanted him to...

"Oh, Bryce," she murmured against his hair.

Taking that as a *yes, please*, he moved his lips higher, kissing her, stroking her flesh with his tongue.

She tightened her hold on his shoulders, then let her nails trail down his chest, gliding over his bare skin. That soft touch. Oh God, *her* touch. It throbbed through him, made him want to give her everything. All of him. He took his time exploring each millimeter of her upper body, moving slowly over the most sensitive parts of her, his own drive spurred on by her ragged breathing.

When he couldn't stand it anymore, he raised his lips to hers, tasting her carefully to protect the wound on her forehead, the bruises on her face.

She pulled away and removed his boots, tossing them to the floor. Then she shimmied his pants right off his body, leaving his boxers on, unfortunately. He dammed back a breath. But no. He wanted it slow, wanted to explore her, to know her, to feel every part of her. Because she wasn't just another girl. She was deep and real, and she'd managed to do what no one else could've. She'd managed to break through the barriers of his guilt and freed him to feel again.

Desire. Want. Desperation.

"You have no idea what you're doing to me," he grunted, then pulled her body over his.

Shooting him that tempting grin, Avery pushed her hands against his chest and sat up to straddle him. "I have an idea..." Her fingernails teased up his chest slowly and lightly until he was almost writhing underneath her.

Lowering her head, she touched her lips to his neck, grazing his skin with her tongue, pounding blood to the lower half of his body, moving her hips over him.

A feeling of pure ecstasy forced his eyes closed. How could he have lived without this for three years? "I want you, Avery," he grunted against her skin. "I want you like I've never wanted anyone."

"Mmm..." her lips worked their way down his chest, and that was that—she had him right where she wanted him, under a spell, breathing so heavily he felt like he was climbing to the top of the Bells.

Reaching over her, he massaged her shoulders, then hitched her up and pulled her over him so he could feel her body against his.

She arched her back, pressing her perfect breasts into him as his fingers dug into the soft flesh on her back. Then he moved his hands up to the sides of her face so he could pull her into another kiss before he slipped off her shorts and got a better look at that thong...

But when his hands cupped her cheeks, the bandage on her forehead came loose, draping over to one side and exposing her wound, the smears of dried blood. He blinked.

The sight of his hands so close to the blood churned the past back into the present until red flooded his vision. Blood. So much blood. He'd held Yvonne's head just like that, begging her to wake up, pleading with her to open her eyes...

"Bryce?" Avery's voice broke through the chaos. She didn't ask if he was okay. She didn't say anything. She simply pressed the bandage back into place and stared down at him, her face warped with pity.

His heart sped into a painful rhythm that tightened his chest and closed his throat. *No. Not now.* But it was too late. The shakes started in his shoulders, convulsing down his back.

Avery slid off of him and bent so her face drew close. "Everything's okay," she whispered in a soothing tone. But she was wrong. Everything was not okay.

Flames of humiliation licked at his face. He tore himself away from her and hunched over on the edge of the mattress. *Breathe. Calm the blood flow.*

Her hand crawled across his shoulder but he didn't want her pity. He stood and faced the wall, lungs heaving now.

"Don't go," Avery's voice wavered. "Not now. Not like this. Please."

"I'm sorry." He didn't look at her. "I have to." He couldn't battle the rising panic there. Not in front of her. He couldn't battle the craving to submerge it with a scotch on the rocks. He had to battle it alone. He'd always battled it alone.

Swiping his pants off the floor, he stumbled to the hallway.

"Bryce. Wait!" she called.

But he couldn't. No matter how much he wanted to.

CHAPTER EIGHTEEN

All set. Avery zipped the carry-on and set it on the floor, glancing around to make sure she'd gotten everything. With her legs confined by her black pencil skirt, feet teetering in her shiny black heels, she edged around the bed and carefully made it, smoothing out the quilt, already missing its weight over her. Who knew quilts were so warm?

After Bryce had walked out on her, she'd found comfort under that quilt, though she hadn't slept much. Every time she closed her eyes, she saw him…*felt* him, his hands on her, his lips against hers. The memory sparked again, moving through her in a slow heat. Battling it back once again, she arranged the pillows on the bed.

As soon as the early pink sunrise had glowed in her window, she'd gotten up and reclaimed Avery King, the professional, because that side of her, the logical and practical side, made much better decisions. So she'd packed away the jeans, the flowered tops, and the hiking boots, and dressed the part she played so well. Maybe a skirt and silky blouse and uncomfortable shoes would make it easier to say good-bye to Bryce.

With one last look around the room and an overwhelming sense of nostalgia, she opened the door. Rolling her luggage behind her, Avery tried to maintain a confident posture as she marched down the hall.

She shouldn't have gotten that close to him. She'd known better, but he'd been so shaken. Goose bumps spread down her arms. God, the way Bryce had held her and touched her...like he *needed* her. A shiver coursed through her body. She hadn't been able to think, not even one clear thought under the influence of his powerful hands, of his body against hers. Seeing him so vulnerable had gotten to her.

This was her fault and now she had to leave. She couldn't stay here every day and see him. Besides, now that she knew he had an investor, it was time to start looking for other build sites. She'd stay at The Knightley in town and start investigating today. It would give her something to focus on, maybe ease the sense of loss that weighed her down, even though she'd never had him in the first place.

Inside the foyer, she inhaled the scent of a hearty breakfast—something crisp and sweet. One of Elsie's masterful concoctions, no doubt, but for once in her life she wasn't hungry.

Rays of early morning sunlight beamed through the picture windows along the back wall of the sitting room. After parking her luggage by the door, she followed her usual path past clusters of furniture and into the dining room, where dishes clanged. The scent of strong coffee reminded her of Dad. She could almost hear him saying, *You're a King for God's sake. Act like it.* In his opinion, Kings didn't sulk and they didn't let regret sink too deep before casting it aside with a new plan, a new deal, a new project.

So she straightened her shoulders, and stalked past the fireplace.

"Morning dear!" Elsie greeted her with a hug.

"Hi, Elsie." The woman's arms felt so warm and welcoming that Avery snuck a couple of extra seconds sheltered in her embrace. What she would give to have a motherly presence, a nurturing voice of wisdom in her life. So much for battling the longing, the regret. It swelled through her until tears heated her eyes.

Maybe she wasn't really a King after all.

Elsie pulled back and looked her over. A frown puckered her lips. "Why, don't you look…" She paused as though searching for the right word. "…businesslike today."

Tears blurred Avery's vision but she fought back with a smile.

Unfortunately, Elsie wasn't fooled. Her head slanted to the side. "Avery, dear. What's the matter?" Her blue eyes might've been watered down with age, but somehow they saw more than Avery wanted them to. "Didn't you sleep well?"

"I slept okay." She quickly ducked to the table and found a seat before Elsie could read the truth in her eyes. "I still have a headache. That's all."

"I'm sorry to hear it," Elsie murmured as she scurried to the other side of the table. "Nothing a good breakfast won't fix, though. I whipped up buttermilk waffles with strawberry sauce." She spread her arms in grand presentation. "There's also a warm bacon quiche. Everyone needs a good dose of protein in the morning."

She gazed at the offering displayed in front of her. Steam curled off the perfectly browned quiche. Plump strawberries swam in a sugary sauce. The mixture of emotions that had filled her stomach seemed to dissipate in the presence of such extravagance. A low rumble somewhere deep inside begged for a taste of the sweet and savory food.

This sure beat the protein smoothies she made at home.

"Elsie." She shook her head in awe. "This is amazing. I've never seen anything like it." Except maybe on the Food Network. "It's a good thing I'm not staying another night. If I keep eating this way, I'll gain a hundred pounds."

"Not staying?" Elsie paused next to her, the coffee pot dangling from her hand. "Whatever do you mean?"

"Oh." She tried to keep her expression neutral—businesslike—and picked up the serving spoon. "I'm going to stay in town. With my father." She concentrated on heaping piles of food onto her plate and ended up with way too much.

"But why, dear?" The older woman's body slowly deflated to a chair next to her, the coffee pot still dangling in her hand like she'd forgotten about it. "Why do you have to stay in town?"

Because I can't seem keep my hands off of your wounded son. He'd already jerked her heart a couple times and it was starting to feel a bit fragile. "Oh, you know. We have projects to start. I've put things on hold long enough. Time to jump back in."

"Have you told Bryce?"

"Not yet." She slipped in a bite of waffle and let it melt in her mouth. One mention of his name was all it took to fluster her. Instead of a dainty bite, it felt like she was trying to swallow a snake. "Will, he, uh, join us for breakfast?"

Elsie popped up as if she suddenly remembered she was holding the coffee pot. She leaned over to fill Avery's mug. "I'll tell you what. That boy is in a mood today." She set the coffee pot on the table. "He never misses breakfast when I'm cooking, mind you, but when I went to find him, he said he wasn't hungry."

"Huh." Avery folded and refolded the napkin in her lap. "That's weird."

"It's a lie, that's what it is. Bryce is always hungry."

Avoiding the woman's curious glance, Avery lifted her spoon to stir the strawberry sauce on the plate. Somehow, that woman saw right through her.

"Anyway," she said through a sigh, "I reminded him we have a guest and told him he didn't have a choice." A quiet *harrumph* accentuated her authority. "He'll be here shortly."

"Good. That's great." The tremor in her voice weakened her confidence. It would be easier if she didn't have to see him, if she could hug Elsie good-bye and waltz out of there without having to look into Bryce's eyes again.

"Are you sure you're all right, dear? You look upset." This time, Elsie scooted into a chair across the table, which made it hard to avoid her eyes.

"Nope," Avery chirped. "Everything's fine. I'm just tired."

"I suppose that's to be expected when you've been through such a terrible ordeal." Elsie held her mug in both of her hands like she wanted to warm them. "Did Bryce call and wake you last night? He was so worried about you."

Her face burned. "Mmm hmmm. Yes. He sure did."

The sweet older woman looked at her thoughtfully. "Did something happen—?"

Somewhere nearby, a door crashed open. Bryce plowed into the room but stopped when he saw her. His entire body went stiff, as if the sight of her had turned him to stone.

She instantly looked down at her plate. He must have blamed her, too.

"There you are." Elsie gestured to the seat on her left. "I've got your plate all ready."

"Thanks, Ma." Without a glance in her direction, Bryce plopped down across from her, chin nearly touching his chest, eyes focused on the food.

Silence expanded in the room until her eardrums thrummed. She stuffed bites of waffle in her mouth and stared at the bacon quiche so hard it seemed to shimmer.

"I guess this will be our last breakfast together," Elsie finally said sadly.

That seemed to get Bryce's attention. His head snapped up and for the first time since he'd come in, he actually looked at her instead of through her. "What?"

Oh, those eyes. Those striking green eyes. She distanced herself from him with a glance at her watch. "I'm leaving today," she said as though reporting it to the board of trustees. "My car will be here any minute."

Bryce's tense face went soft and, damn him, he looked at her the way he had right before he'd kissed her. "You don't have to leave."

"Actually, I do." *Smile.* "My father and I have to research a new site for the resort. There's so much to do." It was a grand performance. Dad would've been proud. Apparently all those years of pretending everything was fabulous had rubbed off on her. Ignoring the elephant in the room had become a carefully honed talent.

Unfortunately, Bryce didn't possess the same skill. He drilled his gaze into hers. She swore he had superhuman powers—he cut straight to her heart with his eyes.

"Avery." The way Bryce uttered her name said so much—that he was as tortured, sorry, and conflicted as she was.

Elsie planted her hands on the table, her gaze bouncing back and forth between them. A worried look crinkled her forehead. "My goodness! I nearly forgot the muffins. I'll be right back." She practically leapt to her feet and bustled away, obviously wanting to give them time alone.

But being alone with him would make it harder for her to stay strong. She breathed in. She had to stay strong...

After the kitchen door shut, Bryce reached for her hand, but she pulled away before he could touch her. "I can't stay here, Bryce. I can't." *I want you too much.* And she had to protect her heart.

His chin dipped toward his chest, but his eyes peered up at her. "I don't want you to leave." The words were raw, so desolate they made her eyes sting again.

"I'm not enough," she choked out. "I can't make you forget. I can't make the memories of your accident go away. I would if I could." But he had to be the one to choose his freedom. Her father never had. "I'm sorry." She wadded up her napkin and let it fall on the table.

It was time to say good-bye.

* * *

He was losing her.

Bryce stared down at the food Mom had piled in front of him, hands itching to launch it across the room, to break it into a million pieces, to break something. *Damn it.* Damn his past. Damn it all.

"Here we are, dears." Mom reappeared in the doorway carrying a tray of freshly baked muffins. She set it down in the center of the table with that bright, world-changing smile of hers.

But something told him it couldn't change this. It couldn't make Avery stay.

"I can't eat another bite." Avery sat back against her chair and rested a hand on her stomach.

He'd felt that exact part of her body last night, her lower abdomen right above her hips. The curve and swell, the warmth...

The weight of desire for her bore down and threatened to crush him.

"I swear, Elsie. I might have to special order your food and have it shipped to Chicago," Avery said with a pained grimace. "You have a gift."

So did she. Did she realize it? How she made everyone feel like they were the best person in the world? Avery loved deep, a lot like Mom—he could see it, and he wanted to feel it, too.

"I won't have to ship the food, dear." Mom reached over and patted her hand. "You'll come back and visit. Anytime you want. Promise me you will."

He detected the gloom in her voice. This was hard on Mom, too. Avery had brought life back to the lodge, with her laughter and energy. She'd brought hope in a way he hadn't felt for years.

"Of course I'll come back and visit." Her eyes met his and he saw right through the words. She wouldn't come back. Not unless he could give her a reason to.

She glanced at her watch. "I really need to go. I'm sure the car is outside."

Feeling the distance grow between them, he forced himself to a standing position, trudged to the front doors, and lifted her suitcase.

Silently, they all walked out to the porch.

"Thanks for everything," Avery said from a good distance away. She seemed afraid to come too close to him, to touch him, and he couldn't blame her. She'd gotten close to him once and now she was afraid of getting burned again.

"Any time." He battled the urge to enclose her in his arms, make all kinds of promises he didn't know if he could keep, and drag her back to his bedroom to finish what they'd started, to show her how much he wanted her. But he only stood there, weighed down by the knowledge that she was right. She wasn't enough. He couldn't use her as a remedy for the things that tortured him.

"Please don't be a stranger." Mom gave her a long hug, but he hung back.

"I won't," Avery lied, pulling away from her. She eased her suitcase down the steps and hurried to the black town car that idled in the parking lot. The driver opened her door and she waved once more. "Thanks again. Take care."

"Keep in touch!" his mom called, sniffling.

He raised his hand in a silent wave and thought he saw

her hesitate. His breath caught, but then she slid into the car and disappeared.

The driver got in and drove away and he watched Avery slip right through his fingers.

"Bryce David Walker." Mom whirled to face him as the cloud of dust dissipated. "What the hell did you do to her?"

Whoa. If she was swearing, he knew he was in trouble.

"She seems positively devastated." Mom stepped closer, those blazing eyes analyzing his face, daring him to lie to her. "And so do you."

She had one of the most well-honed B.S. detectors he'd ever seen. So he opted for the truth. "She didn't answer the phone when I called last night, so I went to her room." It wasn't as if his mother would be surprised. She probably knew anyway. She had that freakish mother's intuition that'd always gotten him busted. Like the time he'd snuck out to meet his friends for a midnight climb. Or the time he'd snuck Yvonne into his bedroom when they were fourteen. Mom had busted right in. Said she'd had a "feeling."

He might've lied back then, but there was no point now. He'd always been able to tell Mom most anything and it'd never seemed to shock her or change her opinion of him. He sighed. "We ended up...kissing. But I had a flashback. To the accident."

"Oh, son." Surprisingly, the words weren't scolding. They were just plain sad. "You have to protect a woman's heart. You can't be with her that way until you're ready to move on."

"I'd sure as hell like to move on." So why couldn't he? Why couldn't he make himself forget?

She expelled the same deep motherly sigh he'd heard

a thousand times and leaned against the porch railing. "How do you expect to move on when you don't even acknowledge Yvonne? When you pretend like she never even existed?"

The accusation raised his defenses. "I don't—"

"You don't talk about her," she interrupted. "Or look at pictures or even let yourself remember. You can't erase her from your heart."

"I wasn't trying to erase her." He was trying to survive.

"You packed away everything in those boxes and shoved it all in the attic," Mom said quietly. "All of the pictures, your wedding album, even that lovely painting of Maroon Bells you got for your wedding. You hid it all."

He'd hidden it all because everything reminded him of her. Everything she'd touched or admired had suddenly made him angry, and it was either pack it away or break it—rip it apart until some of the agony subsided.

"I know it hurts to think of her, to let those memories be real." She squeezed his hand tightly in hers, and somehow that small gesture made him feel stronger. "But if you want to move on, son, you have to embrace that pain. You can't forget her. You have to embrace her as part of you before you can open your hands and let it all go."

He smiled down at Mom, the one who'd always held his hand, the one who'd spanked him more times than he could count, the one who'd loved him no matter what, the one who'd picked him up off the ground every time he fell, literally and figuratively.

She smiled back, her eyes shining with tears. "You're worthy of a good life, Bryce. A future. A family. You're worthy of love."

"Thank you," he said, for all of it. For refusing to give

up on him. For telling him the truth, day after day, year after year, even when he refused to hear it. "I know what I need to do," and even just the thought of it raked him with fear.

But he'd do anything. Now that he'd met Avery, he finally had a reason to let the past go.

CHAPTER NINETEEN

Avery wrapped the bathrobe tighter around her shoulders and perched on the edge of the soft leather sofa. Directly across from her, a massive window framed the craggy peak behind Aspen Mountain. Below it, ski runs stretched down, glowing green islands in the sea of shimmering pines and golden aspen trees. Overhead, dense gray clouds had started to crowd out the blue sky, giving the scene a gloomy feel, which fit her mood perfectly.

She panned her gaze across The Knightley suite. From the mahogany four-poster bed, piled high with white pillows and a fluffy comforter, to the sparkling granite countertops in the fully-stocked kitchen, the place exuded opulence. Everything seemed to be plated with silver or gold. The fabrics shone with that silken look. Even the wood floors gleamed with what looked like a fresh coat of wax. When she'd walked through the door, she'd discovered an extravagant array of fruits and vegetables, meats and cheeses, along with collection of fine red wines. An hour later, some poor bellboy had had to come and gather it all into the refrigerator.

This was her life—money and extravagance and all of the notoriety that went along with her father's name. But for all the hotel offered her, it didn't comfort the way the lodge had, with its musty smells and faded quilts and dusty log accents. It didn't offer Elsie's hospitality or her warm accepting hugs. And though the food looked good, it couldn't possibly compete with one of Elsie's meals.

She missed the ranch.

Across the room, a plasma television perched precariously on the mantel of a grand fireplace encased with white and silver-swirled marble. The Cubs game hummed in the background.

There was a time she would've been glued to the game, biting her nails even, but she could hardly pay attention. For the last half hour, she'd been perusing the Internet instead, trying to find a new site for the resort before she broke the news to her father that Bryce's ranch wasn't available. Good thing he'd gone golfing with Mayor Pendleton for the day. That had given her time to prepare.

She'd found a couple acreages that could work, though both were much farther outside of town. One near Snowmass and one up north. Neither one had the views but that simply meant they'd have to build something extraordinary to make up for it. She shut down her laptop, snatched the remote off the coffee table, and turned off the game. Dad had planned some big dinner with the mayor, a couple of city council members, and who knew what other bigwigs tonight, which meant she had to get dressed.

A knock halted her progress and damn it if she didn't gasp in a hopeful breath. *Bryce?*

"Avery! It's Vanessa!"

She squealed and leapt off the couch. Not as good as her first choice, but definitely the next best thing. She padded to the door and unlatched it, swinging it open wide to give her friend a hug. She so needed a friend right now, and Van was about the best friend anyone could ask for.

Vanessa bounded in, bringing along the happy scent of perfume as peppy and bright as she was.

"Hey, chica." She fluffed Avery's damp hair and cycloned into the sitting room, dragging her suitcase behind her.

Avery followed. "What are you doing here?" Already her presence had taken the edge off the loneliness that had made her feel as heavy as those clouds outside.

"Edward flew me out," Van informed her. "He's got some project he wants me to work on, though I have no idea what it is." She turned and slapped a hand on her hip, eyeing Avery up and down. "Besides that, I had to get out here and find out what the hell is going on with you."

"What do you mean?" Avery asked, trying to sound as innocent as a Disney princess.

"Uh huh. Don't bother with me, missy. I know you too well." She meandered to the bar and picked up one of the wine bottles, studying the label carefully. "You've been gone almost two weeks, girl." She stabbed the corkscrew into the cork and twisted until it popped. "I've never known you to stay on a business trip for more than three days. Not even in Barbados."

Yes, that was true. Yet another reminder of her workaholic tendencies. Until this week, that was: she'd hardly worked at all since meeting Bryce. Even then, when she'd been checking e-mail or looking over a project proposal, he'd crept into her thoughts and derailed her productivity. And yes, of course, her heart started to flutter just thinking about him, which meant it was only a matter of time before her face flushed. She gazed out the window at the emerald mountainside so Vanessa wouldn't see. "Things haven't gone as smoothly as I'd hoped."

"No shit." Vanessa sipped her wine and perched on the sofa. "How's the concussion?" she asked, her tone teetering on sarcasm.

"I feel great." She would've sounded a lot more convincing if she could've mustered some enthusiasm, but she was clean out, which meant it was time to change the subject. "How's Logan, by the way?" Yesterday, Vanessa had sent her a text to let her know she was taking Logan to Avery's place so he could pick up some of his things.

"You know him," she answered with a smirk. "Always the eternal optimist." Her grin faded. "By the way...I took him out for a drink after we locked up at your place. I hope that's not weird or anything."

"Are you kidding?" Avery gasped and turned to face her friend. Those two would be perfect for each other! Why had she never thought of it before? "That's great, Van. Really. He's a quality person."

A grin brought out Vanessa's dimples. "Yeah. He really is." She scooted to the edge of the couch. "But enough about him. I want to hear all about *Bryce Walker*." She rolled the *r*'s in an exotic accent.

A prick on Avery's cheeks warned of another oncoming blush. Her eyes wandered back to the safety of the window. "What do you want to know?"

"Let's start with why you two were on some secret, romantic horseback ride in the middle of nowhere, shall we?"

"I was trying to get to know him better. So I could convince him to sell."

"Mmmm hmmmm." Van set her wineglass on the coffee table. "Don't you hold out on me, sister. I Googled the man and he is one fine example of God's talent, I'll tell you that much."

Van had no idea. Her body temperature shot up about thirty degrees. *Yeah.* She needed a drink, too. Trying to outrun Van's questions, Avery hurried to the bar and poured a glass of wine.

When she turned back around, her friend looked her over, one brow raised in omniscience, then slapped a hand over her mouth. "You slept with him!"

"Not exactly." She sank into the chair next to the sofa and sipped the dry red wine. "I guess we almost did, but…"

"But what?" Van demanded, as if no possible explanation could possibly suffice.

"His wife died three years ago. He's definitely not over her." A long sigh pushed her back against the plush leather. "He's amazing, though. So real and thoughtful."

"Yeah, yeah, yeah." Van motioned for her to get to the point before she lost interest. "And he looked like he could bench press a pick-up truck, too. Let's discuss that. I'm guessing he has a six-pack. Am I right? Surely you saw it…" Her teasing expression fished for details.

Avery tipped her glass and sipped more wine to fend off that annoying burn deep in her chest. "He's definitely good looking."

"Good looking?" her friend blurted. "*Mamacita*, he's hotter than a July night in a Vegas strip club."

"Sure. Yeah." She wasn't about to deny that Bryce had some serious sex appeal. "But he's also one of the best people I've ever met. Complicated." That was for sure. "But one of the best."

Her friend's dark eyes gleamed. "You have feelings for him."

"Yes." Her body sunk under the weight of it. "I see something in him I've never seen in anyone."

Van's smile got all dreamy, like she was watching the end of a chick flick, but then her eyes went wide like she'd just realized the story wouldn't end in a happily ever after. "Shit, Avery. Have you told Edward?"

"No," she admitted. "There's no reason to. I can't be with someone who's clearly still in love with someone else."

"Are you sure he's still in love with her?"

"Pretty sure." Why else would he have walked out on her? She still didn't know what had triggered his hasty retreat. One minute, he was kissing her, telling her he wanted her like he'd never wanted anyone else, and the next he was sitting on the side of the bed looking like he'd just witnessed a train wreck.

Van crossed her long legs and donned her know-it-all frown. She considered herself skilled in a variety of areas—therapy, medical mysteries, supernatural phenomenon. The woman watched a lot of TLC.

"Sometimes people hide behind loss when they're afraid of what they're feeling," she intoned as if she'd suddenly earned a PhD.

Today, apparently, Van was a grief counselor. Smiling at her friend's suddenly serious face, Avery finished off her wine and slid the glass onto the table. "Maybe. But I can't fix that for him." Just like she hadn't been able to fix it for her father. She'd tried. God knew, she'd tried. And meanwhile, her life had passed her by, the minutes ticking away while she sat in meetings and wrote e-mails and traveled to various sites around the world, pumping every ounce of energy and inspiration into work. All of which she did while sleeping alone. She didn't want her bed cold anymore. She wanted it the way it had felt with Bryce, warm and intimate. Even if she couldn't be with him, he'd opened her up to new possibilities; he'd revived her and exposed her to a depth of passion she hadn't even known existed. He'd made her want more.

Her heart shifted hard in her chest, making her feel reckless and free as she gazed out at the mountains. Just like Bryce, she had a choice. She could choose her own freedom. "I don't want to go back," she said, eyes captivated by the swirling clouds.

It looked like change was coming, a storm...

"What do you mean?" Van asked.

"To Chicago. To work. I don't want to go back." Now that she'd said it, it felt like the easiest decision she'd ever made.

"Whoa, chica. That's huge. Let's take a step back here..."

She turned to her friend, the fiery energy inside of her gaining momentum. "I know it sounds crazy, but I don't belong there."

Van blinked at her a few times, as if letting the information soak in. "What do you want to do, then? Stay here?"

Yes. That was exactly what she wanted, but life had taught her that you don't always get exactly what you want. "I can't stay here." This was Bryce's community, his life. "I don't know where I'll go. Maybe to California." That's where a group of her grad school friends had started their own consulting business. They'd been trying to recruit her for years.

"What the hell would you do in California?" Van demanded, as if insulted that Avery would even consider moving away from her.

"I don't know." The spinning wheels in her brain propelled her body into motion. She paced across the soft shag rug in front of the fireplace. "Whatever I want. I have a marketing degree. An MBA from Harvard, for crying out loud. I can get a job."

"Oh, boy," Vanessa mumbled with a worried shake of her head. "Edward'll have a coronary, Avery."

"He'll understand," she insisted, her fists clenched. Eventually. He loved her. She had to believe he loved her enough to accept her decision, to let her go. Maybe not now...

But hopefully someday he'd understand.

* * *

Why the hell had he suggested this, again?

Bryce glanced out the passenger side window of Ben's rented Jeep. The two-hundred-foot dropoff below him seemed to roll on and on forever, all twisted tree roots and piles of boulders and loose shale that had slid down from the cliff hovering precariously above them. He cleared his throat so he could breathe. Small puffs of steam rose from his mouth, but it still felt like someone had shoved their fist all the way down into his chest.

It didn't help that the clouds above them had sunk low, shrouding the peaks in a dull gray. He inhaled the crisp, cold smell that warned of an incoming blizzard. Bad time to be caught in an open-air Jeep. On the side of a cliff. He zipped up his fleece and blew warmth into his freezing hands.

"You okay?" Ben asked, eyeing him, but also keeping his focus on the rutted Jeep road, thank the lord, because one wrong move and they'd roll down the cliff. Been there, done that. Had no desire to do it again.

"I'm great." His voice had gone hoarse. Truth was, he hadn't been out in a Jeep since the accident. Hadn't had a reason to go back to the place that haunted him. Not until now, that was. Not until the day Avery King had walked into his office.

Fear clashed with resolve and started an uprising in his stomach. *Moving on.* He was moving on, and this had to be done. For three years, he'd avoided coming out here, to the backcountry where he and Yvonne had spent so much time together. This was where most of his memories lived—all those times they'd hiked and fished and camped out, making love under the stars. He hadn't been able to face it, like being alone out here would somehow make her death real.

But it was time.

"Now that's a cliff." Gritting his teeth, Ben slowed the Jeep and leaned over the steering wheel. "Good thing I opted for the insurance package."

Bryce laughed. Felt good to release some of the pressure. "Just make sure you hug the right side of the road."

"Road? You call this a road?" Ben asked, but his eyes

held that look of conquest. That's why he'd asked Ben to do this with him. The guy lived for adventure. Well, that and he'd recently lost his father so Bryce figured he'd understand why he had to go to the last place he'd seen Yvonne alive. He couldn't have driven himself. Didn't know if he'd ever be able to drive on a Jeep road again without dry heaving the whole time.

Even with someone else driving, it was tempting, but he took slow, deep breaths and tried to think about something else. Good thing they had other matters to discuss. "So, have you heard anything from your contacts?" he asked and grimaced at the series of bumps that shook him right down to his bones.

Ben slowed the Jeep to a crawl and eased it over a boulder in the center of the road. "Yeah. I've got a few buddies interested. You still want to go the investors route?" His hands were securely fastened at ten o'clock and two o'clock. "Or do you want me to give you the loan? It's no problem, Walker."

"I won't take your money," he said tightly. Hell, he didn't even want a bunch of investors telling him how to run the place, but if that's what it took to be free and clear, he'd do it. Once things were up and running again, he'd buy them all out.

Ben hit the brakes and shook his head at him. "Still one of the most stubborn SOBs I know." He grinned. "I'll have my business manager schedule a call. We can set it up next week."

"Sounds good." But Avery's words echoed. *Don't wait.* Did she know something he didn't? "Let's make it early next week." Preferably before his Notice of Election and Demand deadline expired.

"Sure thing." Ben threw the gears into drive and eased the Jeep onward.

Landmarks passed by Bryce's window and made it harder to focus on something else. There was the rock shaped like a heart. White heat flashed across his eyes as he remembered Yvonne's smile when she'd pointed it out. *Stop! We have to take a picture*, she'd said.

He'd told her they'd have time to take it on the way down...

"How much farther?" Ben's standard upbeat tone had gone somber.

"We've got about another mile." He'd never forget the exact spot they went off the road. Two more curves, then the road would dip right where he'd gone too far to the left to avoid a deep rut. "Then I'll hike down." To the place he'd left her. To the place he'd returned with the search–and–rescue crew to find her dead.

"I should probably warn you..." Ben braked again and the Jeep stuttered to a stop. "I called Sawyer. Asked him to round up a few of your friends to meet us here."

"Friends?" Anger pumped through him and repelled the chill. What right did Ben have to invite people, like this was some kind of party?

"Yeah." His friend looked apologetic. "He said he knew who you'd want there. Mentioned something about Meg. Paige. And someone named Dinger?"

"Shooter?" It had to be Shooter. He wouldn't hang out with anyone named Dinger.

"Yeah. That's right. Hope you're not too pissed off. I thought maybe after you took some time, we could all go for a hike or something."

"Yeah. Sure." Fury still simmered under his skin, but it

wasn't because of Ben. It was because this was hard. So damn hard. He could see the spot, up ahead. The left side of the road was still eroded, crumbling down the steep grade below. *Embrace it*, he reminded himself. He had to embrace the pain that thrashed his gut, even though it felt like it had the power to kill him. If he did this, maybe the past would lose its power over him.

"Stop." He gagged on the word. Right here, on this very stretch of road, he'd had his hand on Yvonne's thigh, as high up as he could get away with. They'd been talking about starting a family. He told her he wanted a family with a lot of kids, the brothers and sisters he'd never had, a whole basketball team, if she was up for it. She'd laughed, that silky smooth laugh of hers, and then leaned over to whisper in his ear. *Then we'd better get started,* she'd said, her voice low and soft.

But they'd never had the chance because right here, at this very place, the ground gave out on his life, and his dreams had plummeted over the edge.

Silently, Ben pulled the Jeep over and Bryce had to remind himself to move.

Swing one leg out the door, then the other.

Stand, even though he wasn't sure his legs could hold him up.

Walk. His feet shuffled like they'd been dipped in concrete, but somehow he slogged across the road and peered over the edge.

Behind him, Ben cut the Jeep's engine, but he stayed in the car.

The sudden silence let in other sounds—the endless whisper of the wind, the rushing of a river somewhere down in the valley—and even though he was full of turmoil, this was a peaceful place, too. A wild and beautiful place. It reminded him that Yvonne had not taken her last breath surrounded by ugliness.

His footsteps pounded the packed dirt in a solemn processional down to the place where he'd left his heart three years ago. He moved slowly, carefully stepping over loose rock, keeping his weight balanced so he wouldn't pitch forward on the steep slope. Lower, he felt his way over the boulders until he found the flat ground where their Jeep had finally rested.

Seeing it opened the vault of memories he'd carefully protected. His legs gave out. He sank to a rock.

Remember. Embrace it. He battled the instinct to fend off the images, and instead let them fill his mind.

When he'd regained consciousness behind the steering wheel, he'd found her slumped next to him. Blood stained everything red, but she was okay, she'd told him. Just cold and her arm was badly broken. Pain fired all over his body just like it had then, remembering how he'd bandaged the gash on her head with his shirt, how he'd used the old sleeping bag he kept in the Jeep to fashion a bed that would keep her warm while he went for help. How he'd stuffed extra fleeces into their backpack to make her a pillow. "I'll be back," he'd promised her.

And she'd smiled up at him. "I know you will." With a light kiss on the lips, he'd whispered *I love you.* And he had.

He'd loved her the best he could.

He hoped she knew that. He hoped she'd felt that as she drifted away from the world.

"I'm so sorry," he said for what had to be the millionth time, but something in him knew it would be the last time.

She wouldn't have wanted him to spend the rest of his life apologizing for something he couldn't change.

Breathing in the purity of the mountain air, he gazed out over the peaks across from him. The gray, swollen clouds draped over the sharp crags, softening them with a light haze.

"I'll never forget you, Yvonne." He hadn't spoken to her since she'd left him, but he had to believe she heard. "You made me want to be a better person." That's how he'd honor her memory. It started with getting sober, and it'd continue with moving on. With learning how to love someone the way he hadn't been able to love her.

A biting wind scraped his cheeks, and a swarm of hefty snowflakes flitted in the air.

Snow in September.

Yvonne had always loved the snow. She said it blanketed everything in a pure, white peace. It made everything beautiful and new. Every year, when the first snowstorm hit, she'd bundle up and beg him to walk with her. They'd stroll down the streets arm in arm, turning their faces to the sky until their noses went numb.

Breathing in the crisp air, he tipped his head back and let flakes pelt his face. He pictured her laughing and happy, cheeks chapped from the cold, and he couldn't hold back a smile. An early September snowstorm...it felt like one last gift for him to take with him.

"Good-bye, baby," he said, standing stronger than he had in as long as he could remember. Leaving the weight of his regrets behind, he tromped back up the slope.

When he got back to the road, everyone was there—Meg, Paige, Ben, Sawyer, and yes, even Shooter. They'd gathered near Ben's Jeep and were harassing each other about their baseball skills, or lack thereof.

Instead of quieting as he approached, they got even more rowdy.

"I could take you down right here, right now," Meg said to Shooter. Everyone laughed.

"How about we drive up to the top of the pass instead?" Bryce called over, fully anticipating the shocked looks they sent his way.

For three years, they'd all invited him to go on their backcountry adventures and he'd always declined. But it was a new day and he wanted to spend it out in the snow.

Everyone exchanged looks and the gasps of surprise dissipated.

"Hells, yeah," Shooter said, leading the way back to their Jeeps. "Let's do it."

The laughter and chatting picked up again, and it was like nothing had changed. But he knew better. The snow. A promise of something new.

It was an invitation for him to finally live in freedom.

CHAPTER TWENTY

Snow? How could it possibly snow in *September*?

Sure enough, when the driver opened her door, a frigid wind delivered a swarm of huge, wet flakes that melted against Avery's bare shoulders. What was up with that? Yesterday she'd watched the baseball game in a tank top. This morning, the sun had made her world feel a little less dreary.

Avery climbed out of the car, suddenly regretting the sleeveless black cocktail dress she'd selected for dinner. Actually, she regretted a lot of things. Like sending Vanessa on without her so she had more time to get ready. Like agreeing to make an appearance in the first place. After saying good-bye to Bryce and Elsie, her emotions were cranked tight, teetering on the edge of a collapse. All she wanted to do was waltz in here, shake a few hands, smile, have a stiff drink, then get the hell out of there so she could pick up some cheesecake brownie ice cream and sneak back to her hotel room to submerge her sorrow in a tub full of suds.

Wrapping her arms tightly around her chest to ward off the cold, she said thank you to the driver.

The thought of a steaming hot bath bolstered her with enough resolve to adjust her posture and march toward the door like a woman on a mission. For ice cream. And a whirlpool tub. She'd masqueraded her way through plenty of high-society dinners, smiling and shaking hands and playing an Academy Award-winning role. Judging from the looks of Elevation 8,000, this dinner would be no different.

The building was one of the oldest in Aspen, with a stone façade that resembled something you'd see on a cobblestoned street in Rome. Black awnings billowed above oversized windows, which were tinted just enough to make the place look mysterious. The sign above the door looked more like a sculpture, with rod iron twisted to impersonate tree branches and white lights twinkling in the gaps.

Beyond those doors, she'd no doubt find herself among pretentious men in tightly buttoned suits, trophy wives clad in low-cut cocktail dresses, dim mood lighting, and a wait staff that kept every wineglass topped off without asking.

Here we go.

Before she could reach the handle, the door magically opened. A young hostess appeared, sparkling in a black sequined dress. Her skin glowed with an ethereal smoothness. Not even one freckle.

"Miss King, welcome to Elevation 8,000." She held open the door and swept out her arm in a grand gesture with which she might've greeted a queen.

"Thank you." Avery sashayed past her, anxious to get this over with.

The inside of the restaurant had a trendy minimalist vibe. All clean lines, natural woods, and symmetrical décor. Hanging lamps with white shades dropped over private booths like upside-down mushrooms. Instead of artwork, industrial metal paneling garnished the walls. The place appeared quite full: beautiful sparkling people set against the lovely background music of refined murmurs, clanking silverware, and soft laughter.

"Your party is in our private room upstairs," the girl murmured discreetly, as though addressing a spy. She'd obviously had plenty of experience dealing with the rich and famous. "If you'll follow me." The girl loomed over her in four-inch stilettos that could've cracked her ankle in half. She traipsed up an iron spiral staircase and stepped aside at the top.

This room was a miniature version of the main floor dining room, with the same metal paneling and soft lighting. Instead of booths, the room held one polished dining table that would easily seat twenty. Floor-to-ceiling windows extended across the back of the room, framing an incredible view of Aspen Mountain. Across the way, leather couches faced off in front of a stone fireplace. Not surprisingly, that was where her party mingled—Dad, Vanessa, Mayor Pendleton and a few men she didn't recognize.

"You can order a drink back there." The hostess gestured to the area behind her where a full bar and bartender became the first bright spot of Avery's day.

"Food has already been ordered and will arrive shortly." Before Avery could thank her, the hostess disappeared down the staircase and left her standing on the outskirts of the dinner party.

No one had noticed her tardy arrival yet. Her father seemed to be in the midst of an intense discussion with two gentlemen she didn't know. From the looks of their arm gestures, it appeared they might be discussing golf.

Vanessa sat on the couch next to Mayor Pendleton, but Avery recognized the blank look on her friend's face. The woman was bored out of her mind.

The volume in the room far exceeded a normal decibel level, which meant everyone had already consumed a fair amount of alcohol.

No fun to be the only sober one at a party. She made a beeline for the bar. "I'll take a dirty martini with two olives," she said to the bartender as if she ordered that same drink every day, instead of the more fru fru drinks she tended to gravitate toward—mojitos, margaritas, anything with a lot of sugar and only a touch of alcohol.

It was a special occasion, though, right? The day she'd decided to quit her job, leave her doting father behind and step out into the unknown? Her stomach clenched. Normally, she didn't drink much. After what she'd seen as a child, she'd always been too scared, but tonight called for an exception.

The bartender passed her a napkin and the telltale wide-brimmed glass. After a quick "Thanks," she sipped the murky liquid.

Ohhhh, it burns. A trail of fire roared up her throat and scorched her eyes. Her sputtering cough caused every head in the room to turn in her direction and a hush fell over the crowd.

"Avery!" Vanessa squealed and leapt off the couch,

no doubt grateful that she didn't have to listen to Mayor Pendleton prattle on and on.

"Hi everyone." She blinked to clear the blur from her eyes and made her way to the fireplace.

"It's about time," Dad grumbled, swirling the ice in his brandy.

Ignoring him, she beamed an apologetic expression to the rest of the room. "Sorry I'm so late. I got held up."

"No problem at all, Avery." Mayor Pendleton rose from the couch with the grace and elegance of a dignitary. He introduced Avery to William something, a city council member, apparently; then to Gary (she didn't quite catch his last name), who was some bank bigwig. Next, he moved on to George something-or-other, CEO of the what's-it corporation and his assistant, Chet. Now *that* she could remember, even with a good amount of vodka coursing through her veins. *Chet.* One syllable. Uncomplicated. That was how she liked a name.

The other men were older than her father, but Chet was younger, good looking in a Clark Kent sort of way, with serious blue eyes accentuated by dark-rimmed glasses and a very symmetrical face. Laugh lines in the corners of his mouth and eyes gave away his propensity to enjoy a good joke.

"It's nice to meet you all." She choked down more of the martini and gagged back the threatening cough.

"Nice to meet you, too, Avery." Everyone else faded back into their own conversations, but Chet's gaze wandered down her dress and back up. A look of appreciation made him look less studious and more laissez-faire. He peered into the almost empty glass in her hand. "Can I get you another drink?"

"Sure!" She started to hand the glass over, but Vanessa clamped a hand onto her arm. "Avery? Can I have a word?"

"Ow." She tried to shake her, but the woman had some grip.

"This won't take long. I promise," Van said to Chet. A fake smile wrinkled her nose as she dragged her away. "We'll be right back."

"Let go of me," Avery hissed once they'd cleared the fireplace. "What is the *matter* with you?"

Vanessa released her, but she confiscated the glass and smelled it. "Seriously? A martini? When's the last time *you* chugged a martini?"

She sighed, but instantly regretted it when she caught a whiff of her own breath. "I'm just nervous, okay?" she whispered to Van. She'd always hated giving her father bad news, and he was in for a double whammy tonight. First, the fact that the ranch was off limits, and second that she'd decided not to go back to Chicago. She couldn't, or she'd get pulled into her old life again before she knew what had hit her.

Her friend's jaw dropped. "You're telling him *tonight*?"

Rolling her eyes, she shushed Vanessa's loud mouth. She obviously had no training in being discreet. Maybe she could take some lessons from the hostess downstairs. Avery escorted her closer to the bar. "I have to. Before I lose my nerve."

"Oh, boy. You're sure about this? Totally, one hundred percent sure this is what you want?"

"Yes." But the consequences of that one word caused a blast of anxiety that nearly blew her back downstairs and out the door. No. She had to do this. She had to be brave. She set her unfinished martini on the bar and straightened her dress, but before she could march across the room and give it to him straight, Dad strode over to her.

Oh, boy. Her head felt light, like it'd somehow disconnected from her body.

"Is everything okay?" Dad gazed down at her with his concerned father expression, mouth tight, eyes narrow and searching.

She searched his face too, and she saw it in his eyes. He cared about her. He might be terrible at showing it, but he loved her and he would want the best for her. Right?

Dad glanced over at the martini glass. "You don't usually drink. What's going on?"

"Um…well…" She leaned into the bar for support. "Here's the thing, Dad." *Whew. Inhale. Exhale.* "Bryce has some investors," she informed him, making sure to pump an appropriate amount of sympathy into her voice. "We have to find another place to build the resort."

She braced for his reaction, but he simply smirked. "No we don't," he said, folding his arms in a foreboding posture. "That's the president of his lending company right over there." He gestured to one of the gentleman standing near the fireplace. "He's a friend of Mayor Pendleton's."

Understanding settled heavy on her heart. Of course he was. That's what this whole dinner was about. Schmoozing the president of Bryce's bank so her father could work out a deal. She yanked on the sleeve of his suit jacket and directed him to a quiet corner. "What are you doing? What are you going to do to him?"

He pulled away and straightened his jacket, adjusting

the gold cufflinks on his crisp, white shirt. "Don't worry about it, Avery. I'll take it from here."

Panic shut down to her lungs. "I *am* worried about it."

"And why is that?" he asked, even though he clearly already knew the answer.

So what was the point of lying? He'd probably known ever since that day in the hospital room. "Because I care about him. I care what happens to him."

"I figured as much." He sipped his brandy, looking so stately and self-important. Untouchable. "Which is why I had to work things from my angle."

Her bravado collapsed and she no longer felt brave, only sick. "What did you do?"

"Your friend has quite the colorful past," Dad said. "Mayor Pendleton told me all about him."

His alcohol problem. He was talking about Bryce's alcohol problem. Anger trampled her fear, and she didn't need courage. Not anymore. She only needed to be real. "I know about his past."

"He's a loser. With a drinking problem and a hell of a temper, from the sound of things."

"No." She knew him. She'd seen his heart. "He made mistakes." But he wasn't that person anymore. "People change."

"Your mother didn't."

The words were a slap, infuriating, sure, but even more than that, so painful her skin stung. He knew exactly where to jab her to make it hurt the most.

"Don't." She pointed a finger in his face. "Don't you compare him to her. He got help. He's stronger than she was." Cotton filled her throat and pressed a dry, bitter taste into her mouth.

Dad's sturdy shoulders caved. "I'm only trying to protect you, Avery. You have to know that. I want what's best for you."

Her hands clenched in a desperate attempt to get a grip on the emotions that exploded in her chest—pain and loss and a deepening sadness that threatened to swallow her. "Don't protect me. Not anymore." She kept her gaze steady on him so he would know she meant it. "I quit, Dad. I'm done."

"What?"

She wasn't prepared for the wounded look that gouged his cheeks, but she had to do this. "I'm sorry. I can't watch you take away the only thing he has left." Tears flooded her eyes and ran over in warm streaks down her skin. "This resort is *not* Mom's legacy." She touched his arm to get past that cold exterior. "We're her legacy. You and me. Our lives are what will honor her memory." And her life hadn't even started, yet. "I'm not coming back to Chicago," she said quietly. "I'm going to live a life that would make Mom proud." A life of the freedom her mother had craved, but was never able to grasp.

As quickly as it had come, the hurt on Dad's face tightened into a look of rage. "You won't get a dime. Do you understand me? Nothing. You walk away from me, Avery, I swear to god you'll regret it."

An alarming calmness steadied her because she didn't want anything from him. Not anymore. "I love you, Dad." She threw her arms around his stiff shoulders.

Then she turned and left.

CHAPTER TWENTY-ONE

Cold. Holy moly she was so cold. Avery stopped at the end of the block and scanned the deserted streets. Maybe she'd made a wrong turn and ended up in Antarctica.

The wind whipped straight through to her bones as she started out again, feet slipping on the few inches of snow and slush that had piled up on the sidewalk. A swarm of snowflakes blinded her and made it hard to read the street signs. Was she going the right way?

In her haste to flee the restaurant, she hadn't thought to call for the car. The hotel was on the other side of town, maybe three miles away, but, technically, it was her father's car and she no longer had any rights to it, no rights to anything that belonged to him. He'd made that clear.

The streets were quiet for nine-thirty, but beautiful, too, frosted by the new snow. It piled up on the black lampposts that lit the sidewalks in an orange glow. Snowflakes cascaded down, slanted sideways, and danced on the wind. It would've been so peaceful if her muscles weren't stiff.

She paused again and wiped her eyes, tried to see past the blinding snow. Straight. She should go straight, then take a right at the next intersection. At least, she was pretty sure...

Move. She had to keep moving. Putting her head down, she fought the wind and staggered past the warm storefronts that were all closed for the night. Of course. That was one good thing about Chicago. Nothing closed early.

A couple of cars passed her by. One slowed, no doubt to gawk at the crazy lady tromping around the snow in the dress. But then it sped away like the driver might be afraid she'd ask for a ride. Which she might've, come to think of it. Because she definitely needed a ride. There was no way she'd make it back to The Knightley on her own.

Shivers coursed through her and rattled her shoulders. She stopped underneath a store's awning and dug her phone out of her purse. Who could she call? No one who would inform her father on her whereabouts. Not even Vanessa, because she'd freak out and tell Dad and the next thing she knew, he'd be there with the warm car, making her feel guilty for wanting to leave and talking her into staying. Then the point she'd just made wouldn't matter. Besides, it was hard enough to walk away from Dad once. She couldn't do it again.

That left one person. The only local number she had. Bryce. As dangerous as that felt after their little rendezvous last night, it did sound more appealing than hypothermia. Besides that, she had to tell him her father had met with the president of his bank. So, yes. She'd call

Bryce and ask him for a ride back to her hotel. She'd even pay him. Like a taxi. Maybe then it wouldn't feel so personal.

Hands shaking, she scrolled through and found his number.

It only rang once before he picked up. "Avery?"

The deep vibration of his voice in her ear sent a rush through her. "Hi," she almost whispered.

"Hey, I'm glad you called. I'm on my way to your hotel. I need to talk to you."

"I'm not there," she said, her voice weak with the cold. But his words wrapped her in warmth. He was on his way to her hotel? He had to talk to her?

"Where are you?"

"Um..." Her teeth chattered, but her insides glowed. "I'm in town." She turned to look at the storefront window behind her, noticing for the first time the colorful teddies and nighties hanging in the window. Of course it would be the lingerie shop. Of course. At least she was dry and out of the wind...

"Avery? Are you there?" Bryce asked with that thoughtful concern he'd offered her in the hospital.

"Yeah." She cleared her throat. "I'm sort of stranded in front of a store." Was it possible for your face to flush when your skin was frozen? "Um, it's pretty cold out. So...I was hoping you could give me a ride back to my hotel."

"I'll pick you up." She heard the engine of his truck in the background. "Which store?"

Yes. Definitely possible to blush in the middle of a snowstorm. "Um...well...it looks like it's called... um...Intimate Intrigue."

"Seriously?" he said through a laugh. "In that case, I'll be right there."

"They're closed," she grumbled. "And I'm really cold. I didn't realize I'd need my winter coat in *September*."

"I'm two minutes away," he promised, all serious again. "Hang tight."

"Thanks, Bryce." Smile beaming, she clicked off the phone, stuffed it back in her purse, and huddled against the glass to wait.

* * *

Come on. Bryce slowed the truck behind a whole line of red taillights that clogged the highway. His fingers drummed on the steering wheel. Traffic was never this bad after nine. Must've been an accident. No surprise there. First snow of the season always snarled things up. Like people forgot how to drive in four short months or something. Normally a traffic jam didn't stress him out, but he had to get to Avery. He hated to think of her out in the cold. Didn't like the sound of her teeth chattering, and her breathing had come across the line in wispy gasps.

Punching the gas, Bryce swerved around a stalled car on the right and sped up Galena Street and through the center of town. This couldn't be more perfect. He hadn't exactly figured out how he would've gotten into The Knightley to see her, anyway. It was the swankiest hotel in town, designed like a castle, with pale bricks, arched windows, and flawless grounds. He tended to steer clear of places like that, maybe because he knew enough to know he didn't belong there.

But picking her up at Intimate Intrigue...well, let's just say that'd be a lot more fun, especially if she had a full shopping bag. And screw giving her a ride back to her hotel. He was taking her back to the ranch. With him.

He whipped around a corner and spotted Avery huddled under an awning. What the...?

She wore a sleeveless black dress and heels. No coat. In a damn snowstorm. His foot crushed the brake pedal and he shifted the truck into park. Leaving the engine running, he sprinted over to her and shimmied out of his coat. "What're you thinking?" he asked, throwing his coat around her bare shoulders. Now that he was close, he realized her dress was soaked and her skin looked red and chapped.

"It's a long story," she chattered, and damn it, she really was freezing.

"Come here." He pulled her against him and bundled the coat tighter, hustling her toward the truck.

"I'm fine," she insisted, but it would've sounded a lot more convincing without those shallow breaths chugging in and out of her mouth.

"Right. Fine." And people thought he was stubborn. He steered her to the passenger door and yanked it open, then thrust her inside and buckled her seat belt for her.

When he climbed in next to her, she smiled and shook her head. "You really do have some kind of hero complex, don't you?"

"You could've gotten hypothermia." Blasting the heat, he peeled out and pulled an illegal U-turn so he could get her back to the lodge. Get her warm and safe. Get her in his arms where she belonged.

"So, Bryce," she said, and did he imagine it or did

she suddenly sound shy? "We need to talk. It's about the ranch. My father—"

"No," he interrupted. "We'll have plenty of time to talk, Avery. Okay?" He glanced over at her, noting the fact that she was still shivering. "First I want to get you warm. Then I have some things to say." He wouldn't let her say anything until he told her what he'd done, how he'd started out on the road toward healing...

"Wait..." She glanced out the window. "This isn't the way to my hotel."

"I know." He didn't bother to hide his smile. Obviously, she didn't like letting other people into the driver's seat, but tonight she didn't have a choice. "Forget your hotel." Reaching over the console, he rubbed his free hand up and down her arm. "I'm taking you back to my place. I'm gonna warm you up, make sure you don't have frostbite and all that." Oh, yes. He would make sure she got warm.

He drove fast, wheels skidding on ice, the truck's backend fishtailing, and finally turned off the highway.

"Slow it down, buddy." Avery laughed. "This isn't the Indy 500."

Even so, he made it home in record time.

After he parked in front of the office, he whisked her out of the truck.

"Bryce!" She gasped out another laugh. "Are you always this crazy?"

"Only when I'm trying to rescue beautiful women," he murmured, gathering her under his arm as they tromped up the steps to his apartment above the office.

"And how often do you rescue beautiful women?" she teased.

"Well, this week I've been swamped." He shot her a meaningful look as he opened the door.

Moose woofed and jumped and sniffed, but he nudged the dog away with his knee and took Avery straight into the master bathroom.

"Um …." She looked up at him, uncertainty blaring in her eyes. "What're we doing in your bathroom?"

Before he could answer, Moose busted through the door and jumped on her, licking her face, nuzzling her chest with his head. And yes, it made him just a little jealous.

"Hey there, Moose." She smiled down at the dog, and Bryce wanted to kiss those flawless lips right then and there, but he had more important things to do at the moment.

"Moose, down," he commanded. The dog dropped to the floor, resting his head on his front paws and peering up at Avery.

"Good dog," she murmured, patting his head.

Lovesick dog was more like it. But he could relate. *Anyway…* "Best way to get warm is to take a hot bath," Bryce informed her as he kneeled down to crank on the faucet in the oversized tub he'd never used.

"That's not necessary," she murmured breathlessly. He'd never heard her sound more afraid.

"It'll warm you up faster than anything else. Trust me." He swiped a clean towel from the cabinet and set it next to the tub. "Don't worry. I'm not planning to hang out and watch." Though he wouldn't mind, but she obviously didn't want that. "You can take your time. I'll go make a fire."

"Okay," she said, but her eyes shifted like she was uncomfortable. Yeah. That was his fault. Last night, he'd walked away, leaving her bare and vulnerable. Hopefully one mistake hadn't ruined his chances with her.

He moved toward the door. "I'll find something dry for you to wear and leave it on the bed." Stepping into his bedroom, he closed the bathroom door, then went to the very back of his closet and pulled out the heavy bathrobe he never wore. At least it'd keep her warm. Maybe he could throw her dress in the dryer...

"Bryce?" Avery's muffled voice came through the door.

He hurried over. "Yeah?"

The door opened and she stood there still clothed in that soaked dress, which happened to accentuate her perfect cleavage.

"Um..." Her face glowed even redder than it had out in the snow. "I can't seem to get the zipper down."

Well, shit. That meant he'd have to touch her, to see what hid under her dress. "Are you sure?" he asked. Because once he touched her, it wouldn't be easy to stop.

"I've tried," she muttered, like this was much harder on her than it was on him. It probably was. It'd be a lie to say he wouldn't enjoy it.

"I pulled on it, but it started to rip."

"Okay." No problem. He just couldn't think about how much he wanted to ravage her right now. Careful not to touch her skin, he gathered her hair in his hand so he could locate the zipper.

As he undid the clasp, a slow breath leaked through his lips. God, she smelled good.

Carefully, he tugged on the zipper. It didn't budge. Of course. Now he'd have to touch her. Sure enough, his fingers grazed the soft skin on her shoulders as he tugged harder. Finally, the zipper gave. "How'd you get stuck in front of the underwear store?" he asked to distract himself from the slow reveal of her bra and underwear.

"I was actually at Elevation 8,000," she said, her voice as guarded as his movements. "With my father and some of his friends."

"Must've been some dinner," he said, studying the sexy cut of the dress.

"Yeah. That's actually what I wanted to—"

"If you went to dinner, how'd you end up at the store?" he asked to take the focus off her body. Because through the zipper's open slit, he caught a glimpse of some tight lacy slip contraption that she'd probably picked up from someplace like Intimate Intrigue. Tightening his fists, he stepped back so his hands wouldn't sneak right in and caress her soft, scented skin...

"I quit my job," she murmured.

"What?" He stilled. She'd quit? She'd walked away from her father?

"I told Dad I wanted to move away." A shaky strength fortified the words. "He got mad and cut me off from everything. So I left."

He slipped in front of her so he could see her eyes. She was moving away from Chicago. His heart thumped hope into his body. "Where are you moving?"

Her eyes avoided his. "I don't know yet. I'm thinking California."

Damn. Not what he wanted to hear.

"Avery..." He went to touch her, but she stepped back.

"Um...thanks for getting the zipper." She shuffled awkwardly toward the vanity, keeping her backside positioned away from him.

"Sure," he said casually, like every pulse point in his body wasn't thrumming with want.

"So I guess I'll take a bath," she whispered, her face blotchy.

"And I'll go make a fire," he replied, his eyes still linked with hers.

Then he'd make her the best mug of hot chocolate she'd ever tasted and prove to her that he was worth a second chance.

CHAPTER TWENTY-TWO

Well...she couldn't stay here forever. Avery sat up in the tub, water trickling down her body. It was a dangerous place to be...submerged in Bryce's tub. In Bryce's bathroom. In Bryce's apartment. At Bryce's ranch. He'd been right. The bath had definitely warmed her up. Blood rushed through her, pounding anticipation into her body. Bryce was there. Right outside the door. Waiting for her.

But he'd seen her—all of her—and it hadn't been enough to keep him from running out on her the last night. Tough for a girl to forget that feeling. Tough to let go of the fear she wouldn't be enough for him now, either.

Straining her ears, she eased out of the water and stepped onto the warm tile. Radiant heat. It rose up her legs as she snatched the fluffy gray towel Bryce had left out.

The bathroom was nicely lit with an oiled bronze

sconce above the double vanity. A light-colored granite countertop highlighted the two copper sinks and their vessel faucets. The place was so neat, it looked lonely, like there should've been hair products and a blow dryer and make-up strewn about. Maybe there had been, once.

Shuffling across the tile, she pressed her ear against the door. Nothing but silence. So Bryce must not be in the bedroom, thank goodness. Just in case, she cracked it open and peeked through. Another neat room. Everything about it was so him, from the hand-built log bed frame, which had to be a California king, to the matching nightstands and dresser. A masculine grayish color dulled the walls, but the old-school Aspen Mountain framed ski posters brought in pops of color.

Satisfied that she was alone, she opened the door fully and looked around. The door to the bedroom had been closed, since Bryce seemed to think of everything. Just like when he'd brought her all that stuff in the hospital...

Nope. Not going there. Not now. Instead, she toweled herself off and slipped on the navy blue bathrobe he'd laid out on the bed. It smelled like him, that hint of mountains and pine, but she couldn't imagine Bryce Walker wearing a bathrobe. He was too manly. She'd pictured him as the kind of man who walked around naked and unashamed. *Oops.* Those thoughts were restricted at the present time. Off limits.

Let's get this over with.

In front of the door, she paused and locked in a breath for an extra dose of strength. Her heart beat like dragonfly wings, too fast and out of control, but she gripped the doorknob and pushed the door open anyway.

Bryce sat on a black leather sectional in front of a roaring fire. She could feel the warmth of it all the way across the room. The whole scene in front of her was so cozy, warm and inviting. She'd missed it on the way in, but his open-concept kitchen and living room weren't quite as neat. Gorgeous, but lived in, too.

"Feel better?" Bryce grinned at her, a sly enticing grin that made her re-tie the belt of the robe into a secure knot. As if he could undo it with one look.

Moose scampered over to her, wagging and licking, which seemed to be his two favorite activities. She ran a hand over his soft fur. "Hey, buddy."

"I made hot chocolate." Bryce's eyes were brighter than they'd been yesterday when she left.

He patted the cushion next to him, and she had no choice. She couldn't turn down chocolate.

"Thanks." She crept over and sat on the couch, making sure to leave a generous space between them, but he scooted closer and reached down to pull her feet into his lap.

"I should check you out for frostbite." He gave her a stern glare, but a grin peeked through. "Can't believe you wore those open heels in a snowstorm." His fingers probed her feet.

Her body hummed with approval, but she cleared her throat and tried to maintain her weakening grip on the cliff of rationality. He was simply inspecting her feet for damage. That was all.

Bryce carefully ran his fingers over the bottom of each foot, and it shouldn't have been sensual because he really was inspecting them, prodding and feeling and rubbing, but she was already so charged that he practically had her squirming with pleasure.

"They look good." He placed her feet back on the floor, and she almost begged him not to stop, but she did have her dignity. Sort of.

Seeming oblivious to her severe disappointment, Bryce lifted one of the ceramic mugs from the coffee table and held it out to her with an adorable look of hope, a silent *I hope you like it.*

She took it from his hands, unable to fight off the smile the rose from deep within her, and when she sipped the creamy, sweet concoction, she fell in love with him a little more.

"I'm sorry I ruined your night." She faced him, not so afraid anymore—of him, of what he made her feel.

"You didn't ruin my night." He shot her that enticing grin, and, yes...she was in trouble. Big trouble.

He could've simply picked her up and dropped her off at her hotel. She would've thanked him and told him to have a nice life. Instead, she was sitting on his couch, wearing his bathrobe, sipping the best hot chocolate she'd ever tasted in front of a romantic fire.

So much for protecting her heart.

"Actually," Bryce sat upright. "You made things easier for me. I was on my way to see you. At *The Knightley.*" He pronounced it with a terrible British accent, which earned a laugh. Or maybe she laughed because he'd been coming to see her. At her hotel. He was coming for her.

"Why'd you want to see me?" she asked, sliding her hair behind her ear, slipping into junior high mode once again, because it felt like she was experiencing all of these feelings for the very first time.

Bryce's face sobered, but his eyes still gleamed. "I went to the accident site today."

She searched his face for the pain she'd seen there, but it had been replaced with a look of hope.

That same hope sparked inside of her. Instead of retreating, instead of pushing her away, Bryce looked into her eyes, clear and steady. Determined.

"I remembered everything about that day. Things I didn't want to remember."

"That must've been so hard," she whispered. The burden of what he'd had to do settled on her chest and commanded her to break the no-touching rule and reach for him. Her hand covered his, fingers stroking the rough skin on his knuckles.

"Yeah. It wasn't easy." He turned his hand up so their palms melded together. "I know it'll take time, but I can see a life now. Not just an existence. I see a future."

"I'm happy for you." The warmth from his hand seeped into her. She'd never felt so connected to someone, so captivated. And now she knew he felt it, too.

"The thing is..." Bryce exhaled and shifted to face her. "I never had a reason to let go. Not until I met you." His hand reached to her face. Tenderly, his fingers swept her hair behind her ear, then trailed down her neck in a soft caress. "I'm not good at this. At words." Eyes flickering with hesitation, he dropped his hand back to his lap.

Smiling, she set her mug on the coffee table, then eased onto her knees and tugged his face close to hers. "I think you're doing okay," she whispered. "In fact, I think you're doing better than okay."

A slow grin changed his face, erasing every trace of that hesitation and drawing her lips to his because she couldn't hold back anymore. He was strong in the hardest way possible and she wanted him to know that, to feel it in the very core of his soul.

Her lips brushed his with a heat like fire, but it wasn't nearly enough. She worked her fingers into his hair and pressed in harder, tasting the salty sweetness of his lips.

He still held his mug, balancing it in his hand, raising it in the air while he kissed her back. "Whoa, slugger," he murmured between kisses.

She stole the mug out of his hand and set it next to hers, then shifted so she could straddle his legs. "I love it when you call me that."

He laughed a low, sexy sound and leaned closer to her ear. "Slugger," he whispered, slipping his hands under the robe, then gliding them up her bare thighs. "Slugger, slugger, slugger." His tongue got involved in the action and sent a shock down to her toes.

She lowered her hands to the edge of his shirt and pulled it over his head in one smooth motion. Then her fingers inched their way down his bare chest and over his tight abs to unbutton his jeans.

"Avery." His hands swallowed hers. "You don't have to...this isn't why I—"

"I know I don't have to," she cut in before he could finish. "I want this." So much she could hardly even utter those words. They were too real, too revealing, but she couldn't contain them because Bryce made her ache, and he was right there in front of her, open and unguarded.

With a surrendering sigh, he reached up and smoothed his hand over her hair before pulling her mouth back to his, kissing her with a restrained desperation. His hands traveled down her sides, slipping under the robe again, skimming her skin, sliding over the curve of her hips, then up her stomach, higher and higher until the hard pound of her heart resounded through her.

"Bryce," she gasped, because that was all she could manage. It was a question, a command, a plea all in one. His eyes connected with hers and the force of his stare pierced her somewhere deep. She could feel it, her heart fusing with his in this mysterious bond that pried her open. Alone she wasn't enough, but he gave her a glimpse of the wholeness her heart craved.

She wanted more than a glimpse.

Keeping her eyes locked on his, she inched off his lap and took her time tugging his pants off of his hips, pulling them down, down, all the way to the floor. When she straightened back up, he stood there with her, hands cradling her cheeks, wrenching her closer, kissing her like he'd only just discovered what it could do to him, how it could free him. And she felt it, too. Free and bold.

Bryce might not have been much of a talker, but the man could kiss. Yes indeedy, he'd obviously spent a good part of his life honing that important skill.

His lips moved down her neck tracing and kissing, lingering at that magical place just underneath her jawbone, while his hands worked at the belt tied so snug against her waist. "It's like a fortress," he complained, hands pulling, fingers untying, while his mouth molded to hers again and they both laughed.

Finally, he freed her of it and slipped the robe off her shoulders. "I haven't stopped thinking about you since last night," he groaned. "About your perfect body..." His lips traveled lower, tenderly grazing each of her breasts until she had to tighten her mouth to keep from crying out. "You're a dream, Avery," he murmured against her, his breath hot on her skin. And that was exactly how he made her feel, treasured and cherished, like he'd searched for her his whole life.

Without another word, Bryce lifted her into his arms as if she weighed nothing, then lowered her to the floor in front of the fireplace.

The dancing light softened his face and flickered on his upper body. Such a scenic body. Her eyes worked their way down to his black boxer briefs. She really should do something about those...

She tried to sit up, but Bryce pressed her shoulders firmly to the floor and rocked onto his knees next to her. "Stay there," he said, and the enticing grin made her back melt into the floor.

Starting at her feet, he slowly massaged his way up her legs, kneading his fingers over her calves, then her knees, pausing to caress her inner thighs before inserting his fingers and stroking her in a gentle, fluid rhythm. And oh wow. He knew exactly where to touch, where to tug, where to press, and he took his time with the exploration of her, slowly taking her over, body and soul, claiming her with a selfless devotion. Lowering his face to hers, he kissed her mouth with a slow, lingering heat, then worked his lips to her ear. "What do you want, Avery?" he droned, sending a deep vibration down her left side.

How could he ask her that when his hand played her body this way, like he'd always known his way around her? How could he even wonder when she was quaking at the sheer extravagance of his touch?

"You," she whispered, turning her gaze to his, losing herself in the promise that softened his eyes.

His fingers plunged deep then, the explosive sensations swelling into her lower abdomen and arching her back. Was she even breathing?

She must've been, but air didn't fill her lungs before she had to gasp to get hold of herself. Heat pulsed so hard between her legs she knew he had to stop. This wasn't enough. She wanted to take him where he'd brought her, to erase the cold loneliness that had edged in around his heart. She wanted to connect with him in the most intimate way possible.

Scooting out of his reach, she rose on her shaky knees and slid those briefs right down his legs until he was exposed before her.

His sharp intake of air was cut off by her lips. Her tongue teased his before she pulled away and trailed her hands down his body, over his hips, taking her time, kissing her way down his neck and across his stationary chest. "Breathe," she commanded him, and his shoulders slumped with a weighted exhale.

"God, Avery, you have no idea what you're doing to me," he uttered as if he'd forgotten how to inhale.

She did know. She understood, felt his needs as strongly as she felt her own. Pressing her lips against his, she breathed him in and closed her hand around him, feeling the hard pulse of his desire. Stroking and tugging, she caressed him until he panted her name.

"Avery...how'd I live without you?" He stared into her eyes, his breaths ragged.

"You don't have to anymore," she murmured against his lips. Somehow, in this world full of pain and sorrow, they'd found each other. And she wouldn't let him go.

"Make love to me, Bryce." She guided his hands to her

backside and he lifted her against him, still on his knees, still hard and strong and powerful.

"Avery," he panted again as he thrust into her. Shards of delight splintered inside of her as she wrapped her legs around his waist and hooked her ankles tight.

Holding her securely against him, Bryce kissed her neck, her cheek, her forehead, and she'd never trembled like this, dangling over that cliff, holding on with everything she had because she didn't want it to end.

"I've never wanted anyone like I want you," he murmured breathlessly against her hair.

"Me either," she gasped, and it was the truth.

Rocking his hips, he caught her in an electrifying rhythm. She murmured words in his ear, though she had no idea what she was saying because the force of him consumed her, pushing her farther over the edge with each thrust. It intensified—the heat, the friction, until she cried out, until she was seizing and gasping in his arms. He came after her, breathing her name, clutching her tight in a series of aftershocks, before pulling out and lowering them both to the floor in a heap of heavy breaths. He fit her back to his chest and spooned his body around hers, stroking her arm with a light touch.

"Thank you." He whispered into her hair, then kissed the back of her head with a cherished sweetness. Wrapping his arms around her, he held her tightly against him so that his heartbeat resounded through her.

And she'd never felt so content.

CHAPTER TWENTY-THREE

The heaviness of a deep, comatose sleep weighted his eyelids. Bryce turned over. His arm landed on the deserted pillow next to him. He yawned, scrubbed open his eyes. It'd been a long time since he'd slept like this, completely oblivious, dead to the world. Had to be the extra warmth in his bed, the feel of Avery's form against his. He'd forgotten how much he missed sleeping next to someone. Not that they'd slept much. After spending most of the night talking and making love by the fire, he'd finally carried her to bed only a couple of hours ago.

And yet somehow he felt energized.

The smell of bacon and coffee wafted through his open bedroom door. He inhaled. There was something so warm and familiar about those scents...

"Breakfast?" Avery appeared in the doorway.

That was all it took to wake the rest of his body.

She wore one of his button-up shirts, but she'd missed

a few buttons. Her hair was pulled loosely on top of her head spilling down over the bare shoulder that peeked out from the unbuttoned collar. In her hands, she balanced a tray that held two plates piled high with bacon and slightly blackened French toast, along with two mugs of steaming coffee.

"You cook?" He almost laughed. Just when he thought nothing in this world could get better than last night...

"Sure. Maybe not to Elsie's standards, but I can fry up bacon and French toast, thank you very much."

She walked toward him, her long, toned legs demanding his attention. Still wrapped in the sheets, he leaned over to steal the tray from her hands, but she swiped it out of reach.

"What's the hurry? I thought we'd have a long, leisurely breakfast. Especially since we never got the chance to have a snack last night." Her smirk reprimanded him.

"Sorry. My fault. It's just..." What could he say? He was making up for lost time. "I can't keep my hands off of you."

The corners of her mouth curled in a teasing smile. "How come?"

Yeah, right. She knew exactly what she did to him.

He ran a hand up her thigh. "You look good in my shirt." His fingers fumbled with the buttons. "But you'd look even better without it."

She laughed. "We don't want our breakfast to get cold." But she perched the tray on the nightstand.

"I like my French toast cold." He captured her in his arms and pulled her down next to him. "Freezing, in fact." He pulled his body over hers. "Which is good. Because what I have in mind might take awhile."

"Oh yeah?" She wrapped her leg around him.

He slid his hands under the shirt and felt his way up her smooth, silken skin. Touching his lips to hers, he groaned. "You're gorgeous. And sexy. And flexible. Damn near perfect."

Avery laughed again but this time it sounded hollow. "Trust me. I'm not perfect. Not even close to perfect."

He pulled back and propped himself on his elbow to study her face.

Her gaze evaded his.

Uh oh. "What's wrong?"

"Nothing," she said, but he recognized the worry in her eyes, the way they shifted back and forth like she didn't know where to look. He'd seen Yvonne do that a number of times, especially when she was afraid to tell him something. Back then, he'd let it go, afraid of her emotions, afraid he wouldn't be enough to help her deal with them. But not now. He wanted to be worthy of Avery's trust.

"Hey." He lifted her chin. "What is it?"

She laid her head back on the pillow. "Sorry. I checked my phone. I shouldn't have. Six messages from my father. I feel awful."

"You've got to be kidding me. Why would he leave six messages?"

"To tell me what a disappointment I am. To remind me how much he's given me over the years. To beg me to come back to work."

"You are *not* a disappointment." He took her chin in his hand and forced her to look at him. "You're compassionate and beautiful and funny and smart." He found his phone on the nightstand. "Want me to call and tell him that?"

"No." She turned her head to the side and looked at him. Curls spilled down over her shoulder and tempted his hand to brush them back.

He ditched the phone and gathered her into his arms, lowering his mouth to her ear. "You don't have to go back. We can hide out all day," he teased.

Avery didn't smile. She stared at the ceiling. "I have no idea what I'll do, Bryce. Where I'll go. Where I'll work..."

Ah, yes. The fear of the unknown. He knew all about that. Ever since she'd told him she'd quit, he'd wondered when the panic would kick in. She seemed like a pretty scheduled person. Not exactly the spontaneous type. Lucky for her, he had more experience in that department. "You have nothing to worry about," he told her with authority.

"Really?" She looked at him, eyes skeptical.

He grinned. "Really. I've got the day all planned out. First we'll take a shower. Then a nap." He emphasized the word so she'd know he didn't mean sleeping. "Then we'll eat. Another nap. Maybe sit in the hot tub..."

Avery's smile returned. That was exactly what he'd wanted to see.

He kissed her lightly, then gazed into her eyes. "Seriously. You can stay here as long as you want. Until things blow over with your father." And a helluva lot longer than that, if she chose to. Not that he would tell her that, yet. He couldn't push her. Not today. In some ways, they were both learning to live in the moment, to move forward, to leap uninhibited into an unknown future. He wanted to walk into that with her, but she needed time to figure out what she wanted.

"Thank you." She traced his lips with her finger. "That means—"

Behind him, his cellphone buzzed and bounced.

"Sorry." He swiped it up and glanced at the screen. "Don't recognize the number." Probably a sales call, but it also could've been his bank. He'd been trying to talk to someone since his conversation with Ben.

"Hang on a sec," he said to Avery, then swung his legs over the side of the bed and clicked on the phone. "This is Bryce."

"Mr. Walker." There was something vaguely familiar about the voice, formal and cold...

"This is Edward King."

Yup. That was it. "Hang on." He glanced over his shoulder at Avery, who had sat up and was leaning against the headboard innocently sipping her coffee, looking bright and happy. Couldn't ruin that moment for her. So he scooted off the bed and covered the speaker. "I'm gonna take this in the living room," he said cheerfully.

"Hurry back," she called.

"Definitely." Unfortunately, something told him this wouldn't be a quick conversation. As soon as he was out of range, he lifted the phone back to his ear. "What can I do for you, Mr. King?"

"Tell my daughter you don't want her. Send her back to the hotel. Don't contact her again. And I'll make sure you keep your ranch."

Was this guy for real?

"I won't do that to her." He couldn't. Not after last night. Not after he knew how it felt to sleep next to her. He couldn't go without that. Not anymore. Besides, he'd be able to hold onto the ranch. With Ben's help.

"I had a feeling you would say that," King said. "So you can consider this your notification that your ranch is going to auction. Next Wednesday. I'll see you at the county building."

Auction? The room closed in on him. He couldn't breathe. The man was bluffing. He had to be bluffing. "That's not possible."

"It is when you know the president of the lending company," the jackass stated.

"You can't do this." But the words were no match for Edward King and he knew it. The man had the money and the notoriety to do whatever the hell he wanted.

"It's already done." King paused. "It's been 120 days since you received your Notice of Election and Demand. Your bank filed the paperwork this morning. The property will be auctioned off to the highest bidder, and I think we both know who that will be."

Shock held him in a vise. He couldn't breathe or blink or swallow. Millions. Edward King had millions of dollars. He couldn't come up with enough to outbid him. Not even if he worked the rest of his damn life.

"I'm surprised Avery didn't mention it," her father droned in that tight grating tenor. "She knew."

"No." He glanced across the room and saw her through the open bedroom door, sitting on his bed. The bed they'd slept in together. "She wouldn't keep something like that from me."

"She's very loyal to me, Mr. Walker. Remember that." He paused. "You can expect your official notice from the bank later today." A click sounded and the line went dead.

The phone fell from his hand and hit the floor. He'd

lost it. Everything. Edward King had taken it all away. And Avery had helped him?

"Looks like our breakfast is getting col—" she stepped through the door, but stopped when she looked at him. "Bryce? What's wrong? Who was on the phone?"

"Why didn't you tell me?" He eased in breaths between the words so he didn't shout at her, but blood pumped through him, hot and fast, and he knew he had to get out of there.

"Tell you what?" Her eyes were round with innocence.

He stepped as close as he dared, but not close enough that she could touch him. "That your father was schmoozing the president of my bank."

Her mouth dropped open in a look of fear, and that was all he needed to see. She knew. She knew and she hadn't told him.

He swept past her, into the bedroom, and blindly ripped clothes out of drawers.

"Stop." She followed behind him. "Bryce, please. Calm down."

"Calm down?" He yanked on his pants and sweatshirt. "I'm gonna lose the ranch. Do you get that? This place is my life, Avery. And next week they're gonna auction it off to the highest bidder. Which'll no doubt be your father."

She smoothed her hands over his shoulders. "I'm sorry, Bryce. I love the ranch, too."

He jerked away from her, fury stinging down his arms. "Don't do that."

"Do what?" she shot back, like she had any right to be mad at him.

"Pretend that you care. Pretend that you're not the same person as your father." He got in her face. "My grandparents built this place themselves. I grew up here. I got married here. Yvonne and I *lived* here together..."

She flinched like he'd slapped her.

His words echoed back to him. *Wait.* That wasn't what he'd meant. He'd only meant this was his home...

But anger tapered her eyes. "I'm not pretending, Bryce. None of that was pretend. I quit my job because I couldn't be part of it anymore."

"Yeah, well the damage was done, wasn't it?" He knew he was being an asshole, but she'd been part of it from the beginning. She'd set the whole thing in motion coming out there, staying with him, feeding information to her father.

She didn't back down, didn't shrink away from him like he wanted her to. "That's not fair," she said, her jaw set with determination. "I started to tell you, but you wouldn't listen. Then I just..." Her cheeks reddened. "I got distracted."

So she was blaming him? "I can't deal with this right now." Once again, he bolted past her, through the living room.

"No!" she yelled after him. "You don't get to leave. We need to talk about this. You owe me that."

"I don't owe you anything." He ripped open the door.

"Where are you going?" Avery demanded.

"I have to talk to Ben," he bit out, then slammed the door behind him.

He had to figure out how to come up with the money to outbid Edward King before he lost everything.

* * *

The slam of the door shook the walls, shook her. A cold loneliness spread all through her until she felt like she was back on that snowy city block again, shivering and alone. Lost.

Bryce was right. She could've stopped this a long time ago. She could've worked harder to talk Dad out of the ranch. She knew what he was capable of. She'd seen him go after properties like that a hundred times.

The burden of it all deflated her to the couch.

"*Mmmwooof.*" Moose pranced over to her, wedging himself as close as he could, then plopping down on her feet. She ran her hand over the dog's soft coat, and he licked her toes sympathetically while she cried. She'd never been much of a crier, but then again, her heart had never hurt like this. She'd given Bryce everything last night, all of her, and it still wasn't enough to make him stay, to make him talk to her. He still chose the ranch, his memories, over her.

They'd spent most of the night curled up together in front of the fire. He'd talked about his grandparents, about growing up here, about how he'd fish in the spring pond that always formed down in the meadow. He'd told her a story about chasing a bear away from his mom's cherry pie while it cooled on the back porch. This ranch wasn't only his home; it was part of his identity.

Moose looked up at her with his doleful eyes and she realized she'd stopped petting him. "Sorry, buddy." She gave him a good scrub behind the ears, then prodded him to the side so she could stand up. Because sitting on the couch crying wouldn't change anything. And maybe, just maybe she could change things for Bryce before she pursued her new life in California.

Maybe she could make sure Bryce didn't lose the ranch.

With Moose hot on her heels, she hurried to her purse, dug out her phone, and found Vanessa's number.

Van answered before it even rang. "Avery? Where the hell are you? I've been worried out of my mind." The words were strung together without a breath. "Seriously. I drove all over looking for you last night."

"I'm fine," she lied. "But I need you to pick me up. At the Walker Mountain Ranch."

Vanessa gasped.

Before her friend could say a word, she cut in. "I need you to bring clothes, too."

"Ohhh...someone had a good night. Do tell, chica. I want details."

"We'll talk when you get here," Avery ground out. "I'm in Bryce's apartment, above the office. Come on up."

"See you soon! Can't wait!" Van sang, then the line went dead.

While she waited, Avery busied her hands with washing the breakfast dishes, wiping up the countertops, and tidying Bryce's place. She always thought best when she was in motion, and as she loaded the ceramic plates in the dishwasher, thoughts and ideas and strategies flooded her, flowing together until the currents of a plan—a good, solid plan—swept away her sadness.

"Avery!" Van sang from the bottom of the steps.

"Coming!" Energy buzzed through her as she dashed over and opened the door.

Moose barked, leaping and bounding, overjoyed with a new person to fall in love with, but Van warded him off with her outstretched hands. "Holy Moses! What the hell is that thing? A horse?"

"His name is Moose, and he's the sweetest puppy ever," she cooed, unfazed by her friend's look of horror.

"Puppy? You call that thing a *puppy*? Back off, killer." Van hid behind Avery, even though she also had a dog, Smidgen the Wonder Yorkie. Of course, he weighed about five pounds and rode everywhere in her purse.

"Go lay down, Moose," Avery commanded him like Bryce. And he listened. He actually slunk to his massive pillow near the fireplace and curled up in a sulk. "Good boy!" She'd have to slip him one of those oversized doggie bones she'd seen in the cupboard before she left.

"So, is Bryce dressed yet?" Van inquired with a smirk. "In the shower, perhaps?" Her shaped eyebrows dipped together. "Don't hold out me. I know he's taken and everything, but I can still peek."

"He's not here." She snatched the bag of clothes from Van's hand. They didn't have much time. If she was going to save the Walker Mountain Ranch, she'd have to get dressed and get to work. Pronto.

"I'm sorry, what?" Van looked around like she thought it was a joke. "What do you mean, he's not here?"

"He left," she said, ignoring the painful tug of her heart.

"Ouch." Van tugged her to the couch. They sat down. "What happened?"

Submerging an impatient sigh, she started at the beginning. "Dad called him this morning and told him the bank was taking the ranch to auction."

Her jaw dropped. "Wow. Talk about bad timing."

"Yeah. He was pretty pissed off." Really pissed off. Not that she blamed him. "I'm pretty sure he'll never talk to me again."

"That sucks," Van offered. "Sorry, Avery."

But there wasn't time to be sorry. Bryce had said the auction would take place next week. That gave her seven days to pull this thing off. And she'd need all the help she could get. "This isn't about me. I have to help him, Van. I have to save the ranch."

"How? I hate to say this, but it's not like you can out-bid your father."

No. She couldn't. But if she rounded up enough people, maybe they all could. Together. "What if we threw a fundraiser? Like a picnic in the park or something?"

"A picnic in the park," her friend scoffed, shaking her head, bouncing those tight black curls. "Honey, if you want to bring in the big spenders, you're gonna need more than a picnic in the park." With an exaggerated roll of her eyes, she practically pushed Avery off the couch. "Go get dressed. We've got work to do."

CHAPTER TWENTY-FOUR

The aftereffects of last night's snowstorm still lingered in the form of slushy roads and a billowing fog, but that didn't stop Bryce from gunning the engine and taking the curves too fast all the way down to the highway. Traffic flowed through the roundabout, splattering muddy sludge across his windshield. Messy. Things had gotten so damn messy. He flicked on the wipers, ignoring the way regret nagged him to flip a U-turn and go back to her. To tell her he was sorry.

He hadn't meant to lose it like that. Not with Avery. Bryce checked the rearview mirror, but there was no way he could turn around. Cars packed him in on both sides; some headed into town, some headed for the hills. Typical fall day in Aspen when the leaves were peaking.

Didn't matter, anyway. He'd walked out on her twice now. Relationships didn't usually recover from things like that. She was probably using his computer to purchase a one-way plane ticket to Cali right now, dreaming up a new life with someone who wasn't such an ass. He knew one thing for sure: she deserved better.

For three years, he'd kept a tight leash on his heart and in less than two weeks, she'd managed to snap it. If he was honest with himself, staying with her, talking things out, would've been harder. There was more risk involved. If she'd managed to do this to him in less than two weeks, what would happen if he lost her in five years?

He accelerated as if he could really outrun the mess he'd made, the memory of the way her face had fallen when he'd told her this was her fault. As if she was to blame for all the shit that had happened to bring him to this point.

She wasn't. He was. Now he only had one option left. Taking the wheel in one hand, he fished out his cell and found Ben's number.

After a couple of rings, he answered. "What's up, Walker?"

Too much to go into on the phone. "Can you meet me for a burger?"

"Uh. Yeah. Sure." Ben hesitated. "What time?"

"Now would be good."

"Wow." A lengthy pause made him wonder if the call had been dropped. "Everything okay?" Ben finally asked.

"Not sure, yet," he answered honestly, because he didn't have time to beat around the bush.

"Where d'you wanna meet?"

Bryce fired off the address to the only place he'd ever eat a burger in Aspen. "See you there." He clicked off the phone and stuffed it back into his pocket, then zipped through town before cranking the wheel to squeeze the truck into the parking lot of the restaurant Paige's family owned.

THE HIGH ALTITUDE CAFÉ
WHERE FUN AND MOUNTAINS MEAT.

A few years back, *Aspen Monthly* had crowned Paige's dad the King of Bad Puns. The name fit the establishment. Cheesy. That was the only way to describe it. Originally the place had been built as a saloon and a brothel, serving the miners who'd settled there in the early 1920s. When the Harper family bought it thirty years ago, it had been condemned. Paige's dad rebuilt it himself, trying to maintain the original integrity of the structure, if there was such a thing. He'd kept the two-story floor plan and imported bricks that matched the originals. The problem was, he didn't know what the hell he was doing, so the place ended up looking lopsided and crooked, though he swore by the stability. Somehow it'd passed inspection, proving miracles did happen.

Bryce chose a parking spot on the outskirts of the lot and got out of the truck. He passed the constellation of neon signs that buzzed and flickered against the large window. *Budweiser. Corona. Blue Moon.* And his personal favorite, *Coors Light.* What could he say? He was a Colorado man through and through. It was cheap and went down easy. A little too easy.

Man, he could use a beer right now. He inhaled until that craving subsided, knowing he couldn't go back. Not after everything he'd been through to get sober.

Shoving open the wooden door, he ducked inside. The place was a total dive, but that was the best part about it. None of that swanky music. No stuck-up celebrities gliding around in their fur and leather and whatever the hell else they wore. Just the local crowd—the ski bums and board rats who worked hard to be able to stuff as many roommates as possible into two-bedroom condos so they could live in one of the most spectacular places in the world—and serve the celebrities.

The inside of the café was as tacky as the outside. The black-and-white linoleum floor didn't seem to match the dark wood-paneled walls. The red vinyl booths looked like they'd been ripped off from a highway diner. Not that he cared. Peter Harper had gotten one thing right. He specialized in meat. All kinds of meat. Bison and elk and beef. Despite the shoddy appearance of the restaurant, the High Altitude Café's burgers had been featured on the Food Network twice.

For a while afterward, there was always a wait, but then the novelty wore off and it usually looked the way it did right now. He glanced around. Not a big crowd. A couple of the regulars. Ted from the dry cleaners. The transient who looked like Santa Claus and lived in a cabin up near Independence Pass...

"Bryce!" Paige rushed out from behind the bar. "Hey." Her face was red and agitated, just like it always was when she had to be around her family.

"What're you doing here?" he asked, trying to hide a grin. Paige was a vegetarian. She hated working at the restaurant. While the rest of her four siblings made it their livelihood, Paige had done everything she could to get away from it.

She rolled her eyes and shook her head. "Filling in for Penny."

He always had to think pretty hard to remember which Harper was which. Didn't help that they all had P names.

Peter and Patsy were the parents. Then there was Paul, the oldest. Penny came next; at least he was pretty sure of that. Then Pearl, then Pete Jr. Paige was the youngest by ten years, one of those little surprises that had seemed to throw her parents off. They'd never known what to do with her.

"What about you?" She laid her hands on her hips, giving him a cross-examination. "What're *you* doing here?"

The door *whoosh*ed open and Ben strode in, always on time.

"I'm meeting a friend," he said, but Paige didn't seem to hear. She was too busy watching Ben walk toward them with that look of awe he'd seen on many-a-woman's face whenever he hung out with Noble. He'd played second fiddle to Ben for years when it came to women. Didn't look like this time would be any different. Paige seemed to forget he was even standing there.

"Nothing like the smell of beef in the morning." Ben greeted him with a hearty handshake.

"Wait 'til you taste it," he said, then nudged Paige. "You remember Ben Noble, right?" They'd met, albeit briefly, when they'd gone Jeeping the other day.

"Uh huh." She didn't blink, so he turned to Noble. "Paige's family owns the restaurant."

"Really?" He shot her that grin that had been making women swoon since 1985. "What a place," Ben said. "Can't wait to try the famous burgers."

Paige smiled softly and smoothed her hair behind her ear.

Huh. Bryce had never seen her act like such a girl.

"Get whatever you want," she said sweetly. "It's on the house."

His friend's eyebrows shot up and he increased his smile by about 500 watts. "What*ever* I want?"

Seriously? Bryce cleared his throat. Couldn't let Ben get any ideas about Paige. She was like his little sister. "So...first thing we'll need is a table." They did have things to discuss. And he needed Ben to stop eyeballing Paige like she was a juicy cut of meat.

"Oh. Sure. Right. Yes. A table." Her face turned as red as those vinyl booths. "Right this way." She grabbed two laminated menus and practically sprinted to a booth in the corner. That suited him just fine. Didn't need anyone else listening in.

Once they'd sat down, Paige and Ben picked up their heated staring where they'd left off.

"So, I'll take a Coke," Bryce interrupted. "What d'you want, Noble?" *Besides* the woman who stood in front of them. Because he couldn't have her.

"Same," he answered without taking his eyes off of Paige.

"Two Cokes coming right up," she squeaked.

Had he ever seen her blush like that?

As soon as she was gone, Ben leaned halfway over the table. "How come I've never met Paige before this week?"

"She's not your type." Ben tended to gravitate toward women who didn't expect much of a commitment, and Paige deserved a commitment.

"We're not in college anymore, Walker," Ben said in his lazy drawl. "Maybe I've changed. Maybe I'm looking for somethin' different."

"Yeah, well, you can keep looking. Got that?" He unrolled his silverware and set it out. "Anyway, I didn't bring you here to hit on my friend, who is also the closest thing I have to a little sister. Understand?"

Ben opened his mouth—probably to argue, knowing him—but Bryce shut him down with a glare. "I got a call this morning. They're taking the ranch to auction. Next week."

His friend's face sobered. "Are you kidding?"

"I wish I were."

"Here we are," Paige busted in on the moment, placing their Cokes in front of them. "Are you ready to order?" she asked Ben with a shy smile Bryce had never even seen her use before.

Great.

"We'll both take the heart attack burger," Bryce answered for him. "Everything on it."

"Sounds perfect." Ben's smile had lost some momentum, thank god.

"Okay. That'll be right up." She backed away, eyes locked on Ben's. Then she turned and disappeared into the kitchen.

Ben's jaw was set in the determined look Bryce remembered from their college days. He'd always been as competitive as hell. The guy had never failed at anything, as far as he knew, but there was a first time for everything.

"I'll try to find the funds. Pull some investments. Light a fire under my buddies. We'll work it out," he said like they were talking about hundreds instead of millions.

"Not sure about that." There probably weren't enough funds in the world. "Edward King met with the president of my bank." He told him about the phone call.

When he'd finished, Ben shook his head. "He won't let it go, then. He's cutthroat."

"I'm guessing he'll drive up the price until no else can afford it." Not even Benjamin Hunter Noble III and his group of investors.

Ben kneaded the back of his neck like it killed him that he couldn't help. "If I wasn't launching the campaign, I might be able to outbid him, but there's no way it can happen right now," he said. "Shit, Walker. I'm sorry. I know how much that place means to you."

It was what he'd expected to hear, but the finality of Ben's response made him feel like the rug had been pulled out from under his life. Suddenly, everything was up in the air, floating above him, ready to hit the ground around him. And he didn't know where it'd all land.

He nodded at Ben. "Figured that was the case, but I thought I'd ask." Then, because there wasn't much else to say, he looked out the massive square window at the town that'd always been his home. For the first time in his life, he was groundless. Even when fate had taken his wife, he'd always had the ranch to hold onto. The familiarity had kept him sane. It'd given him a place to heal.

Now, he'd have to learn how to survive without it.

* * *

Ben & Jerry's Cheesecake Brownie ice cream…the breakfast of champions.

Avery slopped another bite into her mouth and let the frozen goodness melt into a sweet cream that soothed all the way down her throat. She eyed the other carton, which she'd practically licked clean, the crumpled frozen pizza box, and the empty bottle of wine that had tipped over on the counter. It appeared that event planning stressed her out. Last night, she and Vanessa had split up to make some phone calls. Then Vanessa had a late meeting with her father and the mayor, so she'd been on her own.

And over the last twelve hours, she'd learned that she sucked at event planning. So far she hadn't even found a venue that was available in three days. She'd failed. Miserably.

But thank god Ben & Jerry didn't judge. Their intricate work in fusing two of the best desserts on the planet proved that they loved her unconditionally, even if she had let Bryce down.

As she dug in for another bite, her phone buzzed for about the hundredth time in an hour. But where was it? Avery tossed down the spoon and raked through the mountain of papers, notes, and pictures strewn across the counter in her suite. *Come on!* She couldn't afford to miss a phone call.

The twinkling buzz of a voice mail ridiculed her. What was she thinking? She couldn't do this. She couldn't pull off a fund-raiser in three days!

Down the hall, the door busted open. "Avery!"

Vanessa's cheery voice inspired a shriek. She tore down the hall and hugged her, nearly knocking them both off balance.

"Wow. You're that desperate, huh?" Van peeled herself away and smoothed out her short, pleated red skirt and sassy, white blouse. Her spiral curls had been pinned to one side, cascading down over her left shoulder. Somehow, the woman always managed to look like she'd just stepped right out of a fashion magazine. Avery looked down at her own attire, which consisted of the hotel's bathrobe. After event planning 101, maybe Van could give her some pointers on her wardrobe.

"Are things really that bad?" her friend asked. "I've only been gone for twelve hours."

"I can't even find my phone," she confessed. "I'm a mess without you."

For any event King Enterprises had ever put on, Vanessa had been the spine, holding it all together, making sure everything ran the way it was supposed to.

"Okay, girl. Settle down." Her friend glided through the hallway and into the kitchen, then stopped when she saw the mess. "Whoa. You've *got* to be kidding me."

Avery shot her a sheepish grin. "Um, yeah. I didn't have file folders or anything. Sorry."

"Are there at least piles?" She shuffled through the papers and held up a torn piece of a magazine. "What the hell is this?"

"Food ideas?" Avery scooted herself onto a stool. "Like I said, I need you. This is never gonna work." Bryce would never get his ranch back...

"Oh, it's gonna work." Vanessa swayed her hips and stood across from her. "We're gonna make it work. Last night, your father came up with a plan for the auction." Her eyebrows peaked. "After he went over the numbers, I figured out we'd need at least twenty-five million to outbid him."

Twenty-five million. *Okay.* That was possible. She'd liquidate all of her assets to get a good start, and she knew for a fact that a million dollars was pocket change for some of her invitees.

"If we're gonna do this, though, we need to get you

organized," Vanessa lamented, and she wasn't kidding. With a militant tone, her friend barked out orders. "Anything that has to do with the guest list goes here." She smacked her palm on the counter. "Food ideas and suggestions go here. Media contact information and appointments go here."

"Got it." She started to rummage through the mess she'd made earlier. "Hey look!" Underneath a copy of *Food & Wine*, she found her phone. "Fifteen messages?" She flicked it onto the counter and backed away. "I need ice cream. Stat."

Prepared with her iPad, Vanessa swooped around her and confiscated the phone.

While she finished off the rest of her ice cream, Van scrolled through her messages, one at a time. "Oh!" She squealed. "Way to go, girl. A local Denver station wants to do an exclusive about the fund-raiser." She checked her watch. "In an hour."

Quickly, she shoveled in another mammoth bite of pure heaven. Truly, it was the break she'd been waiting for, the perfect opportunity to tell the story of the Walker Mountain Ranch to the world.

"I can't." She shook her head, wiping a droplet of ice cream from her chin. "I can't do it, Vanessa. Look at me. I'm a mess." She was too shaky and scatterbrained. And how would the media treat her after the Wrigley Field debacle?

Without a response, Vanessa turned her back. She held up the phone to her ear. "Hi, this is Vanessa Martinez. Miss King's assistant."

"Wait! No! Stop!" She leapt off the stool and made a grab for the phone, but that woman was quick.

"Miss King is happy to do the interview." She snatched a wooden spoon from the counter to ward Avery off.

And she didn't doubt Van would use it.

"You can have your crew here in an hour." After a pause, Vanessa shot her a gloating grin. "You're so welcome. We'll see you soon." She clicked off the phone and raised her hand in victory. "Looks like you're doing the interview."

Avery opened her mouth to stage a protest, but Vanessa silenced her with a single wave of her hand, the way only she could do. "This is part of it, Avery. The more people who see the story, the more donations you'll get. For Bryce. You know this could go national."

She was right. Avery hated it when Van was right. But it happened all the time.

Still gloating, her friend linked her arm with hers. "I'll be with you every step of the way. Now let's get you in the shower and find acceptable interview attire. You wait, girl. I'm gonna turn you into America's sweetheart."

"Fine." She let Van lead her away. "But I'm only doing it for Bryce."

CHAPTER TWENTY-FIVE

The attic had never been Bryce's favorite place. Even as a kid, his stomach got all screwed up tight when Mom asked him to bring something up there. *It stinks*, he'd tell her with a scowl, but really, the damp smell didn't get to him as much as the eerie dim light, the ghostly creaks and moans, the shadows that seemed to shift and spread until they'd captured him in their darkness.

One time, Mom made him haul up a box of winter clothes. He'd pulled on his headlamp, determined to get over his fear, but the second he'd reached the top rung of that pull-down ladder, the attic lights flickered and buzzed out. Shrieking like a little girl, he'd dropped the box of clothes on the floor below. When Mom came running up the stairs, he'd tried to save face and told her he'd run straight into a coon. Mom spent all afternoon searching the attic, but couldn't find even one trace of the coon.

That's because it's a ghost, he'd wanted to tell her. But he'd kept his lip buttoned.

Bryce didn't believe in ghosts anymore, but the stacked boxes in the attic haunted him. They were the sum of his memories, carefully packed away to be forgotten. After the funeral, he'd come home and thrown everything he could find in those boxes. All of Yvonne's clothes and keepsakes and anything else that would dare spark a memory of her. When Mom had come into the room, he'd never forget how she knelt by his side. Silently, reverently, she pulled everything out of those boxes, carefully wrapped any breakables, and took great care fitting the pieces of Yvonne's life back into the boxes. When they were finished, she'd squeezed his hand in her affectionate way. "There's a purpose, Bryce. Even in this. Pain and loss push us to find our true selves. Sometimes we have to reach farther than we ever imagined we could."

Maybe he hadn't reached far enough. Maybe that was why he'd lost the ranch, too.

Bryce pulled down the attic ladder. It crashed to the floor with a thud. One week didn't give him much time to sort through the scenes of his life with Yvonne, to decide what would accompany him to the next, unwritten chapter.

His gut twisted as he pulled himself rung after rung into the cavern of the past. It still smelled like wet dust. His eyes burned and adjusted to the faint light. The outline of the boxes loomed over him like a solid wall. Floorboards creaked as he eased over them, still remembering where the soft spots hid. The first box he removed from the stack was light. He set it on the floor and dug out his pocketknife, slicing the tape in one quick motion.

His hands dug through paper, piles of old cards that he and Yvonne had given each other over the years, love notes they'd written. At the bottom, hidden underneath the paper, was a photo album. He cracked open the binding and found himself staring at pictures of their road trip to Canada the first year they'd been married. Wow, they looked young. Her dark hair was so long, almost down to the middle of her back. Bryce held the picture up to the light, gazing at Yvonne's dark, exotic eyes. But they didn't jolt him like they once had.

They'd been gone on that trip for three weeks, driving all the way up to Banff, then over to Vancouver. God, it was so long ago. Things had been so different. For the first time, it felt like he was looking at pictures from a past life. He flipped through picture after picture, reliving those days, but that trip hadn't all been as blissful as the pictures made it look.

Neither one of them had been good with words, good at talking things out, good at dealing with the shit between them. Instead, they'd pretended everything was fine, his drinking, her depression. Both of those things hid beneath the surface of their life together, making it impossible to build that deep connection they both craved. Maybe things would've gotten better after that fight they'd had before the accident. Maybe. But he didn't know for sure. He'd never know if they would've been able to find that intense connection that would've gotten them through anything.

The kind of connection he'd felt with Avery.

He slammed the book closed and placed it back in the box. Man, he was such an idiot. He'd met Yvonne when they were kids and in some ways their relationship never grew up. He'd loved her the best he could. He'd been committed to her. But Avery made him want to be a better person. She challenged him. He needed that. He needed someone who would put him in his place when the situation demanded. Someone who wouldn't ignore the issues. Someone who could stand against him and stand with him at the same time.

He needed Avery and he'd walked away from her.

Wiping the sweat from his face, he kicked a box out of the way and started down the ladder. He had to find her. He'd drive all the way to California if he had to. He had to tell her that she *was* enough. Even without the ranch, she was more than enough for him.

He'd just stepped a foot down on the hallway carpet when his phone rang. Mom's number glowed on the screen. He brought it to his ear. "Hello?"

"Bryce? Are you at home?" she asked frantically.

"Yeah. Why?"

"Turn on the television right this minute."

He started to fold up the ladder. What, was there another *Murder, She Wrote* marathon on? "I'm kind of in the middle of something." Or at least he would be as soon as he got in his truck and tracked down Avery.

"Bryce Walker, you listen to me," Mom ordered. "This is important. Go. Now."

"Okay, okay." Bracing the phone between his shoulder and ear, he pushed up the ladder and shut the attic's trapdoor, then jogged to the family room and flipped on the television.

"Channel nine," she instructed. "Hurry!"

When the pictured cleared, Avery stared back at him. "What's she doing?"

"Listen," Mom practically sang. "Just listen!"

A blond woman sat across from Avery in a living room. He studied the screen. Looked like a hotel suite. Was she still in Aspen?

"So, Miss King," the blond woman said. "We all know there are plenty of rumors going around, but we want the scoop. Why didn't you marry Logan Schwartz?"

The camera zeroed in on Avery again. The sight made his heart flip. Even as nervous and stiff as she looked, the woman was hypnotizing. She wore a soft sweater and tight black pants. Her hair was loosely pulled back, the way he liked it.

Unable to take his eyes off of her, Bryce sank to the couch.

Avery seemed to hesitate. She uncrossed her legs and sat taller. "Logan is an amazing person, but we wanted different things for our lives."

Her smile nearly made him dizzy.

"He won't have any problem finding a wonderful woman. We're still great friends. I wish him all the best."

Mom clucked in his ear. "Now wasn't that so classy? Bryce? Are you there?"

He grinned. "Yeah. I'm here."

"You're listening, aren't you, dear? Doesn't she look lovely?"

"Lovely," he repeated. *Sexy.* But Mom might not approve of that description.

Blonde interview lady smiled and batted her fake eyelashes. "So, Miss King. You wanted to tell us about a fund-raiser you're hosting in Aspen?"

Fund-raiser? Bryce grabbed the clicker and turned up the volume.

"Did you hear that?" Mom squealed. "A fund-raiser! Isn't it amazing? Can you—"

"Shhh." He meant it as nicely as possible.

Avery still sat ramrod straight, obviously uncomfortable, but she had a fervent glow on her face. "The Walker Mountain Ranch has been a fixture in Aspen for years. The owner is facing a foreclosure auction if he doesn't come up with enough money to pay off the bank."

His shoulders let down, and he leaned back into the couch cushions as he sat there transfixed by her. She was doing this for him. After the way he'd treated her, she was trying to save the ranch.

"Tomorrow night, I'm hosting a fund-raiser gala on the patio of The Knightley to help save the Walker Mountain Ranch. There'll be local bands and some of the best food in the valley." She listed a bunch of other details about the black-tie event, but he didn't hear them.

"Seriously?" He hadn't meant to say it out loud, but... wow. All that for him?

"I knew she loved you!" Mom celebrated so loudly, he had to hold the phone away from his ear. "Why else would she go to all this trouble?"

He couldn't come up with a reason. Not one damn reason. After the way he'd treated her he didn't deserve it. He didn't deserve her.

"You really think she could love me?" A surge of hope almost lifted him off the couch. "Because she's way out of my league. You know that, don't you?"

"Don't be ridiculous, dear! You're perfect for each other."

On the screen, the interview lady leaned close to Avery. "So, what's the story here? How did you hear about the Walker Mountain Ranch?"

"I stayed there a few days ago and fell in love with it," Avery answered brightly, but then her smile faded, and he knew why.

"The owner is a friend of yours?" Interview Lady asked.

Avery flinched—there was no mistaking it—but she recovered quickly. "Yes. I'm a friend of the Walker family," her voice was strained, but Interview Lady didn't seem to notice.

Mom, however, gasped. "What. Did. You. Do." It was the closest thing to a growl he'd ever heard come out of her mouth. "That poor girl. She's heartbroken."

He winced at the memory. "I may have overreacted when I found out about the auction."

"Oh Bryce," she sighed. "Well, you are going to march yourself to that gala and apologize to her, mister. And you'd better hope she forgives you."

"I've never been to a gala." What the hell was a gala, anyway? What did that word even mean?

"Well, you absolutely have to go. There's no other way."

"Can't I just call her?" Even as he said it, he knew it wouldn't be enough. Avery had done all of this for him. God, he needed her back.

"Where's the chivalry in calling her?" Mom moaned. "She just went on a television show for you. And she hates the cameras!"

"You're right." He glanced at the television again. "What does 'black tie' mean?"

"That means you have to clean yourself up and wear a tux, dear. You know, one of those black and white numbers with a bow tie?"

"A tux, huh?" Despite the fact that he'd have to actually comb his hair, he grinned. He could find a tux, no problem. He'd take Mom's advice, clean himself up, dress in a monkey suit.

Then he'd show up at The Knightley and give Avery King a night she'd never forget.

CHAPTER TWENTY-SIX

Avery glided under the canopy of twinkling white lights that dangled above The Knightley's lovely patio, her head tipped back, eyes wide with awe. In between the small globes, white paper lanterns swung in the gentle breeze and made her feel like a little girl walking through a fairy's garden. Magical Night. Vanessa had chosen the theme for the fund-raiser, and it was perfect. Beautiful and elegant, but rustic, too. She weaved between the round tables, which had been covered with white silk. Large Mason jars, decorated with burlap ribbons, sat in the centers, plumes of wildflowers spilling over the sides. Heat lamps were scattered around the patio, just in case, but even at seven o'clock, the temperature hovered at sixty-five degrees. No snow tonight. Apparently, high altitudes made Mother Nature moody.

Guests had started to arrive, and were mingling near the elegant hors d'oeuvres tables and a flowing champagne fountain that seemed to be keeping everyone's spirits high. Soft jazz hummed in the background, courtesy of a local band Van had hired.

Not to brag or anything, but she highly doubted The Knightley had ever seen a more classy affair. Especially one that had been thrown together in three days.

Three days.

Three days of phone calls and media interviews and decorations and catering decisions and shopping. The result still earned a surprise gasp every time she gazed over the patio. It was lavish without being pretentious, a place where Bryce's friends could come together with hers for a common purpose—to raise a ton of money and hopefully have a good time in the process.

"Avery!" Van barked from over by the catering tent. "Get back to your post!" She threw up her hands. "You have one job. One job! Greet the guests. Charm them into parting with their millions, *capiche*?"

"*Capiche!*" she answered with a snarky salute. She never missed a chance to mock Van when she was running an event. The woman transformed into a drill sergeant, barking out orders, pointing her finger, clapping her hands as she ordered people to *move, move, move*!

Her friend flipped her off.

"I love you!" Avery called in response, then resumed her position beneath the arbor that curved over the patio's entrance.

A mixture of nerves and excitement swirled in her stomach, making her crave one of those delicious cupcakes she'd seen the baker setting out. This could work. This really could work. She'd gotten a huge response to the media interviews she'd done. In addition to the money she'd come up with after liquidating her own assets, they'd already raised twelve million through online donations. Another lucky thirteen, and Bryce just might be able to outbid her father...

Around the corner, voices drifted on the night air.

Here we go. She smoothed the bodice of the shimmering blue gown that Vanessa had insisted matched her eyes perfectly, and smiled like she had Vaseline slathered on her teeth. Honestly, the whole act was starting to wear her out, but benevolent rich people always expect an overly gracious greeting from the host. If she had any hope of bringing in enough money, she couldn't disappoint.

Instead of yet another wealthy concerned animal activist or philanthropist, Paige and Shooter sauntered through, followed by Sawyer and his cute wife, Kaylee, then Meg and her fiancé, Nelson. "You're here!" she cried, clapping her hands. Hiking up her gown, she rushed to greet them all with a hug, even Shooter. "Thanks so much for coming everyone."

"Don't mention it," Shooter murmured to her cleavage. At least he'd cleaned himself up, though. He actually looked nice in a tux.

Paige glanced around the room with wide eyes, looking like a little girl who'd stepped into a fairy-tale land. She smoothed her red, strapless gown and glanced at Avery. "We're not in Kansas anymore."

Avery laughed. "You fit right in. That dress is perfect on you." The second she'd seen it hanging on the rack a few down from her own dress, she knew she had to buy it for Paige.

"Yeah, but this Spanx thing is gonna kill me." She gripped at her dress, twisting it and shimmying it up. "Seriously. It's reducing the oxygen to my brain. I can't even think straight." She leaned in close. "Just make sure I don't do anything stupid, like hook up with Shooter. Okay?"

"Got it," she promised. "But...you do realize you don't need Spanx, right? You've got a great figure." Paige was small, yet still toned and athletic.

"That's not what my love handles told me in the mirror," Paige insisted, loudly enough that the whole group laughed.

Avery admired the dress again. Red fit the woman perfectly, fiery and vivacious, eye catching. And she definitely seemed to be catching some eyes from across the room.

"Where's the food?" Shooter asked, resting a hand on his belly.

If anyone could use the assistance of Spanx, it was him.

She pointed to the tables near the catering tent. "Over there. Just make sure you leave some for the rest of the guests."

"Can't make any promises," he said with a jovial smile, then plodded away.

"Personally, I like to start with alcohol," Sawyer joked, and everyone else heartily agreed.

"The bar is that way," she directed them past the bubbling stone fountain.

"Perfect." Sawyer linked his arm through Kaylee's. "We'll catch up with you guys later."

"I'm with them," Meg said, dragging Nelson away.

When they were gone, Paige adjusted her Spanx again, grimacing and twisting. "So is Bryce here?" she asked casually, even though she knew there was nothing casual about Avery's feelings for him. She'd pretty much told Paige every ugly detail.

"No." The happy, alive feeling she'd had only minutes before dulled. She'd thought about inviting him, but every time she got out her phone, she chickened out. It would be torture for her to see him, knowing she had a flight to L.A. early the next morning. "I never told him."

"Why the hell not?" Paige demanded with one hand on her hip and her usual amount of sass.

"It's better if he doesn't come," she answered firmly, if only to remind herself. He'd made it clear how he felt, and she didn't want him to think she was doing this to manipulate him into changing his mind. That wasn't what this was about.

"Sorry, Avery." Paige snagged two glasses of champagne from a passing waiter and handed one to her. "I know how you feel about him."

Instead of answering, she sipped champagne. The thought of losing Bryce forever made her want to retreat upstairs and bury her face in a brand new carton of Cheesecake Brownie comfort. Unfortunately, that wasn't an option. So she put on a brave face. "Hey, what about you? Do you have a date?"

"Evening, ladies," Benjamin Noble drawled from the other side of the garden arch. "This where the party is?"

"Hi!" Avery hadn't meant to shriek, but Ben Noble had a reputation for being quite the generous benefactor, and they were in need of some serious generosity. "I'm Avery King." She extended her hand and he shook it warmly. "Thanks so much for coming."

"Wouldn't miss it." He grinned, and even she had to admit he had one of those all-American smiles that had the power to make a woman forget her last name. Except his grin wasn't directed at her; it was aimed at Paige, who stood still and silent, her cheeks nearly matching the color of her dress. The woman smoothed her hands down her sides self-consciously.

Hmmm. Avery eyed her. She wasn't usually the self-conscious type…

Ben waved a check in the air. "Where do I turn in this baby?"

While she couldn't see the amount, she did glimpse a whole lot of zeros. *Oh, wow.* She fought the urge to throw her arms around him. Not appropriate for a first meeting. Besides, she didn't want to steal Paige's thunder. The chemistry in the air was so palpable she was almost blushing, too. "Checks go over there." She pointed out Vanessa, who was posted by the catering tent, meticulously eyeing every tray that came out. "Paige?" She elbowed her lightly. "Would you take Ben over and introduce him to Vanessa?"

"I'd sure appreciate it," he drawled, holding out an arm like a true southern gentleman.

"Of course," Paige practically gasped, then linked her arm through his, giving Avery a bewildered look.

Happiness bubbled through her as she watched them walk away. Those two would be so cute together…

"Hey, Avery." Logan's voice startled her. She turned in time to see him saunter under the arch.

"Logan!" She reached out to hug him, then stopped, unsure if he even wanted her to. "What a surprise."

His quick grin broke through her awkwardness. He leaned in to hug her. "Vanessa invited me. Hope that's okay."

"Of course it's okay." It was more than okay. He deserved someone like Vanessa. "It's so good to see you." She meant it. He looked great, as optimistic and happy as ever.

"So is Vanessa here?" He glanced around and stuffed his hands in his pockets, which she happened to know he only did when he was nervous.

"Why, yes she is." She couldn't hide a smile. Feeling like Cupid, she pointed him to the catering tent. "She's over harassing the waiters."

"Thanks," he said. "I'm sure you're busy right now. Hope we can catch up later."

"Definitely." She waved him away. "There's a great band here tonight. You should ask her to dance." Logan had some crazy fun dance moves. Come to think of it, so did Vanessa.

He only smiled as he sauntered away, hands still deep in his pockets.

At least it was turning out to be a magical night for *some* people, she thought as she went back to her job as greeter. When the traffic slowed, she left her post, mingling and schmoozing with the best of them, all the while keeping an eye on Ben and Paige, who were dancing near Meg and Nelson. Shooter was at the bar chatting up one of the waitresses—unsuccessfully, judging by the scowl on her face. Then there were Vanessa and Logan, engaged in deep conversation on the outskirts of the party. Her friend no longer looked stressed, only happy and engrossed in whatever they were talking about.

She waited for a lull, and when Logan walked away from Van and headed for the bar, she hurried over, brandishing a wide smile. "How's it going?" She swiped a lamb lollipop topped with mint pesto from another passing waiter.

"Okay," her friend replied, but her happy expression went flat. "Except…" Her head bent and her fingers tapped the screen of her trusty iPad. "Avery…the donations have stopped coming in."

A sinking feeling weighted her stomach. Suddenly the lamb lollipop wasn't so appetizing.

"I wish I had better news." She switched off the iPad and tucked it under her arm. "But even with the online donations, we're only at sixteen million."

It felt like someone had stabbed the heel of her stiletto right into her chest, then twisted it for good measure. That wasn't enough. Not even close.

Eyes burning, she tossed the half-eaten lamb lollipop into a nearby trash can. She couldn't cry. Not there. Not in front of all of these people.

"You did everything you could," Van insisted with an uncharacteristic quiet.

"But it wasn't enough." The burn in her eyes intensified until she couldn't see, but she bit into her cheek and froze her face. One wrong move, one small twitch, and she wouldn't be able to stop crying for a very long time.

"Crap. Why'd the music stop?" Van glared at the stage. "I have to go check in with the band." She gave her a lopsided hug. "Sorry, girl."

Still silent, still frozen, Avery waved her away like it was nothing, like her heart wasn't broken for Bryce, but those tears built with a vengeance and started to spill over, probably dragging her mascara with them. All she needed was to walk around the rest of the night looking like a blond Marilyn Manson.

With nowhere else to hide, she put her head down and
elbowed her way through the crowd, then ducked into the
ladies' room. Leaning over the sinks, she inspected her
face. At least her mascara was still intact. If she could just
make it through a couple more hours . . .

Inside of her beaded purse, her phone chimed and announced an incoming text. She ignored it and blotted a
Kleenex under her eyes, but it chimed again. And again.

Leave me alone. She unearthed it from the mess of
receipts, mints, and tampons ready to click it into silent
mode, but his name lit up the screen.

Bryce Walker.

Hey, Avery.

It's Bryce.

Watcha doin?

Her heart tumbled into a free-fall. He didn't know?
How could he not know? Sure, she hadn't told him, but
she'd figured he'd find out. All of his friends were there.
And of course there were the media interviews . . .

Okay. Not important. What really mattered was . . . he
cared what she was doing?

Her fingertips buzzed. What should she say?

Nothing important, she sent back, then regretted it.
Nothing important? How could she lie like that? This
might've been the most important thing she'd ever done.
Even if she'd failed.

The phone chimed again. Slowly, she raised it to eye
level, almost afraid to look.

You're pretty dressed up to be doing nothing important.

She looked left, then right. Yeah. Like he'd be standing
in the ladies' room at The Knightley! He must've
heard . . .

You look beautiful.
Blue is your color.
Love the flower in your hair.

Heat snaked through her veins and made her heart feel like it would burst. He was there? He'd seen her?

More important... he thought she was beautiful?

She sank to the flowered bench in the corner because her knees had quit working, just like that. He'd come. How could she have missed him? How did—

The door opened and Bryce sauntered through like he walked into ladies' rooms every day.

"Hey." He stopped a few feet away. "Can we talk?"

Talk? Yeah, right. She couldn't utter a word. One hundred percent pure infatuation tangled her throat. He stood there in a tux. A tux! And his hair... God, his hair. He'd tamed it into waves that made her fingers long to feel them, to glide through their softness. He looked so... well, the sight of him was enough to make a nun feel lust.

His eyes connected with hers and her heart floored it, because this was the same way he'd looked at her right before he'd made love to her, his gaze steady and sure, mesmerizing.

"I'm sorry," he said, still two feet away from her. That was her fault because she still hadn't answered his question. But how could she when her tears were welling up again? Because he was there. In the ladies' room. With her.

She dipped her chin to her chest so he wouldn't see her cry, but then he got on his knees in front of her, holding her face in his hands and looking straight into her heart.

"Walking out on you was the stupidest thing I've ever done, Avery. And I've done a lot of stupid stuff."

She shook her head against the regret in his voice. "You were right. I could've done more. I should've." The tears did fall then, because it was the truth. "I could've stopped it." If only she'd been paying attention. She'd would've seen what her father was planning to do.

"Hey." His thumbs stroked her cheeks, wiping away those unrelenting tears. "None of this is your fault." He inched closer; his elbows resting on her thighs, his face drawing so near that her body ached for him to pull her into his arms.

"We didn't raise enough money," she whispered, because he should know that before he made another mistake. "Not even close." Waves of her sadness rippled through the words. "I can't stop the auction."

"Avery."

She closed her eyes at the way his lips formed her name, with great care and tenderness.

His hands lowered and swallowed hers. Under his protective hold, her heart picked up and found a new rhythm.

"It doesn't matter." He smiled, still holding her hands in his, still looking at her like no man ever had, open and defenseless. "You were wrong. You are enough."

The words reached the hollows of her heart, those empty places carved out by loss and disappointment, filling them until they brimmed over.

Bryce moved his hands to her face and brought it in line with his. "You're so different. So strong. Compassionate. Vibrant." He shook his head. "God, I'm so in love with you, Avery," he uttered with a helpless vulnerability. "I didn't even know it could be like this."

"Me neither," she murmured, peering into his eyes, letting him see the truth because she couldn't hide it anymore. She couldn't pretend. She couldn't walk away. Somehow her heart had found its true home in him. A surge of emotion tangled her throat. "I feel like I've loved you my whole life."

Still on his knees, he inched closer, until his upper body pressed against hers, until not even air could fit between them. "When I thought about my life without you, I couldn't picture anything." The words were rough, almost frantic. "I don't need the ranch. I need you. I'm sorry it took me so long to figure it out."

But she wasn't sorry. Without the last couple of days, they wouldn't have known. They wouldn't have caught a glimpse of life apart. They wouldn't have discovered that they belonged together. She tugged his face closer, watching his eyes carefully the whole way, feeling that sharp, beautiful sting of anticipation spiral through her. "I'd say you figured it out just in time," she whispered, right before his lips melded to hers. The warm softness of his skin spread through her, loosening her joints, brewing a heated desire in the deep recesses of her soul.

His hands glided up her bare arms, then cupped her jaw, the manly roughness of his fingers scraping her in a lovely, tingling way.

He pulled back, his shameless gaze seeming to take in the details of her face, moving over her lips and her nose and her forehead.

"You combed your hair," she whispered, because she couldn't resist.

"Don't get used to that," he said with a sly, heart-stopping grin.

"I wouldn't dream of it." She tangled her fingers in his soft waves, mussing his hair just enough that he resembled the real Bryce. The one she'd fallen for. "There. I like it better this way, anyhow."

Bryce pushed to his feet and pulled her up, bringing her close against his body, sliding his hands down her back, stopping them on the curve of her hips. "Don't go to California, Slugger," he begged. "Stay with me."

And even though her feet were technically touching the ground, her body threatened to float away. She stood on her tiptoes so his lips were within reach. "Okay."

It was the simplest decision she'd ever made.

"Okay," Bryce repeated before his lips teased hers, then sank in, silencing the rest of the world, drowning her in a warm rush. He wrapped her in his arms, bringing their bodies closer, caressing his hands down her back. His lips were solid and demanding, so dominant over hers that her lungs ached with a groaning breath. Grinning against her mouth, Bryce backed her into the wall, pinning her body with his, working his lips down her neck...

Creak.

The door *whoosh*ed open.

Avery froze, trying to focus past the blur of passion in her eyes. Under the doorframe, a white-haired woman gasped and clutched her chest. "Oh, goodness! I'm so sorry," she called as she hurried out.

Laughing, Bryce rested his forehead against hers. "I guess we'll have to hold that thought."

"Not necessarily." She tugged on his bow tie and widened her eyes into an invitation. "I have a suite upstairs..."

"You have no idea how much I want to see it," he said, in that hungry, gravely tone. "But there's someone who wants to see you, first."

Hadn't she already seen everyone who'd walked through the door? "Who?" she demanded, because she'd rather not see anyone except him at the moment.

"You'll see." He took her arm and escorted her out of the ladies' room, back toward the party. When they turned the corner and walked under the arch, the flutter in her heart turned violent. "Dad."

He stood near the fountain, dressed in his classic shawl-collar tuxedo.

Wriggling out of Bryce's grasp, she stopped. "What is he doing here?" she asked, torn between tears and anger. He'd cut her off like she meant nothing to him, and she hadn't heard from him for three days...

"I asked him to come." Bryce's hand landed on the small of her back, nudging her forward again, soothing her with a gentle touch.

Her feet shuffled, but she couldn't seem to draw in a stabilizing breath. She turned to Bryce. "You *asked* him to come?" When? Why would he do that?

"Yeah." He gazed down at her with a small smile, but it wasn't apologetic. "I'd give anything to have my dad around, Avery. So I called and told him that I was coming here. To convince you to stay with me in Aspen. I thought he should know."

In other words he'd done this for her. He'd graciously gone to the man who was taking away his home and tried to make things right between her and her father. The anger crumbled, exposing her sadness, but Bryce was right. She couldn't move on like this, not without seeing Dad, not without making sure he knew how much she loved him. Even if he'd cast her aside.

"Besides, we had a great talk. I think you should hear

him out," Bryce said, and this time when he nudged her toward Dad, she didn't resist. But she didn't have to move far because he met her in the middle.

"Avery...I'm sorry," he said. His gray eyes were rimmed with red.

It took so long for those words to come together in her mind, to make sense to her heart. "What?" she gasped, not bothering to hide her surprise. Dad never apologized.

"After Bryce called me this morning, I realized something." His jaw twitched like it always did when he was trying to hide his emotions. "I should've given up everything for your mom. The way Bryce did for you."

Her throat stung like she'd swallowed glass. She peered up at Bryce. "What is he talking about?"

Bryce simply looked at Dad.

He cleared his throat. "I called him three days ago and told him he could have the ranch back if he broke things off with you."

A swell of anger forced her back a step. "How could you do that?" The tears were blinding now, sloppy and everywhere...

"It was a mistake." Dad rested his hand on her forearm. "And he refused," he said, looking at Bryce with obvious respect. "It made me think. I wish I would've chosen your mom over everything else. Maybe things would've been different."

Okay. Okay. Breathe. But that was much harder than it sounded at the moment. She held back a sob.

Bryce rubbed a hand over her shoulders, and she loved him so, so, so much. She loved them both.

"You were right," Dad said with a hitch in his voice.

"You're her legacy. You're like your mom in every way that made her good. I'm so proud of you."

"Thank you," she whispered, gripping his hand in hers, savoring the feel of a connection that felt like it had only just started.

He squeezed back, his eyes glassy with pent-up tears. "I want to make this right." He looked between her and Bryce. "For both of you. I'll see to it that you can buy back the ranch at the auction. You two will do more with it than I ever could."

And that released the sob. She threw her arms around him, hugging his neck so tight he started to cough. But she held on anyway.

When she finally let him go, Dad righted his suit coat. "I want you to be happy. That's all that matters. You'll always be my little girl, Aves."

"I know," she answered, those sneaky tears pricking again. For all of those years, they'd survived together, but now she was ready to live, deeply and boldly. Unafraid. And she hoped he would, too.

Bryce pulled the hankie out of the pocket of his tux and offered it to her, then reached out to shake Dad's hand. "Thank you. For everything." He smiled down at Avery. "We'll make the ranch something your mom would've loved."

She slipped her hand into his. "That sounds perfect."

Dad sniffed, then blinked hard. "I could use a stiff drink," he said, his gruff tenor making a comeback. He gazed at the bar. "I'll be over there if you need me."

"Okay." She smiled, offering him one more hug. He pulled back and strode away, but not before she saw more tears in his eyes.

As soon as they were alone, Bryce pulled her close. "You're serious, right? About staying in Aspen? About working on the ranch together?"

"Yes." She rested her palms against his chest and batted her eyelashes. "I mean... if I have a reason to stay."

"Oh, I'll give you a reason." He brushed his lips against hers and inched his hands up the sides of her ribcage until her lungs felt ragged from lack of air.

"I'll need a marketing queen. You know anyone like that?"

"Maybe." She drew out the word in a tease.

Bryce's gaze lowered down her body. "She has to be as hot as you are."

"Isn't that a little sexist?" she asked sweetly.

"You wanna play hardball?" He held up his hands. "I get it. Okay. Fine. I'll even throw in room and board. You can have my bedroom."

She exaggerated an eye roll. "How generous of you."

"I'm all about sacrifice." He straightened, but his eyes never left hers. "Think of everything we could do together."

"In your bedroom?"

"You said that. Not me." But then his easy expression evaporated. After a glance around, he linked her arm in his and escorted her to a quiet corner near the garden arch where she could hear the fountain trickle nearby. Then he looked down at her, his green eyes solemn. "Seriously, Avery. I never thought I'd feel like this. I didn't even know it was possible." He brushed her hair behind her shoulder, his fingers grazing her neck, weakening her legs...

"I'd given up. Didn't think I'd get another chance to

share my life with anyone. You changed that." The words were rough, so full of emotion that she had to hold her breath so she didn't ruin the moment with more tears.

"You changed how I saw everything. When you walked into my office that day, I came alive."

"Me, too," she whispered, clasping his hand in hers. And she had. Without Bryce, she never would've known her life was missing something. She never would've realized there was so much more.

He lifted her hand and kissed her knuckles. "I promise I won't walk out on you again."

"I believe you." And right then, she knew it was over. She knew no one else would ever own her heart the way he did.

A burst of a commotion broke their spell. She peered over his shoulder and everyone was there—Ben and Sawyer and Kaylee, Meg and Nelson, and, yes, even Shooter—all closing in on them. *Wait.* Where was Paige? Avery studied Ben, who no longer seemed to be smiling, but before she had time to investigate, Sawyer slung an arm around her and Bryce. "Get these kids some champagne!" he shouted, and that's when the party really started. There were whistles and whoops and before she knew what was happening, she held the stem of a crystal glass.

Worried, she glanced at Bryce. It couldn't be easy for him to be around alcohol...

But he grinned at her like he knew exactly what she was thinking. "Never been much of a champagne guy so Sawyer made sure I got a Coke," he explained, showing her the vintage glass bottle. Then he drew closer. "And right now, I'm only craving you, Avery."

She knew exactly what he meant.

Clasping her hand in his, he raised his glass. "To the future."

There were more cheers, a couple of hearty sniffles, but then everyone quieted to wait for her.

She paused for a moment, to breathe it all in, to etch every detail into her memory. Then, drawing close to Bryce's side, she raised her glass. "To the Walker Mountain Ranch," she sang.

Then she clanged her glass against his and sealed their new partnership with a long, lovely kiss.

EPILOGUE

Eight months later...

I am *not* getting on that thing." Avery crossed her arms and gave Buttercup the evil eye. "She's mocking me. Look at her grinning like that. She's waiting for me to put my foot in that stirrup so she can rear up and buck me again."

Bryce laughed. "You wouldn't do that, would you, Buttercup?" He leaned in and kissed the horse's nose, and while it was disgusting, it also stirred that warmth Bryce had infused into her heart.

God, she loved this man.

He came up behind her and pulled her against him, and even after eight months, her knees went soft and her lungs opened up and she let herself melt in his arms. "We can both ride Hoolie then," he murmured in her ear.

She turned into him, so they were face to face, body to body. Maybe her favorite place to be in the entire world. "Why do we have to ride at all?" Her fingers pulled at the collar of his shirt and she shot him her best seductive smile. It hadn't failed to distract him yet. "We could go upstairs instead…"

"Nice try." Backing away, he caught her hand in his and towed her over to Hooligan. "I need to show you something." He touched a light kiss to her lips. "And I'd love to take you up on your offer but everyone'll be here for dinner in a half hour."

"Fine," she grumbled, but secretly reveled in the feel of his hands tight on her backside as he boosted her onto the saddle. He hoisted himself up behind her and yes, she could ride like this, shoulders snuggled against his chest, feeling his heart beat into her back.

"Come on, Hoolie." Bryce's heels nudged the horse, and Hooligan obeyed, trotting out of the brand new stables that housed not two horses, but six, just in case families wanted to ride together, Bryce had said.

The movement was jarring, but Bryce's form held her steady, and truthfully she would've ridden anywhere with him if he would've asked. She'd go all the way to Denver on horseback, if he wanted her to.

The sun warmed her face as they trotted up the road behind the lodge. Bryce nuzzled her neck, sending sparks down the left side of her body. The wind puffed her hair, blooming with the scent of honeysuckle and fresh green grass. Love like an old quilt wrapped around her. She loved these mountains. She loved the newly renovated lodge. And she loved Bryce more deeply than she'd ever thought possible.

"Where are we going?" Her chin grazed her shoulder as she turned to peer into his eyes.

"If I told you that, it wouldn't be a surprise, would it?" His arms tightened around her and he kicked his heels into Hooligan's side again. The horse's neck strained. His hooves pounded harder, faster, up the road, through the aspen grove where the brand new leaves were still budding.

The temperature dropped, but the cooler air only chilled her cheeks. The rest of her glowed with a warmth stirred from deep within.

At the top of the road, Bryce steered Hooligan into an emerald meadow overrun with purple asters and yellow alpine buttercups.

"Whoa, Hoolie." He pulled the horse to a stop and helped her climb down. Capturing her from behind, Bryce held her tight. Once more, his lips pressed into her ear. "Close your eyes."

As soon as she squeezed them shut, he led her a few steps, then turned her around.

"Okay. You can open them."

Color flooded her vision, so bright and clear it was almost overwhelming. The whole valley stretched out below, vast and open. Far in the distance, Aspen looked like a miniature town, the pointed roofs and squared brick buildings crowning the main streets. But closer, almost right below them, the ranch sat like a beautiful refuge, sheltered in the trees. Eight months of hard work had paid off. They'd done a complete renovation, leaving the old lodge's structure intact, but adding on two new guest wings and six family cabins. The whole place matched the mountains, with its rock and log façade. A wide porch wrapped around the entire structure, and in the back, stepped down to an intricate stone patio, where the brand new swimming pool gleamed a shimmering puddle of blue.

The inside of the lodge was almost as impressive as the outside. The floors were tiled with a grayish slate that resembled the granite peaks. Exposed log beams held up the vaulted ceilings and opened the great room. Each suite had been redesigned based on different themes—romantic getaways, family vacations, corporate team-building retreats.

As she looked down on it now, she realized all of their hard work—all of the long days and the sleepless nights were worth it. The Walker Mountain Ranch was a master-piece. Their masterpiece.

Bryce slipped in front of her, taking both of her hands in his. "You always say you never felt like you belonged anywhere." Eyes fixed on hers, he lowered to one knee. "You can't say that anymore."

Something inside of her broke. A breath whooshed out. "Oh wow. Oh. Bryce…" Tears flooded her eyes and ran over, pure love and joy and the hopefulness of a new life sprinkling down onto the collar of her fleece.

"This is your home. Our home," he said, and the words were so sincere, so sure. "You'll always belong here with me." Smiling up at her, he reached into the pocket of his fleece, then opened his hand. A ring sat on his palm, the diamond gleaming in the sun.

"I love you, Slugger," he said, and she laughed through her tears. "And I promise to prove it to you every day. Marry me."

Weak trembling overtook her legs. She lowered to her knees across from him, so she could look into his eyes, so she could remember this moment. "Of course I'll marry you," she whispered.

He kissed her then, lips working hers over with a slow grace, and when he pulled back, his face beamed like they'd just won the town championship baseball game.

Capturing her left hand in his, Bryce slipped the ring on her finger.

She gasped. It was from another time, a sparkling European-cut diamond set in an intricate Art Deco platinum band.

He clasped her hand in his and ran his thumb over the diamond. "Mom gave it to me. She wanted you to have it. It belonged to her mother before her."

"I love it. It's perfect." It was everything she'd ever wished for, a legacy of love on her finger, giving them something to hope after and strive for.

"I can't wait to marry you." Bryce kissed her cheek and stroked her hair. "And I really hate to say this, but we have to get back. Everyone's waiting."

"Okay," she grumbled playfully.

While she hated to let the moment pass, she couldn't wait to see everyone. They had so much to celebrate. After eight months of renovations and new hires and plans and reservations, they had their first summer completely booked. Tomorrow, they would welcome their first guests. Eight families would stay at the lodge, do the brand-new ropes course, and take a guided excursion up the Maroon Bells. Tonight, the staff was gathering in the newly renovated dining room for dinner so Elsie could test out her brand-new gourmet kitchen.

And soon, very, very soon, she would be Mrs. Walker.

All the way back to the lodge, they talked about the wedding. Something in the fall when the leaves were changing. It would be at the ranch, of course. Small and intimate.

After they got back to the stables, Bryce drove her up to the lodge on the ATV. He hurried her up the steps, across the porch, and into the foyer. Obviously he was as excited to make the announcement as she was.

Right inside the door, he paused. "You ready for this?"

The sounds of laughter and competing voices drifted from the dining room. She held her breath to listen, to soak them in. Once the lodge had been so quiet and gloomy, but now it was full, the seams in the walls barely able to contain the love and togetherness their little circle had built over eight months.

"I'm so ready."

His arms wrapped around her, tense and solid. So safe.

That was the moment Moose chose to gallop into the room, running circles around them and woofing madly, while his whole backend wagged with excitement.

They were encircled then, by the laughter and the voices that had crammed the dining room only minutes before.

But that was okay because she couldn't wait to tell them. All of them.

"Well, it's about damn time. I'm starving," Shooter muttered. Yes, Shooter. Turned out that Bryce thought he was qualified to manage the horse stables. And... well, he was kind of growing on her.

"Good lord, you two. Get a room." Then there was Paige. Sweet, honest Paige, whitewater rafting guide extraordinaire.

Other members of the baseball team snickered near the couch, while Sawyer huddled with his wife in the far corner of the room.

"Shush, everyone. Quiet down." Elsie elbowed her way through the circle, eyes twinkling in the soft light. "I do believe these two have news to share." A bounce of her eyebrows prompted them.

Bryce positioned himself next to Avery, and she fit so perfectly against his side. He waited until the group quieted, then rubbed his hand up and down her arm. "Avery said yes." His broad grin lit up the whole room, the whole town.

"Guess that means you're off the market," Shooter muttered.

Paige gasped. "Congratulations!" She hugged Avery tight. "This is amazing! Don't worry. I'll clue you in on all of his annoying habits so you can be prepared ahead of time." She winked.

The rest of them shook hands, patted their backs and, yes, razzed Bryce about his silly grin.

"Oh, my." Elsie sniffled and dabbed at her eyes. "Come on, dears. We have to celebrate. I'll break open the champagne."

The others followed Elsie to the dining room.

As Bryce led her across the foyer, Avery took in the beautiful architecture, the walls they'd designed and planned themselves, the furniture they'd picked out together. The Walker Mountain Ranch wasn't a lodge. It was a grand palace that promised love and laughter and peace. That promised her the freedom she had craved her whole life.

Outside the dining room, Bryce pulled her close. She inhaled him, the smell of the evergreens and dried leaves. His hands cupped her cheeks. They were calloused and rough, but so real. He pulled her face closer until the ends of their noses brushed. "I love you, Avery King."

"I love you, too."

Without another word, he swept her into the dining room, and for the first time in her life, she was home.

Please see the next page for a preview of

SOMETHING LIKE LOVE

CHAPTER 1

Here we go. Paige's heart launched into a tumbling routine that could've rivaled Gabby Douglas' Olympic gold performance. She eased her Subaru into a parking spot outside the Walker Mountain Ranch office and cut the engine. Being summoned to the office was never a good sign. Didn't matter if you were in high school or at a Catholic Church camp, the words, *Can I see you in my office?* infused a sense of dread into your bloodstream. Especially when it came in the form of a voice mail from your boss.

Not that Bryce Walker scared her. No, it wasn't about fear. She hated disappointing him, that was all. She'd been a disappointment her whole life, as nearly every member of her family liked to remind her. But when she'd started working for the Walkers in high school, they'd treated her more like a person instead of a pest and now she hated to let Bryce down.

She obviously had, somehow. His voice mail had an unmistakable undertone of disappointment. She should know. She'd heard that tone her whole life.

The parking lot sat empty, as it typically did in the middle of the week. Most of their outfitting clients came in on a Thursday or Friday and left on a Monday or Tuesday. Wednesday was their day off. Not that she minded coming in. She spent most of her free time around here, anyway, helping groom the horses or mucking out the stables or chatting with Elsie and doing whatever else needed to be done. The Walker Mountain Ranch always hummed with life, with people coming and going, sharing a meal, laughing and chatting. It was the one place she fit.

Besides all of that, if she spent time at the ranch she wouldn't risk one of her siblings stopping by her apartment to ask when she planned to stop being so selfish and come work at the café so Dad and Mom didn't have to work so much. That happened at least once a week.

A foreign sense of dread pulsed through her as she shuffled up the porch steps. Once a one-room dungeon, Bryce and Avery had transformed the Walker Mountain Ranch lobby into a palace with three offices—one for Avery, who did most of the marketing; one for Bryce, who handled all of the facilities and trip planning; and one for Kaylee, Bryce's cousin, Sawyer's wife, who did all of the booking and finances. There was also a gorgeous waiting area for clients who were checking in or out, complete with a grand stone fireplace, heavy pub tables, and leather seating. Oh, and who could forget the espresso machine and freshly baked goods case that Elsie kept stocked with every temptation known to mankind? She never missed a chance to stop by and check out the day's selections, but for once her stomach didn't tempt her.

Usually pushing open the solid pine door made her grin, but now she plowed through with her head down, apprehension about the impending meeting knotting up her neck.

"Hey, Paige."

She looked up.

Bryce stood behind the check-in counter, changing the light bulb in a stained glass lamp.

As usual, he was dressed in his khaki Carhartts and a short-sleeved blue button-up shirt with a monogrammed Walker Mountain Ranch logo on the pocket.

"Hi," she replied, trying to sound chipper, but her tone had gone flat. Normally when she saw Bryce, she'd bound right up to him and punch his shoulder, give him a noogie, or maybe tease him about how short Avery made him keep his hair now. A pang of sadness drew her gaze back to the floor. He was her true big brother, even though she had two others who could claim blood relation. But they'd never looked after her the way Bryce had.

"I'm all set here." He flicked on and off the lamp, as though making sure it worked. "Let's talk in my office."

In the office. Not a casual conversation in the hall...

"Okay," she squeaked, and followed him across the lobby sitting room into his office. Right outside the door, she stopped.

Bryce's wife, Avery, was lying on his couch, eyes closed, fanning herself with the latest issue of *Backpacker* magazine. Her three-month baby bump poked out the front of a cute, fitted red maternity shirt. Even three months pregnant, the woman had the best sense of style Paige had ever seen.

"Hey, baby, look who's here." Bryce skirted her and sat on the arm of the couch, resting his hand on Avery's belly. It would've been the cutest scene if Paige hadn't felt so cold. Avery had been called to the meeting, too. And yes, they were friends, but Avery was also Bryce's wife, and kind of her boss, too, though no one at the ranch thought of her that way. She was too sweet.

"Hey, Paige," Avery said in that groggy voice she'd grown accustomed to hearing over the last few months. "Sorry. I'm tired and hot. Again."

Bryce slid down next to his wife, kissing her on the cheek and then resting his hand high on her thigh.

Normally, Paige would've made some joke about how they couldn't seem to be in the same room without touching, but this was not a normal day, not a normal meeting, and, for the first time ever, she felt like she didn't fit there.

Somehow, Avery seemed to sense it. She sat up straighter, smoothing her long, blond hair down over her shoulders while beaming what was probably supposed to be a reassuring smile at Paige.

"Why don't you sit?" She gestured to the chair across from the couch. "I'll make us some lattes." She raised her sculpted brows at Bryce in a secret message.

In response, he reached up and scratched his head.

What the hell were they doing? Baseball signals?

"I don't want a latte." Paige had never been good at decoding signals, at politely stepping around issues. "I want to know why I'm here. In your office." She shot Bryce her own coded look. He knew her. He knew she preferred a more direct approach. *If you have something to say, get on with it.*

He acknowledged her with a sigh. Obviously got her meaning.

"Paige...you should sit," Avery insisted, her tone softened into a careful gentleness.

The ache in her stomach twisted into a nauseating whirlpool. No, make that cesspool, churning over and over. She'd heard that tone before. It was the tone a mother would use with a wayward child.

An itch crawled over her skin. Summoning the same courage she always relied on with her own father, she perched on the very edge of the squeaky leather cushion. What had she done wrong? Were they going to fire her? Her mind catalogued back over the last several months. There'd been the time she'd forgotten to log her trip miles, but that was weeks ago...

Bryce and Avery exchanged a pained look, their carefully guarded expressions communicating things she couldn't understand.

Her eyes heated. The three of them had always been on the same side, ever since Avery had come to the Walker Mountain Ranch, ever since she'd joined the baseball team. Paige had been the maid of honor in their wedding, for crying out loud.

Bryce's sharp inhale cut off her thoughts. With a glance and a nod, he seemed to offer the floor to Avery.

"Paige, honey...we've, um, well ..." She folded her hands in her lap. "We've gotten some complaints about you. On your guide evaluations."

"Complaints." The fear that swirled in her stomach quieted. That was it? Complaints? Shoot, people might complain about her after the trip, but she never heard any complaints when they stood on top of a mountain or made it through a Class IV rapid. Sure, her methods might be unconventional but she always delivered. She shot Avery her own smile. "Maybe this is a good time to talk about the customers you keep assigning me. Seriously? Why does Shooter always get to take the fun groups while I'm stuck with people like the Funklemans?"

Neither one of them smiled back. Bryce glared right into her eyes. "Thing is, customers say you're too harsh. You don't listen." His raised his head so he was looking down on her. "Then there was that whole fiasco with the Funklemans."

Heat pierced her, remnants of her mother's Irish temper flaring. "Fiasco? *Fiasco?*" She shot to her feet. "I got them up that mountain and back down before the lightning hit. I'd hardly call that a fiasco!" She had a feeling Hal would rather follow her up that mountain than sit there by himself. And she was right. He thought he was bear bait. Little did he know, black bears almost always spooked when they even heard a human anywhere in the vicinity...

Bryce swiped at his face, a frustrated gesture she'd seen him make a number of times, but it had never been directed at her.

She sank back to the couch. He wasn't messing around, giving her a flippant reprimand. He was mad.

"Sure, you got them up the mountain. But Mr. Funkleman had plenty to say about *how* you got him up there," he said.

"I did my job. I'm good at my job." She worked harder than anyone to prove herself...

"You are, Paige." Avery leaned over and patted her knee. "You're great. We know that. We appreciate your skills." She nodded in Bryce's direction as if encouraging him to agree, to reinforce her.

He didn't. "We need people to like you, too. We need 'em to tell their friends about their great experience. They're getting hung up on your personality."

The comment stung. He'd never had a problem with her personality before. He'd always accepted her, despite her personality. But he of all people had to know why she took her job so seriously, why she was so careful. He'd been a guide once, too.

"I do what I have to do to keep people safe." Because she could never live with herself if something happened to someone out there. That was why she never left without being overly prepared. She carried more weight in emergency supplies than she did in personal items. She kept an eye on the weather. She forced people like Hal to do what she said, even if it meant she had to yell at them.

Bryce and Avery looked at each other, that same coded language firing back and forth between them.

"The thing is…" Avery paused. "We're still trying to establish our brand. Poor customer service won't help."

She stared at her hands. They were weathered for someone her age, chipped nails, cracked, dry skin.

"We can't grow with bad word of mouth." Bryce's gaze drilled into hers until she felt herself start to shrink.

Oh, god. They were going to fire her. What about the program she'd been begging Bryce to start? The equine therapy program? Ever since she'd watched MS slowly kill Gramma Lou, she'd wanted to help people with physical challenges experience the peace and solitude of mountains. She'd been training the horses for months. Bryce kept telling her they'd talk about it as soon as they were more established...

In a swift blink, she saw her dream start to disintegrate. If Bryce fired her, she'd never find another job around here. Everyone would know. She'd never have the chance to start the program.

"You can't let me go. Please," she begged. "I'll do anything. More customer service training. I'll change. I know I can—"

"Oh, sweetie." Avery laughed softly. "We're not letting you go. We just wanted to have a chat about it."

She snapped up her head and gaped at her friend. They weren't firing her? Her hands clasped together in her lap. "O...K..."

"We've got an important group coming in." Bryce took over again. "This'll be highly visible, and I need everything to be perfect. Including my guides."

"Of course. No problem." This was the perfect opportunity for her to prove herself, to show them she could handle any client.

Avery and Bryce looked at each other. "Um..." Avery's nose twitched. "The thing is...you kind of already know this friend."

"Really?" That was a good thing, right? It'd make it easier. But if that was the case, then why did Avery look so worried?

"Yeah," Bryce said. "You remember my buddy, Ben? Ben Noble?"

Blood surged to her face, then drained too fast, a hot flash that ended in a wintry cold. Ben fuc—bleeping—

Noble. *He* was the big client? *He* was the customer she had to take on a rafting trip?

"It'll be huge publicity for us," Avery gushed. "He's bringing his whole campaign up here. They're donating the acreage they own west of town to a new land trust."

Shit. Okay, yes, she was trying to cut back on the swearing, but shit. *Shit, shit, shit on a stick.*

"He wants to do a rafting trip," Bryce said. "All the way down the Fork. His land is just past Enderson Falls, so you can pull over and deliver him right to the signing ceremony."

Bryce went on about how important it was that this all went off without a hitch, but all Paige could see, all she could hear, was the scene on the night she'd last seen Ben Noble.

They'd been dancing at a fund-raiser gala that Avery had thrown for Bryce nearly two years ago, and the man knew his way around a dance floor. Wearing that million-dollar smile, he'd twirled her and dipped her and charmed her all night with that damn southern drawl of his. Then he'd kissed her, brushing his lips against hers until her knees gave and she heard herself agree to go up to his room.

It was a damn good thing that busty blonde had stopped him to throw her drink in his face before she'd made the biggest mistake of her life. It seemed Ben Noble enjoyed the dance but not the morning after, and she didn't do one-night stands. Especially with a man who'd turned it into an art form. She'd never put herself in that situation again. Not after what Jory had done to her when he was nineteen, convincing her to sleep with him then tossing her aside like a ruined pair of those Nike basketball shoes he always wore.

She'd only been humiliated that way one other time i
her entire life, and she'd sworn then that it would neve
happen again.

"Paige?" Avery waved a hand in her face. "Are yo
okay with this?" she asked, wearing that furrowed frown
girl code for *I know things didn't end well between yo
two*...Thank God she refrained from saying those word
Bryce had no clue that she'd been anywhere near Be
Noble. He'd been too busy kissing Avery that night.

"Because if you're not—"

"Of course I'm okay with it," she said, mentally hikin
up her big girl panties and snapping the elastic. Th
was her chance. If she did this, if she made Ben's trip
success, Bryce couldn't put her off about the therapy pr
gram. Not anymore. "It'll be great." She chiseled out
smile. "Ben is *so*...great."

Avery slanted her head and called her out with anoth
look, but she fired up the smile again. "Seriously. I'm fir
with it."

Bryce looked back and forth between them. "Wh
wouldn't she be fine with it?" he demanded.

"No reason," Avery murmured, suddenly appearin
very interested in a loose thread on her shirt.

She was so believable.

"It'll be a chance to get us some publicity." Bryc
stood and folded his arms, ever and always the worrie
boss. "I need to know you'll give them—Ben, his cam
paign guys, the press, *everyone*—a good experience."

"I will." She was vaguely aware that she was noddin
too quickly but she couldn't seem to slow it down. "
swear. I'll be so sweet you won't even recognize me."
might require a roll of duct tape, but she'd do whatever

ook. "You have nothing to worry about," she assured him
with a syrupy sweet smile.

Her on the other hand? She had plenty to worry about.

The biggest thing being how she would spend a whole
week with Benjamin Noble and somehow be able to resist
his charm.